THE GIRLFRIEND EXPERIENCE

THE GIRLFRIEND EXPERIENCE

Charles O'Donnell

Moon Lit. Publishing
Westerville, Ohio
www.moonlitpub.com

THE GIRLFRIEND EXPERIENCE

5-10-2019

Author's website: www.charlesodonnellauthor.com

ISBN: 1-970041-09-9
ISBN-13: 978-1-970041-09-5

To my wife Helen
Without your support and advice I never would have finished this book.
To all my former bosses from whose mistakes, missteps and
misjudgments I have learned
Without your inspiration I never would have started this book.

Also by Charles O'Donnell

Moment of Conception (Matt Bugatti #2)
Shredded: A Dystopian Novel (Shredded #1)
Shade (Shredded #2)

Contents

1

THE PROGRAMMER

A THIN BEAM of orange light broke through the blinds and fell on the opposite wall, moving slowly downward as the sun rose. Before the morning light filtered through the windows the room was dark except for one glowing computer screen; deserted except for a figure leaning forward in his chair; silent except for the sound his fingers made on his keyboard.

Matt Bugatti focused on the lines filling his display. There were a few recognizable words, and some numbers, but mostly they consisted of symbols, some familiar— parentheses, brackets, semicolons, asterisks—and some less so, arcane symbols representing mathematical and logical operations. To one familiar with computer languages they were readable, and a good programmer could understand how a computer would interpret them. To Matt they had a meaning at a level inaccessible to all but three or four people in the world.

As Matt composed his program his thoughts shifted fluidly, beginning with an abstract concept, often indistinct, hardly more than a feeling. Out of this nebulous beginning he invented detailed calculations which he translated into lines of computer code, instructions so precise an unthinking machine could follow them flawlessly. He closed the loop as he mentally tested the code against his original idea, following this spiral path repeatedly from pure intuition to unambiguous commands and back, sometimes completing a dozen cycles in a matter of minutes. It was a feeling he knew well, somewhere between anxiety and exhilaration, when his creativity was at its peak. Matt had a word for it—the *vertex*.

As Matt finished the last few lines, he dimly perceived the sound of a door opening, followed by the overhead lights flickering on. He blinked at the sudden brightness, putting his elbows on his desk and pressing his palms against his tightly shut eyes.

"You did it again," said the voice behind him. "You were here all goddamn night. Did you eat anything?"

"Anson, I wonder if you could turn off the lights for a minute," Matt sighed.

"Sorry, Matt, I'm not like you. I can't work in the dark. I need to *see* what *I'm* doing," said Anson Polk.

Matt raised his head and looked up at the man next to him through the narrow slits of his eyelids. As his eyes focused he saw the outline of a tall, dark-skinned figure against the blinding ceiling lights. He could just make out his broad grin.

"What have you got?" he asked.

Matt rubbed his eyes with his fingertips. "I was at the vertex," he replied through his hands. "I think I'm on to something."

"Jon's meeting is in one hour. You can tell us all about it." Anson walked off toward his computer.

Matt turned back to the screen. He clicked a menu on the banner and selected *Build - Project Cygnus*. A window opened, filling with status messages, scrolling too fast to read. The last message said:

Build Complete. No Errors.

After a few more keystrokes the screen flashed and a window appeared containing a short white line against a dark blue background. Matt watched as the line sprouted branches, which themselves sprouted more branches, until it resembled a densely tangled bush. A second window appeared in the right half of the screen: a list of numbers, each number increasing, ticking off like the mileage indicator of a car, as if the car were traveling at the speed of an airliner. He used the computer mouse to change the view of the branching tree, rotating it, magnifying it, watching the structure evolve. *Beautiful,* he thought. He checked the numbers, nodding very slightly, then allowed himself a thin smile of satisfaction, exhaling heavily as he leaned back in his chair. At that moment he became aware of two sensations: acute pangs of hunger, and an urgent need to use the bathroom.

❖ ❖ ❖

At twenty-five minutes past eight the first attendees of the weekly program status meeting of the Connectrix Corporation of Eau Claire, Wisconsin, began drifting into the small conference room next to the office of Jon Ames, founder and Chief Technology Officer. Some seated themselves at the small table in the center of the room; others chose one of the shabby chairs lining the walls, in front of white boards that stretched from floor to ceiling. The boards were covered with numbers, equations, and diagrams, some of which resembled the tree-like structure on Matt Bugatti's computer screen. Within a few minutes eleven people had entered the room. They moved slowly; many had a haggard look. A few spoke but most remained silent. Matt was not among them.

At precisely eight-thirty, Jon Ames entered the room and took the last empty seat at the table opposite the door. It was the same chair he always chose—*Jon's chair.* Everyone knew not to occupy Jon's chair. He laid a bound journal on the table and opened it to a blank page. He wrote the date at the top and underlined it. Beneath the date he wrote *Cygnus Project—Status Update.*

"Good morning, team," he said, looking up from the page. His eyes scanned the faces in the room.

"Where's Matt?" he asked. No one answered.

"Anson, you're his buddy. Go find him."

The tall black man lifted himself from his chair and left the room.

"Let's make good use of the time it takes Mr. Polk to track down Dr. Bugatti, shall we?" Jon said. He picked up his pen and positioned it at the first line of the blank journal page, ready to write.

"Hardware?"

A husky man seated in the corner of the room spoke up.

"First prototype is on schedule. We'll have hardware in six weeks. Final draft of the specification is out for review; we should release it on Wednesday. First boards are due in four weeks. That's sixty-four nodes plus four spares," he announced in rapid cadence, as if rehearsed.

Jon transcribed the report verbatim. "Two weeks for configuration, Eric?"

"One week for configuration, one more week for debug and shakedown."

"Let's spring for eight spares," Jon instructed. "I don't want to take any chances. Systems?"

At that moment Anson re-entered the room with Matt close behind, looking disheveled and carrying a large cup of strong black coffee. Jon's eyes followed them, his face expressionless as they made their way to their seats against the wall.

"Matt, we're pleased to have you among us at last. And, may I say, you look disgusting."

Matt looked at Jon with half-closed eyes. "Sorry, Jon."

"Right. Where were we? Systems?"

A thin woman with long straw-colored hair, wearing a bulky sweater took a step forward.

"Delta release is in simulation now. Burn-down is on track with one week remaining. We'll be ready for hardware in one week. I don't want to start Echo release without an honest-to-god hardware test."

"Kathy, you'll have to keep going. You'll have the hardware in six weeks."

The young woman shifted her weight to her other foot and crossed her arms.

"Jon, if we find any hardware-related issues we'll have to scrap everything we've done on Echo. We'll lose that time and whatever time it takes to debug Delta."

"Understood. That's my decision. It's a chance we'll have to take."

"You're not taking chances with the hardware," Kathy protested, pointing at Eric, "but with the software, it's okay to take chances?"

"Kathy, please. Let's move on."

Jon scribbled notes for a few moments before looking to Anson. "Applications?"

Anson stood and took a step in Jon's direction. "User interface is on schedule, ready for acceptance testing in four weeks. Five more weeks for testing followed by final build. If we can get time on the hardware for a short test that would be great, but if we can't, no biggie. We could sure use some of the communications functions planned for Echo release. I wonder if we could pull some of those into Delta release as long as we're waiting for the hardware."

"The comms functions are all there is in Echo," Kathy said loudly. "They'll delay Delta release by eight weeks, maybe more. That'll put me on the critical path."

"I don't think you have to worry about the critical path," Anson countered, sounding amused. "Matt *owns* the critical path."

He turned back to Jon. "The application is on schedule, but without Matt's algorithm, Cygnus won't fly."

Jon summarized Anson's report in his journal. "Matt?" he said, without looking up.

Matt lowered his cup from his lips and paused a moment to swallow.

"I'm still behind but I made up some ground last night. I had an idea on how to predict a search point based on previous results. The algorithm breaks off the search tree to a promising point in factor space with no intervening search path. I started a test run this morning."

Jon's pen hand froze in mid-stroke. "That's…that's not…" he stammered. "…*possible*." He paused, cocking his head. "Is it?"

"We'll see. The test run looks promising. Extrapolating the results so far, it looks like it could solve in twelve hundred to twenty-four hundred hours."

There were murmurs in the room as Matt's report sank in. Few in the room had even a vague understanding of Matt's algorithm. What they *did* know were two numbers: the *goal*, and the *best time*. At the prior week's meeting, Matt reported the best time as four thousand hours. The goal was eight hours.

Anson turned toward Matt with eyebrows raised. "You mean on the hardware, right?"

Matt paused for another sip of coffee. "No—on my workstation."

The room broke into a buzz. They all knew the significance of Matt's accomplishment, even if they didn't understand exactly how he did it. To cut the best time from four thousand hours to twelve hundred, or even twenty-four hundred, in one week was unexpected. But they all knew what *best time* meant. It was the time needed to solve a well-defined problem on the hardware under development. That hardware consisted of sixty-four powerful computers, communicating at high speed, all working together in one system. To achieve a time of between twelve hundred and twenty four hundred hours on a *single* computer was a thunderbolt.

"People!" Jon shouted. "One conversation!" The buzz trailed off.

Jon stared at Matt. "A two-thousand bit key?"

"Of course. It's the standard benchmark."

"When can you confirm your estimate?"

"I can't say for sure until we actually find a solution. The algorithm is not deterministic. We can't know for sure if it'll *ever* finish. But everything I've learned about factoring large numbers tells me that there is a better than ninety-five percent chance that there will be a solution in twelve hundred to twenty-four hundred hours. I can refine that estimate in a few days, but I doubt it'll change much."

Jon lowered his eyes slightly for a moment before continuing. "If you're right, how long will it take on the hardware?"

"On the sixty-four node prototype I expect the algorithm to run about thirty times faster. The nodes aren't as powerful as my workstation, and there's some overhead in the parallel algorithm that will hurt our efficiency. That puts solution time on the hardware at forty hours best case, but eighty is more likely."

The droning in the room returned, more intensely than before, but a stern look from Jon quieted them.

"Matt, I have to remind you that we proposed a system that could break a two thousand forty-eight bit encryption key in eight hours or less. We've got a long way to go."

The room erupted in derisive laughter. Jon was unable to restore order. Anson spoke above the noise.

"Jesus Christ, Jon, did you hear what Matt said? This is big! Ten years ago nobody thought you could break a two thousand bit key in less than an eon. Not long ago we had no reason to believe it could be done in less than a year, no matter how much computing power we threw at it. Yesterday our best case was six months. Matt pulled an all-nighter and got it down to three days!"

"We can't lose sight of the goal," Jon answered, in the low, even voice he reserved for his stock phrases.

Anson smiled and shook his head as the commotion continued. "No one is losing sight of the goal, Jon. Just the opposite. Until this moment, none of us was sure the goal was even possible."

The room sounded like a crowd at a rally. Some shouted *"That's right!"* and *"Way to go!"* Those close to Matt leaned toward him and touched his shoulder or shook his hand.

"Jon, it's major," Anson said. "For once, just enjoy it, okay?"

The noise in the room rapidly died away as one by one they noticed a man standing in the doorway. He was considerably younger-looking than his seventy-three years, slightly less than six feet tall, wearing a tweed jacket over a colorful sweater. Josef Hofbauer, Chief Executive Officer and Chairman of Connectrix, stepped into the room. He looked around a moment before speaking.

"Something has happened, no? Something good, no? *Ja?*"

Jon stood. "Josef, Dr. Bugatti seems to have had a breakthrough. We still need to validate his estimate, but if it holds up, it puts us much closer to our goal."

"That is good, no? Dr. Bugatti, you have had a brainstorm, no? *Ja?* What is the best time?"

"Forty hours, maybe. Eighty is more realistic."

Josef took off his glasses and tapped the earpiece on his lower lip. "This is very good. You are doing well. And the rest, Jon? All the rest is good, too?"

Jon glanced down at his journal. "The algorithm is critical path. Hardware and systems are on schedule."

Josef replaced his glasses and smiled broadly. "Dr. Bugatti, it seems all our fortunes rest with you, *ja?* You keep up with the brainstorms and you'll make us all rich."

Josef turned in military fashion and exited the room. The team remained silent, but the mood had changed, from anxiety and uncertainty to excitement and determination.

❖ ❖ ❖

An hour later Anson found Matt at his computer examining the diagram, which by now had evolved into a finely detailed structure.

"Matt, you just gave all of us a shot in the arm. I haven't seen folks fired up like this in months."

Matt studied his computer screen as he rubbed one eye, then the other, with the palm of his hand.

"Good to hear. We're not there yet. Still a long way to go."

Anson rolled his eyes. "Oh, brother. *Jon* is the company buzz-kill, not you. Is this a big deal or not?"

Matt turned slightly toward Anson, keeping his eyes on the screen for a moment before looking up at his friend.

"Take a look at the factor space diagram. Can you see what's going on?"

Anson leaned down, his face just inches from the screen. He scrutinized it for a moment before standing up. He put his hand behind his head, scratched his scalp and smiled.

"It's not connected. The graph is broken up into isolated subsets. It looks like thousands of disconnected sets."

Matt smiled back. "That's right. That's the breakthrough—a disconnected search path. It's ten to a hundred times faster. But there's more. Remember what I said about the algorithm not being deterministic?"

"Yeah, sure. It's based on probabilities. You pick the best place to look and you take your chances. We're all betting on you to find the good spots."

"Well, last night it came to me." Matt tapped his forehead with his fingertips. "This thing. It's just a feeling right now. I have to work it out. But it *feels* right. I think…" He took a deep breath. "I think it *is* deterministic. I think I can show that the prime factors will *always* fall in the subset I'm searching." He spoke softly and shakily, as if saying his conjecture out loud could invalidate it.

Anson's face went slack. "I'm not sure what that means."

"It means another ten-times improvement. It means we hit our goal—eight hours." Matt leaned forward, with his hands clasped between his knees. He lowered his voice, speaking with almost electric intensity. "It means the world of mathematics turns upside-down."

Anson looked into Matt's face. His cheeks were dark with two days of stubble. His eyelids drooped. But Matt's grey eyes, focused intently on Anson's, hinted at a vision only Matt could see and few others could understand.

"How close are you?"

Matt squeezed his eyes shut. He ran his fingers through his thick black hair, oily and unwashed since the previous morning.

"I *could* figure it out tomorrow," he sighed, "or it could take years."

"We don't have years."

Matt grinned and shook his head. "Yeah, tell me. If I ever forget it I'm sure Jon will remind me—and Hofbauer to lay the fate of the free world on my back. I really don't need *that* kind of pressure."

"How can I help?"

"You can't. I've got it."

Anson put his hands on his knees and stood. He tapped his closed fist on Matt's shoulder.

"Don't worry about what Hofbauer says. Christ, you had a major breakthrough today. Everyone in this place is jazzed. *You* did that. Why punch yourself in the face while others are patting you on the back?"

Matt smiled weakly. "Thanks for the perspective."

Anson smiled back on Matt, still hunched over.

"Perspective is free, any time. I'll go one better. Meet me at Stella's after work and I'll buy the drinks. You deserve it. All I ask is that you go home, get some sleep, and make yourself presentable. You won't attract any ladies looking like that."

Anson patted Matt once more on the shoulder and walked back to his workstation. Matt straightened himself in his chair, closed his eyes and inhaled deeply. He held it in for a moment before exhaling. Then he turned back to his computer.

❖ ❖ ❖

At six-thirty that evening, Matt arrived at Stella Blues, an Eau Claire landmark and a favorite after-hours venue for Connectrix employees. Matt wore a light jacket zipped up to his chin in the cool mid-September evening. He scanned the room for Anson, spotting him at a table against the wall, holding a bottle over his head in one hand and pointing in Matt's direction with the other.

"Bugatti, get your ass over here. We've got a bucket of Leinie longnecks and you're way overdue for a good time," he shouted.

Anson sat next to Eric, the husky hardware team leader. Kathy, the systems team leader, sat across from Eric. Matt dropped wearily into the chair opposite Anson, his hands still in his jacket pockets.

Anson took a bottle from the ice bucket at the center of the table and popped off the cap.

"Unzip and unwind, my friend. It's Friday and you've had a big week," he said as he handed the bottle to Matt. Matt took the bottle with one hand and unzipped his jacket with the other.

"Oh, man, look at you," Anson remarked. "I told you to go home, take a nap and a shower, and try to look like a human being. And you didn't. You stayed at work all day. I know you did because I could smell you three cubicles away. At least tell me that you ate."

Matt tipped back the bottle, enjoying the feel of cold beer on his parched throat. After several gulps he set the bottle on the table. Foam welled up and spilled down the sides, puddling on the table. He looked at Anson through half-closed eyes.

"Anson, I have a mother who keeps pretty close tabs on me, and I don't need a mom substitute when she's not around."

"Oh yeah, how is your mother? Does she know you're slowly dying of exhaustion? Does she know about your pathetic attempt to starve yourself to death?"

The two men looked at each other with mock sternness.

"My mom's just fine, thanks. And I ate before I left the office."

"Let's see if I can guess what you ate…Fritos. Am I right?"

"Fuck you, Polk."

Anson laughed a low, warm laugh.

Eric and Kathy watched the exchange without a word, their expressions halfway between amusement and boredom.

"Is this the fun evening you promised? Beer and insults?"

"Yeah, mostly. But there's a waiter headed this way with two orders of sliders. I'll have to feed you if you won't feed yourself."

The waiter arrived at the table with a platter of miniature burgers. "What else can I get you?" he asked dutifully.

"You've done all we've asked of you and more," Anson replied ceremoniously. "But when you get back to the bar, see if they have any grappa."

Matt winced. "Anson, forget the grappa, okay?"

"Nonsense!" Anson waved a hand at Matt. "This man's drink is grappa—*grappa*—the drink of his ancestors! Nothing else will serve on this auspicious occasion!"

"I don't know if we have…whatever you said…grappa? Is that right?"

"Yes, yes, grappa. The national drink of Italy. Good God, man, you work at a bar in Eau Claire, Wisconsin, a center of international culture." Anson bellowed with indignation. "You must have grappa! You have at least *heard* of grappa?"

"I'll go see right away," the waiter answered as he hurried off.

Kathy had already started on the platter of appetizers. Eric was drinking the last of his beer. Anson took a slider for himself and bit into it.

"Matt, eat up before you pass out," he mumbled through his half-full mouth.

Matt helped himself as Eric set his empty bottle on the table.

"Gotta go, guys," Eric said. "I told the wife I'd be home by seven."

Anson threw his arms in the air, looking as if he were calming a riot.

"No! No! No! We have eight more bottles and a dozen baby burgers. Do your part, Eric."

Eric stood up and pulled on his jacket. "You've never needed my help to drink a bucket of beer, Anson."

"That's where you're wrong, big guy. You're the anchorman. You're the cleanup batter. Abandon us now and we'll leave money on the table."

Eric grinned. "Sorry, man, you're on your own. You all have a great weekend." He turned to leave, but paused and turned back.

"Matt, congratulations. That was some great work you did this week. I finally feel like there's an end in sight." He gave

Matt a tired but sincere smile, and then walked away, just as the waiter returned with four generous shots of grappa.

"Perfect!" Anson cried. "One for me, one for Kathy, and two for Matt."

Kathy wrinkled her nose. "Yuck. I can still taste the last one of those you got me to drink. I hate that stuff."

Matt leaned back and studied the four narrow glasses filled with clear liquid. "This isn't like the grappa I drank at home," he said, his voice saturated with weariness and nostalgia. "That was some good grappa. Dad had it sent over from Italy. He gave me my first glass when I was twelve, on Christmas Eve." He lifted a glass, staring at it, before looking at each of his companions in turn. He grinned.

"Well, the old man's gone, we're here, and I've had a triumph." He brandished the glass at Kathy. "Anson, I guess we can't count on this slip of a girl to help us with this round. It's all ours. *Salute!*"

"To the genius of our age," Anson responded as they each downed two shots in rapid succession. Kathy raised her beer and took a sip.

Anson and Matt winced as they set down their glasses, exhaling through pulled-back lips.

"Kathy, what's your thinking on getting this man a social life?" Anson asked, gesturing toward Matt. "Do you think he's completely hopeless?"

"Like Eric said, you're on your own," she said flatly. "I've got my own love life to think about."

"Kathy," Anson responded, "you're a female in a company dominated by males. You can pick and choose. It's like a smorgasbord."

Kathy grinned. "First, I don't fish in the company pond. Second, you guys are males in the technical sense only. Engineers are about as romantic as a textbook—hopeless geeks with no social skills." She sipped her beer. "Connectrix isn't so much a smorgasbord as it is a White Castle."

Anson's laugh reverberated in the bar, now crowded with Friday-night patrons. A few turned to him with startled looks, then smiled and went back to their conversations. A man with dark, wiry hair, wearing a black hooded sweatshirt, sat alone at a table against the opposite wall. He turned along with the others but did not smile. As the laugh died away, his gaze returned to its former direction toward the door. His expression remained unchanged.

Matt smiled wearily. "Anson, I really could go the whole night without discussing my social life. If I want to hear about how disappointing it is, I'll call my mother."

❖ ❖ ❖

Kathy left the bar before nine. It was another hour before Anson decided that Matt had faded beyond recovery and declared the evening at an end. As they left the bar they pulled the collars of their jackets to their chins against the cold for the walk of a few dozen yards to Anson's car.

"Matt, when are you going to get your own ride? What are you saving your money for?" Anson said as he opened the door and climbed in. Matt entered from the opposite side.

"Why do I need a car? I live a half mile from the office. I'm within walking distance of the supermarket. And if I need someone to drive me home after beer and grappa you're right there."

Anson started the car. "You've got no ride and no girlfriend. Do you think these things might be connected?"

"I thought we agreed my love life was off-limits. Besides, I don't see you fighting off the girls."

"Fair enough," Anson said as he pulled away from the curb. He wrinkled his nose and sniffed loudly.

"Wow. I guess I need to change the air freshener in this car. That is really weird. It smelled fine this morning. Now it smells like dirty laundry gone rancid."

Matt could not suppress a faint smile as he replied, "You're a funny man, Anson Polk."

❖ ❖ ❖

Matt entered his apartment at ten-thirty, a little less than forty hours since he'd left it. He shed his jacket, letting it drop to the floor on his way to the bedroom. The answering machine on the nightstand blinked in the darkness, its display indicating one new message.

Matt sat on the bed, staring at the blinking light. He hesitated, and then slowly reached for the playback button, as if he were completing an unpleasant but necessary chore.

"*Ciao, Matteo caro,*" the message played. Matt recognized his mother's voice.

"I left the restaurant early tonight. I told Marie to close for me. I just wanted some time to myself but I got to the house and it seemed so empty. It always seems empty without you and your father. Tonight, though, it seems really big and lonely. Isn't that strange? After all these years since Giovanni died, I still get lonely. So I thought maybe if you're lonely too I'll call you and we can talk.

"But I guess you're not at home. I hope you're out with your friends, meeting new people, and not working all night. I think you work too hard. You are so much like your father.

"Well, I'll call you again soon. Take care, dear. I love you."

There was a click, followed by the mechanical voice of the answering machine: *Received Thursday at nine-twenty p.m.*

Twenty-four…no…twenty-five hours ago thought Matt. He leaned forward, cradling his head in his hands, before falling back on the bed, exhausted. He was asleep in seconds, still fully clothed.

❖ ❖ ❖

In the street, alone in his nondescript car, a man with dark, wiry hair made his report.

2

THE DIRECTOR

ALVIN XIAO LEFT the Zhaolong Hotel, Beijing, shortly after eight-thirty in the morning, trailing a suitcase on wheels and a leather briefcase containing his computer, a few file folders, and a thick bound report of the details of all operations of the Mechanized Minds Corporation in the United States and China, along with forecasts of the Chinese market for industrial computers.

Alvin, who used his given name Xiao Weiguo when in China, glanced at his watch. His meeting with officials of the Chinese Ministry of Commerce was to start at nine. The drive to the Ministry offices near Tiananmen Square would take less than fifteen minutes. He was early.

As Alvin emerged from the hotel, the door of the limousine parked directly in front of the entrance opened. The driver was tall, more than six feet—unusual in China, even for the northern region—dressed in an ill-fitting black suit and tie. He walked briskly toward Alvin, pausing just long enough to ask "Mr. Xiao?" before reaching for his suitcase. Alvin offered the suitcase but politely withheld the briefcase. The driver stowed the suitcase in the trunk of the limousine, then held the door for Alvin as he entered the car.

The limo was small by American standards, accommodating four people, possibly more if they were willing to sit close. Alvin was alone on this trip. During the ride he reviewed the report for the twentieth time, concentrating on projected sales volumes for Mechanized Minds computers, based on estimated market growth in China and his company's share. The estimates were conservative, perhaps overly so, but the projections were impressive nonetheless. If his mission to Beijing was successful, Alvin expected his company's sales to triple in the next five years.

Alvin was Chairman and CEO of Mechanized Minds, a maker of industrial computers—small, rugged devices used to control machinery and electrical systems. He had built computers in China for several years, mostly for export to North America, at a contract manufacturer in Shenzhen who simply built designs to order. To expand into the Chinese market, Alvin needed his own operation, one that he controlled directly, located in China, with Chinese engineers under the direction of Chinese managers. And that required the consent and cooperation of the government of the People's Republic of China.

The route to the Ministry offices took the limousine past the eastern wall of the Forbidden City. Alvin viewed the Beijing landmark with curiosity. It was only his second visit to the city, and he'd had no time during either trip to tour the medieval palace. *Someday, perhaps,* he thought, *but not today.* He had much to accomplish, and little time.

The driver expertly negotiated the Beijing traffic, arriving at the Ministry of Commerce ten minutes before his scheduled appointment. The driver opened the door for Alvin, who slipped the report into his briefcase as he stepped from the car. He looked up to see two smiling figures, both dressed in the same drab fashion as the driver. The shorter of the two stepped forward and extended his hand with a slight bow. He addressed Alvin in Mandarin.

"Xiao Weiguo, welcome to Beijing. I am Chen Baoshan from the Ministry of Commerce, and this is my colleague, Liang Zhongwei. I understand you arrived from Shenzhen last night. I trust the arrangements we made for you are to your satisfaction?"

Alvin took the man's hand. He'd had meetings with government officials before, but they had never met him at the curb to escort him. *Good*, he thought, nodding. *My reputation in China is finally paying off.*

"They are quite satisfactory, thank you," Alvin responded in slightly accented Mandarin. Although Alvin left his native Taiwan at age twelve, his mother spoke only Chinese at home, and Alvin continued to study the language at her insistence. He prided himself in his mastery of the language, and counted it among his most important assets when doing business in China.

"Wonderful, we are very pleased to know that," said Chen. "You need not worry about your luggage. Your driver will keep it safe for your return."

Chen Baoshan accompanied Alvin to the meeting room with Liang Zhongwei trailing behind. It was a small, windowless room, with a half-dozen chairs surrounding an oval table on which sat bottles of water and a platter of fruit. Sitting against the wall was a smiling man, wearing the same nondescript outfit as his colleagues, as if they were all in uniform. His olive complexion was smooth and unblemished; his smile was fixed and his narrow eyes unblinking. Alvin thought he looked like a mannequin. He did not stand when Alvin and his two hosts entered the room. Chen made the introduction.

"Mr. Xiao, this is another of our colleagues, Wang Shutao, of *Guoanbu*."

Alvin tensed. *Guojia Anquan Bu—Guoanbu* for short—the Chinese Ministry of State Security, was responsible not only for foreign intelligence, but also for surveillance of the Chinese people. To Alvin, *Guoanbu* was the brutal arm of the Communist regime, an instrument of repression.

Why would they bring the Chinese CIA into this meeting? Alvin fretted. He shot a concerned glance at his hosts.

"Mr. Xiao," Chen said, "you may wonder why Mr. Wang is with us today, but you have no need to be concerned. We are taking a very big step in your relationship with the People's Republic. It is perfectly normal, routine, in fact, for our security ministry to take an interest in your enterprise. Really, you have nothing to worry about."

Alvin said nothing, but circled the table and offered a hand to the seated Wang Shutao. He rose halfway from his chair to shake it before sitting down without speaking. His smile never wavered. Alvin paused just long enough to show deference to his hosts before taking the seat at the head of the table. *Whichever one of you is in charge*, he thought, glancing alternately at Chen and Wang, *I'm running this meeting.*

"As you know," Alvin began, "our contract manufacturer in Shenzhen has been a great partner in our success. With Chinese labor and suppliers, we have reduced our costs substantially. This has allowed us to remain competitive in the North American market. And the quality of the products we receive from Mr. Luo's factory is excellent."

Alvin reached for the report in the briefcase beside his chair. "But the market for our products is expanding much faster in China than it is in America," he said, placing the report on the table. "I will need Chinese designs for the Chinese market. It will not be enough to have Mr. Luo build products that sell in America, but don't meet the needs of our Chinese and Asian customers."

Chen lifted his hand from the table, palm toward Alvin.

"Yes, we received your report and we have studied it. This is a great opportunity, and the People's Republic of China is prepared to partner with you to realize its full potential."

Alvin felt a moment of satisfaction, but sensed that Chen had more to say.

"We believe it would be to your advantage to locate near Chengdu, in Sichuan," Chen continued. "Many American companies are considering that location for expansion."

Alvin shifted in his chair. "That is an interesting proposal. But should I be concerned about the transportation infrastructure in Sichuan? I understand the logistics of shipping large quantities of products can be difficult."

Chen's smile grew wider. "This should not be a problem, Mr. Xiao. As you know, the State Council has made infrastructure development a priority. And your prior experience may be misleading. Shenzhen's location near the coast is good for exports, but its advantage is not so great for products that are destined for internal markets."

"That is reassuring, Mr. Chen. However, I still believe that locating my operation in Shenzhen would be most expedient. I already have many contacts there, and good relations with local suppliers."

Chen nodded an acknowledgement. "That is an important consideration, Mr. Xiao, but we believe that Chengdu offers many advantages. You will find the labor force to be of high quality and their wages to be quite reasonable, especially compared with what you are paying in Shenzhen. And as more companies locate there, the supply base will expand, further lowering your costs. Besides, we have already made arrangements with a company in Chengdu to construct your facility, which you may lease at a very attractive rate."

Alvin's mind raced—the Chinese were not only agreeable to his plans, but anxious to proceed. *But on their terms*, Alvin thought. *Who calls the shots?*

"I see you have given this some thought," Alvin answered. "We can move forward without delay. Of course, my staff must work through the details with the appropriate people. I assume you can make those arrangements?"

Chen nodded slowly. "Excellent, Mr. Xiao. Yes, of course we will arrange for detailed discussions. Mr. Liang will be your contact. I believe I can say with confidence that the sales forecast in your report do not reflect the potential of this venture. You stand to make a great deal of money. We will be honored to have been a part of your success."

Alvin put his hands together and pressed his index fingers to his lips. *Too easy*, he thought. He shot a quick look at Wang, the *Guoanbu* man, before offering the only acceptable reply.

"And I will be grateful."

"Very good, Xiao Weiguo. We are of one mind. All that remains are the details, which we can delegate to our subordinates."

Chen stood, followed by Liang. Alvin placed his briefcase on the table before standing himself. For the first time since entering the room, Wang stood, hands folded in front of him.

"I have been told your flight leaves this afternoon," said Chen. "You have time to enjoy some of the sights of Beijing. We understand that you have never visited the Forbidden City. We have arranged a tour for you."

Alvin reacted with surprise and genuine interest. "Wonderful! It will give us more time to become acquainted."

Chen gestured as he had before, showing Alvin the palm of his hand.

"Xiao Weiguo, we will have many opportunities to become acquainted in the future. We anticipate a long and fruitful relationship. But I regret to say that today Liang Zhongwei and I are occupied with other matters. Wang Shutao will accompany you on your tour."

❖ ❖ ❖

Alvin and Wang boarded the limousine for the short drive to the Forbidden City. Wang's expression remained tranquil, while Alvin's face betrayed mistrust. They remained silent for a moment before Wang spoke.

"You are called Alvin in America?" he asked in English, with a thick but not impenetrable accent. "May I call you Alvin, if it is not too forward?"

"I am," Alvin replied tersely. "You may."

"Alvin, I must compliment you on your Chinese. It is excellent, much better than my English, I must admit."

Alvin said nothing. Wang continued.

"It is a good thing for our partnership that you speak our language. It is also a good thing that you understand our culture. It will make our dealings much simpler. There is so much that is lost, and much more that is misunderstood, when bridging the gulf between our peoples."

It took only a few minutes for the car to reach the northern end of Tiananmen Square. Wang exited the car, followed by Alvin, still carrying his briefcase.

"Alvin, you may leave your things with our driver. He is quite trustworthy. They will be safe."

"If it's not a problem, I'd prefer to keep this briefcase with me," he objected. "It's not heavy."

Wang nodded. "Of course, that is your choice, but the tour is quite long. What is not so heavy at the beginning of your journey may become a burden by the end."

Alvin and Wang stood before the central arch leading to the Forbidden City, dominated by an enormous portrait of Mao Zedong. Alvin had seen photographs of the scene, but now, in person, the immense image of Mao with his serene expression had an impact on Alvin that he did not expect. He was raised to loathe the memory of the man, in a home where Mao was mentioned only rarely, and with disgust. But it was not disgust that Alvin felt. It was reverence, bordering on awe. It was involuntary, and when Alvin took stock of his emotions, his awe turned to shame. His cheeks burned as he read the inscriptions on either side of Mao's likeness: *Long live the People's Republic of China. Long live the great unity of the people of the world.*

Alvin and Wang followed the crowd through a tunnel which opened onto a promenade. Ahead of them was a gate at least as imposing as the one they had just come from.

"We're in the Forbidden City?" asked Alvin.

"No, Alvin, we must pass through the gate ahead and another before we enter the City."

The crowd surged forward, through another tunnel, along a tree-lined path leading to the courtyard at the Meridian Gate, the south entrance to the Forbidden City.

It was a spectacular sight. The plaza was bounded on three sides by walls nearly thirty feet tall. The structure ahead was meticulously decorated in the medieval style that was so common in China, but on a scale Alvin had never seen. Alvin was not quite awestruck, but he was visibly impressed. Wang took notice.

"It is said that the emperor wished that any man who approached this gate would be humbled. Those who sought an audience would know who was their master. It was not necessary to say it in words."

Wang led Alvin toward the center opening in the gate. The pair bypassed the ticket booth as well as the line of visitors waiting to enter. Wang produced a thin wallet from his jacket pocket and showed it to the attendant. They were admitted immediately.

Alvin and Wang passed through the third tunnel, emerging into an open space paved with stone, divided by a serpentine canal spanned by five bridges. The area was bounded by structures in the same medieval style. The throng of people which had squeezed through the tunnel spilled out into the plaza and began to congregate in small clumps, widely separated. Alvin and Wang were alone, the closest person being at least twenty yards away. Wang calmly enjoyed the surroundings, hands clasped behind his back. Alvin did not speak as he and Wang made their way across the central bridge, up the stair and through the second gate.

"This is *Taihemen*, the Gate of Supreme Harmony," Wang intoned, sounding more like a tour guide than a spy. "This stair was reserved for the emperor alone. Of course, now it belongs to the people."

They passed through the fourth passageway of their tour, entering yet another stone-covered expanse, facing the grandest structure yet, a two-story building on a tiered platform with three levels. Each gate seemed to lead to a space grander by far than the one they left. The impression was of ascending to higher and higher levels, with no end in sight. "This is *Taihedian*, the Hall of Supreme Harmony," Wang explained. "By tradition, it is the most important building in the empire."

"It seems there is nothing small in China," Alvin remarked.

Wang turned to Alvin and nodded. "We are a great people, with a great history, and an even greater future."

A great future, indeed, Alvin thought. *Where does it end?*

"How do the Chinese people regard the Forbidden City?" Alvin asked. "It seems so excessive—inconsistent with the aims of the 'People's Republic.'" Alvin said the words *People's Republic* with a slightly sarcastic tone, easily detectable by a native English speaker. It appeared to make no impression on Wang.

"An interesting question," Wang replied. "To me, the Forbidden City is a reminder of what one man's ambition can achieve at the expense of others, if left unchecked. That is certainly not consistent with the aims of the People's Republic. Instead, I imagine what the ambitions of a billion Chinese can achieve together, if properly channeled."

"You mean if properly *controlled*."

Wang looked directly at Alvin with raised eyebrows. His smile disappeared but quickly returned.

"*Controlled*—that is a word *you* might use. I prefer *channeled* —or *directed*. Our goal is for a great people to realize their destiny."

"What about *individual* destiny? What about *individual* ambition?"

The questions seemed to please Wang. "Is not the destiny of the individual bound together with the destiny of all? And as for *individual* ambition, you have only to look around Beijing, or Shanghai, or even Shenzhen to see that anyone can realize his ambition in China, the same as he can in the United States. We have more billionaires in China than any other country except yours. But that is not what you are talking about, is it? No, you are talking about *freedom*. We have freedom in China, but we do not fool ourselves into believing that unlimited freedom is either possible or desirable. That is a delusion that seems peculiar to America."

Alvin glared. Wang looked surprised. "Alvin, please do not take my words as a condemnation of your beliefs. We are sure to have disagreements, but that is the nature of relationships. We can pursue our goals with mutual respect, even if we disagree."

Alvin and Wang continued the trek through the ancient palace grounds, leaving the square surrounding the Hall of

Supreme Harmony. This was the dividing line between the ceremonial Outer Court and the Inner Court, where the emperor and his family lived and worked. They again found themselves separated from the crowds, outside of the hearing of the nearest tourists.

"Wang Shutao, can I expect *Guoanbu* to be involved in all stages of our negotiations?" Alvin asked in a low voice he was sure would not be overheard.

Wang let out a restrained laugh. "No, no, Alvin, of course not! We are not interested in the workings of your venture in China. Our colleagues at the Ministry of Commerce are perfectly qualified to manage those details."

Wang unclasped his hands from behind his back and held them out to Alvin. "You are embarking on a new relationship with the People's Republic. I am here to see that your business interests and China's do not conflict, but also that both you and the People's Government realize the benefits of cooperation."

"Of course the people of China will realize benefits," Alvin responded quickly. "My company will create jobs. We will create value, and the People's Government will certainly get their share."

"Yes, yes, of course, Alvin, that is expected. But we already have Chinese companies that make computers much like yours. Our Chinese companies create jobs. They create value. The people will benefit from that value, and the profit our Chinese companies retain will stay in China, to create more jobs."

"If that's your concern, I can assure you, we intend to expand in China as our business expands."

Wang laughed with less restraint. "Alvin, you misunderstand me! Of course, we are happy to have your investment in China. We expect you to expand as your fortunes permit. In fact, it is to your advantage to invest your dollars in China, rather than repatriate them to your country, where you would pay the American tax rate instead of the much more reasonable rate in China. No, we are not concerned about that, and if we were, Chen and Liang would negotiate an agreement. But I ask you: would we make the most of this opportunity, and our relationship, if your company's only contribution was computers that Chinese companies could make as well?"

Alvin flushed at a sudden realization. His company's largest selling computers were simple, low-tech devices. Their most important features were ruggedness and low cost. But Mechanized Minds also manufactured sophisticated, high-end computers for specialized applications that required proprietary technology. It was a small but growing and highly profitable business.

"Wang Shutao, if you're suggesting we manufacture our high-end computers in China," Alvin said quietly, "I'm afraid that's prohibited by U.S. customs laws. They're considered sensitive technology."

At this, Wang laughed out loud. "Xiao Weiguo," he said, calling Alvin by his Chinese name, "that is an interesting thought, but it is not at all what I had in mind. Besides, that would be too obvious and far too easily detected."

Wang paused to survey his immediate surroundings. For the first time, he seemed concerned that someone might overhear their conversation.

"Alvin, you understand our culture. We know from your reputation in Shenzhen and elsewhere that you value the Chinese way of doing things. It is also your way of doing things. It is your culture. You will find that the People's Government is a powerful friend, and if you are a friend to the People's Government you can rely on our support. And we hope that we can come to rely on yours as well."

Alvin and Wang continued through the last section of the Forbidden City, the elaborate Imperial Garden. The lush surroundings contrasted pleasantly with the imposing splendor and monumental scale of the courtyards and halls. It was peaceful, but it gave no comfort to Alvin.

A memory from Alvin's upbringing troubled him, a principle deeply embedded in the Chinese culture—the custom of *guanxi*. He had expected his negotiations with the People's Government to go well, in part because of his prior experience in China, and from the many personal contacts he had cultivated as a result. During that time he had granted and received many favors. No favor was ever granted with an explicit agreement that it would be returned, but instead with an unspoken understanding. It was this exchange of favors with no overt expectation of *quid pro quo* that cemented his reputation as one who could be trusted. It was Alvin's *guanxi*.

Alvin was sure he would incur a deficit as a result of this venture, and that he would have to balance the account at some point. But the speed with which the agreement was struck, the deference paid by his hosts, and above all, *Guoanbu's* involvement suggested that the Chinese expected a big payback. It was impossible for him to discover what was expected—that would be revealed in time. He briefly considered asking outright, but thought better of it. That would be an unforgivable breach of etiquette.

The two of them exited through the rear of the garden and crossed the bridge spanning the moat surrounding the walled compound. The limousine was waiting on the street at the end of the bridge, its driver leaning casually against the fender while smoking a cigarette. When he saw the pair, he sprang from the car, dropping his cigarette as he opened the rear door. He motioned for Alvin to enter.

"Xiao Weiguo, the driver will take you to the airport," Wang said in Mandarin. "I wish you a good journey."

Alvin stood next to the car, still holding his briefcase, trying to discover in Wang's face any hint of what he wanted from him. He swallowed hard before responding in Wang's native language.

"Wang Shutao, I look forward to our next meeting. I assure you, I understand what it means to be a friend, and I will be a friend to the People's Government, though I fear I have little to offer."

Wang placed his hand along Alvin's forearm. "You need not fear, Xiao Weiguo. You are more valuable than you know."

Wang Shutao entered the office of the Minister of State Security. He waited patiently as the Minister read the last page of a report before he removed his reading glasses and looked up.

"Wang Shutao, what did you learn about Xiao? Can we rely on him?"

"Minister, I can't say with certainty. If he were a native-born American, I would say yes, we can rely on him. Most of the Americans we encounter don't believe that rules apply to them. Indeed, they boast that they write their own rules. If they see an advantage for themselves, there is little they will not do to realize it."

The Minister folded his hands together and pressed them to his chin. "But Xiao isn't native-born American. He's Taiwanese."

"Yes, and that's why I can't say confidently that he will cooperate. Although he is ambitious, it's clear that he is not sympathetic to the People's Government. But that's not what concerns me. His knowledge and understanding of Chinese culture are impressive. He understands his place in the arc of history, and that his actions have consequences beyond himself. He may hesitate to cooperate if he thinks it will harm the greater good, even if it's to his own benefit."

"Should we continue the operation?" the Minister asked.

"Yes. He is still our best prospect to obtain access to this technology."

"And remind me, what is Xiao's connection?"

Wang reached into his jacket pocket and took out a folded paper which he had carried since that morning, through the meeting at the Ministry of Commerce, and the tour of the Forbidden City. He opened it and read its contents before continuing.

"He is a director on the board of a small company called Connectrix. We believe that his company, Mechanized Minds, supplies sophisticated computers to Connectrix for the system they are building."

"Yes, the system you think will break encryption keys," the Minister said with palpable skepticism. "Our scientists have been working on this problem for years. They have failed. Tell me why you think this small company will succeed with none of the resources we have at our disposal."

"We only suspect that they are working on this problem. Clearly, this project is of importance to the American government. They have brought in an old Cold Warrior named Hofbauer from the West German intelligence agencies to run the company. But the real reason for our interest is that they have recently hired a man we have been watching for some time."

Wang read from the paper, pronouncing the name with difficulty.

"Matteo Bugatti."

3

THE ENTREPRENEUR

FOLLOWING THE STATUS meeting, Jon returned to his office. He dropped wearily into his chair, looking quite unlike the driven, efficient leader who had conducted the session just minutes before. Matt's announcement at the meeting was encouraging, but it barely dented months of accumulated stress.

Jon's desk was simple, almost spartan, consisting of little more than a long table with a shallow drawer. The only objects on the desk were a flat screen computer, a keyboard, a mouse, and Jon's bound journal. The credenza behind him, unlike his desk, was cluttered with photos and mementos of a twenty-five year career. The walls of the office were decorated with more photos and plaques, and a few framed prints, all with a technical theme, all limited editions, signed and numbered by the artists.

Jon leaned back and stared at the ceiling before closing his eyes. He cleared his mind, breathing slowly and deliberately, before leaning forward. He opened his journal to the meeting notes and began typing:

From: Jon Ames, Chief Technical Officer
To: Josef Hofbauer, Chairman and CEO
Cc: Connectrix Board of Directors—Technical Committee

Subject: Cygnus Program Progress Report—CLASSIFIED

As Jon began transcribing his notes, he heard a tap on the open door to his office. He looked up to see Josef Hofbauer precisely centered in his doorway.

"Jon, do you have a moment?" he said in his clipped German accent.

"Of course. Come in."

Josef entered with short, quick steps and seated himself in the chair in front of Jon's desk.

"You had some excitement this morning, no? We have made a leap, no? *Ja?*"

"It would seem so. If Matt is right, of course."

Josef pursed his lips as he took off his glasses, using them to point at Jon. "You think there is reason to doubt him?"

Jon marked the open page in his journal with a paper clip. He closed it and carefully positioned its edges parallel to the edges of his desk. "I can't say. I have a fair understanding of how he's going about solving this factoring problem but he caught me by surprise this morning. I don't know if it's real or if he's digging a dry well. He's operating way above my level."

Josef nodded slightly as he leaned forward, looking at Jon over his glasses. "What exactly has he done?"

Jon bit his lower lip as he took a deep breath. He leaned his elbows on the desk and held his hands out as if holding an invisible basketball. "You generate a public encryption key by multiplying two large prime numbers. Anyone can encrypt a message with the public key, but you need the two prime factors to decode the message. There are billions of known prime numbers and trillions upon trillions of possible keys when you multiply two primes."

Josef pressed his lips together tightly in a look of annoyance. "I know all this. You could take centuries testing all the pairs of prime numbers. But he does this in hours, not years, no? How does he do this?"

It was a familiar conversation. *Every time I explain this he tells me to start from the beginning,* Jon thought, *and when I start from the beginning he tells me to get on with it.* He continued, slowing his pace, pronouncing each word with exaggerated clarity.

"Think of a flat surface, with two dimensions, like width and length. Each dimension consists of all the prime numbers. You multiply one prime number on the width dimension with another on the length dimension, and you get a product." Jon traced an outline of a rectangle on his desk with his fingers. "That product can be used as the encryption key. Since a prime number can't be evenly divided by any other number besides itself, the product is one single point on the surface. If we can figure out the prime factors, we can decode a message that used that key."

Jon paused, expecting another interruption, but Josef remained silent, still peering unblinking over his glasses, annoyance frozen on his face.

"He doesn't just multiply prime numbers at random. He tests the properties of each prime. Depending on the test, two primes are more or less similar. The more similar they are, the closer together they are on one dimension of the surface."

Josef unfroze his expression with raised eyebrows. "Then they are not in order, small to large?"

"No, they're not. But it's even more complicated. The size of a prime is only one of its properties. Matt has discovered multiple properties of primes. Each property is a separate dimension. Matt told me he searches for the factors not on a flat surface, but in a space with seventeen dimensions."

"Seventeen! *Allmächtiger Gott!* How does one deal with seventeen dimensions?" Josef scoffed, more skeptical than impressed.

Jon shook his head. "I couldn't say. It's not something you can visualize. At least *I* can't visualize it. As for Matt, who knows?"

Josef stood and walked to the wall. He touched his finger to his chin as he examined one of the framed prints on the wall, an ultra-realistic drawing of a steam locomotive. "I wonder—perhaps he can see this in his mind, no? But in any case, how does this help? He still has to try all the pairs, no? *Ja?*"

Jon continued, quickening his pace. "No, he doesn't. He picks a starting point based on the properties of the key, but then he does a test to decide which nearby points are the most likely factors. Then he tries those points, and other points close by those points, and so on. He follows each path until he either finds the factors, or he reaches a dead end. The result is millions of search paths, branching off one another, like the branches and twigs of a tree."

Josef turned toward Jon with a look that seemed just on the edge of comprehension. "So he explores a large space, but he tests only a few points. How does he know he is looking in the right place?"

"He doesn't, at least not for sure. He can only know with a certain probability. It's possible he may never find the answer."

Josef scowled. "Unacceptable! How can we have a system that cannot find a solution in a fixed time? Have you conveyed this to Dr. Bugatti? I cannot tell the National Security Agency that our system only works *some* of the time!"

Jon inhaled, closing his eyes. He opened his eyes to see Josef glowering from across the room.

"Josef, we've discussed this before. We can only calculate the *probability* of finding a solution in a given period of time. But there's a chance it will take a *very long* time. Our job is to reduce that chance to as low a value as possible."

Josef gazed intently at Jon for a moment before looking at the floor, appearing to collect his thoughts. He put his arms behind his back as he moved deliberately toward Jon. He walked behind Jon's desk and stood next to him. He straightened himself to his full height. Jon remained seated, appearing small and subservient next to his CEO.

"The NSA is expecting our progress report by the first of October—just *two weeks*. We have committed to demonstrating the system by April of next year. We will show them a system that will break a two-thousand forty-eight bit key in eight hours or less. *Every time, ja?*"

Jon's jaw clenched and his stomach churned. He stared at his desk as he pressed the knuckles of his tightly closed fist against his lips. His other hand rested on his desk, his fingers tapping as he spoke in a low, strained voice.

"Josef, *you* made that promise, *not me*. You knew from the start how risky this program would be. You knew because *I told you*."

"Jon…"

"*Josef!*" Jon rasped. "We had a perfectly legitimate product plan for a clear text analysis system. If we don't solve the factoring problem we can still fall back on that." He looked up as he gestured toward the door. "Those people out there —*my team*—are frustrated and scared. Matt's breakthrough was the first good news they've had in weeks. But if we continue to hold them to this impossible goal, we'll lose them. And then we'll lose this company. I'm not letting another company go down."

Josef's expression did not change. He looked down at Jon for a few seconds before he removed his glasses and rubbed his eyes.

"If you are quite finished, I will tell you what I thought you already knew. You can sell your *clear text analysis* system if you want. Your brilliant designers and your brilliant programmers will make a system that can analyze a million messages in one second. You will build a big system and you will sell it and then perhaps you will sell one more and then you will run out of customers. Do you understand? It is a simple problem and because you are so good at solving it you will saturate the market very quickly."

Josef broke away and walked back to the locomotive print and resumed his study of it.

"But this system you are making…*Cygnus*, you call it, *ja?* This is very different. Reading an encrypted message no one else can do, not in weeks, not months, not even years. If you could read such a message in weeks, it would not be of interest. But in hours, that is very interesting. If we want to sell this system, I tell you, it must break the code in eight hours, no more."

Jon was still smoldering, but he was listening intently. Josef turned toward Jon. "If they only need to read one message every eight hours, they will only need one machine, no? If they need to read one message every hour, they will need eight machines, no? *Ja?*"

Josef lowered his voice, barely whispering. "This is the NSA. They read *everything*. They need to read thousands, hundreds of thousands, *millions* of messages every day."

Josef paused, never breaking eye contact. "Jon. If you want to sell thousands of systems, they must be very fast, *ja? But not too fast!*"

Josef cleaned his glasses with a small cloth he took from his inside coat pocket, inspecting them repeatedly as he continued.

"You are a good technical man. You have good technical people, and a few geniuses. I have no doubt you can complete any project you undertake as well as anyone, anywhere." He motioned toward the collection of memorabilia on the credenza. "But your history as a businessman is, should we say, somewhat checkered, no?"

Jon felt himself flush, but kept quiet.

"That is why I am here. This technology has great potential, but it must be managed. I have worked with the NSA for many years. I know them. Your board of directors brought me here to run this company because I am the one who understands this customer."

He inspected his glasses one last time before replacing them.

"If it were up to you, you would have set a goal you felt confident you could obtain, no? Perhaps a thousand or two thousand hours. I would have pushed you to be more aggressive and you would have perhaps given me a goal in the hundreds of hours, no? Hundreds of hours. Weeks, in other words. And no one would want your machine that can read a secret message weeks after it was sent."

Jon listened as the blood continued to rise, burning in his cheeks.

"I did not set a goal of eight hours because I thought you could accomplish it. I set a goal of eight hours because it will make us the most money. It was a risk you would not have taken, no? That is why I am running this company instead of you."

Jon stood. "This is *my* company. *I* built it. You're my superior, but it's *my* company. You can go to the board if you don't like the job I'm doing but it's still *my company, not yours.*"

Josef sighed deeply as he walked toward the door, turning back before leaving. "*Ja,* it is your company. But you need to keep some things in mind. First, if I did not set this very aggressive goal, your boy Bugatti would not have had his breakthrough. People rarely do more than they're expected to do, but they will often surprise you when the task is sufficiently challenging. Second, it is a very good thing for your company to deliver on a large government contract. And third, it is a very *bad* thing for your little company if you do not deliver." He gestured again toward the credenza. "Then your company, and all your work, and the work of your very talented team will be just another souvenir on your trophy shelf."

As Josef left Jon remained standing, fighting off his anger before sitting again.

❖ ❖ ❖

Connectrix was the third company Jon had founded since leaving the supercomputer maker Cray Research more than twenty years before. His first company, American Computation Incorporated, known as ACI, was one of a number of companies that made smaller versions of the powerful Cray computers, with only a fraction of their power but vastly cheaper. It was a competitive market with multiple players chasing a few specialized customers. Jon did well when ACI was acquired, making his first million before he was thirty-five. But Jon aimed higher.

Convergent Concepts, Jon's second company, provided tools to develop programs for parallel computers. It was a unique product, with enough promise to justify a public offering, and for a short time Jon was wealthy, on paper at least. For the second time he found the market limited, serving narrowly defined applications, and within a few years the company was acquired at a fraction of its initial share price.

Jon made money on both ventures, but not an extravagant amount. It was enough to live well, even luxuriously, but it was not enough to satisfy his ambition. It was certainly not enough to rank him among the legends of the tech revolution: Bill Gates, Steve Jobs, or even Cray Research founder Seymour Cray, a mercurial genius who never achieved fabulous wealth but who nonetheless made history. Most men would have been satisfied with Jon's accomplishments. Jon was not.

❖ ❖ ❖

Jon looked over the memorabilia on his credenza, accumulated over twenty-five years and four companies: a photograph of himself with Seymour Cray next to an early model Cray supercomputer, a gold-plated circuit board from an ACI computer, a champagne bottle from a party held on the evening of Convergent Concepts' initial public offering. There were paperweights and more framed photographs, scattered among a dozen more pieces of gilded electronic gear, each with an engraved plaque listing the date, the names of its inventors, and a description of its now obsolete function. Jon did not keep them in his office to boast of his accomplishments. They were a reminder to himself of his own lofty goals and the degree to which he had fallen short.

A few moments passed before Jon shook himself out of his funk. He turned back to his desk to continue his report.

But he thought again before opening his journal to the marked page. He went to the office door and looked out on the small open space, broken up by cubicle walls. He spotted Eric Reilly, the Cygnus hardware team leader, standing in the opening of the cubicle of one of his designers. Eric was half a head taller than Jon and weighed nearly two hundred fifty pounds, though he carried his weight well.

"Eric," Jon called out. Eric turned to Jon without lifting his hands from their resting places on the cubicle walls.

"Do you have a minute?"

Eric spoke a few words to his designer before ambling toward Jon's office. Jon made way for Eric and closed the door behind him as he entered. Eric paused and gave Jon a questioning look. Jon rarely held impromptu closed-door meetings, and when he did, it usually signaled some urgent matter. As the door closed, Eric anticipated a prolonged interruption to his day.

"What's up, Chief?" Eric said evenly, with just a hint of anxiety.

Jon recognized the note in Eric's voice. He'd heard it hundreds of times in the thirty years they'd known each other. They had roomed together during their college days in Madison. When Seymour Cray recruited Jon after graduation, Jon insisted that Eric come along. When Jon left Cray to start his own company, Eric was the first man he recruited to his startup team, not because he was a virtuoso designer, but because he was a steady, practical, no foolishness hardware man who could solve problems and get things done. Whenever Jon left one company to start another, Eric was quick to follow.

Jon took his seat behind his desk and motioned to Eric to take the chair opposite him.

"Don't look so worried. I've just been thinking over a few things and I want to get your perspective."

Eric relaxed a bit. "Sure, Chief. What's on your mind?"

"Tell me how the team is reacting to Matt's report."

Eric smiled slightly. "They're reacting pretty damn good. I haven't seen them this fired up in weeks."

Jon's eyes dropped, as if he were contemplating his clasped hands resting on his desk. Eric's smile disappeared and his look grew more anxious.

"Wait a minute," he said, "are you going to tell me it's not real?"

It was Jon's turn to smile. "Always the alarmist, aren't you?" He unclasped his hands and gripped the edge of his desk, leaning back slightly in his chair.

"To be honest, I don't know if it's real or not. I don't know if Matt knows. But I'm taking it at face value. That's not what I wanted to talk to you about."

"Okay, I'm listening."

Jon relaxed his grip. "I want to know how Matt's doing. The whole program depends on him. I want to know if he's holding up, if we can count on him to keep the program moving forward."

"Oh," Eric responded, "good question. I don't have a good answer." Eric leaned forward and rested his fleshy forearms on the desk.

"Jon, we've worked with some smart guys but Matt is the smartest. He's a genius. I used to say that about Seymour Cray but Matt's even smarter than Seymour. He's brilliant. But here's the thing."

Eric removed his arms from the desk and laced his fingers behind his head. "He's wrapped tight, really tight. He works ninety hours a week and barely stops for bathroom breaks. Usually he's a nice guy but when he gets rolling you don't want to come near him. If he doesn't ignore you he bites your head off. I know the whole program depends on him, but I think he could lose it at any time."

It was what Jon expected, but didn't want to hear. "I was afraid of that," he said with a mix of frustration, despair, and residual anger from his encounter with Josef. "Any idea how we can keep him cheerful until we finish this program?"

Eric pressed his lips into a thin, straight line and shook his head slightly. "Well, I could give you my opinion, but if you really want the inside story, talk to Anson. He's the closest thing Matt has to a friend."

"All right," said Jon. "See if he's free to talk to me."

Eric chuckled lightly. "Jon, you're the boss. You tell any of us to come and we'll come. For you, we're always free."

Jon chuckled back and stood up to signal Eric that the conversation was over. Eric paused as he walked toward the door and looked back through narrowed eyes.

"Jon, how's this thing going to come out?"

"What do you mean?"

"ACI didn't pan out like we planned. I thought we had the big score when Convergent went public, but that fizzled."

Jon looked pained.

"Hey, I don't mean anything by that," Eric assured him. "Hell, we both did okay on those deals. I could retire today and live very comfortably. But I like working for you. And I know you want more. Is Connectrix going to be the big score?"

Jon forced a confident smile. "If we have anything to say about it, it will."

Eric left the office, reassured, as Jon looked after him.

And if we deliver on this contract, he thought. *And if I can keep Matt Bugatti happy.*

Jon had just returned to his seat when Anson Polk tapped on the door frame.

"Hey, Jon, the big guy says you want to talk to me."

"Come in, Anson. Shut the door."

Anson complied, showing none of Eric's apprehension.

"Man, the place is on fire, Jon. Nonstop chatter. We're hitting on all cylinders again," Anson said cheerily as he sat. "I hope you're in the mood to enjoy it. Seemed like you were doing your best to pee on the Froot Loops this morning."

Jon winced. "Glad to hear it, Anson. How's Matt taking it?"

Anson's mouth spread into a wide grin. "How do you think? He left the meeting and went right back to work. A couple of folks stopped by his cube to congratulate him and he barely grunted. When he's at the vertex, nothing makes an impression on him."

"He *is* a machine, isn't he? That's what I wanted to talk to you about. I'm worried about him. We're depending on him for so much and I need to know he's holding up."

Anson rubbed his chin. "Holding up? Hard to tell. He's got a lot of pressure on him, and not just from the Connectrix Mental Ward."

Jon reacted visibly to *mental ward* but let it slide. "What kind of pressure?"

Anson gestured as he spoke, with his wide, pale palms facing upward.

"Jon, you think Matt's this cool, calculating wonder boy, but he's got another side to him. His family is first generation Italian, very traditional, very old school. If it was just his mama putting the arm on him to get married and make babies he could handle it. But that's not just what his mother wants. It's what *he* wants. He goes on and on about his home life, or lack thereof, and how this place is eating him alive. His love life is the shits, so he throws himself into his work. Then he spends all his time at his keyboard instead of the Knights of Columbus mixer meeting a nice Italian girl. It's a vicious circle."

"Is it affecting his work?"

"*Yeah*, it's affecting his work—for the *better*. He's channeling all that sexual tension into his programming. I think we owe this breakthrough to a severe bout of horniness."

"So there's no problem, right? Matt keeps working and we hit our goal."

Anson shook his head. "Jesus Christ, Jon, were you ever young? How long do you think Matt can keep that up? Sure, he's making history right now, but if he doesn't get laid soon he's going to snap."

Jon pressed his fingers against his eyes. "Okay, Anson, I get the picture. Do me a favor. Take him out tonight and get him to let off some steam. The last thing we need is to lose Matt. He means too much to the program."

Anson stood up and rubbed his palms together. "Is that an order? Because if it is, I'm turning in an expense report."

"Go ahead, I'll sign. Take the whole group. Have a good time."

"I'll ask around but I don't know how many takers I'll get. Have you gotten close to Matt today? I don't know when he last took a shower. He reeks."

As Anson left, Jon opened his journal to the marked page and resumed typing his report. Less than a minute later, the phone on his desk rang. Jon recognized the number on the display—the cell phone number of his wife, Hannah.

Perfect. Just what I need right now. He picked up the handset.

"Connectrix, Jon Ames," he said flatly.

There was a moment of silence before Hannah replied, "Why do you do that? You know it's me."

Answered your own question, didn't you?

"Sorry, I was working on something. I just picked up. Anyway, should we even be talking? Shouldn't your lawyer be talking to my lawyer?"

Hannah's voice sounded as it always did in the weeks since they agreed to a divorce—carefully measured, but with undertones of fear and anger.

"I talked to my lawyer and he suggested I call you directly with an offer."

"I'm listening."

"I know you've got your money tied up in your company so I'm willing to settle for a third instead of half."

Jon's stomach tightened. The idea of parting with *any* substantial portion of his assets, much less a third, brought him to the edge of physical illness.

"That's very generous of you but I still don't see why you should even get a third. I was the one that worked my ass off for the last twenty years. Besides, I can't even come up with that much without liquidating my shares in the company. I've offered you twenty-five percent and I'll have to mortgage the house to get that much. If that's not good enough for you we'll let the judge decide."

There was a pause of perhaps ten seconds, during which Jon anticipated the possible responses. His offer of one-fourth of his worth was only his latest; he had wanted to deny his wife any settlement but his lawyer convinced him that was unreasonable. But he also knew he couldn't offer much more. His liquid assets were limited after he put most of his money into Connectrix—over his wife's objections. It was this act which finally broke a marriage that had barely survived years of inattention, uncertainty and brutally long working hours.

"Damn it, Jon, why are you such a bastard?"

Jon kept quiet during the pause that followed. Hannah spoke first.

"All right, if that's what it will take to get past this, I'll take it."

Jon exhaled as silently as he could, but he didn't get a chance to respond before Hannah continued.

"But I get the house."

"Forget it!" Jon shouted. *Bitch!* he added silently.

"That is as much my house as it is yours."

"I paid for it."

"But I made it. I was the one who had to deal with the builder, the decorator, the landscaper. That house is more me than you."

You're breaking my heart, Jon thought.

But it was true: the style of the house, its furnishings, its surroundings, were all a reflection of his wife's tastes, which he admired. But Jon regarded his house as the principle outward sign of his accomplishments, the most tangible proof of his success.

"You have my offer and it doesn't include the house. From now on, if you want to talk, have your lawyer call me."

Before Hannah could respond, Jon dropped the handset in its cradle.

Jon sat motionless for a long time, left arm across his chest, right hand propping up his chin. He turned slightly in his chair, back and forth, as he tried to calm his mind. As he turned, he caught sight of an empty champagne bottle on the credenza. He leaned forward and picked it up, examining the inscription etched into the glass.

Convergent Concepts Initial Public Offering
August 14, 1999

Offer Price $15.00
Closing Price $27.00
Congratulations Team!

Jon rotated slowly in his chair as he studied the relic. Then he threw the bottle toward the door. It caromed off one wall near the corner, then the adjacent wall, before spinning across the floor, coming to rest against the wheels of his office chair. The force of the collision was not enough to break the heavy glass bottle, but the noise was audible throughout the office. The normal, constant buzz of conversation and key clicks outside Jon's office ceased. Eric Reilly peered around the doorframe.

"Chief, are you okay?" he asked uncertainly.

"Fine, Eric. No problem. I'm just fine." He went back to typing his report.

4

THE AGENT

Neither Anson nor Matt noticed the car that followed them from Stella Blues to Matt's apartment—a dark green Ford, not new, but well maintained. At night, under street lights, the car appeared black. Anyone trying to identify the car would very likely describe it as black. The illusion was intentional.

The driver was a man in his late thirties with dark, wiry hair, wearing a black hooded sweatshirt. The dark car, being driven by a dark man in a dark shirt was not supposed to draw attention to itself. And the fact that the driver was trained and well practiced in the skills of surveillance virtually guaranteed that he would not be noticed.

He parked his car a discreet distance from the apartment building, far enough to avoid detection but near enough to observe Matt as he stepped out of Anson's car and closed the door behind him. Matt turned back and leaned into the open window. *Subject paused for brief conversation with driver after exiting the vehicle*, the man noted. After a moment Matt stood up and slapped the top of Anson's car, as if it were the hindquarters of a horse. As Anson drove off Matt turned and walked unsteadily into the apartment building.

The man in the black sweatshirt watched the window of Matt's apartment for a few minutes. The light did not come on. He considered whether he should enter the building and verify that Matt had returned to his apartment but decided against it. *I've been watching this guy for months*, he thought. *He's in there. He has got to be leading the most boring life in this god-awful boring town.*

He let another minute pass after he was certain Matt was back in his apartment. *The guy probably passed out from exhaustion*, he thought. The man opened his laptop computer and began typing, finishing in just a few minutes, having previously summarized most of Matt Bugatti's activities for the prior forty-eight hours.

He picked up his cell phone, an elaborate device that opened to reveal a keyboard and a touchscreen. He tapped the screen a few times before closing the device and pressing it to his ear. The phone rang only once before the other party answered.

"Good evening, Agent Gutierrez. You're later than usual. Dr. Bugatti must have had an enjoyable evening."

"Good evening, sir," responded FBI Special Agent Anibal Gutierrez. "The subject has just returned to his residence. He left Connectrix at approximately six-fifteen after spending the entire day, last night, and the previous day at work. He went immediately to an establishment known as Stella Blues, where he remained until approximately ten-fifteen, during which he drank four beers and two shots of liquor. In addition to Matt Bugatti I observed Anson Polk, Eric Reilly, and Kathy Darling. Mr. Reilly and Ms. Darling left early in the evening. Mr. Polk drove Dr. Bugatti home, arriving approximately five minutes ago. There was no contact with any party beyond those mentioned, other than the waiters at the bar."

"Thank you, Agent Gutierrez. I have no questions."

Anibal hesitated, but finally decided to rid himself of a burden he'd carried obediently for months.

"Well, *I* have a question. I want to know why I'm giving my report to you before I give it to my supervisor. You're not even in the Bureau. I've never been asked to report outside the Bureau before and it's not right."

The voice at the other end of the conversation responded coolly, with no indication of irritation or indignation.

"I understand your concern, Agent Gutierrez, but you should have had this conversation already with your supervisor. This is a special assignment. I have made arrangements to be kept informed of the activities of Dr. Bugatti, and for you to make these reports directly to me as they become available. These arrangements should have been communicated to you by your supervisor."

"Yes, we discussed it. I know what I'm supposed to do. What I don't know is *why*. I don't know who *you* are or why the Bureau would deviate from policy just for you."

"Agent Gutierrez," the voice responded, now with a hint of impatience, "you have your instructions, and you've executed them admirably these past weeks. It is not necessary for you to know any more than you've been told. I expect your reports nightly. If you have further concerns, please take them up with your supervisor."

Anibal grumbled to himself but let the matter drop. The man was right. He had his orders. The fact that the orders were unorthodox, indeed, unheard of, should be of no concern. But it bothered him anyway.

"All right, sir. I'm sorry I brought it up. Have a good evening."

"And good evening to you, Agent Gutierrez. By now I'm sure Dr. Bugatti is sound asleep. I think it's time you went home and got some sleep yourself, no? *Ja?*"

5

THE CONFERENCE

NELS COFFMAN RELAXED during a rare free moment the afternoon before the International Number Theory Symposium, to be held for the first time at the University of North Carolina at Chapel Hill. Hosting the conference was a personal coup for Nels, evidence of his success as head of the Department of Mathematics. The world community of mathematicians considered North Carolina a leader in number theory research, the result not only of Nels's own tireless efforts, but of a few lucky breaks that concentrated an awesome pool of talent at the university. It was a lineup that produced a steady stream of publications, more than a few considered seminal works. Although his most brilliant and productive researcher had left the department almost a year ago, he left behind a legacy of accomplishment that inspired the rest to push the boundaries of this obscure field. Nels gave himself credit for having placed North Carolina among the leading mathematics research institutions, but he also gave much of the credit to Matt Bugatti.

With success came rewards, which Nels enjoyed freely. His office was richly decorated with antiques: a massive, ornately carved desk and matching sideboard, and a similarly ornate bookcase housing several first edition volumes on mathematics, some inscribed by the authors. Vintage scientific instruments and artifacts covered nearly every horizontal surface. He had accumulated his collection over many years, but his acquisitions became rarer and more expensive as his department's reputation grew, raising the prestige of the university, attracting grants from government, industry, and foundations. Although Nels was a competent mathematician, his real talent was finding young geniuses, turning them into productive researchers, and parlaying their success into a bigger department budget and a higher salary. He had achieved nearly legendary status among his peers, having co-authored more than a hundred papers in the last five years. It was a period he contemplated with pride as he took a bottle of frightfully expensive scotch from his sideboard and poured himself a generous drink.

As Nels stood at the window behind his desk he heard a timid tapping at the door.

"Dr. Bugatti," Nels said, smiling and nodding, as he motioned for Matt to enter. "Welcome home."

Matt entered and glanced around the office. "Dr. Coffman, your collection has grown," he remarked as he shook hands with his former mentor. Matt's ill-fitting and well-worn outfit contrasted sharply with Nels's tailored shirt and designer suit. The men grinned at each other through their extended handshake, until Nels gestured toward one chair and sat in another.

"Collecting is an addiction, Matt. I think cocaine would be cheaper."

"But not that scotch, if I remember your tastes."

Nels held out the elegant cut crystal glass. It caught the sunlight and sprayed the walls with rainbow specks.

"Would you like some? It's against the rules to drink in the offices, but I won't tell if you don't."

"No, thanks. I think that particular brand might be wasted on me."

Nels took another sip and set the glass aside. "I was happy to hear that you'd be attending our symposium, Matt. But I'm disappointed that you're not presenting."

"We're working on a sensitive project," Matt explained as he ran his fingers awkwardly along the length of his tie. "Everything that goes public has to be reviewed and approved. I thought about writing a paper, but I just didn't have anything to offer that could get past the censors. I wasn't even sure they'd let me attend the conference."

Nels pressed his fingers against his lips, then let his hand fall to the drink on the table beside him. "Matt, our field is mathematics. Its discoveries belong to posterity. You're destined to make history—if you don't hide your genius from the world." He idly rotated the glass. "This secrecy will only slow progress, not stop it. Research will go on, and others will get credit for your discoveries."

Nels held his glass in front of him, lifting one finger to point at Matt. "You can have a position on the faculty of this department any time you want it. You'll be tenured before you're thirty." He looked directly into Matt's eyes. "You can remain obscure, or you can share your talent with the students of this university and with your peers and get the recognition you deserve." He paused before delivering what he hoped would be an irrefutable closing argument. "Come work for me, and you'll win the Fields Medal."

It was not the first time that Nels had suggested that Matt could win the prestigious award for young mathematicians. Matt was sure he had the talent to do so. The idea appealed to him, and Nels knew it. It was the most persuasive argument Nels could have made.

"I appreciate the offer, Dr. Coffman," Matt said softly, "but I've got to see this through."

Matt leaned forward, hands folded, elbows resting on his knees. "Do you know that quote from Samuel Johnson? 'Nothing focuses your mind like knowing you're going to hang in the morning?' That's what this project is like. I've come up with new, fundamental theories, on the fly, turned them into computer code, and proved that they work, all on a deadline. That kind of pressure forces me to take risks. It forces me to think in ways I wouldn't otherwise. It makes me a better mathematician." Matt lowered his voice to a whisper.

"I'm doing the best work of my life. You would not *believe* what I've come up with."

Nels sat up straight, a startled look on his face. Matt's whispered revelation convinced Nels that Matt had achieved a breakthrough, possibly revolutionary—and that he could not share it with the world. That prospect made Nels all the more determined.

"Matt, you are uniquely qualified to lead our research in computational number theory. You have a premier reputation in the field and with your degree in computer science we could build a whole program around you."

Matt looked down between his knees and smiled before looking into Nels's eyes. He could see the man was sincere, but he also knew where Nels's loyalties lay. Every word Nels said was true, but to Nels, Matt was a means to an end—the elevation of the University of North Carolina, and, ultimately, of Nels Coffman.

"I'm sorry, Dr. Coffman, but I'm sticking it out," he repeated. "I've got to get this system into production."

Nels lifted his glass and sipped the last of his scotch. "Good god, you've become an engineer. I can't imagine a more dismal fate."

"It's not that bad," Matt chuckled. "My love life is non-existent, but what else is new?" He straightened himself in his chair. "It's good to know I've got a place to land if it doesn't work out."

"Yes, you do," Nels said as he set down his glass. "But don't wait too long. If you don't publish, your standing in the academic community will slide. Besides, you only have another dozen or so years to win the Fields Medal, and they don't award it every year."

Matt stood and Nels followed suit.

"Dr. Coffman, I'll see you at the conference tomorrow," Matt said as he extended his hand.

Nels took Matt's hand. "We're having a reception tonight for the speakers, and dinner tomorrow night. You're welcome to come as my guest."

"Thanks, Dr. Coffman. I'd love to come to dinner tomorrow. I have plans for tonight."

◆ ◆ ◆

Matt crossed the courtyard along the same path he'd traveled hundreds of times during his years at the university. It was a typical glorious October afternoon in North Carolina, still comfortably warm, with a hint of cooler weather to come. Matt took his time as he strolled among the trees, their sunward leaves just starting to turn their brilliant fall colors. He slowed his pace, then stopped. As he took in his surroundings, he noticed his own breathing, measured and regular. He closed his eyes, feeling the stress drain from his body for the first time in months.

The building that housed the Department of Philosophy was warm and inviting—wall coverings and furnishings gave the surroundings the feel of a traditional Southern home. Matt paused in the reception area, enjoying the feeling of nostalgia, until the receptionist called his name.

"Matt Bugatti!" she cried with delight as she stood and hurried from behind her desk. She was a substantial woman in her late fifties, her face framed in graying curls, her eyes narrowed to joyful arcs by her ecstatic smile. Matt smiled back as she trotted toward him with her arms wide.

"How *are* you? Come here, give me a hug!" Her smooth Southern accent fell musically on Matt's ears.

"Jenny, I'm wonderful," Matt said as their arms encircled each other in an affectionate hug. "You look great."

"And you look skinny, darling," she observed as she held Matt at arms' length. "I don't think you were this skinny when you were a teenager. You're not sick, are you?"

"I'm fine, Jenny. I guess I miss my mom's cooking."

"How is your mama? How is her restaurant doing?"

"Mom's doing well. Her restaurant is doing *really* well. She hired more help so she can have some time to herself."

"I need to get over there to Raleigh sometime to see your mama."

Jenny went back to her desk. "Emmett's here. He would kill you if you didn't stop in and say hello."

"Jenny, I came here to see *you*, but I suppose I could say hi to Emmett," he said, grinning widely.

"Oh, go on," she laughed. "I'll call and let Emmett know you're on your way back."

"No, don't call. I want to surprise him." He took a step toward the hall, then paused.

"Jenny, I've missed you."

Jenny rested her chin on her hand, smiling more enthusiastically than before. "We *all* miss *you*, darling. You take care now." Her eyes followed Matt as he walked down the hallway before she turned cheerfully back to her work.

Matt walked to the last door, layered with clippings, cartoons, class schedules, test scores, announcements, and dozens of other odd snippets, some more than a year old, surrounding the nameplate: *Emmett Komalski*. The door was slightly ajar. Matt quietly pushed it open and stood silently in the doorway.

The room was riotously disarrayed. Piles of books and stacks of paper nearly concealed a well-used metal desk, spilling over its edges and pooling on the floor, spreading in all directions. Shelves lined the walls, stuffed with books of all sorts, most with ragged scraps of paper sprouting from their edges. Posters hung above the bookcases, held in place with pushpins. Amid the chaos sat a disheveled man in a wrinkled white shirt, reading a heavy volume, oblivious to all else. Matt stepped quietly into the room.

"Hello, Emmett."

Emmett barely reacted other than to raise his hand, signaling that he knew he was not alone but that he could not respond immediately. He continued to read another thirty seconds, then laid the book carefully atop the shallowest pile on his desk. As he peered over his reading glasses his face registered a look of recognition which transformed slowly to one of warm greeting.

"Matt Bugatti. Come in, boy!" He beckoned with his hands as he blazed a trail through the underbrush of printed matter to embrace Matt. After a moment Emmett broke the embrace and took a step back, considering Matt with a clinical expression.

"You've lost weight, boy. Should I be worried about you?"

"Jenny said the same thing, and no, you shouldn't be worried about me."

"Sit, sit! I'm sure we have a lot to talk about. I want to hear what you think of the real world. Is it what you expected?"

Matt removed a book from a wooden chair and looked for spot to put it. Emmett took it from him and set it on the corner of his desk where it perched unsteadily for a moment before slipping to the floor. Emmett reacted with mock horror as he picked up the book and placed it carefully on a shelf and then took his seat behind his desk. He folded his hands on the desk and looked at Matt over his glasses, his sparse hair forming a halo illuminated by the late afternoon sun streaming through the window.

"So, Matt, tell me. Are you happy?"

It sounded like a simple question, but between Matt and Emmett it was profound. Through five years of study and two post-doctoral years, Emmett provided Matt with sanctuary from the awful pressure of high expectations in a demanding profession. Matt was years younger than his classmates when he entered college, having graduated from high school at fourteen with several advanced placement and university-level courses to his credit. From his first day at college Matt saw himself as others saw him—an awkward boy, a socially isolated curiosity.

In his second year Matt chose as an elective an introductory course in philosophy, taught by Professor Emmett Komalski. For the first time in his academic life, Matt struggled. The problems of philosophy didn't lend themselves to the methods of analysis with which Matt was most comfortable. He was forced to think in new directions, wrestling with problems not of logic, but of meaning and belief. To Matt, the conceptual landscape of mathematics was intricate but well defined, governed by rules, whose propositions could be clearly stated and unambiguously proved. Philosophy was a jungle with no single destination and no clear path. Matt found it at once frustrating and irresistible.

Midway through the semester Matt's life suffered an upheaval: the death of his father, Giovanni. It was a blow that might have shattered Matt had it not been for Emmett Komalski. Emmett was a patient listener, counselor, and friend as Matt questioned the foundations of his beliefs, his morals, and his personal motivations. Together, Emmett and Matt explored the meaning of life in general and of Matt's life in particular.

Between Matt and Emmett, the definition of *happiness* could fill a book.

"No, Emmett, I'm not happy. Not yet."

Emmett nodded with understanding.

"Emmett, I'm doing things now I didn't know I could do. The stuff I'm coming up with—it's incredible. I don't know where it's coming from. I don't think it's too much to say that no one else could do it. I didn't know *I* could do it."

Emmett raised one hand from the desk and rested his forehead against it.

"That's good. Self-actualization. Using your talents to their full potential. That's necessary, but not sufficient. What about recognition?"

Matt looked down. "Not much of that, I'm afraid. The program is classified—top secret. I do get props from my teammates, though."

Emmett raised his hand with two fingers extended, as if he were offering benediction. "But that's not enough, is it? Your achievements deserve acclaim. It's not your nature to toil in obscurity. That's not pride or arrogance—your sense of fairness *demands* it. You owe it to your chosen field, to the memory of your father. You owe it to yourself. And you owe it to *posterity*."

"Posterity," Matt repeated. "That's the second time I've heard that word in the last hour."

"Matt, you have a voice in a centuries-long dialog. You need to be heard."

Emmett leaned back in his chair and contemplated the young man. "You have a conflict. How do you resolve it?"

Matt squeezed his eyes shut and massaged his forehead. "I don't know, Emmett. If I stay with the program, everything I'm doing stays a state secret. If I opt out, I lose my edge."

Emmett nodded. "And what about your family life?"

"Not much is happening in that department. I'm working eighty and ninety hour weeks. It doesn't leave much time for a social life. And Eau Claire, Wisconsin is not exactly a Mecca for singles."

Emmett chuckled.

"But how important is that, anyway?" Matt asked, as much of himself as of Emmett.

"Matt," Emmett replied, no longer chuckling, "we've discussed this many times. Your need for a relationship and a family are as much a part of who you are as is your talent with math. You know, don't you, that if you neglect that need, you'll come to resent your profession. What will that do to your 'edge?' You'll risk your happiness just as certainly as if you were to waste your gifts on trivialities."

Matt nodded. "I know, Emmett. It's just going to have to wait, that's all. I don't want to pressure myself to find a girlfriend with everything else going on in my insane existence, not right now, anyway."

"Matt, you know how important perspective is. Of course you should allow yourself to choose your priorities, and you understand that priorities change. But don't compromise your goals. If you have to make a temporary concession to practical demands, acknowledge that, but hold on to your aspirations." He leaned back in his chair. A hint of a smile appeared. "Success isn't guaranteed, but if you go down…"

"…go down with guns a-blazing!" Matt interrupted, completing a phrase he and Emmett had repeated innumerable times over many years.

❖ ❖ ❖

The last remnants of daylight remained as Matt pulled into the driveway of the Bugatti home. He turned off the engine and rested a moment, looking at the house in the fading light, a modest but well-tended home, close to its neighbors, all on a row of small, neatly trimmed lawns. An oak tree towered over the house from behind, its first few fallen leaves scattered on the roof and collecting in the gutter. A cropped hedge spanned the front of the house below the windows, which glowed through closed drapes, illuminating the bushes from behind as the last rays of sunlight vanished.

As Matt stepped out of the car the front door of the house opened. Flora Bugatti stepped onto the small porch as the light streamed through the opening, casting a shadow on the front walk. She was tall, almost as tall as Matt. Her dark hair, sparsely streaked with gray, framed her Mediterranean features. She was elegantly dressed, and a person could accurately describe her as striking.

Flora stepped off the stoop and strode toward Matt in the slow, even style she had practiced over many years as the hostess of an upscale restaurant, appearing not so much to walk as to glide. She reached Matt shortly after he closed the car door and turned to face her.

"*Matteo caro*," she greeted Matt as she enveloped him in her arms. She kissed him warmly on his cheek.

"Hi, Mom. You look good," Matt replied. Although they had not seen each other for nearly nine months, Matt was certain that Flora had not changed at all.

"So do you, dear. But you're thin. You look the way your father looked in the middle of a project, when he wasn't eating or sleeping," she said as the two of them walked toward the house, her hand on Matt's arm. "It always worried me. I worry about you, too."

"Mom, I'm fine," he reassured her. "You don't need to worry about me."

"I hope not, dear. You know, your father had his attack when he was in the middle of a big project, when he wasn't taking care of himself. So I think I have cause to worry." She put her arm around his shoulder and pressed him to her side. "I don't want to lose you, too."

As the two of them entered the meticulously maintained home, Matt recognized the scent of his mother's *braciole*, a favorite of Matt's, and time consuming to prepare. *She's been cooking all day*, he thought. He flashed a smile at Flora and hugged her again.

"When did you find time to make *braciole*?"

"Marie is hosting for me at the restaurant today," she answered. "I wanted dinner to be special for you. And I knew you'd be thin."

Flora had prepared a meal as elaborate as any she served at her restaurant, *Da Flora*. Through the early courses, Flora reported the local gossip. Matt recognized the names and acted interested as Flora gave an account of who were engaged, who had married, and whose marriages had produced children. Occasionally she would tell him about a neighbor's vacation, or a friend's illness, but for the most part she stuck to the family theme.

As Flora served the *braciole*, she took the conversation to the next stop along the path to its logical conclusion.

"Matt, are you working so hard that you can't meet new people?"

Matt felt a twinge of queasiness. "Are you asking me if I'm working so hard that I can't meet a girl?"

Flora smiled weakly as she reached across the table and placed her hand on his.

"Matteo, you're my only child. You know I'm just concerned for your happiness."

Happiness, Matt thought. *Meet a girl and be happy. I wish it were that simple.*

"I know, Mom, but wouldn't a few grandchildren make *you* happy? That's not your motive, is it?"

"*Matteo caro*, of course I'd like to have grandchildren, but I know it would also make *you* happy to have children of your own. That will happen in its own time—if it happens. Meanwhile I worry about you, the way mothers worry. I want to know that your life is good."

Flora patted Matt's hand as she spoke. "Your father was not a joyful man. He worked too hard—like you do. Such a stubborn man. And impatient." She smiled. "But on the day you were born you would have thought that he ruled the world."

She folded both her hands around Matt's hand and squeezed it gently.

"So, Matteo, tell me. Are you happy?"

Until that moment Matt had noticed no changes in Flora's appearance since he had last seen her. Now he saw shadows and lines of age in her face. The independent, resilient woman who had raised him, who had started a business and made it successful, who had suffered the loss of a husband and endured, suddenly seemed vulnerable and frail.

"Matteo?" Flora said, squeezing his hand again.

"Yes, Mom," Matt answered at last. "I'm happy."

❖ ❖ ❖

The next morning Matt arrived early to the symposium. The international gathering would be the perfect occasion to announce a breakthrough in number theory. This was Matt's primary reason for attending, and it was the justification he had offered when he requested permission to attend. Matt anxiously reviewed the titles of the sessions, looking for any hint that others were pursuing lines of thought similar to his. None seemed directly relevant to his own discoveries—to his great relief.

Throughout the day Matt was reminded of how much he enjoyed these meetings. He renewed old acquaintances and made new ones, some with persons whose names he had known for years but had never met. Nearly all had heard of Dr. Matteo Bugatti.

❖ ❖ ❖

Nels had arranged for dinner at a local restaurant to which he invited the general session speakers and a few guests. Matt arrived shortly after six and was shown to a private room where Nels and the others were enjoying cocktails and appetizers

"And here is our Dr. Bugatti, who has been absent too long," Nels announced with a raised glass. "Matt, come here. I don't know if you've met Dr. Petrescu."

Matt made his way toward Nels, who was standing beside a young woman with straight black hair and a smallish man whose thick glasses nearly obscured his eyes. Matt offered his hand to the man.

"Dr. Marku Petrescu, I'm pleased to meet you. I enjoyed your talk today."

The man looked up with a thin, nearly imperceptible smile. "Thank you, Dr. Bugatti. I hope you found my theories credible. I must say, I was hoping to hear from you during the conference. I was disappointed when I didn't find you on the program. Your papers on properties of prime numbers were astounding. I owe much of my own progress to you. But you've gone silent these past months. Where have you been?"

Before Matt could answer Nels jumped in.

"Dr. Bugatti has been doing some important work that he's not yet ready to publish. But I'm hoping I can convince him to come back to North Carolina to continue his research."

"That's right, Dr. Petrescu," Matt added. "I'm afraid my research is incomplete. I can't say when I'll be ready to publish. As for coming back to the university, who knows? For the time being I'll remain in my current position, but Dr. Coffman is very persuasive."

Nels laughed as he placed a hand on Matt's shoulder. "I haven't yet tapped my most potent powers of persuasion. For example, you will work with some of the finest young mathematical minds in the world." He motioned in the direction of the young woman. "You do remember Connie, don't you?"

"Of course I remember Connie," Matt said, shaking the woman's hand. "You should be very close to completing your doctoral thesis by now."

Connie smiled warmly. "I am, in just a few months, in fact. I'm very proud of it. You should be, too. I give you more than a small amount of the credit."

The waiter offered Matt a glass of wine and refilled the others' glasses. After a brief pause, Dr. Petrescu spoke.

"Dr. Bugatti, I wonder, have you explored the application of your theorems on properties of primes to the problem of factoring large products of prime numbers?"

Matt swallowed hard at such a direct question. "It's occurred to me. It's an important problem, of course, but very difficult to solve. Perhaps impossible."

Petrescu's gaze remained fixed on Matt through his substantial spectacles.

"History has taught us that what is impossible in one age becomes possible in the next," Petrescu countered. "But I would agree with you that the problem will remain intractable. You have described eleven properties of prime numbers that could be utilized in a factoring algorithm. My own research indicates that these properties are insufficient to construct a practical factoring algorithm."

"True," Matt responded. "And if there were only eleven such properties I would agree that the problem would be intractable."

Nels, Connie, and Petrescu all froze. Petrescu was the first to speak.

"Although I have not yet proven it, I have reason to think that there are no others."

Matt sipped his wine. *Seventeen*, Matt thought, *and perhaps more*. "What we have reason to think in one age becomes unreasonable in the next," he said.

"No. I will prove this," Petrescu maintained. "And I will welcome your response if you dispute it."

"I look forward to it," Matt answered.

"And once I prove it, I will then show that any search algorithm in factor space is computationally impractical with existing methods." Petrescu spoke rapidly, with agitation. "And even if there *were* more properties the fact that the search path is connected is the final proof that the solution time is unbounded."

Matt sipped again, and then appeared to study his wineglass as he spoke. "You said the *fact* that the search path is connected."

Petrescu stood on his toes. "Of *course* it is connected! It *must* be connected!"

Matt smiled. "Are you *sure?*"

❖ ❖ ❖

The cell phone of Stephen Quan rang as he drove home from his office at the end of an eleven-hour day. The display announced the name of the caller: *Marku Petrescu.* He answered the call immediately.

"Dr. Petrescu, how is the conference going?"

"Not so good, Mr. Quan. Your man Bugatti is a bit of a loose cannon. I quizzed him on a few points during dinner and he revealed a little too much."

Stephen sighed. Among his duties as an analyst for the National Security Agency was responsibility for secrecy surrounding a system under development by the Connectrix Corporation—a system that could break strong encryption keys. If there was a breach in security, he would have to do damage control.

"How serious do you think it is?"

"Not too serious, but I thought you should know about it. He implied that he had discovered more prime number properties than he had already published. And he let on that he had discovered that the search path might be disconnected. But I think I covered it well."

"Who else was there?"

"Coffman, and a graduate student. Her name is Connie, but I don't recall her last name."

Stephen sighed with exasperation. The use of operatives such as Petrescu, who were experts in specific subjects but unskilled in gathering intelligence, was a necessary, if inconvenient part of his job.

"Do me a favor, will you, Doctor?" he snapped. "Find out who that grad student is. And write down everything you and Bugatti said. Word for word, if you can remember it. Then call me back."

Stephen abruptly ended the call. *Shit*, he thought. *Maybe I shouldn't have cleared Bugatti for this conference.* He continued his drive home, trying to convince himself that the incident was of no concern.

❖ ❖ ❖

Wang Shutao entered the office of the Minister of State Security and waited to be acknowledged.

"Wang, what have you got?" the Minister demanded.

"We have new information about the Connectrix affair. We believe that Dr. Bugatti has developed new theories that could be applied to an accelerated factoring algorithm. I have turned over this information to our scientists for evaluation. It is not too specific but it suggests some new lines of research."

The Minister seemed pleased. "Who should I thank for this new information?"

"It was overheard at a recent conference by our operative Hu Zhixian."

"Hu Zhixian," the Minister repeated. "Have I heard of this person?"

"You may have, Minister. Her American name is Connie."

6

THE ACCIDENT

ALICE HUBER ALWAYS cautioned her children to be safe when making their Halloween rounds, but in their ecstasy they rarely took her warnings to heart. Her boy Carl was six, the youngest she would allow a child of hers to Trick or Treat unaccompanied by an adult, although she insisted that he stay close to his ten-year-old sister Joanie.

Carl had decided to dress in an oversized suit, complete with an outrageously patterned tie and fedora that Alice had found at a thrift store. Alice laughed out loud as Carl shuffled out of his bedroom in full attire, eyes wide and grinning like a maniac. Joanie, costumed convincingly as a zombie, joined in. The sight of the tiny suited man next to a gruesome undead apparition laughing hysterically was enough to touch off another round of laughter that none of them could suppress.

After the ritual photographs and safety lecture, Joanie and Carl started their rounds. It was late twilight as they headed down the near side of the tree-lined street, kicking up damp leaves, releasing the musty scent so characteristic of late autumn in Wisconsin.

It took nearly forty minutes to reach the end of the street. Carl's costume was a hit at every stop. It was usually the lady of the house who answered the door and most insisted on calling their husbands to laugh at Carl before giving him his candy bribe and sending him on. Carl was delirious with joy, and Joanie shared his bliss. She held his hand, helping him keep his balance as he shambled along with twelve inches of excess pants pooled around his shoes.

At the corner Joanie and Carl stood behind a small group of children in all manner of costumes waiting for a break in the traffic to cross. As the last in a line of cars drove past, the children moved forward with Joanie and Carl trailing. Joanie pulled Carl forward as he struggled to keep up while the gap between them and the crowd grew. As they crossed the center line they heard the sound of a car approaching from the right, along a portion of the street that curved out of sight. Joanie picked up the pace, tugging at Carl's hand. As Carl hurried to keep up he stepped on the cuffs of his pants and stumbled as the car rounded the curve.

The car's wheels locked as the driver applied the brakes, losing traction on the wet leaves. Joanie pulled hard on Carl's hand. Her feet slipped out from under her, ending up just inches from the tires of the car as it slid by. The car came to a stop with its passenger door in front of Joanie. Joanie's hand, which had held Carl's hand tightly just a moment before, was empty.

The driver's side door sprang open and the driver leapt out, struggling to keep his balance on the slippery surface. As he came about the front of the car he stopped short, supporting himself with his right hand on the hood for an instant before sinking to his knees. He scrambled forward on all fours until he reached the small form in its oversized suit wedged under the right front tire. He placed a hand tentatively on Carl's cheek, just able to make out his face, eyes open, two scarlet threads issuing from his nose and mouth.

He pulled a cell phone from his pocket and fumbled with it as he punched three digits.

"Eau Claire 9-1-1. What is your emergency?"

"There's an accident. A little boy's been hit," he choked.

"Is this a car accident?"

"Yes, yes, the boy was hit by a car."

"Yes, sir, can you tell how badly the boy is hurt?"

"It's bad. I think it's bad. I don't think he's breathing." The caller had difficulty speaking, as if he were suffocating.

"Where are you?"

"I'm on Ridge Drive near Orchard. Hurry, please."

"We're sending an ambulance right away. Do you know if the driver of the car is there?"

"I'm the driver."

"What's your name, sir?"

"My name is Anson Polk."

"Please stay where you are and don't move the child. The ambulance will be there shortly." There was a click as the operator ended the call.

Anson dropped his phone and looked into Carl's eyes until his vision became clouded with tears. He covered his head with his hands as he pressed his forehead against the pavement. His sobs were barely audible over the screams of Joanie Huber.

❖ ❖ ❖

Matt Bugatti was at his workstation at six o'clock on Monday morning, testing a new variation of his algorithm. Since his breakthrough, just six weeks before, he'd made modest progress. He was able to improve his test function, which yielded a small gain, but the next big leap eluded him. He was convinced that his search algorithm was correct, despite Dr. Petrescu's objections, but he hadn't come up with a proof—the proof that Matt was sure would be the key to his next breakthrough.

By eight o'clock a few others had arrived, and the background noise of keystrokes and chatter had risen to its normal level. Matt tuned out these distractions as he focused on his tasks.

After forty-five minutes and another disappointing test run, Matt paused to collect his thoughts, leaning back in his chair, pressing his hands against his face. As he thought, he became uneasy. His hands dropped to his desk as he realized that the sound of keystrokes had ceased. The murmur of voices continued, but in hushed tones.

Matt stood and scanned the room. He saw a few small groups of people scattered throughout, their heads visible above the cubicle walls. One group stood outside Jon's office. *What's this about?* Matt thought. He looked around for Anson.

Matt's uneasiness changed to angst as he searched. Anson wasn't there. He jogged to Jon's office. As he approached, the group gathered at the door went silent and turned toward Matt with looks of dread. Matt glanced from face to face without a word as he elbowed his way past them to Jon's door. He expected to find Anson there, but instead found Jon seated at his desk and Josef standing to one side, both with grim looks.

"Matt, come in," Jon said. "Close the door."

Matt did so.

"Jon, what's going on around here?" he asked shakily, afraid to hear the answer.

Jon and Josef exchanged a glance.

"I got a call from Anson this morning," Jon said. "He's not coming in to work today."

Matt looked at Josef for a reaction and, seeing none, turned back to Jon.

"Is he all right?"

"He was in an accident last night. He's not hurt. Not physically, anyway."

Matt's stomach churned. "What does that mean, 'not physically?' What happened?"

"He was driving home. He hit a child, a boy" Jon gulped. "The boy died."

"Oh, sweet Jesus," Matt whispered. "I've got to go."

"Matt…" Jon said as Matt opened the door and left without answering.

❖ ❖ ❖

Matt alternately jogged and ran the four miles to Anson's building. He sprinted up the stairs and found Anson's place, pausing with his fist an inch from the door before knocking softly. After a minute with no response he knocked again. The door opened a few seconds later.

Matt gasped at the sight. Anson's eyes were red and swollen. He was still wearing the same clothes from the day before, wrinkled, dirty, and stained heavily at the knees. Anson let Matt in without a word and returned to his kitchen to retrieve an open bottle of beer, leaving the door open behind him.

"Anson, are you okay?" Matt asked tentatively.

"Me? Okay?" he snorted, holding his arms outstretched. "*I'm* just fine. No marks on *me*."

"Anson, what happened?"

Anson laughed. It was a laugh quite different from his usual boisterous, joy-filled laugh.

"Let me give you the rundown. Wait. Bad choice of terminology." He worked at pronouncing his words. "After… what was it…twelve hours? Yes. After working *twelve hours* on that fucking prototype on a *Sunday*, I decided I wanted to get back to…home? Is that the right word? Can I really call this dump a home? Anyway, I just wanted out of there so I could have some time to myself. No hardware, no software, just some stinking down time. Went a *little* too fast. Came around a curve and *wham*. What else do you want to know?"

Tears welled up in Matt's eyes. "Are you in trouble?"

"Hell if I know. I spent two hours with the cops last night making a statement. They said they'd let me know." He drank the last of his beer and retrieved another from the refrigerator. He held it out to Matt. Matt shook his head.

"I talked to a lawyer. He says I shouldn't worry. He'll get to work on it right away. Good thing I have someone looking out for *me*."

The two stood wordlessly for a minute.

"Matt, buddy, thanks for coming over. Nice gesture. Highly appreciated."

"I'll stand by you, Anson. Always."

Anson smiled wearily. "No need, my friend. I've been drinkin' and thinkin' all night. There're whole big parts of life that other people get to experience and I don't. This high pressure, top secret bullshit doesn't fill out my bingo card. I'm going to find out what I've been missing." He took another long pull on his beer. "I'm getting out of here. I called Jon this morning and quit my job."

◆ ◆ ◆

The Cygnus program status meeting began, as always, precisely at eight-thirty on Friday morning. Jon Ames entered the room but did not sit in his customary spot. Instead, he stood at the head of the table and addressed his team.

"I'm sure you've all heard about Anson by now," he began. "First, I want you to know that he's in good spirits, considering what he's been through. Also, he told me that no charges will be brought against him."

There was a conspicuous release of tension in the room.

"What you may not know is that Anson has resigned from Connectrix, effective immediately."

The team reacted with a few whispers, but nearly all of them had already heard the news. Over the past week, Matt had made no secret of Anson's decision, which he'd discussed with anyone who would listen. Matt's reaction surprised some—not regretful, nor sad, nor angry. He was envious.

"We tried to persuade him not to leave but his mind was made up," Jon continued. "He doesn't plan to stay in Eau Claire. I've asked Kathy to assume Anson's responsibilities in addition to her own. Her first task will be to report on the state of the system and what impact Anson's leaving will have on our schedule."

Kathy exchanged a few timid glances with the others.

"Unless you have questions, we'll get on with the meeting."

Jon paused three seconds and then took his seat. He opened his journal. "Hardware?"

◆ ◆ ◆

Kathy found Jon in his office after the meeting, entering and closing the door without knocking.

"Jon, you've got a problem."

Jon stopped typing his status report to listen.

"I can do my job *and* Anson's job, and the program will survive. But if we lose Matt, we're fucked."

Jon winced. "I know that, Kathy. Why are you bringing it up now?"

Kathy brushed the hair from her face and put her hands on her hips. "I'm bringing it up now because if we don't take action, Matt's gone."

Jon's throat went dry. He felt a constriction in his chest. He forced himself to breathe.

"Why do you say that?"

"All week long he's been talking about how he's got no family, no relationship, how nobody knows what a fucking genius he is, and how lucky Anson is for getting out. He's not doing any work, he's pissing off everyone else and he's *this close* to bailing." She held her thumb and forefinger in front of her eye, separated by a millimeter.

Jon tried unsuccessfully to swallow. "What do you think we should do?"

"*I* don't know. *You're* in charge. Talk to him. Make promises. Do *something*," Kathy demanded. "But do it quick. He's talking about going home to mama and teaching school."

Kathy spun on her heel and left the office.

Jon remained motionless for several minutes as his mind raced. He remembered what Anson had said to him weeks ago. As he sorted through his thoughts, taking stock of his options, he returned to it again and again.

"*…if he doesn't get laid soon he's going to snap.*"

7

THE OPERATION

JIMMY LIU WAVED to Alvin from the crowd as Alvin exited the gate area of Shuangliu airport in Chengdu. Jimmy had preceded Alvin to China two months earlier with instructions to hire staff, install equipment, bring on workers, and begin production at the new Mechanized Minds factory. When he heard Jimmy's description of the 20,000 square meter facility, complete and ready for outfitting by the time he arrived, four weeks after Alvin's visit to Beijing, Alvin would not have believed it, had it not come from Jimmy. Such a structure would have taken many times longer in the United States. Alvin had to see it for himself.

But Alvin had another reason for his trip. While the building itself went up in record time, Jimmy's progress reports were disastrous. Jimmy was working on a deadline and every task was late. Alvin decided it was time for personal intervention. He came loaded for bear.

"Good morning, Boss," Jimmy said grimly as he took the handle of Alvin's carryon. "How was Shenzhen?"

"Just like always, Jimmy," Alvin snapped. "Luo keeps cranking them out. When are we going to move some of that production up here?"

"I can't say, Boss—feels like my feet are stuck in goo. It takes forever to get the stupidest little thing done."

"And why's that? Huh?"

"It's this government guy—he has his fingers in everything. Insists on approving every hiring decision, even the factory workers. I can't take a shit without clearance."

Alvin halted suddenly. Jimmy's momentum carried him forward a few steps before he stopped and turned back.

"The government has to approve hiring of *factory workers?*" Alvin asked incredulously. "That's not their normal procedure!"

"Normal?" Jimmy sneered. "What normal? This is fucking *China*. There's no *normal* here."

Alvin gritted his teeth as they exited the terminal. "Jesus, Jimmy, they built the whole goddamned factory in a month. They couldn't *wait* for us to move in. Now we can't even hire a fucking *janitor* without approval? How does that make any sense?"

"Boss, you know me. I'm no slacker. I'm busting my ass here. If you ask me, someone, somewhere, has a hard-on for you."

The two walked silently to the car at the curb. The driver put Alvin's carryon in the trunk and offered to take his briefcase. "Not necessary," Alvin told the driver, and followed Jimmy into the car, briefcase in hand. The car pulled away and made it to the airport exit before Alvin spoke.

"How's your Chinese?" he asked Jimmy.

"It's coming back to me," Jimmy said, smiling for the first time since Alvin arrived.

❖ ❖ ❖

The Mechanized Minds building was gleaming white, surrounded by fresh landscaping. The grounds were spotlessly clean. As Alvin and Jimmy got out of the car, Alvin stopped to admire the sign on the side of the factory facing the main road. Alvin himself had designed the Mechanized Minds logo, a stylized human head with a clockwork brain. Seeing his company's name prominently displayed near a public road in Communist China felt like a personal coup.

Jimmy escorted Alvin to a meeting room on the second floor. The space was beautifully appointed—to one side a wall of glass from floor to ceiling overlooking the factory, with an elegant wooden railing extending the length of the room. Four elaborate Chinese scrolls hung on the opposite wall, immediately behind Jimmy's staff members, who stood in line at attention.

Jimmy began the introductions, addressing Alvin by his Chinese name. Alvin smiled and nodded politely as Jimmy identified each person by name and function. At the end of the ceremony Jimmy and the staff remained silent, awaiting Alvin's next words. Alvin didn't speak, but instead turned toward the windowed wall.

From the second floor vantage point the entire factory was visible. With the exception of two idle workstations and a few stacked boxes, the area was deserted. Alvin recognized the boxes—they contained material that he had personally arranged to ship from his subcontractor in Shenzhen. *With the exception of those boxes,* he thought, *there's not one thing in this giant, expensive factory that can be transformed into industrial computers.*

He turned from the window toward his managers. The looks on their faces satisfied Alvin that his brief, silent observation of the empty factory conveyed his displeasure as eloquently as any words. He paused a moment longer, as if to emphasize the point before speaking.

"Greetings. I am proud to be here at this beautiful facility. I look forward to hearing your progress reports."

For the next four hours, each staff member in turn gave an account of his responsibilities, objectives, schedule and current status. Alvin questioned each presenter at length, exploring the reasons behind the delays. All the staff members had excuses for falling behind schedule that seemed out of their control. In many cases they blamed extraordinarily long times to get government approvals, but they had no explanations for their problems with suppliers, shippers, and distributors. It seemed that every outside company was reluctant to do business with Mechanized Minds and no one in the room could say why.

◆ ◆ ◆

Jimmy arranged a banquet in Alvin's honor that evening which all staff members were required to attend. Jimmy and Alvin were the last to arrive. As they entered the banquet room, they found eight staffers in a few small groups talking quietly. The discussions ceased instantly as Alvin came in.

Alvin went around the room and greeted each person individually, calling them by name, then took his seat at the circular table. The early courses were already laid out on a glass turntable in the table's center. When the last person was seated, Jimmy stood to speak.

"Good evening everyone. We are pleased to have our president, Xiao Weiguo, visiting from America. He has asked me to thank you for your preparations and to tell you that he looks forward to working with you. We are greatly encouraged to have Xiao Weiguo's counsel and advice as we continue with our great undertaking."

Jimmy lifted a glass resembling a tiny wine goblet. It was filled with *baijiu*, a clear, viscous liquid with a potent scent some likened to sweat socks, and others to diesel fuel.

"To Xiao Weiguo. To your good fortune, good health, and long life and to our glorious enterprise. *Gambei!*"

Everyone tapped their glasses on the table and drank the *baijiu* in one motion. Alvin drained his own glass of the fiery liqueur slowly and deliberately. As the glasses were replaced on the table, a young girl appeared and scrambled to refill the glasses before disappearing behind a curtain. Jimmy lifted his glass again.

"We are also pleased to have with us our liaison to the People's Government, Deng Yang. His support has been invaluable. To Mr. Deng, and to the People's Republic of China. *Gambei!*"

The ritual was repeated, as it would be a dozen more times over the course of the meal. It was a custom which Alvin detested, but performed dutifully. By the time the main courses were served, the *baijiu* had done its work, and everyone was chattering noisily. In the midst of the din, Alvin turned to Deng.

"Mr. Deng, this afternoon my staff gave me an update on our progress. They are working hard, but their progress is much slower than I expected."

Deng listened to Alvin as he rotated the turntable to bring a steaming tureen within reach. As he ladled the soup into his bowl he nodded to indicate that he was listening. He lifted his bowl and manipulated a dull, chocolate-colored lump into his mouth with chopsticks and chewed slowly. He was still chewing when Alvin finished speaking and continued for a few seconds longer before answering.

"We are always very careful during our first venture with a company in China," Deng said through a full mouth. "Every decision which affects the local economy must be reviewed. I think you will agree that we cannot let this undertaking fail because we were careless." As he spoke, he remained focused on his soup, searching for another lump.

"Yes, of course," Alvin said with feigned diffidence. "Yet these delays are not without a cost. If we don't make progress, I have concerns about the success of our project."

Deng set down his bowl and chopsticks before turning to Alvin. "That is a valid point, Mr. Xiao. But my superior has instructed me to be especially careful with your applications. He and I are jointly responsible for the success of the startup and the factory's continuing operation. I send every application to my superior with my recommendation within a day or two of receiving it. I remind him daily of all outstanding requests. When I receive an approval, I communicate it to Jimmy immediately." Deng turned back to his soup. "The delays are not due to any actions of mine."

Alvin gripped the edge of the table.

"Mr. Deng, I would not question your commitment to this project. Perhaps you can make a suggestion."

Deng leaned close and lowered his voice. "I will say—confidentially—that my superior has hinted of an unusual interest in your company—from Beijing. This factory must be very important to someone far above me in the bureaucracy. Perhaps that person is responsible for the delays."

He went back to fishing for lumps. "You must try some of the duck blood soup, Mr. Xiao," he said. "The chef at this restaurant prepares it wonderfully."

❖ ❖ ❖

Alvin and Jimmy rode alone in the car back to the hotel, Alvin venting the frustration that had built up during the meal.

"That fucker Deng is holding back. Someone is trying to screw us and I think he knows who and why."

"Boss," Jimmy said in an even voice, "you might be right. Someone might be sabotaging our startup. But I don't think Deng is in on it. I talk to him every day. He copies me on *everything*. He's just as frustrated as we are."

"He didn't look frustrated to me."

"Alvin, trust me. He thinks *his* boss is hamstringing *him*. If he hid that from you it's because he doesn't want to blame the higher-ups."

Alvin looked at Jimmy, his face illuminated by the occasional passing headlights.

"So, he doesn't want to blame the higher-ups, huh? Well, that's odd. That's just what he did. And he didn't stop at his boss. He went straight to the top."

Alvin settled back in the seat. "Tomorrow I'll make a few phone calls."

❖ ❖ ❖

Jimmy arranged a temporary office for Alvin during his visit. Alvin had thought he'd be inspecting his production line, meeting suppliers, or discussing strategy with his product developers on his first trip to Chengdu. Jimmy had set up a few meetings with potential customers, but with the factory in its current state, Alvin had a lot of time on his hands. He asked the administrator how to get an outside line to call Beijing. To Alvin's mild surprise, the administrator assured him that the phone system was fully functional and gave him simple instructions for placing an inter-city call.

Alvin punched in the telephone number as he mentally rehearsed the conversation. After penetrating two layers of the People's Ministry of Commerce bureaucracy, he reached his target.

"Hello, Chen Baoshan. This is Xiao Weiguo calling from Chengdu," Alvin began cheerily. "I hope you have been well."

"Yes, Xiao Weiguo, I was told you were in the country," Chen replied, equally cheerful. "I am delighted to hear from you. I trust the commissioning of your factory is proceeding without incident."

Alvin gritted his teeth. "It is good to speak to you again so long after my very enjoyable visit to Beijing. The factory building is splendid."

"It pleases me to hear that. I have not visited the factory myself. Perhaps I may once the factory is fully operational."

"We would be happy to have you," Alvin said, choosing his words carefully, "but I fear it may be some time before the factory is running at full capacity."

"Oh? But you are already producing some products now, correct?"

Alvin thought he detected a hint of mock surprise. *Don't pretend you don't know what's going on*, he thought.

"I'm afraid not, Mr. Chen. We've been plagued with setbacks. I'm really very concerned about the pace of progress."

"Xiao Weiguo, this is disturbing news. What sorts of setbacks?"

Alvin described the hindrances his staff had reported the previous day, careful to avoid assigning blame to anyone, particularly the People's Government. Chen clicked his tongue as Alvin went through the list.

"Xiao Weiguo, this is very distressing. This is not at all representative of the experience of our foreign partners. I will personally look into this situation. We cannot allow your venture to fail."

"Mr. Chen, I hope you can help," he said, pausing before he continued. "I would be most grateful."

"Not at all, Xiao Weiguo. Let me work on it. I will call you in five days to see if your situation has improved. Until then."

As Alvin hung up the phone, he was certain that Chen was responsible for his idle factory.

❖ ❖ ❖

Alvin spent the rest of the day with a prospective customer, learning his requirements for industrial computers. The evening banquet with the customer, including the obligatory *baijiu* toasts, laid the foundation for a lasting relationship. Alvin was pleased with how his meeting with the customer had gone, but on the ride to the hotel, he wondered if he would ever be able to sell him any products from his Chengdu factory.

❖ ❖ ❖

Alvin arrived late the following morning, nursing his second hangover in as many days. As he entered the building, he sensed a change, like an subtle alteration in the atmosphere. Instead of going to his office, he took a route down a hallway, past a row of lockers for workers not yet hired, through a door to the factory floor.

It was a beehive of activity. The receiving dock to Alvin's left was crowded with stacks of large boxes and more boxes were being unloaded from a flat-bed truck. Alvin recognized his senior managers as they lifted the boxes, carried them to the factory floor, and unboxed one gleaming white workstation after another, assembling them in place. There were already two rows of workstations set up and there seemed to be enough boxes for at least two more rows. In the middle of the chaos, Jimmy was directing the installation, occasionally pausing to sign a shipping document proffered by a truck driver. Alvin watched, mute, until Jimmy noticed him. He grinned to the point of beaming as he headed toward Alvin.

"I don't know who you called yesterday but you got to the right person," he shouted above the commotion.

Alvin was dumbstruck. "When did this stuff arrive?"

"It started around lunchtime yesterday. We ordered this furniture six weeks ago. The inventory racks are on that truck over there and we're expecting a shipment of tools by noon."

Alvin speculated about the chain of events that began with his conversation with Chen Baoshan and ended with this blur of activity. He abandoned all remaining doubts that someone at the Ministry of Commerce—probably Chen Baoshan himself—had intentionally sabotaged his operation.

"We should have all four lines set up by the end of the day," Jimmy explained as he turned back to check on the progress of the construction.

"A lot of good it'll do us with no workers and no suppliers," Alvin complained.

"We got approvals on our supplier contracts," Jimmy said. "We should have parts by Thursday, and a consignment shipment to our circuit board contractor by Friday."

"Who's going to build them?" Alvin asked with a sweeping gesture toward his senior management team. "These guys?"

"This is just temporary. Our employment contracts got approved. Twelve associates will start tomorrow." Jimmy perused a clipboard holding a sheaf of papers. "We'll have our first shipment ready for export by late next week, assuming the test equipment shows up on time."

Jimmy was clearly delighted with the progress, in no small part because Alvin was there to witness it. Alvin was restrained, and would remain so until he knew the reason why one phone call could have brought about such a change.

"Carry on, Jimmy," Alvin said as he turned to go back to his office.

"Sure thing, Boss," Jimmy chirped, and added as an afterthought, "Oh, and we got our private network connection. You can get to the company internet now."

Instead of going to his office, Alvin set up his computer in the conference room, where he could watch the action on the factory floor. The production area was quickly transforming into what he had expected to see when he first arrived. He stood at the window watching Jimmy direct traffic as the line of workstations grew. He seemed to be in complete control. But that was an illusion.

Whose factory is this? he thought. *And what does Chen want?*

❖ ❖ ❖

Over the next three days Alvin's time was occupied from morning until late evening. He immersed himself in the countless details of running a factory. The nagging question of the Ministry of Commerce's objective intruded during rare moments of inactivity but never completely left Alvin's mind.

At mid-morning on Friday Alvin was inspecting the first of his fully configured assembly lines. Alvin was notorious for fussing over minutiae, and on this day he lived up to his reputation. As he and Jimmy discussed changes to the details of a work instruction, the factory receptionist trotted across the floor to interrupt their conference.

"Mr. Xiao, you have a visitor. He's from Beijing."

Jimmy looked at Alvin with an expression of surprise and concern.

"It must be Chen, the Ministry of Commerce guy," Alvin speculated in a tone that said *let's get this over with*. "He said he would call. I didn't think he'd pay us a personal visit."

Alvin followed the receptionist to the lobby, ready to offer Chen his gratitude. He entered the reception area and extended his hand before stopping short. Waiting for him, smiling placidly, was not Chen Baoshan of the People's Ministry of Commerce, but Wang Shutao, *Guoanbu*.

Alvin blanked but he recovered quickly. "Wang Shutao, this is a pleasure I did not expect. Welcome to our factory." He stepped forward and took Wang's hand, bowing slightly.

"Xiao Weiguo, thank you for receiving me unannounced," he replied in a manner as smooth as his olive complexion. "I apologize for my sudden appearance. I was in Chengdu for another matter and I found myself with some free time. Do you have a moment to chat? Someplace where we will not be distracted? I understand you have a fine conference room with a view of your factory. If it's not occupied, perhaps we could talk there."

Alvin escorted Wang to the second story conference room. Wang turned and faced the window.

"You have an impressive operation, Mr. Xiao. You have made much progress."

Alvin stood next to Wang and pretended to study the activity below.

"Thank you, Mr. Wang. I'm pleased with the facility but it was not so impressive when I arrived. We've made all this progress over the last four days." Alvin turned to look at Wang's face, hoping to detect some reaction. "Mr. Chen has been most helpful."

"Yes, I received a call from Mr. Chen on Monday," Wang said, never looking away from the window. "Between the two of us we were able to—let's say—*expedite* many of your requests for approval that had accumulated in the bureaucracy. They were not getting the attention they deserved. It was an unfortunate situation that we have rectified."

Alvin gripped the railing.

"We were also able to…*persuade* some of your suppliers to deliver your equipment and materials right away. Without guidance from us, they were uncertain about what priority they should assign to your needs. That was also an unfortunate situation."

Wang turned back toward Alvin and looked directly into his eyes. Wang's smile faded slightly, a subtle, yet chilling effect.

"It would be *most* unfortunate if these situations were to reoccur."

Alvin's knees buckled. He caught himself on the railing. Wang put his hand on Alvin's elbow to steady him.

"Xiao Weiguo, are you all right? You look ill."

"I'll be fine," Alvin said as he straightened himself. "You're right, Wang Shutao, it would indeed be unfortunate if our progress were to falter. You have my gratitude."

Wang's smile returned. "It pleases me to have been of service, Xiao Weiguo. And I'm looking forward to our continued cooperation."

Wang turned again to the window. "In fact," he said, "I have a service to ask of you."

Alvin tightened his grip.

"How may I help?" Alvin asked with a catch in his voice.

"Oh, it's a very simple request," Wang replied, "but one which you are uniquely qualified to satisfy. You sit on the board of directors of a small company called Connectrix. They are developing a system with some exceptional capabilities. We merely want to know more about it. Whatever you can find out."

Alvin blanched. Before he could protest, Wang continued.

"When you return to the United States, you will be contacted by one of our operatives. His name is Tan Yingqun."

Alvin's eyes grew wide as his mouth dropped open.

"Tan Yingqun? The dissident? He's a critic of the Communist regime! He had to flee China for asylum in America!"

Wang nodded and turned to Alvin with a look of satisfaction. "Yes, I thought you might have heard of him. Whatever you discover, you will communicate directly to Tan."

Alvin squeezed the railing with both hands. He surveyed the factory, which just days before had been vacant, now filled with equipment, material and people. He looked at the floor, then at Wang.

"Wang Shutao," he rasped, "I know the program you're talking about, but it's very sensitive. They haven't shared any details with the board. I don't know what more I can learn."

Wang put his hand on Alvin's arm, as he had outside the wall of the Forbidden City.

"Xiao Weiguo, I know much about you. I know what you have accomplished in America and what you hope to accomplish in China. You are a determined and ingenious man. I have faith in you. If you cannot help us, of course, we will be disappointed. But I believe you will help us."

Wang leaned closer and gripped Alvin's arm with both hands.

"And then you will have *our* gratitude."

83

8

THE GIRLFRIEND EXPERIENCE

JON CALLED MATT into his office less than a minute after Kathy left. Jon never let personnel problems go unaddressed for long, but Kathy's warning left him in a state of near panic.

He listened as Matt vented, continuing for more than an hour, during which Jon spoke fewer than a dozen sentences.

Matt held nothing back. The torrent of grievances spanned the range from work environment to compensation to personal relationships. At the end of his rant, Jon thought the situation had stabilized just by having talked it out. Jon had dealt many times with young people in high-stress environments, and he recognized the signs of a man close to the edge. Jon knew that simply by allowing Matt to air it out he would relieve his stress, but unless the causes were dealt with, the pressure would build again. A resolution was inevitable. Jon was sure that unless he acted, Matt was gone.

For the rest of the day Jon was functionally inert. He mentally reviewed Matt's list of gripes, trying to concoct some ploy that would keep Matt content long enough to complete the program. *Just five or six months*, he thought. *I don't have to make him happy. I just have to give him a reason to stay.*

Matt touched on many themes, but one stood out. It came up in different contexts, described in various terms: *I have no social life, I miss family, I could use a real relationship.* What Jon could do about that, he had no idea beyond what Anson had suggested weeks ago, succinctly, if crudely: *The boy needs to get laid.*

The idea seemed obvious but insufficient. A talk in Jon's office or a night of drinking might distract Matt temporarily, but the underlying discontent would remain. An evening of passion might do the same, but with no lasting effect. *No,* Jon thought, *Matt needs a steady girl.*

Through that afternoon and evening Jon played out alternate scenarios. He could arrange for Matt to meet someone on the chance they would take to each other, but that would be time consuming and unlikely to succeed. Even if they did hit it off, there was a risk that the relationship would sour, turning Matt's outlook even worse. Besides, Jon could come up with no pretense for an introduction, and he didn't know anyone suitable anyway.

It wasn't until sometime after two in the morning that the solution came to Jon as he awoke from a fitful sleep. *I need a willing, attractive woman I can rely on—right away.*

Now wide awake, Jon turned to the Internet, searching clumsily for a promising prospect. Jon had never done such a search before; in fact, the raciest item Jon had ever come across was a video of Anna Kournikova in a bikini which appeared after he innocently clicked a link in an email of uncertain origin. After a few false starts, Jon entered a world he had only heard about and scarcely imagined.

Jon's options were endless and varied. Bewildered, he navigated from one explicit offering to the next, most with pictures. He pressed on, at the brink of nausea, until he hit upon a website named *Diana's Parlor.* After a moment of wide-eyed uncertainty, Jon understood that it was an advertising site for freelance escorts.

Unlike the lurid offerings Jon found in the assortment of personal ads and porn sites, *Diana's Parlor* had an upscale look, with muted colors, elegant titles and a professionally designed layout. To the left was a list of large cities and states. Jon scrolled down and selected *Wisconsin.*

An array of photos appeared of women in various states of partial dress, most of them tastefully composed and professionally shot. Each was captioned with a first name and a location: *Jocelyn, Madison; Mira, Milwaukee; Tanya, Green Bay*. Jon scanned the array for Eau Claire and found a few offerings. One caught his eye: *Gina, Eau Claire (visiting)*. Jon clicked the listing, opening a page with a gallery of glamour shots, personal statistics, and a sales pitch:

I'm Gina, and I'm ready to serve your personal needs with just a phone call. Sensual and sophisticated, perky and playful, I'm at home at a ball or a ballgame, at a dinner party or on the dance floor. You'll enjoy my loving attention and stimulating conversation. Whether you seek a brief, but memorable encounter or the full girlfriend experience, your pleasure is my passion. Available for outcall or incall at my luxurious Minneapolis apartment. Call me today! No blocked numbers, please.

The girl in the pictures was strikingly beautiful, dark haired and perfectly proportioned. The poses included nude shots, carefully composed to avoid revealing too much, as well as some in lingerie and a few in stylish evening dresses. None exposed Gina's full face, but she was obviously stunning. He looked over Gina's personal information.

Age: 23
Ethnicity: Caucasian
Hair: Black
Eyes: Brown
Height: 5' 4"
Weight: 105
Measurements: 34" 22" 35"

There was a telephone number with a Minneapolis area code. Jon checked the time: seven-thirty in the morning. He bookmarked the web page and went back to bed.

❖ ❖ ❖

At ten o'clock, Jon returned to his computer and began the long process of talking himself into calling the number and rehearsing what he would say. By eleven he had mentally scripted the conversation. He nervously entered the number on his cell phone and waited through several rings. He was about to end the call with a mixture of disappointment and relief when he heard a click and a voice.

"Hi, this is Gina. What's *your* name?"

Jon paused a few seconds, having forgotten his rehearsed response.

"Ah, hello Gina. My name's Jeffrey."

"Hello, Jeffrey. Thanks for calling me. Tell me what you're looking for and maybe I can help you find it."

"I saw your advertisement online. I was wondering if we could meet."

"I'd like that, Jeffrey. I have a few questions first. Is that okay?"

"Questions? Sure, I guess so. What questions?"

Gina laughed, a low, soft, and smooth laugh, halfway between a giggle and a purr. Jon thought it almost musical. He reacted with an involuntary stirring, causing him to shift in his chair.

"Jeffrey, you sound nervous. Tell me—is this your first time?"

"What?" Jon blurted. "I'm not a virgin, if that's what you mean."

Gina repeated her endearing laugh, which only served to further stimulate.

"No, Jeffrey, I mean is this your first time answering an ad like mine? I think it is, isn't it?"

He gulped. The call was not going as expected. "Yes. Yours is the first number I called."

"You made the right choice, Jeffrey. I specialize in first-timers. Just relax, okay?"

Gina's reassurance and tone of voice effectively calmed him. The feeling was short lived.

"Jeffrey, are you a police officer?"

"No!" Jon blurted. "Of course not!"

"I didn't think so. Cops are never as nervous as you are. They try to sound nervous but they're never very convincing."

"Does that mean we can meet?" Jon blurted, having abandoned his script, now speaking extemporaneously.

"We'll get together really soon, Jeffrey, but we have to get acquainted first."

"Oh. Okay. What do you want to know about me?"

"Let's start with the basics. I see you're calling from a cell phone with a Wisconsin number. Where are you?"

"I'm in Chippewa Falls, but I can come to Minneapolis."

"That's a good idea, Jeffrey. My place is very comfortable. You'll like it."

"I can come tonight. How do I get there?"

"Oh, sweetie, you *are* new at this. One step at a time. I need to know a few more things. Like where you work—and your work number."

Jon squeezed his cell phone as he fumbled for a response.

"Why? Why do you need to know that?"

"Jeffrey, I don't know what you do for work, but my job is a little risky. I need to take precautions. Here's what will happen. I'll call you at your place of work so I'll know for sure who you are. If we have any problems, I'll know where to find you. But I don't think we'll have problems. You seem like a nice guy. You'll be good to me. And I'll be *very* good to you."

"Gina, that's a problem for me. I'm not sure this will work out. I'm sorry I wasted your time."

Jon was about to end the call when Gina's voice gave him pause.

"Jeffrey, let's talk a bit. I like you. I think we could have a good time together. And I think if you don't spend time with me you'll find someone else, someone who isn't as careful as I am. That's a risk you don't want to take."

Jon kept listening, persuaded as much by her soothing voice as by her logic.

"I'm a professional. I don't take risks, so you won't take risks. You can call another girl, but if she doesn't ask you the same questions *I'm* asking, you're taking a chance. That really would *not* work out."

The line was silent for more than ten seconds. Jon wrestled with the decision. Gina waited patiently, recognizing the moment of commitment was imminent.

"I work at Connectrix, in Eau Claire."

"Connect Tricks? I don't think I've heard of that one. I'll need the number. The general number, not your direct one. I'll call your office and ask for you by name."

He gave her the main number of Connectrix, passing the point of no return.

"Gina, you should know something else."

"Your name's not Jeffrey, is it?"

"No. My name's Jon."

"Just 'Jon?'"

"Jon Ames," he surrendered.

"Hello, Jon Ames. I'm glad to meet you. I'll call you on Monday. Is ten o'clock good for you?"

"Yes, thank you," he said quietly, like a child submitting to punishment. "I'll talk to you then."

"Okay, Jon. I can't wait!"

"Gina," he said hurriedly. "What about you? What should I know about you?"

"Me?" she giggled melodiously. "I'm Gina. I'm just a nice Italian girl."

❖ ❖ ❖

After Gina ended the call she secured the sash on her robe, a prune-colored garment of a sheer silk blend that covered her to mid-thigh and conformed resolutely to her otherwise nude body. She ran her fingers through her dark, nearly black medium-length hair, coaxing it into a semblance of its previous night's coiffed perfection. She was still waking up, having been roused from a sound sleep minutes earlier by the persistent ringing of the cell phone on her nightstand.

She touched a button on her Solis coffee maker, a gift from a satisfied client. It came to life with a growl which rose in pitch before ceasing, followed by a soft gurgle as the porcelain demitasse filled with aromatic liquid, topped by thick *crema*, the mark of a perfectly brewed espresso.

Gina remained standing at her kitchen counter as she lifted the lid of her MacBook Air. She had bought the sleek laptop computer just a few weeks before, choosing it over bulkier models because it fit easily into the oversized Reed Krakoff handbag she kept with her constantly, adding almost nothing to its weight. As she lifted the miniature cup to her lips, she typed *connect tricks eau claire* into the search bar of the browser with one hand. After a moment the screen displayed search results under the question "Did you mean *Connectrix?*"

The first entry was titled "Home—Connectrix Corporation, Eau Claire, Wisconsin." The short blurb following the link included the company phone number, matching the number Jon had given her. Immediately below were several more links: *Our Products. Press Releases. Investor Relations.* Gina clicked on *Leadership Team.*

The screen displayed a catalog of Connectrix executives, each with a portrait, a title, and a short biography. Jon Ames, Founder and Chief Technology Officer, age 50, was second on the list. His face was not unpleasant, Gina concluded, within the range of what some might call "handsome." Gina suspected the photograph was not recent, but she was nonetheless relieved. *Not bad,* she thought, *not exactly easy money, but not a chore, either.*

She added a new contact to her address book, adding Jon's name, company, and the Connectrix telephone number. She retrieved Jon's mobile number from her cell phone and entered it. She copied and pasted Jon's picture from the Connectrix website. To her calendar she added a reminder— *Confirm Jon Ames*—at ten o'clock Monday morning. She shut the lid of her computer with a feeling of accomplishment as she sipped the last of her espresso. *Score one for Gina,* she mused to herself. *It pays to advertise.*

Gina turned and leaned back against the counter, gazing across the living room of her twelfth-floor apartment, through the large picture window framing the Minneapolis skyline. Her eyes closed as her hand slipped under her robe to massage a tender spot on her inner thigh. The pain caused her to wince slightly. She wondered if she would develop a visible bruise. The minor contusion had been inflicted the night before by a middle-aged, somewhat overweight, but otherwise healthy and enthusiastic Senior Director of Procurement, a repeat customer who, on this occasion, had retained Gina for an evening of dinner, theater, and affection for a flat fee of twelve hundred dollars—Gina's going rate for the full Girlfriend Experience.

9

THE BOARD

CROWDED INTO A van with his fellow Connectrix board members, Alvin Xiao spent the ten-minute ride from the hotel contemplating the events of the previous week.

Late morning of the day after his return from China, Alvin sat in his St. Paul office, immersed in a lengthy dispatch from Jimmy when his assistant Melissa knocked at his door.

"There's a man here to see you," she said quietly, reluctant to interrupt his concentration. "He says you're expecting him. A Mr. Tan. Do you know him?"

Alvin froze, his eyes fixed on the memo. "Tell him I'm not available."

From behind Melissa came a mild, slightly accented voice.

"Xiao Weiguo, it would be a great disappointment to me if we were unable to spend at least *some* time together. I've come such a long distance to meet you."

Tan Yingqun stepped into view. Alvin recognized him instantly—a tall, lean man, with fair, almost feminine features framed in thick, wavy hair, a pair of black-rimmed spectacles atop his thin nose. He wore a calf-length camel-hair coat, unbuttoned, revealing his immaculate white linen jacket over a black crew-neck shirt, perfectly pressed khaki pants and glossy black shoes. He resembled nothing so much as a male model.

"I know we haven't met, but we have a mutual friend," he continued. "Mr. Wang sends his greetings."

"Melissa," Alvin croaked, "Mr. Tan and I have some business to discuss. Please see that we're left alone."

Melissa stood to one side as Tan entered the office and then shut the door behind him. Tan strode smoothly toward Alvin until he stood in front of his desk. He put out his hand. Alvin remained seated with his hands on his desk. Tan closed his hand and pressed his fist to his chest and sighed.

"Xiao Weiguo, we will be spending quite a bit of time together in the coming months. I had hoped we could at least be cordial to one another."

Alvin remained silent as Tan removed his coat and draped it carefully over the back of one chair and sat in another. He crossed his legs and rested his hands on his knee, one atop the other. His movements were deliberate and graceful, as if they'd been choreographed.

"I apologize for my unannounced visit. I was afraid you would have avoided me had I called in advance." Tan's voice was thin, with a slight tremor, as if he were fearful. But he didn't appear afraid. He looked sad. His eyes were large and liquid, the corners of his mouth turned down. He seemed infected with a contagious melancholy.

Alvin gripped the edge of his desk as he sat straight in his chair.

"Wang Shutao told me you would be in contact. He didn't tell me anything else."

Tan nodded. "There was no need. I will explain everything."

"Then start with this. You're Tan Yingqun, a critic of human rights abuses by the Chinese regime. The Communists threw you in prison after a show trial lasting less than an hour. Thousands here in the United States and around the world campaigned for your release, until you were finally granted asylum in this country. You're an inspiration to them and to millions more as a defender of freedom. You were an inspiration to me." Alvin's grip on his desk tightened, until his fingers turned white. "Explain to me how you became a spy for your oppressors."

Alvin looked directly into Tan's face, a face he had seen many times on television and in print. Tan looked back for a long moment before breaking away, turning toward the window with glistening eyes.

"It's pointless to discuss my motivation," he said in a barely audible voice. "It's enough to say that I have my reasons, as you have yours."

Alvin relaxed his hold on the desk and slumped slightly in his chair.

"I'll tell you what I told Wang Shutao. This program is highly sensitive. I'm aware of it, but I know very little about it."

"You mustn't discount the value of what you know, or what you can discover," Tan countered. "Even mundane facts can be useful, if only to suggest further lines of inquiry." He paused to smooth a wrinkle from his slacks with the back of his hand. "Perhaps you should tell me what you do know, rather than dwell on what you don't know."

Alvin folded his arms across his chest before pressing a knuckle against his chin. The events of the prior week in Chengdu, alone with Wang in the conference room, replayed themselves in his mind as he studied Tan's face. It remained impassive.

"The program is classified. There are a few board members with security clearance who get detailed briefings. The rest of us rely on their assurance that the program is consistent with the company's objectives and that it's making appropriate progress. I don't have clearance. I only know that the product is on schedule and will be demonstrated for the customer sometime in April."

Tan nodded slightly as Alvin spoke, pausing briefly before asking, "Who is the customer?"

"The board meeting discussions suggest that it's a government agency."

"Indeed?" Tan said with raised eyebrows, as if Alvin had revealed some surprising fact. He flicked a tiny bit of lint from the lapel of his jacket. "When this program is discussed, how do they refer to it?"

"The program name is Cygnus."

"Cygnus?" Tan repeated. "Like the constellation?"

"Yes—Cygnus, the Swan."

"And how did you become associated with this company, Xiao Weiguo?"

"Connectrix is using computers designed and built by Mechanized Minds for the Cygnus program."

Again Tan's eyebrows rose. "Then you have access to the system's design?"

Alvin hesitated before answering. "The design is classified. Only the designers have clearance to access its details."

"But you are the president of the company. You have seen the design, haven't you?"

"I don't have clearance," Alvin repeated.

Tan leaned forward. "That was not my question," he said in a low voice.

Alvin glanced at the report lying on his desk. It described the Chengdu factory's current status in detail. More than half of Mechanized Minds' production had been moved from their Shenzhen contractor to Chengdu. Jimmy had shipped samples of computers to prospective Chinese customers, and some had promised to order large quantities of the new design when available, providing that time was not too far in the future. Jimmy continued to marvel at how the barriers they had encountered had vanished—*thanks to you, Boss*, he wrote. Things were going well. There seemed to be no limit to the potential of the Chengdu operation.

Alvin looked up from the report. "Yes," he said, "I've seen the design."

❖ ❖ ❖

Jon Ames, Josef Hofbauer, and Connectrix CFO Cooper Hodge entered the Connectrix Corporation board room discussing last minute tactics for the presentation of their fourth quarter results—*getting the story straight*, as Josef put it. Cooper carried a dozen bound copies of the presentation, each marked "CONFIDENTIAL" in large red letters. He dropped one copy at each position. Jon followed close behind, aligning the books in a precise row. As Jon and Cooper performed what by now had become a familiar ritual, they continued their tactical discussion as they awaited the arrival of the van carrying the directors from their hotel.

❖ ❖ ❖

The directors filed into the board room and sat at their assigned places. Josef called the meeting to order, starting with finances.

The company was burning cash. It was not a happy situation but it wasn't a surprise. The company was bringing in some income from the sale of several product lines, but Cygnus was the big payoff. Meeting the goals for Cygnus, on schedule, would be the difference between lucrative success and costly failure. The discussion of finances went quickly in anticipation of the program progress reports.

"We've briefed the technology committee on Cygnus," Jon began. "This slide summarizes the committee's report." He used a laser pointer to highlight each item in the presentation. "The program is on schedule for its first demonstration in April. We still anticipate meeting all the promised performance targets. That said, the program's key performance measure *has* hit a plateau, improving only slightly over the past few weeks. But our principal investigator, Matt Bugatti, assures us that another breakthrough is imminent.

"We did incur some additional risk with the departure of our lead application developer, Anson Polk, but our lead system developer, Kathy Darling, has assumed Anson's responsibilities and the program is back on track."

The three members of the technology committee nodded slightly while the rest of the board exchanged nervous glances. Jon continued his report.

"In summary, Cygnus is on track, risk is manageable, and we hold to the financial forecast given in the previous section."

Jon laid his laser pointer carefully on the table in front of him, perpendicular to the edge. "Questions?"

Alvin was the first to speak.

"Jon, we're all counting on the success of Cygnus. My company is providing hardware for the product and I don't even have access to the details of the design. I'm aware of the sensitive nature of the program, but I'm accountable to my own board. And since we're a public company, I also have to answer to the shareholders. Cygnus represents a big percentage of our projected sales, yet I know almost nothing about it. Can you tell us *anything* more about this program that you haven't already?"

Jon was about to speak when Josef cut him off.

"Alvin, I sit on your board. I know all about your forecasts. Our Cygnus product is less than ten percent of your projected sales, no? And if your expansion in China is successful, even less than ten, no? *Ja?*"

Alvin tightened his grip on the table., feeling a tremor in his hands. "Josef, it's *not* an insignificant amount and if the program fails it could severely impact our performance in the coming fiscal year. I've already given guidance to the analysts. If we find out in April that the program is in jeopardy I'll have to adjust our projections and the impact on our stock could be severe."

"Alvin!" Josef interjected. "I know the guidance you have given to the analysts. The range of your projection is very wide, and I know also you have been very conservative in your plans for China, no? If you removed Cygnus entirely from your forecast your guidance to the analysts would not change one bit!"

Josef sat down with a thump and stared at Alvin over his glasses. "The committee has reviewed the program and given their report. It is the procedure we have followed for a year, no? Up to now their assurance has been sufficient, no? *Ja?* What has changed?"

Alvin pressed his palm against his mouth.

"I don't like being uninformed about a program as important as this."

"You know everything you need to know," Josef said dismissively. "Now, if there are no more questions, we are ready to vote on the matters before the board."

"I have a concern," said a large bald man two seats from Alvin. "You've already lost one critical contributor. You say you've recovered, and that's great. But the key investigator—Bugatti, right?—he's crucial. He's irreplaceable. If you lose *him*, you *can't* recover. What are you doing to make sure *he* doesn't leave?"

Josef turned toward Jon. The eyes of every director followed.

"You're correct," Jon said. "Dr. Bugatti is essential to the program. It would be very difficult to meet our program goals if he left; almost impossible, I'd say."

"And my question?" said the bald man. "What are you doing to keep him?"

Jon looked at the floor, a string of images flashing through his mind like a highlight reel: *The phone call…the drive to Minneapolis…the luxury apartment…the beautiful, charming escort…the negotiation…the agreement.*

"We're taking appropriate measures," he answered. "Dr. Bugatti is safe."

10

The Encounter

Matt felt only a little better after his talk with Jon. For an hour afterwards he fiddled with his program before he stopped and closed his eyes with his fingers still on the keys. He exhaled halfway between a sigh and a sob. He opened his eyes to stare at the screen of cryptic symbols. With resignation he tapped into his one reliable source of consolation: He threw himself into his work.

For a week Matt focused on proving the conjecture on which he'd built his algorithm. Every distraction—Anson's departure, Nels Coffman's offer, his loneliness—faded into the background as he committed himself to the strenuous, yet delicate process of teasing the elusive proof from a tangle of conceptual threads, as he picked up each one in turn and followed it to its intersection with another thread or to its unproductive end. He alternated between his computer and the conference room, which he had commandeered for this purpose, scrawling panel after panel of equations and diagrams on the walls then erasing them and starting again. All other Connectrix employees gave him his space, recognizing the depth of his reverie and fearing to disturb it. More than once they had left at the end of the day with Matt transfixed, staring at a patch of mathematical symbols, only to find him in the same spot the next morning, seemingly frozen in place. By Friday, Matt felt he had closed off some avenues of inquiry, but was no closer to his goal. He was ready for a break.

❖ ❖ ❖

Matt, Eric and Kathy were at their usual table at Stella Blues by seven o'clock, and by nine they were cheerfully tipsy. Eric entertained Matt and Kathy with stories from the old days at Cray. His young colleagues were transfixed, sometimes open-mouthed, as Eric casually referred to Seymour Cray as "Seymour," as if he were talking about a pet. Eric might as well have been Thor come down from Valhalla to dish the latest gossip on Odin.

They took turns buying rounds. The only rule was that no one could repeat a previous selection. After Eric bought a round of Jim Beam, and Kathy a round of *Jägermeister*, Matt looked at Kathy with as straight a face as he could muster and ordered grappa.

"Oh, yuck," Kathy grunted. "Why are you doing this? You don't even like the grappa at Stella's. You just want to make me sick."

Matt grinned. "If you can handle Eric's moonshine, or that German cough syrup you like, then you can stomach the grappa. Besides, I've been working with the management. They've got the good stuff now."

"Hmph," she snorted. "I liked this game and now I don't like it so much." She crossed her arms and glared at Matt as the waiter set three small stemmed glasses on the table. Each raised a glass as Matt offered a toast: *"Cin cin!"*

Matt and Eric drained their glasses. Kathy continued to hold her glass as she looked past Matt into the distance.

"Come on, Kathy, drink up," Matt commanded. "We did our part, now do yours."

Kathy seemed not to hear Matt but after a moment looked at him with a hint of a smile.

"Don't look now, Matt, but that woman at the bar is checking you out."

Matt spun in his chair to look behind him. Kathy slapped her forehead and planted her elbow on the table.

"That was really smooth, Matt. *So* sophisticated. I think you got her attention."

Through the crowd Matt saw a young woman on a high-backed stool at the corner of the bar. She wore a black knee-length skirt, revealing a pair of shapely calves, and a low-cut, close-fitting top which accentuated her perfect breasts. She leaned forward, resting her right hand on the bar next to a cocktail in a stemmed glass, and her left elbow on the edge of the bar. Her slender fingers idly traced the line of her jaw. Her dark, medium-length hair framed a face that Matt found hauntingly beautiful, with large, dark eyes and full lips that glistened in the dim light. She did indeed seem to be looking directly at him, even as she sipped from her cocktail without breaking eye contact. She replaced the glass on the bar and gave Matt a smile.

Matt turned back to his companions. "She's not checking me out," he huffed.

"She's checking you out," Kathy repeated.

"Matt," Eric said, "I've been married since before you were born, so I'm a little out of practice, but that girl looks to me like she's interested."

Matt lowered his head. "Hey, guys, look at her. She's out of my league. She's in the majors. I'm in T-ball."

"Go talk to her," Kathy said.

"What? No!" Matt turned just enough to get a glimpse of the woman from the corner of his eye. She was still looking.

"No way," he said, shaking his head.

Kathy leaned forward and spoke in a low voice resembling a growl. "Matt, you fucking idiot. You spend half your time complaining about your miserable love life. I'm sick of it. If you don't go over there and talk to that woman I will make sure that everyone at work knows what a pussy you are." She pushed the grappa toward Matt. "Here, have another shot if it'll get you off your candy ass."

Matt pulled the glass toward him and drained it in one gulp.

"All this fuss just to get out of drinking a little grappa," he said as he stood, a little unsteadily.

As Matt made his way across the bar, the woman turned toward him and crossed her legs at the knees, never looking away. Matt hesitated for an instant. Had it not been for his state of inebriation and Kathy's threat, he might have returned to the table, or left the building. Instead he kept going until he reached the bar and propped himself against it.

"Hi. I'm Matt."

The woman smiled. Matt was transfixed.

"Hi, Matt. I'm Gina," she replied in a voice that Matt found viscerally sexy.

"Gina. I was just noticing how out of place you seem here," Matt said, over-pronouncing every word.

Gina turned her head slightly, looking at Matt sideways. "Really? Why do you say that?"

"Just look around," Matt said with a sweeping gesture. "Look at 'em." He placed a hand on his chest. "Look at *me*. We are *not* the classiest crowd. I estimate that the classiness of this place increased four-fold when you walked in."

Gina laughed softly, with such intense femininity that it startled Matt. "Wow, you're quite the charmer, Matt. You'll turn my head."

"I'm not always so charming," Matt replied, as he repositioned a stool next to Gina and sat in it. "I guess I brought my 'A' game tonight."

A bartender materialized in front of the couple. "Another cosmo?" he asked Gina.

"In a minute. Why don't you take care of my friend here?" she said, tipping her head in Matt's direction.

"Sure thing. The usual, Matt?" he said.

"No, thanks, Ziggy. I'll have a club soda."

"So, Matt, you're a regular," Gina said, leaning closer.

He smiled as he turned toward her. His face blanked involuntarily as he looked into her eyes from less than a foot away. He was sure at that moment he'd never seen a woman so beautiful.

"A little too regular, I'm afraid," he said, his besotted smile returning. "But you're not. I would definitely have noticed you."

She rested her chin lightly on the curled fingers of her hand. "I'm new in town. I'm just getting to know the area. So far the people seem very friendly."

The bartender returned with a tall club soda and placed it in front of Matt.

"I'm curious," Gina said. "What's your 'usual?'"

"Grappa. At least that's what Ziggy thinks. I don't drink it that often but I'm practically the only one in here that drinks it at all. So Ziggy calls it my 'usual.'"

"Is it at least a decent brand?" Gina asked.

"It is, actually," said Matt. "Nonino. They used to serve stuff no better than cheap gasoline. I got them to order Nonino. It's the brand I grew up with."

Ziggy appeared a third time. "So what do you say, sweetheart? Another cosmo?"

Gina pushed the empty glass toward Ziggy. "No, thanks. I'll try the grappa," she said, looking directly at Matt.

Matt saw himself reflected in her eyes, tiny images of a young man looking as if he were seeing something wonderful for the first time. "Make it two, Ziggy," he murmured.

❖ ❖ ❖

Kathy and Eric watched from a distance as Gina and Matt drew closer.

"What do you make of that?" Eric asked.

"Who'd have thought it?" she answered. "Beauty and the geek. I wonder what the attraction is."

"Maybe Matt reminds her of her father," Eric deadpanned. Kathy punched his arm.

"You pig," she said with feigned disgust.

"Ow!" Eric complained, rubbing his bicep. "You asked the question. I just answered. What's *your* theory?"

"Who knows? Maybe she's a pro."

"A hooker? That's harsh."

"You don't think so?"

"She's no pro. I've lived in this town for thirty years and I can tell you for sure that there are no whores in Eau Claire who look like that."

❖ ❖ ❖

By midnight Kathy and Eric had left and others taken their seats while Matt and Gina stayed where they were, discussing topics ranging from the best restaurants in Eau Claire to the history of mathematics to favorite colors. At every turn of the conversation Gina was irresistibly charming. The intimidation Matt felt at first sight had vanished. He was utterly at ease.

"Gina, I seem to have robbed you of your evening," Matt said, noticing the clock behind the bar.

"What a way to put it!" Gina laughed. "You haven't robbed me of anything. I wouldn't want to spend my time any other way."

"Me, neither. But I'm afraid I can't offer you a ride home. My own ride left two hours ago."

"Not a problem," Gina said. She retrieved a large handbag leaning against her chair and fished out a set of keys. "I can find my own way home. I can even give you a ride."

"I will take you up on that offer, lady," Matt said. His words seemed warm and thick, the combined effect of contentment and intoxication.

Matt followed Gina out of the bar and across the street to a parking lot. Gina walked steadily in her high heels while Matt struggled to navigate a straight line. Gina pressed a button on her key as they approached her car, a two-door Mercedes-Benz coupe. The interior lights came on as the door locks clicked open. Matt was visibly impressed.

"A very nice car, Gina. How do you like it?"

"I love it!" she said brightly. "Hop in and tell me what you think."

Matt eased himself into the passenger's seat. He resisted the temptation to run his fingers along the trim as he sank into the leather seat.

"You know, Gina, we talked about almost everything but I don't think I asked you what you do for a living."

A faint smile appeared on Gina's face as she started the car. "I'm a graphic designer."

"Graphic designer," Matt repeated, as he examined the interior of the car admiringly. "I'll bet you're a good one."

❖ ❖ ❖

Gina followed Matt's directions to his apartment and parked at the curb. The car was silent for a moment before Matt spoke.

"Gina, it was nice meeting you."

Without a word Gina leaned across the console and pressed her lips against Matt's. He gasped slightly, as much from the softness of her lips against his as from the suddenness of it. Her fingers tangled themselves in his hair as she kissed him harder. After a few seconds she broke away and looked into Matt's eyes.

"Aren't you going to invite me in?"

Matt examined her face. The features he had admired all evening were even more alluring in the faint light. Her eyes seemed especially large and deep, her lips full, her cheeks perfectly contoured. He placed his hand against her face, feeling its warmth, fearing to move, content just to feel his flesh against hers.

"I…" he said haltingly. "I can't. Not tonight."

Gina placed her hand on Matt's and pressed it tighter against her cheek. "It'll be all right," she said.

Matt smiled weakly. "It's not you, Gina. There's a lot going through my mind right now. I'm afraid I'd be distracted, and that's not how I want to be with you."

Gina gave Matt's hand a final caress before taking it from her cheek and placing it on the console. She reached into her handbag and produced a card. She handed it to Matt. It read simply

Gina Bianchi
612 555 8800

"I want you to call me, Matt. I'll be very upset if you don't."

"Count on that," he said, pocketing the card.

As he made a move to open the door Gina leaned across once more to kiss Matt on the cheek. With a grin he stepped out of the car, and then leaned inside, supporting himself with one hand on the open door.

"Gina, where do you live?" he asked.

"It's a ways from here," she answered. "I've got a bit of a drive ahead of me."

"Be careful. Drive safe."

Matt closed the door. Gina pulled away from the curb and started the drive back to Minneapolis. Matt watched the taillights disappear in the distance before heading into the apartment building. Neither he nor Gina took notice of the dark green—almost black—late model Ford parked less than a block away, or the dark man with dark wiry hair watching them intently.

❖ ❖ ❖

Matt entered his apartment and flipped on the light switch. The remains of his breakfast were still on the table. Four days' worth of dishes lay in the sink. A river of soiled laundry snaked from Matt's bedroom to his bathroom with a tributary leading to the small laundry room off the kitchen. The floor was sparsely dotted with spills that had long since dried in place. Sheets, blankets, and pillows formed a flattened ball in the center of his bed. Compared with the scent of Gina's perfume, which still lingered in his nostrils, the place smelled rancid and stale.

Matt surveyed the scene wearily. He checked his watch—nearly one in the morning. With a sigh he went to the sink and turned on the faucet. He reached under the sink for a bottle of detergent. In a few minutes the sink was filled with sudsy water and Matt began going through the backlog of dirty dishes. By three o'clock the laundry was in the dryer and the apartment was spotless.

❖ ❖ ❖

Gina arrived at her Minneapolis apartment and checked her phone messages—four calls from regular customers and two new prospects. It was going to be a busy week.

11

The Arrangement

By mid-morning Jon Ames had dealt with the usual flurry of minor crises he faced daily and had settled into his weekly review of the Cygnus project schedule. Jon required updates before nine o'clock every Monday and all but one of his project leads had met their deadline. Both Eric and Kathy provided detailed reports with each milestone identified, and although they had suffered minor setbacks, none threatened the planned demonstration in April. At ten o'clock Matt's report was still absent. *As usual,* he thought.

Jon hadn't yet set out to track down the missing report when Matt appeared in his doorway. He as well groomed as Jon had ever seen him, hair combed and clean shaven, wearing a new shirt and slacks. He looked Matt over from head to toe. His shoes were shined.

"Jon, here's my report. I wish it were better news. I made some progress—not much. But I'm right on the edge—I feel it. I'm not giving up on the April demo date."

Jon took the report and skimmed it. It was the first time in nearly a year that Matt had prepared his status report in the proper format. He looked up at Matt open-mouthed.

"Any questions?" Matt asked.

"No. No questions. Thanks for the report."

Matt gave him a grin. "Not a problem," he said as he turned to leave.

"Matt?" Jon asked after him. Matt turned back with a questioning look.

"I like your shirt. Is it new?"

"This? Yes, it is new. I got it over the weekend. I decided the old wardrobe was getting a little threadbare. Thanks for noticing."

"Not at all, Matt," Jon said. "And thanks again for the report."

Jon was still marveling at Matt's transformation when his phone rang. He recognized the number on the display as Gina Bianchi's.

"Call me back on my cell phone," he said before Gina could utter a word.

He hung up the phone and closed his office door. His cell phone buzzed a few seconds later.

"Yes, what is it?" he answered.

"Hi, sweetie," Gina responded cheerfully. "How was your weekend?"

"It was fine," he said brusquely. "Tell me what happened on Friday."

"Oh, I get it. Straight to the point. All business," she said. "Well, Matt and I had a very nice conversation. Then I drove him home and dropped him off."

"That's it? Nothing else?"

"Jon, I'm surprised at you. Do you want all the dirty details?"

"No, no, spare me," Jon said with his fingers pressed to his eyes. Gina laughed.

"There's nothing to spare. I asked him to invite me in and he didn't. Otherwise we had a good time."

"Then we're even, right?"

"Not quite. You took care of my time up to midnight. I left at one, so that's another five hundred."

"But nothing happened!"

"Jon, remember our deal. Fifteen hundred for the evening, plus another five hundred if I go past midnight. Three thousand if I spend the night. We went through all of that during your very enjoyable visit last week."

"Okay, okay, fine," Jon sighed. "How do you want to get paid?"

"I run a cash business. We can meet the next time I'm in Eau Claire. I'll trust you until then."

"Do you know when you'll be back?"

"Sometime this week. It depends on Matt. When he calls me we'll work out an arrangement."

"When he calls? How do you know he'll call?"

Gina laughed again. "Oh, Jon, he'll call. He will definitely call. And when he does, what should I tell him?"

Jon hesitated. "I'm not sure what you mean."

"I need to know you'll take care of my time. When Matt calls should I tell him I'll let him know? That wouldn't be very encouraging. Should I tell him I have to call his boss to make sure I'll get paid?"

"Oh, Jesus," Jon muttered. "Why can't you just say you'll meet him, or go out with him, or whatever, and I'll pay you afterwards?"

"We can handle it that way, if that's what you want. I trust you. And if you try to stiff me I'll just show up at Connectrix one morning and we'll settle the bill. But I have another option for you."

"What option?" he asked anxiously.

"Yours is an unusual account. Normally, I deal with my clients directly. I don't keep them in the dark, and they all know exactly what they're getting. When I can't accommodate a request, they handle it like big boys."

"Are you asking me for more money? I'm already paying you more than your regular rate. That's what you told me, anyway."

"The money's fine. We agreed on a price and I'll honor it. I'm a professional. But Matt thinks I'm his girlfriend. I'll need to hold time open for him. I need a retainer."

"What?" Jon asked in a strained voice. "What kind of retainer?"

"I'd say ten thousand to start, with one thousand per week minimum. But if I'm any judge, you'll cover your minimum every week. That boy is smitten."

At the mention of the sum Jon sat down with a thump. He laid his forearm on the edge of his desk and rested his head on it as he pressed his cell phone to his ear. "Ten thousand," he muttered. "That's going to be a problem."

"How big a problem can it be? You didn't have any trouble with the fifteen hundred. Besides, I'm sure a Chief Technology Officer can cover that amount."

"I paid the fifteen hundred out of my own pocket. I can't come up with ten thousand on my own. I'm going through a divorce. My wife's lawyer is crawling through every bank statement and credit card bill. I can hide fifteen hundred but not ten thousand."

"Suit yourself, Jon. We can do a pay-as-you-go arrangement. But I can't promise I'll always be available when Matt calls. I have my other clients to think about. And they usually book way ahead."

Jon let his head rest on his desk as he considered his options. *The last thing I need is for Matt to be disappointed after he gets his hopes up. And ten thousand is just for starters.* He did a quick mental calculation—*four and a half months until the Cygnus demonstration. Eighteen weeks at fifteen hundred to three thousand per week. Between twenty-seven and fifty-four thousand dollars. If they see each other more than once a week it could top eighty thousand. Maybe a hundred.*

"Gina, when he calls, tell him you'll see him. Contact me and we'll meet ahead of time. But I'm not kidding when I say that ten thousand is going to be tough. How about five?"

"I'm sorry, Jon, I really need ten thousand. I'm putting my regulars at the back of the line. But here's what I'll do. When we meet, you can settle up for Friday plus half the retainer— fifty-five hundred in all. You can pay me the other five thousand the following week. I have a feeling I'll be visiting Eau Claire on a regular basis."

"All right," Jon surrendered. "Call me when you know you'll be in town. I'll pay you then."

"Thanks, sweetie. It's a pleasure doing business with you."

"Just one thing," Jon said sternly. "Matt needs to feel loved. I need him happy and productive for the next five months at least."

"Oh, Jon," Gina laughed. "He'll feel loved. He'll be the center of my world. It's what I do."

After the call ended Jon remained in the same position with his head on his desk as he let his cell phone fall on the desk in front of him. After a few seconds he went to the door and looked around the workspace. He saw Eric and Kathy having a conversation with a programmer and a hardware designer in a cubicle just outside his office.

"Kathy, Eric," Jon called. "Have you got a minute?"

The two entered Jon's office as Jon closed the door behind them.

"What's up with Matt?" Jon asked.

The two looked at each other for a moment before Kathy burst into laughter and Eric grinned.

"He cleans up nice, doesn't he, Chief?" Eric said jovially. Kathy held her hand over her mouth laughing through her fingers. Jon watched with a blank expression.

"We can't be sure exactly what happened but we think Matt had a good weekend," Eric deadpanned. "Starting about midnight on Friday." Kathy's laughing spell had tailed off but began anew. She sat down as she strained to stifle her laughter.

"What are you talking about?" Jon asked with pretended ignorance.

"He hooked up," Kathy said, still wheezing.

"Yeah," Eric added. "She was hot, too. From where we were sitting they looked like they were hitting it off. We didn't stick around too late but we're guessing they didn't split up at closing time. Not if Matt's mood on a Monday morning is any sign."

"And a welcome change it is," Kathy added. "I've had enough of his attitude. Maybe now he can get some work done without whining and acting all moody."

Jon looked at Eric, then Kathy. "Well, that's good news. So we can stop worrying about Matt and move this program forward, right?" he said.

"You bet," Kathy answered. "I guess the boy just needed to get laid."

12

THE LIAISON

"Unfortunate," Tan Yingqun said, "but not surprising."

Tan and Alvin sat at a table in a remote corner of a lounge near Alvin's office. Alvin had reported what happened at the board meeting, and then he scrutinized Tan's face in the subdued light for his reaction. He determined that Tan was not pleased, but neither was he angry, or even disappointed. He acted as if he were expecting the news.

"You don't understand what you're up against, do you?" Tan continued. "The chief executive, Hofbauer, is an experienced intelligence man and a veteran of the Cold War. He is more than careful. He's paranoid. Paranoia is an occupational hazard in a business where carelessness can be fatal. You can't possibly ask a question in Hofbauer's presence that could yield useful information—and you will only bring suspicion upon yourself."

Alvin closed his fists and said in a strained voice, "In that case, I don't know how I can provide anything useful. The board meetings are the only interaction I have with Connectrix. And since Hofbauer presides over every meeting, it seems that I will not be of any use to you."

Tan lowered his eyes and pushed at his glass of scotch with his fingertips. "Now *that* is surprising," he said. "I thought you to be cleverer than that. You're a self-made man,

113

wealthy, in fact. As your company expands into China you could become spectacularly wealthy. Could you have achieved all that if you were not ingenious and resourceful?"

"That's very flattering, Tan. I'm sure I could teach you all about how to start a company. But in the field of espionage *you* are my teacher. Tell me—what should I do?"

Tan sipped his scotch before answering. "It's true that your primary interaction with Connectrix is through the board meetings—*at present*. Since, as we have concluded, that is not a useful forum for getting information, you must find other opportunities."

"Such as?"

"Surely you have working relationships with other board members at Connectrix besides Hofbauer, don't you? Many of them have valuable information. It's a matter of creating the opportunity to ask the right questions."

Alvin leaned forward, straining to catch every word.

"If you ask a direct question," Tan continued, "you will undoubtedly reveal your intentions. Then how can you expect a direct answer? You cannot. You must *draw out* the answers from your sources slowly, with subtlety. And the secret is this: *You must give the appearance of knowledge.* Your questions should seek only clarification rather than new information. If your source thinks you already know, he will tell you what you do not know."

Alvin nodded. "I think I understand."

"Let me use an example. Your engineers have security clearance, and you do not. They also know that the Cygnus hardware design is classified. Yet you have detailed knowledge of it. How did you obtain it?"

Alvin sat up in his chair. The corners of his mouth turned slightly upward.

"I knew it was a parallel computer. I guessed at the approach my engineers would take. I've known many of them for years and I know how they think. When I suggested it to them, they validated my guess."

"Is that all they did?"

"No. They described the design to me."

"But you have not only knowledge of the design. You also have diagrams and other documentation. Did your engineers give those to you the first time you discussed it with them?"

"No," Alvin answered.

"Of course not. You discussed the design with them over many days and weeks. During each conversation your engineers revealed a bit more. Over time there was nothing in the design you did not know. By then it was a small thing for them to hand over the documents. At least that's how I suspect you accomplished this bit of espionage. But perhaps I'm mistaken. Am I?"

Alvin laughed quietly as he shook his head. "No. You're not mistaken."

"You see, you can't convince your engineers to break security for you simply because you have power over them. They don't suspect you, but they won't tell you what you're not allowed to know *unless they believe you already know it.* I suggest you use a similar technique with your counterparts at Connectrix. You'll be surprised at what you will learn."

Alvin straightened himself in his chair.

"All right, I get it. But still…"

Alvin's voice trailed off. His eyes narrowed and his mouth clenched. He glared at Tan for a few seconds before turning away.

"Xiao Weiguo," Tan said, "I understand what you're feeling. I've been through it myself. You have compromised your principles to achieve a goal, a goal which has great importance for you. And yet you also believe that your principles are equally important, perhaps more so. But who doesn't compromise his principles a dozen times a day? Or hundreds of times in a week?"

Tan placed his hand on Alvin's in a comforting gesture, a move which took Alvin by surprise.

"If you knew what I have sacrificed," Tan said, "you wouldn't feel so conflicted."

Alvin withdrew his hands from the table and placed them in his lap. There was a period of awkward silence before Tan spoke.

"Xiao Weiguo, how did you know the design was a parallel computer?"

Alvin looked up with raised eyebrows. "I knew how many prototypes Connectrix had ordered. And I knew what price we had quoted. It had to be a parallel design."

Tan nodded, smiling for the first time that evening. "You are ingenious and resourceful after all. And why did you go to such lengths to learn about the design? You knew it was classified."

Alvin looked directly at Tan with his jaw set. "I need to know what's going on in *my* company."

Tan lifted his glass and drained the last of his scotch. "I have one more question before we part to enjoy the remainder of the evening. Why do *you* not have security clearance?"

"My family history," Alvin said softly. "My mother brought me to America when I was twelve. My father stayed behind."

"In Taiwan?"

"No," Alvin said. "In China." A tear rolled down his cheek.

Tan stood and put on his coat.

"Tan Yingqun," Alvin said in a low voice. "What if I can't do this?"

Tan buttoned his coat as he spoke. "You wouldn't be the first to doubt your own resolve, Xiao Weiguo. But I have confidence in you."

Tan wrapped a scarf around his neck. "You called me your teacher, but you already know how to do this. I have been told of your reputation in China. You understand the Chinese ways. In China, the spoken word is like the tip of an iceberg. You must perceive the hidden meaning, even as you conceal your own intentions behind a veil that is neither transparent nor opaque. It's an art, one I hear that you have mastered."

"We're not in China, Tan."

"Very true," Tan answered. "We are in America, and in America, a man often speaks his mind, even if to do so is counter to his purpose. That is the approach you took in the board meeting, and you see what that has achieved. You know what to do. And you have the motivation." Tan put on his gloves and put out his hand. Alvin hesitated before shaking it. "As long as you are useful to the People's Government, Alvin, your business in China will thrive."

13

The Payment

THE CUSTOMER STEPPED up to the window and laid a credit card on the counter, the name *Jon Ames* embossed on the card immediately above *Connectrix Corporation*. He pushed it toward the teller.

"I'd like a cash advance, please. Five thousand, five hundred dollars."

"Yes, sir," the teller replied. "May I see some identification?"

Jon fumbled as he removed his driver's license from his wallet. The teller checked the photo and compared it with the credit card. He smiled.

"How would you like that, sir?"

"Hundred dollar bills will be fine," Jon answered quietly.

The teller swiped the card and entered the amount. She produced a statement for Jon's signature. After he signed, she carefully counted out fifty-five bills and pushed the stack toward Jon.

"Do you have an envelope I could put this in?" he asked with one hand resting on the cash. The teller produced a heavy brown envelope and slipped the money inside. Jon put the envelope in a pocket inside of his jacket.

As Jon left the bank he glanced at his watch. *Quarter to five.* His appointment with Gina Bianchi was more than an hour away.

❖ ❖ ❖

The drive to the Target store on the outskirts of Eau Claire took a little more than ten minutes. By the time Jon entered and found the coffee shop another five minutes had passed. He ordered a cup of decaf and sat down to wait for Gina. He spotted her a few minutes before six, walking toward him and looking as elegant as ever. She smiled as their eyes met, a wide smile of straight, even teeth. She took the chair opposite Jon, laying her handbag on the table and unbuttoning her coat.

"Hello, Jon. How have you been?" she asked cheerily.

"Fine, thanks," he answered. "I have your money."

"Jon, slow down!" Gina laughed. "You don't have to be *all* business, *all* the time. We have an hour. I'm meeting Matt at seven. He's taking me to dinner."

"So, he called you?"

"Of course he called. I told you he'd call." She pulled a compact from her handbag and checked her herself in the mirror, lightly coaxing a few stray hairs into place. "Jon, I wonder if you could bring me a skinny latte, two sugars?"

Jon fetched the coffee and returned to the table. As he sat down, he took the envelope from his jacket pocket with his free hand and laid it on the table. He pushed the coffee and envelope toward Gina at the same time. She lifted the coffee to her lips, ignoring the envelope.

"What's your opinion of Matt?" Jon asked, keeping a nervous eye on the cash.

"Oh, he's cute, in a goofy, awkward kind of way. He's not exactly what I'm used to."

"What do you mean?"

"Jon, I cater to a specific demographic—forty-five to sixty year-old men with six figure incomes. You know—like *you*. They have life experiences I find interesting. And they know how to treat a girl." She sipped her latte carefully, avoiding damage to her lipstick. "Matt's a boy. He hasn't had much time to experience anything. Does he know to treat a girl? I have no idea. I might find out tonight." She took another careful sip. "But I don't have high hopes."

Jon thought back on the prior week. The brooding, untidy malcontent had transformed himself into a presentable and personable young professional. Jon didn't doubt that Gina was the cause. It was yet to be seen if that same influence would translate into progress on the Cygnus program. He hoped it would but feared it might not—especially if Matt got a good look at Gina's cynical side. But it was too late to back out now.

"Matt's changed since the last time you saw him."

"Oh? How?"

"He looks different. He acts different. Better."

She seemed pleased. "I hope I had something to do with that."

"It would appear so."

Gina picked up the envelope and glanced at its contents before slipping it into her handbag.

"Are you going to count it?" Jon asked.

"Oh, I'll count it later. I told you I trust you. If you're short, you'll hear from me."

"Just remember what I'm paying you for," he warned her. "Make him feel good about himself. I don't want him hurt."

She closed her eyes and shook her head, looking annoyed. "Jon, have some faith in me. I know what I'm doing."

Jon stood and pulled on his coat. "I guess you'll be calling me next week."

As he walked past Gina she put her hand on his arm. "Why are you in such a hurry? You're always rushing! We have plenty of time. Let's chat."

Jon returned to his chair but kept his coat on. "I'm not sure what we have to chat about."

"We're always talking business. I don't know anything about you. Tell me about yourself. You're going through a divorce, aren't you? That must be difficult."

"Difficult," Jon replied sullenly. "That's one way to put it."

"I'm sorry. Do you want to tell me about it?"

"Not really. I can't talk about it without sounding bitter."

Gina leaned forward and looked at Jon with raised eyes. "Sometimes people do things to hurt you and when you share your feelings about it, it sounds like bitterness."

"Ha," he laughed. "That sums it up."

She slid her hand along the table until her fingertips touched his.

"She must really have wounded you."

He left his hand as it was, with his fingertips touching hers. Her fingers were slender and perfectly manicured. "I worked my butt off for twenty-five years to make a good life for her. Okay, maybe I wasn't the attentive, romantic husband all the time, but she never complained about all the nice things she has. Now, when I've gotten to this point, with the business and all, just when I could use some support, all she can think about…"

He hesitated before repeating, "…all she can think about is the fucking house."

Gina's fingers inched forward, taking his hand in hers. Her hand was soft and warm and smooth. He looked at her face and her large, liquid eyes which conveyed genuine sympathy.

"You should be getting to your date with Matt," Jon said as he withdrew his hand. He stood again and buttoned his coat. "And I should be getting home."

Gina's sympathetic expression vanished, replaced by her self-assured smile. "Enjoy your weekend." She stood and extended a hand to Jon, who took it in a polite handshake. "You know, dear, if you want some company some night just call me. I'll give you my standard rate."

Jon looked mildly disgusted as he dropped Gina's hand. "That would be very unlikely," he said. He turned to leave.

"You know how to reach me, sweetie," she called after him, wearing the same confident smile.

14

THE DATE

THE PRIOR WEEK had been unlike any other in Matt's memory. For months he'd focused on the solution to one excruciatingly difficult problem to the exclusion of all else, including relationships, nutrition, and hygiene. After his encounter with Gina, what had before seemed inconsequential—his filthy apartment, his shabby clothes— took on new significance. He could no longer ignore nor tolerate them.

He'd slept late Saturday following his marathon cleaning session, on sheets that were freshly laundered for the first time in weeks. He'd spent the rest of the day clothes shopping, an activity he detested, but which now seemed essential. On Sunday he'd deposited a bundle of used clothing at a nearby Goodwill drop box.

Matt called Gina on Tuesday evening. She agreed to meet him for dinner on Friday. Over the next three days Matt continued to apply himself to his proof, but without the all-night sessions. In the evenings he continued to think on it, but in his own apartment and without his usual intensity. It was a departure from Matt's normal pattern. His co-workers noticed and decided that the change was good. Matt himself wondered if distracting thoughts of Gina might dull his edge but ultimately he was unconcerned. It wasn't that he couldn't focus on his proof—he could, but without the anxiety he had experienced almost non-stop for the last two months. By Friday afternoon his intuition told him he was close. The answer still eluded him, but he was as certain as ever that there was an answer and he would find it.

❖ ❖ ❖

Matt arrived at *Il Traghetto Ristorante* a half hour before his seven o'clock reservation. He nursed a glass of wine as he glanced frequently at the entrance, trying to look relaxed.

Matt jumped up when he spotted Gina as she handed her coat to the hostess. He held her chair as she approached. Gina leaned toward Matt and kissed him briefly on the lips, pressing her palm against his cheek. Over the past week Matt worried that his glowing memory of Gina had been clouded by alcohol and embellished by his own hopes. As he seated himself, he dismissed those concerns. Gina was perfect.

"Gina, you look…" he said, and then paused as he searched for the right word. He finished simply, "…great!"

"Thank you, Matt," she answered, giving Matt's hand an affectionate squeeze. "I'm so glad you called. I've been looking forward to seeing you all week."

He gazed at her for the first time with clear, sober eyes. She was every bit as beautiful as he remembered, but now he had a feeling about her that he hadn't before, like a joyful childhood memory that hovered just beyond his recollection —what it was, he couldn't say.

"I'm glad you could make it." He filled her wine glass. "I think you'll like this place."

"That's what you said last week. It's one of your favorites, isn't it? Almost as good as your mom's restaurant."

Matt eyes widened. His memory of their evening together was sketchy. He remembered the general topic of restaurants but none of the specifics. The fact that Gina recalled the details flattered him.

"That's right! They're very good, but they're not quite as good with the details."

"You mean, not quite as good as your mom. She's quite the perfectionist, isn't she?"

"Oh, wow," he chuckled. "I can't believe I told you that. I must have been hammered."

"You were," she laughed. "But in a good way. You were cute. Adorable, in fact."

"She's only that way with the restaurant. She was always particular about things, but after my dad died she took it to a new level."

"That's understandable," Gina said in a soothing tone. "From what you told me, that was a really difficult time for her."

"Gina, just how much of my life story did I tell you?"

She reached across the table and put her hand on Matt's. "You sounded like someone who hasn't opened up in a long time, like someone who's been carrying a lot inside and just needed to let it out. I'm glad you decided to talk to me."

Matt took Gina's hand in his. "I guess I could blame the grappa, but that's not why. I just feel...*good* with you."

"You're so sweet to say that," Gina said, squeezing Matt's hand softly.

Matt was transfixed by Gina's perfect smile and impossibly large and lovely eyes.

"I don't want to give you the wrong impression," he said. "About my mom, I mean. She's really a loving, giving person. Just wait until you meet her."

Gina's mouth dropped open as her eyebrows rose. Matt closed his eyes and hung his head.

"Did I just say what I said?" He unfolded his napkin and placed it on his lap. He handed Gina a menu and took one for himself.

"Before I take you home to meet Mother we probably should have dinner."

❖ ❖ ❖

The first bottle of wine emptied before the main course arrived. Gina chose the second, and, at Matt's insistence, sampled and approved it. She chose a label Matt hadn't tried before. It was splendid—*of course*, he thought.

Their conversation resumed where it ended a week before. There seemed to be no topic on which Gina was not well informed, and on some she was brilliant. When she wasn't, she listened intently as Matt educated and entertained her. When he first took notice of the time, three hours had passed.

"Did the whole evening just evaporate before our eyes?" he asked, checking his watch.

"Not the *whole* evening. We're just getting started."

"What did you have in mind?"

Gina took his hand in hers and leaned forward, speaking softly. "I'm still waiting for that invitation."

Matt smiled hesitantly. "Let's go," he said as he stood and held Gina's chair. "But I'll have to bum a ride."

Matt opened the door to his apartment with apprehension. Although he had cleaned and straightened up a second time during the week, and the stale smell had dissipated, it was the first time he had had a woman as a guest. As Gina entered the apartment, dressed elegantly, having just come from her Mercedes Benz, he was anxious about entertaining her in an apartment that was little better than a college dorm room.

"You have a nice place," Gina chirped. She unbuttoned her coat and pulled it off her shoulders.

"I'll take that," he said, removing her coat and hanging it in the small closet near the door. "Would you like a little more wine? I have some white wine. Not as good as the wine you picked, but not too bad."

"I will, thank you," she said as she looked around the room. There was a couch and a glass-topped coffee table opposite a television on a small stand, two end tables and a lamp, all very ordinary. Gina's eyes were drawn to one item that was not ordinary—a six-foot tall cabinet with a video screen and a shelf holding what looked like two semi-automatic pistols on heavy metal tethers. The box was gaudily decorated with combat scenes filled with grim-faced soldiers. Emblazoned on each side, in military-style stenciled letters, were the words *Army Marksman*.

"Here you go," Matt said, approaching from behind, a glass of wine in each hand. Gina turned toward him, accepting her glass as Matt raised his.

"To new friends," Matt said.

Gina smiled. "To new friends."

They each drank, looking into each others' eyes, until Gina's eyes darted toward the arcade game.

"You're wondering about that big thing," he said, with a hint of embarrassment.

"It does seem to dominate the room. Is there a story behind it?"

"Of course," Matt said between sips. "I won't promise that it's a *good* story."

"Tell me."

Matt set his wine on the glass-topped table and stepped up to the game. He drew one of the pistols from its holster and examined it briefly. He smiled. "It's from an arcade back in Raleigh. I spent way too much time playing this game when I should have been doing something useful. I had the high score four years running. When the owner closed the arcade he gave it to me. Everything else he sold, but not this."

He leveled the faux pistol in a two-handed military grip, sighting along the barrel, taking aim at a spot on the wall.

"His name was Andy. He said to me, 'Matt, you've owned this game from the first time you played it. Now it's yours.'"

Matt let the pistol drop to his side as he reached behind the console and pressed a switch. The box came to life.

"I'm not even sure why I brought it here. I had to rent a trailer to haul it here from Raleigh. It took four guys to muscle it up the stairs. It takes up way too much space."

He pressed a button on the console.

"I guess it reminds me of home."

He took aim as enemy soldiers appeared from behind buildings, vehicles, rocks and trees. He pressed the trigger in rapid succession, picking off one combatant after another with unerring accuracy.

"I don't even play it that much anymore, probably once or twice in the last six months," he shouted over the sound of gunshots and screams, the background music rising as Matt conquered each level. He continued his withering assault, mowing down attackers, tallying forty-two kills before he missed, taking two shots to claim his forty-third casualty. He held his fire as the screen filled with the muzzle flashes of enemy weapons until it went red and announced over ominous chords that Matt was dead.

"Damn it, I never would have missed that shot in my glory days," Matt said. He reached for the game's switch and shut it down.

"Who knew you were such a killing machine?"

"Oh, you have no idea," he said as he holstered the prop gun and retrieved his wine glass. "Maybe someday I'll show you what I'm really capable of."

Gina put her arms around Matt's neck, pulling him close, until her body pressed against his and their lips were separated by inches.

"I'm intrigued," she said, her voice hardly louder than a whisper. She drew him closer. "This dark side of yours is terribly exciting."

They kissed, a deep, soulful kiss. Matt lost himself in the moment, forgetting everything, his mind and body devoted to this one sensation, the feel of Gina's lips on his. The strain of a hundred incessant and conflicting demands accumulated over weeks and months dissipated in a moment as his arms folded around her.

Their lips parted but remained almost touching for a moment until Gina pulled away. She took Matt's wine from him and set both glasses on the table. She began to unbutton his shirt. As she did so Matt placed a trembling hand on Gina's cheek.

She paused between buttons and looked into the boy's face, wearing a look of almost painful vulnerability. She leaned against his hand, pressing it between her cheek and her shoulder, until the tremor stopped. She continued removing Matt's shirt, until it dropped to the floor. She placed both hands on his bare chest.

Matt's hand closed around Gina's as he led her silently to the bedroom. In the darkness they undressed each other slowly, until they stood naked among the scattered clothes. Gina led Matt to the bed, laid down and pulled him after her.

Matt's touch was hesitant, as if he were afraid that Gina might push him away. She patiently guided his hand, first to her breast, then further, until he felt her warmth under his fingers. She moaned into his mouth as she stroked his body. Unlike Matt's inexpert caresses, every movement of Gina's hands, each touch of her lips seemed spontaneous, yet perfectly placed to heighten Matt's passion. Within minutes he took the initiative, losing all trace of shyness. He positioned himself over her; she lifted her hips receptively, guiding him into her.

Matt's climax came embarrassingly soon but he recovered quickly. They made love for nearly an hour, until Matt's stamina failed and he fell to the bed, breathless.

They lay facing each other, a sheet covering them to the waist and the blanket on the floor.

"That was wonderful," Gina said as she stroked Matt's cheek.

He took her hand and pressed the palm to his lips.

"Do you have to go home tonight?"

"Not if you don't want me to."

"I'd like you to stay."

"Then I'll stay," Gina promised. She pulled herself closer, resting her head on Matt's chest, unmoving, until they both slipped off to sleep.

❖ ❖ ❖

Matt woke as the waning moon rose, shining through bare-branched trees, casting a silver shaft of light through the bedroom window. It fell squarely on Gina's sleeping face, rendering her features in shades of grey. She took on the appearance of sculpted marble, a perfect, incorruptible statue.

His breath caught as he understood suddenly the feeling he'd had in the restaurant, a memory he'd tried to but couldn't recover.

A large framed picture hung in Matt's childhood home for as long as Matt could remember, a photo of Michelangelo's *Pietà*. The statue of Mary cradling the dead Christ was a favorite of his mother's, and the photo was embedded in Matt's earliest memories. Michelangelo had interpreted the Virgin not as a grieving middle-aged woman but young, hardly more than a girl, her expression a miraculous picture of piety, serenity and sorrow. As Matt gazed on Gina's face he was overwhelmed by the memory of the image and all its associations of childhood, family and home. He felt an involuntary sob welling up in his chest. He stifled it silently, so as not to rouse the sleeping Madonna.

❖ ❖ ❖

The cell phone on the bare kitchen table buzzed to life just before twelve-thirty in the morning. Josef Hofbauer looked up from his book, set down his tumbler of brandy, and retrieved the phone as it rattled away from him. He didn't bother to check the number. Only one person could be calling at this hour.

"Good evening, Agent Gutierrez. I trust your report will be as uneventful as ever, *ja?*"

"The subject met a young woman for dinner at seven p.m. at *Il Traghetto*, an Italian restaurant, where the couple enjoyed dinner, wine and conversation, leaving the establishment shortly after ten p.m. They went directly to the subject's residence. Both entered the apartment at approximately ten-fifteen and neither has left. From the looks of things I doubt they will until morning."

Josef leaned back in his kitchen chair. He removed his glasses and tapped the earpiece on his lower lip.

"This is the same young woman you reported last week?"

"It is," Anibal answered. "She drives a Mercedes Benz C-class coupe, one of the pricier models. Minnesota tags. It's registered to Gina Bianchi, Minneapolis address."

"I see," said Josef. "Well, Agent Gutierrez, you had better find out what you can about Dr. Bugatti's new friend, no? *Ja?* Do you have anything else?"

"No sir, nothing of consequence." *Unless you want to know what they ordered for dinner,* Anibal thought.

"Very well," Josef replied. "Good evening, Agent Gutierrez. I look forward to your next report."

Josef laid the cell phone on the table and stared into space for a moment before deciding that Agent Gutierrez had the situation under control, at least for the present. He took a generous swallow of brandy and returned to his book.

15

THE OUTING

GINA WOKE SHORTLY before nine, alone in bed. After moment of disorientation she recognized the surroundings: a bedroom as sparsely furnished as Matt's living room, not even pictures on the walls. She sat up and raised her arms over her head, the light from the window casting an elongated shadow of her naked body on the sheets. As she stretched she became aware of an extraordinary aroma—an omelet, she guessed, but more. It was enticingly earthy and herbal, layered over the smell of fresh coffee.

Matt was hunched over his tiny stove, obsessively tending a skillet, when he felt Gina's arms encircle his waist. Matt turned to face her, careful to avoid injuring her with his spatula. Gina pulled Matt's body to her and pressed her lips to his. "Hello lady," Matt said after a lengthy kiss. "Hungry?"

"Ravenous," she answered, resting her head on his chest. "Who wouldn't be after last night?"

Matt laughed gently. "You were unbelievable. You *are* unbelievable." He cradled Gina's face in his hand.

"Where did you come from? What world did you come from? Not my world. I live in a cave, surrounded by walls made of rock. It's pitch black except for a hazy glow coming from the hole I crawled through to get here. What are you doing here in the cave? Why aren't you out in the light with the real people?"

Gina kissed Matt again. "I'm right where I want to be."

"Welcome to the cavern. How about some breakfast?"

Gina sat at the small table next to the kitchen as Matt turned back to the stove. She wore a T-shirt with *North Carolina Mathematics* printed across the front in block letters. It hung loosely on her, covering her to just the tops of her thighs.

"I hope you don't mind me stealing one of your shirts."

Matt studied her, tilting his head to one side, then the other, as if he were judging a fashion show. "It looks better on you than it ever did on me." He tested the edges of the eggs in the skillet and decided they were perfect. He slid them onto a platter and took it to the table.

"This is a Bugatti family specialty," he said, slicing two wedges from the thick omelet and setting them on plates. "A recipe handed down from Bugatti to Bugatti."

Matt fetched a pot of coffee and held it aloft. Gina nodded. He filled her cup as she sampled the dish.

"It's wonderful!" she blurted, around a mouthful, as she covered her mouth with her hand.

Matt smiled as he took a healthy bite. "Holy smokes, it *is* good!" he said with a full mouth, nearly spilling its contents before covering up.

"I don't think I've ever had an omelet like this."

"You don't grow up in the home of Flora Bugatti without spending time in the kitchen. But if she were here she'd tell you, 'It's not an omelet! It's a *frittata!*'"

"Oh, I'm sorry," Gina said gravely. "A *frittata.* Whatever it's called, it's delicious."

For a minute there were no sounds except for forks against plates, chewing, and slurping.

"Gina, when do you have to leave?"

"I have plans tonight, but my day is free. Do you want to do something together?"

"I had an idea—a surprise. But I'm not sure you'd be dressed right for it. And judging from that T-shirt, I don't think I have any casual clothes that will fit you."

Gina got up from the table and kissed Matt on the cheek. She picked up her handbag from its spot near the door and reached inside.

"I have some things in my overnight bag," she said, producing a set of car keys and holding them out to Matt. "It's in the trunk."

Matt took the keys with a mock grimace.

"You brought an overnight bag. Well, *that* was presumptuous." He went to the door and reached for the handle, turning back before leaving.

"I just want you to know—I don't fall into bed with every smart, charming, smoking hot girl that comes along."

❖ ❖ ❖

Gina followed Matt's directions north of Eau Claire to a fenced area of gently rolling terrain, through a gate and past a sign:

Chippewa Valley Shooting Club

"What are you getting me into?" she asked with apprehension.

"I come here almost every week. You were so impressed with my murderous rampage last night I thought you might like to come along. Usually I ride with a friend but I'd rather ride in your car than his pickup truck."

They parked in a gravel lot next to a wide, low building. Matt retrieved a case from the trunk, a container made of dull, textured metal less than two feet long and a foot wide. There were small dents scattered over the sides and scuffs on every edge and corner, giving it a well-used and vaguely menacing look.

❖ ❖ ❖

"A hundred rounds for Doctor Bugatti!" shouted the man behind the counter as they entered the building. The walls were covered with firearms of every kind and from every era.

A row of windows lined the wall at the far end through which a half-dozen firing ranges were visible. The ambient noise was punctuated by the muffled *pop! pop!* of gunfire.

The man disappeared below the small counter near the entrance. He came up holding two boxes of shells.

"Doc, you've been holding out on me!" he said with a loud voice as he laid the ammunition on the counter. "Who's your friend?"

"Chuck, this is Gina. Gina, Chuck."

Chuck held out his hand as he slowly ran his eyes up and down in a way that bordered on sexual harassment. Gina took his hand while ignoring the ogle.

"Gina, I'll bet a sexy chick like you knows how to protect herself. Are you packing a piece in that big fancy bag?"

Gina turned to Matt with a look of astonishment. Matt rolled his eyes.

"No, Chuck," Gina answered, "no guns in here. But I usually don't need drastic measures to take care of myself."

Chuck pursed his lips and nodded slowly as he held Gina's hand. He continued to scan Gina with narrowed eyes.

"Yeah, I can believe that. Yep. I bet no one messes with you." He let her hand go. "But all that said, we have some fine lady-friendly firearms that would go real good in your nice handbag."

"If I decide I need protection I'll know where to come," Gina laughed. "But today I'm just here with Matt."

"Suit yourself, sweetheart. Doc, is sexy Gina going to shoot with you today?"

"I hope so," Matt replied. "But it's up to Gina."

"What? Oh, yes. Sure," Gina answered.

Chuck rang up the cost of one hundred rounds of nine millimeter ammunition. He pulled two paper targets from under the counter and laid them on the glass top. He lifted ear protectors and safety glasses from pegs on the wall and held them out to Matt.

"Gina's new here. She needs to watch the video. We have rules for a reason."

Matt gathered the ammo and paraphernalia. He led Gina toward the video screening room.

"Hey, honey," Chuck called after them. "Stick close to the Doc and you won't need a gun. You'll have all the protection you need. He's a total badass."

❖ ❖ ❖

After the safety video, Matt led Gina into a window-lined hallway to the third of six doors. The persistent *pop! pop!* was louder but still tolerable. Gina followed Matt's lead as he donned his eye and ear protection before entering the booth.

Even with her ears covered, Gina reacted with a start to each gunshot as it erupted from either side. The shooters in adjacent booths fired their pistols in rapid succession with grim, passionless faces, twitching barely a muscle except for their trigger fingers.

Matt laid his metal case on the ledge in front of him, snapped open the latches, and lifted the lid.

In the case lay a nine millimeter semi-automatic pistol and two empty magazines. The weapon resembled the toy pistols on Matt's video game but were immensely more threatening. Matt opened one of the ammo boxes and began pressing cartridges into the clip.

"It's a good pistol if you're not a regular shooter," Matt shouted. "The recoil is very manageable." He finished filling the second clip. "Do you want to go first?"

Gina shook her head.

He clipped a target to the overhead carrier and pressed a button to the side of the booth. With a whirr the target retreated to a distance of forty feet. He inserted the clip and pulled back the slide, leveling the weapon toward the target. His face assumed the same passionless expression as his fellow shooters.

Matt squeezed off shot after shot. Gina flinched with each round, keeping her eyes on Matt instead of the target. He appeared to be counting: *Fourteen…thirteen…twelve.*

After emptying the clip he released the magazine and inspected the chamber. He pressed the button to return the target to the front of the range. The only damage done to the target was a ragged hole in the center of the bull's-eye. Matt took one edge of the target and pulled it closer to inspect the grouping.

"That looks pretty good," he shouted. He replaced the target with a fresh one and sent it to the twenty-foot mark. He slapped the second magazine into the pistol and chambered a round, then presented the firearm to Gina. With wide eyes, she shook her head. Matt looked the target for a moment, then nodded. He sent the target to forty feet and emptied a second clip into it with the same deadly accuracy.

❖ ❖ ❖

The shooting club had a small café where Gina and Matt relaxed after the session. Gina still looked shaken. Matt was quiet for some time before he spoke.

"I can see you didn't enjoy that. I'm sorry."

"That's not true," Gina protested. "I just didn't expect it. You surprised me. I mean, you *really* surprised me. When that man called you a badass, he wasn't kidding. Where did you learn to do that?"

"I've been shooting almost twenty years, since I was seven," he answered. "Another Bugatti family tradition. My grandfather, my *Nonno Matteo*, was *carabinieri* in Italy during the war. He was deadly with a gun. He taught my dad, and my dad taught me. I won my first competition when I was twelve. *Nonno Matteo* rewarded me with that pistol."

"That was your grandfather's gun? Did he use it during the war?"

Matt shook his head. "No, they didn't even start making that model until the seventies. *Nonno Matteo* bought it in Italy and sent it over. But it's a Beretta, a fine old Italian make. I'm sure *Nonno Matteo* had a Beretta or two in his collection."

She reached across the table and took his hand. "What other surprises will you spring on me?"

"You'll just have to take them as they come."

Gina studied Matt. She had to remind herself that this deadly marksman was the same awkward boy she'd made love with the night before.

136

"Matt."

"Yes?"

"When you were shooting—you looked like you were counting."

Matt laughed a little. "Yeah. My dad taught me that. Always know how many rounds in your clip."

16

The Favor

"Good morning, Jon."

Cooper Hodge stood in Jon Ames's doorway shortly before ten o'clock on Monday morning. Jon looked up from his stack of progress reports and motioned for him to enter.

"What's up, Coop?"

Cooper stayed silent, looking as if he needed to say something but didn't want to.

"Are you here for a reason, Coop?"

"I have a question." Cooper held up a sheet of paper. "There's this charge on your company card, a cash advance of fifty-five hundred dollars." He turned the page around so Jon could read the statement. "What's this about?"

Jon nodded as if he had expected the question. "Yes, I can explain that. It's a consultant. I hired a consultant, to work on some system issues."

Cooper turned the statement around and scrutinized it, as if he were trying to find some detail he'd previously overlooked.

"What kind of consultant?"

Jon placed his hands flat on his desk. "It's very technical, Coop. We're having some operating system problems. We've been shorthanded since Anson left and I needed some special expertise."

Cooper examined the statement again. "And you paid him in cash? Why would you do that?"

"It was his idea, but I agreed. The work was highly sensitive. This consultant has top security clearance. And he's well known. He didn't want to raise his visibility."

Cooper held the statement inches from his nose and scrutinized it a third time. "So, if I ask the other members of the technology committee, they'll confirm this? If I ask our security officer, Hofbauer, he'll say he approved this?"

"No. I didn't share it with the technology committee and I didn't clear it with Hofbauer."

Cooper stared blankly at Jon for a moment before he shut the door and sat down.

"Jon, what's going on? I know you're in the middle of a divorce, and money's probably tight. But this…" He laid the statement on Jon's desk and tapped an index finger next to the questionable entry. "This is serious. You need to tell me what this is about."

Jon's fingers drummed on the desk. "God damn it, Coop, I did tell you. We're on a deadline. I can't report every action I take to the technology committee. I can't run everything past Hofbauer. We'd never get a god-damned thing accomplished." Jon slid his hands off the desk and let them drop to his lap, rubbing them together as he spoke. "Coop, we've known each other for twenty-five years. We've started three companies together. You *know* me. I've never done a shady thing in my entire professional life. And you know the deadline we're up against on this program." He stopped rubbing his hands and gripped his knees. "I know I should have done this by the book but there was just no time."

Cooper studied Jon's face, unsure if he was being truthful. He sighed. "Next time *you* need a consultant, *I* need a professional services contract. We'll send the man a check through payroll and a 1099 at tax time. Understood?"

"Coop, it was sensitive. Top secret. If I have to write a contract…"

"Jon, I'm giving you the benefit of the doubt based on our long friendship. If this comes up in an audit we'll both have a lot of explaining to do. I'm doing you this favor, but next time, get a contract. You can redact it if you have to, but *get a fucking contract*."

Cooper stood, turned, and left the office without another word.

Jon sat motionless, trying to quell a rising feeling of nausea, then rested his face in his hands and pressed his fingers against his eyelids.

His cell phone vibrated in his pocket.

Slowly he lifted the cell phone to eye level. He recognized the number as Gina Bianchi's. The nausea began to rise again as he answered the call.

"Let me call you back in a few minutes." He hung up before Gina could say a word.

Jon stayed motionless, head in hands, until he summoned the energy to go to the door and close it. He returned to his desk and waited another minute before calling Gina back.

"Hello, Jon," she answered. "Why didn't you tell me Matt was such a dangerous man?"

"A *dangerous man?* What are you talking about?"

"He took me to shoot guns. He's a scary good shot."

"His pistol shooting," Jon said with relief. "Yes, everyone knows about that."

"Well, *I* didn't know. It came as a shock. But I must say, it *does* make him more interesting."

"I thought you were going out to dinner."

"We did go to dinner, and we had a lovely time. Matt took me shooting on Saturday."

His eyes snapped opened. "You spent the night?"

"Yes, I did," she answered cheerily. "The bill comes to three thousand for Friday and Saturday. In the future I'm going to have to ask for another five hundred if Matt keeps me past noon. We didn't discuss it before so I'll let it go this time. That leaves two thousand on your retainer. I'll let you know about this week as soon as Matt calls. You and I can meet at the same spot."

Jon listened silently to Gina's accounting, one hand pressing his cell phone to his ear and the other hand on his forehead.

"The rest of the retainer is going to be a problem," Jon confessed.

"I'm sorry to hear that," she responded without hesitation. "I'll try to keep this weekend free if I can. Without at least three thousand on account I really can't keep my time open. I would hate to disappoint Matt, but we have rules for a reason. Is that all right, dear?"

Jon mentally replayed his options. His encounter with Cooper Hodge still painfully fresh, he briefly considered ending his arrangement with Gina on the spot and taking his chances, but quickly dismissed that alternative. Matt's change in demeanor had had a stimulating effect on the entire team. *I'm not going to risk a setback now*, he thought. *I've got to stick to the plan.*

"No, let me work on the money. We'll meet this week and I'll pay you."

"That's good news. I'll make sure I keep my calendar free for Matt."

"Thank you," Jon answered in a strained voice. "Is there anything else?"

"Yes, there is. I told Matt that I live in Eau Claire on the weekends but I'm working in Minneapolis during the week until I get my business going. He hasn't been too inquisitive about it but it's only a matter of time before he asks some hard questions. He may be goofy but he's not dumb. Besides, I can't keep spending the night at his place without inviting him to mine. It's not polite."

Jon noticed a hot, throbbing feeling between his eyes. "Can you get to the point, please?" he croaked.

"I need a place to stay in Eau Claire, someplace I can come on the weekends without driving back and forth to Minneapolis. It doesn't have to be fancy, but it should be clean and comfortable. And furnished, of course."

"Out of the question."

"Just think about it, okay? I'm sure I can keep Matt in the dark for the time being. I'll let you know when it starts getting too awkward. Bye for now!"

Jon put his cell phone on his desk and sat straight up. His distress intensified. He made it out the door and to the men's room as quickly as he could without actually running. He opened the door to the stall and fell to one knee just in time to vomit into the toilet.

17

THE ULTIMATUM

THE FLIGHT FROM Chicago to Beijing lasted nearly fourteen hours, giving Alvin Xiao plenty of time to think.

The factory had gone from a smooth-running machine to a wheezing contraption in less than a week. Jimmy's last report from Chengdu was filled with red flags, nearly every aspect of the operation having been affected by slowdowns and shortages. They had lost personnel and replacements were hard to find. Jimmy offered no explanation; "We're all baffled," he wrote. Alvin's jaw clenched as he re-read the report while 30,000 feet over the Bering Sea.

Alvin arrived in Chengdu shortly before eleven in the morning, looking grumpy and disheveled. Jimmy, grim-faced, met him at the gate.

"Good flight, Boss?" Jimmy asked as he took Alvin's bag.

"It sucked," Alvin snapped. "First class was booked. Business was booked. If you had given me some advance warning I could have traveled with some shred of comfort. Why am I always coming over here when things are fucked up? When will I get to come here to celebrate?"

Alvin walked at a fast clip toward the exit with Jimmy, silently fuming, close behind. Neither spoke a word until their car left the airport en route to the factory.

"Tell me again what happened, day by day," Alvin demanded.

"Last Friday everything was fine. We finished the week on quota. Saturday shift replenished floor stock and posted orders to refill inventory, just like we've done every week for the last month."

"You haven't met your quota all week. What went wrong?"

"When the trucks got here on Monday, they were missing parts. They were still short on Tuesday. We tried to build around the shortages but it wasn't just one or two parts. There're more than ten suppliers who haven't shipped us anything all week."

"*Ten?*" Alvin shouted. "Which ten? Are they related in any way?"

Jimmy shook his head. "Not that I can see. We're missing rivets and screws, sheet metal, circuit boards—all from different companies."

Alvin pinched his lip, keeping his eyes fixed on Jimmy. "What do you think's going on?"

"No clue. But I'll say this—it's like someone deliberately picked *the* ten suppliers that could shut us down. Every single thing we make is short at least one part."

Alvin fell back in his seat and turned to the window. *I've been summoned*, he thought. *And the levers have slipped from my hands.*

"Arrange meetings with the delinquent suppliers as soon as possible," Alvin said without turning from the window. "I'll put pressure on them personally. We've got to get control of this situation."

"Yes, Boss," Jimmy sighed with relief.

"What have you got the workers doing?"

"They're building what they can with what they have. It's actually been pretty easy to keep them busy. A third of the workers called in sick on Monday. We've been shorthanded all week."

❖ ❖ ❖

When Alvin arrived he found the factory in chaos. Every work station was clogged with partially assembled computers, each missing one or more critical parts. The half-finished products were stacked on benches, on carts, on the floor—one station even had computers stacked unsteadily on the steps of a ladder.

None of the suppliers gave explanations for their missed deliveries. None promised shipping dates. Alvin visited the Chengdu suppliers personally, but rarely talked to anyone in a position of authority. His dealings with the suppliers had an eerily consistent character: Whenever he pressed for a commitment, or a reason for the shortages, the response was always the same, as if read from a script—*we are very sorry, but we cannot commit to a delivery date at this time.*

Deng Yang, the government liaison, was all but mute when questioned about the situation. He still insisted on approving each applicant to replace the missing factory workers, despite Alvin's polite protests. When asked about the shortage of supplies, he simply repeated that he could not interfere with daily operations.

"Deng Yang," Alvin said to him at one point, "as you can see, our factory is struggling. Can we not rely on our partner, the People's Government, to help us? You've said that you are responsible for the success of this venture. How can we work together to resolve this crisis?"

"I am very concerned," Deng replied. "I've reported it to my superior, with whom I share this important responsibility. He has assured me that everything that can be done *is* being done."

"That's very comforting to hear, Deng Yang," Alvin said, before dismissing Deng from his office.

Alvin waited a few minutes after Deng left. He picked up the phone but hesitated. *Who do I call?* After a moment he placed a call to the People's Ministry of Commerce and asked to speak with Chen Baoshan. After a few soft clicks a voice came on the line.

"Xiao Weiguo, welcome back to China." Alvin immediately recognized the voice of Wang Shutao.

Shit, he cursed to himself.

"Wang Shutao? I didn't expect you. I called Chen Baoshan at the Ministry of Commerce."

"I'm very sorry for intercepting your call," Wang said in his oily manner. "I was told of your visit and I asked that any calls to Chen be directed to me. I wanted to express to you personally my thanks for the very useful information you have provided on the Cygnus project. Our scientists have been able to confirm their theories about the purpose of this system. You have our gratitude."

Alvin's throat went dry. "I'm pleased that I could be of some small service to the People's Government," he rasped.

"Indeed," answered Wang. "You have justified my faith in your ingenuity and resolve. I'm sure we can look forward to our continued cooperation."

"Yes, Wang Shutao," Alvin said with as much restraint as he could summon.

"Now, tell me," Wang continued. "Are things going well in Chengdu?"

As if you didn't know.

"No, Wang Shutao, they're not. That's the reason for my visit. Some key suppliers are late with their shipments. We've lost many of our workers. I haven't had any luck fixing these problems. I'm afraid I'm at the limit of my ingenuity and resolve. I had hoped the Ministry of Commerce could help me."

"Xiao Weigou, this is terrible news! I will certainly relay your situation to Chen Baoshan, and I will personally see that every effort is made to reverse this situation. We cannot allow our venture to fail. Please, don't worry yourself any longer."

"Thank you," Alvin said, concealing his contempt. He hung up, uncertain whether his production problems would persist.

He need not have worried. The following morning eleven absent workers reported for their shift, all deeply apologetic for having missed so many days. They arrived just in time to help receive a week's worth of inventory from the trucks that queued up in the drive leading to the Mechanized Minds Chengdu factory.

❖ ❖ ❖

By the end of the following week the backlog of half-finished computers had cleared and production resumed a steady flow. Jimmy was relieved that the factory was back to normal but quickly grew annoyed with Alvin's interference in even the most routine decisions.

"Boss, you're undermining my authority," Jimmy complained privately after Alvin had rearranged the tools at a workstation with a dozen confused employees looking on.

"That workstation was a disaster."

"Alvin, it was *not*. Even if it was, just tell me and I'll fix it. Now when I give those workers an order they want to know if it's all right with Mr. Xiao."

Alvin glared. After a moment his expression softened. "You're right. You run the factory. I was out of line."

Jimmy crossed his arms and shifted his weight. "Alvin, what's going on? I know you're a stickler for details but you've always trusted me to run the shop."

Alvin didn't answer but gave a slight shrug. Jimmy took it as a sign of agreement and left Alvin's office. As he did so Alvin reminded himself that Jimmy Liu was not Wang Shutao.

❖ ❖ ❖

Alvin joined the line for passport control at the Beijing airport, anticipating an hour of relaxation in the lounge before boarding the flight for Chicago. Alvin approached the agent offering his passport, his boarding pass and departure card. The agent accepted the passport with a weary expression, verified the picture was Alvin's, and scanned the document. A moment passed before the agent's expression changed from boredom to surprise. The agent waved in the direction of a uniformed guard.

"Is there a problem?" Alvin asked in Mandarin.

The agent said nothing as the guard approached the agent's booth and peered at the computer monitor. He looked at the passport, then at Alvin, and then returned his attention to the screen.

"Mr. Xiao," the guard said, "you must come with me."

Alvin followed the guard to the far wall of the security area. The wall was interrupted by a row of alternating windows and doors, each window-door combination belonging to a separate small room, each furnished with a table and chairs. A few rooms were occupied by officials in nondescript suits and travelers looking distressed. The guard left Alvin alone in one of the unoccupied rooms with the door closed.

Fifteen minutes later the door opened. Wang Shutao entered, wearing his usual placid smile, followed by Tan Yingqun.

"Good afternoon, Xiao Weiguo," Wang said, speaking in Mandarin. "I must apologize for intercepting you. I know you don't have much time but you need not worry. You will be at your gate well before your flight leaves. But it would be a shame if you came all the way to China and we didn't have a chance to meet face-to-face."

Alvin looked first at one man, then the other, then said to Wang in English, "What's *he* doing here?"

"Tan Yingqun is here at my request," Wang answered in Mandarin. "What I am about to ask is best said among the three of us, and in person, so there can be no misunderstanding."

Alvin continued in English. "He's not even supposed to be here. The terms of his release were that he agreed never to return to China."

"Yes, that is what we announced when we allowed Tan Yingqun to leave the People's Republic. This is his first visit to China since then. It required some planning to bring him here without alerting the American authorities." Wang looked at Tan and widened his smile. "The Americans believe he is in Thailand, and as soon as we're finished here, he'll return to Bangkok—under an assumed identity, of course."

"What do you want, Wang?"

Wang took the chair opposite Alvin and placed his hands on the table.

"May I tell you again how grateful we are for the information you have provided?" Wang began. "We now know the purpose of this system and the approach to its design. This is great progress. But—what is the English expression?—*the devil is in the details.* We need to know more. We must ask you for more information. And it must be specific."

Wang slid his hands along the table toward Alvin.

"You have provided schematic drawings. But there is only so much we can learn from them. With no context, our analysis is mostly speculation." Wang curled his fingers under his hands. His fists edged closer. "You will also get us detailed specifications. We need to know what this machine is capable of."

Alvin closed his eyes and slowly shook his head. "No. I've given you everything I have."

Alvin stood, leaning against the table. "Wang Shutao, I know you can shut down my factory. So let's stop playing games. I've given you complete details of the Cygnus design —everything you need to reproduce it." Alvin stood straight. "There's nothing more. The well is dry."

Alvin sat down. He gripped the edge of the table. "Shove the bullshit aside and tell me what happens next."

Wang's expression didn't change; Tan looked as if he were in pain.

"Xiao Weiguo, you disappoint me. We have only the best intentions with regard to our partnership. Didn't we take extraordinary steps to establish your presence in Chengdu? Haven't we intervened on your behalf when you encountered problems, not once, but twice?"

Wang lifted a hand from the table and held it out to Alvin. "In all of our actions we have demonstrated our friendship and good will. And up to this moment you have done the same. So this refusal is a great disappointment." He stood and paced. "You suggest we stop playing games. How odd that you put it that way. A game has rules. In a game, no matter how unevenly the sides are matched, the outcome is always in doubt."

He turned and looked directly at Alvin. "We are not playing *games*," he said in English. "Perhaps you are thinking you can survive the loss of your business—that an intelligent, ambitious, industrious man such as you can suffer such a setback and still recover. It's quite another thing to lose your reputation—to lose your family."

Alvin leaned against the table and wheezed, *"What do you mean?"*

"You are compromised, Xiao Weiguo. You have betrayed your country." Wang leaned closer. "It's a sad thing when friends must resort to threats, but if you do not help us Tan Yingqun is prepared to expose you as a Chinese spy."

"You wouldn't," Alvin whispered. He turned toward Tan. "You'd be implicated yourself. We'd go down together."

Wang stood up straight. "We may be able to protect him, but if not, that is a risk he is willing to take. Isn't that so, Tan Yingqun?"

Tan looked down as he broke his silence: "Yes."

"You see, Xiao Weiguo?" Wang said. "No games. No *bullshit*."

Alvin stared fiercely at Wang. His grip on the table's edge tightened.

"I'll try. But I can't promise. I can only say I'll try."

Wang's tranquil expression reappeared.

"I'm pleased." Wang gestured toward the door. "Now, you may go. I wish you a safe and pleasant journey."

Alvin said nothing else as he took his briefcase and left the room. He walked slowly to the gate and boarded the plane for the long flight to America.

❖ ❖ ❖

Tan remained in the room after Alvin left. He closed the door after him, then faced Wang.

"I will never admit to collaboration," he said with uncharacteristic ferocity. He pointed at the door through which Alvin had just passed. "That pathetic man can rot for all I care but I will not accuse him to help you."

Wang sat down, crossing his legs and folding his hands over his knee. "Please, Tan Yingqun, there is no need for such drama. He will help us. He'll find a way to get us the details of this new system. His business in China will thrive, and your part in this affair will remain secret."

"And if you get your precious information," Tan hissed, "you'll keep your promise?"

Wang held his hands out. "Tan Yingqun, you wound me. We are friends. Friends keep their promises."

"Say it to me," Tan snapped.

Wang stood and faced Tan, taking his hand.

"Yes, Tan Yingqun. Of course. Our operation will succeed. We will learn all we need to know about the Cygnus system, and we will nullify the Americans' advantage in espionage. Your reputation will remain unblemished."

"Say it."

Wang let Tan's hand drop. "We will release your wife and daughter. They will join you in America." He smiled and continued in English, "The Land of the Free."

18

GUANXI

JON SPENT MONDAY evening combing through his finances, looking for five thousand dollars he could appropriate for Gina without raising the suspicion of his wife or her lawyer's army of forensic accountants. Small withdrawals from multiple accounts consistent with past transactions sufficed to raise fifteen hundred dollars without raising suspicion. Accumulating five thousand using the same approach would certainly be noticed. He continued to sort through statements, bills, and ledgers to come up with enough money to get him through the week. He refused to let himself think about the long-term expense of Gina's services, or where *that* money would come from—one hurdle at a time. By midnight he surrendered and went to bed for an uneasy rest. It was small comfort that he still had four more days to find the money.

❖ ❖ ❖

Jon was late to work on Tuesday, the first time that had happened as far as any Connectrix employee could remember. Eric Reilly decided to investigate.

"Hey, Chief," Eric said softly as he tapped on Jon's half-open door. "Is everything okay? We're a little worried about you out here."

Jon looked up, eyes drooped with fatigue, his face drained of color.

"I'll be okay. I had a back-and-forth with Hannah last night. I don't think I got more than an hour's sleep." His words were heavy and slow.

"Chief, that's a shame. I'm sure you'll be glad when that stuff is all behind you."

Jon laughed a weary, deflated laugh. "Glad, lonely and broke. That's what I'll be. I'm *so* looking forward to that day."

After many years, Eric had learned when to talk and when to shut up in Jon's presence. He said nothing more, but simply remained in the room.

"It'll all be fine," Jon continued. "Whatever doesn't kill you, right, Eric?"

"Right, Chief."

Jon smiled and shook his head. "Back to it, eh? We have a world to change. Anything I should know about?"

"No, we're all keeping our heads down." Eric turned to leave but stopped and turned back. "There is one thing I've been meaning to tell you," he said. "You know we're doing everything we can to hit the release date, right?"

"Yes, of course. Everyone's busting hump."

"Well, here's the thing. We've scheduled four weeks each for system and application testing, but I think that's optimistic. Six is more realistic. And the tests are scheduled one after the other with no overlap."

"What does that mean?" Jon asked, too tired to analyze the impact to the schedule.

"Even if we run multiple shifts, we're going to miss the deadline. By a lot."

Jon closed his eyes and let his chin fall on his chest. Everything he'd done to keep Matt on schedule could count for nothing if the rest of the project slipped.

"Why didn't Kathy tell me this?"

"She still thinks she can meet the goal. She won't admit that she's late until she's late. But I've seen this before. We're going to miss our date."

Jon's body went limp as he yielded the last of his strength. As he slumped in his chair he mentally ran down the usual list of options.

Add people. Reduce scope. Reallocate resources. Parallel tasks.

His eyes snapped open.

Parallel tasks.

"Eric, what if you had a second prototype?"

Eric cocked his head to one side. "With a second prototype we ought to be able to overlap four or five weeks of testing. That would help." He nodded. "Yes. We could make it."

The two men studied each others' faces before Eric frowned.

"But that's another half million bucks. And we'll never get it built in time. Delivery from Mechanized Minds is at least a month, maybe more. Then we'll have to build it and debug it." Eric shook his head. "Nice try, but I don't see how we could pull it off."

Jon stood up. "Let me worry about the money. Besides, we can always sell the prototype to recoup the expense. And I'll negotiate the lead time myself. It might cost us a little more, but I'm sure I can work out an expedited delivery."

Eric smiled. "Okay, Chief! Make it happen!" Eric's smile became a grin as he turned to leave. He stopped in the doorway and looked back. "It's like old times, isn't it? Pushing the limits, hanging it out over the edge."

"Always fifteen minutes from disaster."

Jon closed his office door after Eric left. He returned to his desk and tapped a few keys on his keyboard to open his contact list. With a few more clicks he located a phone number. He made the call and waited for an answer.

"Good morning, Mechanized Minds Corporation. How may I direct your call?"

"I'd like to speak with Alvin Xiao, please."

❖ ❖ ❖

Alvin could only imagine what Jon wanted. Jon had been vague on the phone, saying only that he had an important matter to discuss, and that it had to be in person. Whatever

Jon had in mind, Alvin saw it as an opportunity. He recalled Tan's advice—*you must perceive the hidden meaning, even as you conceal your own intentions behind a veil that is neither transparent nor opaque.*

Melissa tapped on Alvin's door. "Jon Ames is here."

"Show him in."

Jon strode into the office, looking energetic and cheerful. He shook Alvin's hand in a friendly greeting.

"I heard you just got back from China. How was your trip?"

"Travel to China is always tiring, but I've recovered," Alvin answered with a smile.

"And your business there? How's that going?"

"We've had a few bumps in the road, but things are running smoothly now."

The two men took seats facing each other. There was a moment of awkward silence.

"You're wondering what this is about," Jon said.

"You weren't specific on the phone. I'm not sure what would require our meeting face to face. But I'm glad to see you. We should spend more time together between board meetings."

"Great idea. I'll make a point of stopping by whenever I'm in St. Paul."

Another moment passed. Alvin raised his eyebrows and gestured toward Jon with open hands.

"I'm working on a couple of thorny issues," Jon said. "I think you can help me with both. Our schedule for Cygnus is under some pressure. If we don't take action we'll miss our deadline. But we think we can get back on track if we have a second hardware prototype."

"Of course, we can provide as many prototypes as you need," Alvin said, nodding. "You only need to submit your order."

Jon shifted in his chair. "I understand, and under ordinary circumstances, we would have done exactly that. But we need the prototype as soon as possible. Your lead time is too long."

Alvin folded his hands and pressed his fingers to his lips. *All this could have been done over the phone*, he thought, *and by lower level people.*

"That won't be a problem," he said casually. "Our early prototypes required design and process verification. That's why they took so long. We're well past that stage." Alvin watched Jon carefully as he continued. "The only concern I have is whether we can get the material but I'm sure we can expedite shipments of key components, and we have adequate stock to cover the remainder of the requirements."

Alvin opened his hands as if to punctuate the end of the conversation. "Have your buyer submit a purchase order and we can ship the product in the same quantities as before in less than a week. Same price."

"That's great news," Jon said unsteadily.

"Wonderful," Alvin said. "I'm glad we could help. And I enjoyed our time together. In the future, it would be a shame if you came all the way to St. Paul and we didn't have a chance to meet face-to-face."

Jon turned pale. He swallowed hard. "I have another problem I'd like to discuss."

Alvin folded his hands and leaned forward. "Of course. Your other problem. What else can we do for you?"

"We have some development expenses of a..." Jon seemed to be searching for the right words. "...a sensitive nature." Jon swallowed hard again.

"Melissa," Alvin called out. "Can you bring some water for Mr. Ames? Would you like some water, Jon?"

"Yes, please."

Melissa brought two bottles of water and handed one to Jon. Alvin held up his hand to decline the bottle when offered. He settled back in his chair and waited for Jon to continue.

"It would be...um...awkward to cover these expenses through the usual accounting procedures. I have a proposal for you that would avoid that problem."

Alvin nodded silently, his serene expression unchanged.

"We would be willing to pay an expedited delivery fee for this prototype, say, twenty percent."

"That's very generous, but unnecessary. As I've said, we can ship these products in less than a week at the same price. Do you need them sooner?"

"No," Jon said. He took a drink of water. "A week will be fine. But I have this other problem, these development expenses."

"I see," Alvin said coolly. "If I follow what you're saying, it would seem that you're asking me to, let's say, *rebate* the expediting fee to cover your development expenses. Am I on the right track?"

"Yes," Jon said quietly.

"What you're suggesting is rather irregular, wouldn't you say?"

"Yes," Jon repeated.

"And to participate in such an arrangement would involve some risk on both our parts, do you agree?"

"Agreed."

"Then why would I do that?"

"We can work out an arrangement. A split, maybe?" Jon waited for a reaction that did not come. "Fifty-fifty?"

"Jon, you disappoint me. Although we're not close friends, you must know me well enough to understand that I would never agree to such a scheme." Alvin paused to smooth a wrinkle from his slacks with the back of his hand. "Not for such an insignificant amount."

Jon's mouth dropped open. "Do you want more?"

Alvin got up to close the door. He sat behind his desk and placed his hands on the surface. "I have an interest in the success of this program, Cygnus. Despite what Josef Hofbauer thinks, this program is very important to my company and to me personally. And yet, the details of the program are kept from me." He lifted one hand and gestured as he continued "I'm willing to assist you with a second prototype, and to rebate a certain percentage of the cost to you. I'm not interested in any split. What I need is far more valuable. I need information. And it must be specific."

Jon blanched. "The program is classified. There's nothing I can tell you that you don't already know."

"I only need this information for my own purposes. I need to know the potential of this program, and its risks." Alvin stood and paced behind his desk. "It's also important to know what other opportunities we can realize from this parallel computing technology, which I have learned is very tightly bound to the software algorithm. The more we know about this software, the greater the potential."

Alvin stopped pacing and faced Jon. "We're partners. This thing you ask me to do, this risky thing, I'll do this for your sake, to help you succeed. And what I ask from you will be to our mutual benefit." He returned to his seat next to Jon.

Jon turned a blank stare downward. "I can't do that." He looked up. "I signed an oath."

"I understand that you're unwilling to violate your oath. But you have already compromised yourself simply by making this proposal. You have a goal, which is very important to you. And your principles are equally important, perhaps more so. But who doesn't compromise his principles a dozen times a day? Or hundreds of times in a week?"

Jon stood up and walked unsteadily to the door. "Alvin, I'm sorry I wasted your time. Please forget this conversation. It should never have happened. I should never have come."

Alvin didn't speak as Jon left the office. His expression didn't change.

❖ ❖ ❖

As Jon drove back to Eau Claire he cursed himself for even considering a kickback scheme. He cursed Alvin for his outrageous proposal. By the time he reached the Wisconsin state line he stopped cursing and his thoughts returned to his two crises, the ones he thought he could solve with one bold, if less-than-ethical stroke.

When Jon arrived home he stopped in his driveway. He got out of his car and looked at his house, a large residence, over five thousand square feet on two acres of carefully managed lawn. It included every feature he or his wife had ever wanted in a home. He thought about the year that he and Hannah had built it. It should have been a happy time, and in many ways it was. But looking back he realized the house, so important to the two of them, meant very different things to each. To Jon, it was a trophy, won by talent and hard work. To Hannah, it was payment for a debt.

I can manage it, he thought.

Jon pulled his cell phone from his pocket and punched in a number.

"Hello, Melissa?" he said. "This is Jon Ames. I'd like to talk with Alvin if he's available."

❖ ❖ ❖

Alvin hung up the phone after the conversation and turned toward the window. He clasped his hands behind his back. He had recovered from his experience in Beijing. He savored the feeling.

Back in control.

19

THE BREAKTHROUGH

MATT IMMERSED HIMSELF the proof of his conjecture. Although the answer still eluded him, each new attempt exceeded the last in elegance and rigor. Glimpsing, however imperfectly, a fundamental truth, and striving to describe it in the austere, hard-edged language of mathematics, kept Matt in a singular state of concentration.

Despite his obsession, Matt took time to arrange a date with Gina the following Saturday. He worried that she might have lost interest after their shooting escapade, but he needn't have. Gina seemed more interested than ever.

Matt rose early Wednesday morning, despite having worked late into the previous night. As he walked to work in the bracing December air, he tried clearing his mind, hoping for a fresh perspective. At one point he stopped to shake his head vigorously, as if he could shuffle the heap thoughts and uncover some new approach.

There had been no snowfall that season, but on this morning every surface wore a coat of delicate frost, catching the glow of streetlights and reflecting it in countless prismatic points. Matt trudged on, mindless of the glittering spectacle, until he chanced to look up into the leafless limbs of a tree, twinkling against a purple sky.

The scene reminded Matt of the tree-like diagram of his factor space. Even the colors resembled the white branching structure on a blue background. Matt stared without appreciating its stark beauty; instead, he wondered what fraction of the tree's envelope was occupied by the tree itself and decided it was very small, perhaps a few percent. He imagined a plane intersecting the trunk, defining a single round section, like the smooth surface of a stump left behind after felling the tree with a mathematically perfect chainsaw. As he mentally raised the plane higher, the round section became smaller as the trunk became thinner, until the trunk branched, and the single round section became two, then three, then six, the circular sections multiplying in number as they shrank in size. Matt wondered how many branches and twigs intersected the plane at the widest part of the tree, each of thousands of intersections forming a circle, all the circles disconnected.

All the circles disconnected.

Matt stood statue-still, afraid the idea whispering to him from the deepest recess of his mind might evaporate if he moved.

Oh, no. How could I have missed that?

❖ ❖ ❖

Matt burst through the front door of the Connectrix building after sprinting six blocks. He went directly to his cubicle and scanned his bookshelf for a thick volume, its title printed in plain capital letters on the spine:

MANIFOLDS

Matt carried the book and a sheaf of paper into the conference room and laid them on the table. He stooped over the book and paged through it until it lay open to a chapter titled *Higher Dimensional Manifolds*. He tried to read the text, realized it was too dark to read, and switched on the overhead lights. He returned to the book and scanned it, page by page, for several minutes, still bent over, until he stopped, stood and surveyed the walls filled with equations and diagrams. He proceeded to erase every square inch. Starting in one corner, he began to write. He was still wearing his hat, his scarf, and his coat, zipped up to the chin.

❖ ❖ ❖

By nine o'clock, word had spread. Singly and in groups of two or three, people visited the room and peeked cautiously in. Nearly half the wall surface was covered as Matt continued to write furiously. His coat, scarf and hat lay scattered on the floor. His sleeves were rolled up to the elbows. Although the temperature in the room was in the mid-sixties, Matt was sweating.

A few minutes after nine Kathy entered the room at the head of her team.

"Matt, we have the room," she said. Matt ignored her.

"Matt," she repeated. "I have my project meeting now. We should only be an hour."

"Not now," Matt said without looking and without slowing his pace.

Kathy looked at the walls. The columns of equations, diagrams and graphs might as well have been alien glyphs as far as Kathy was concerned, but she sensed that they were somehow different than the symbols and drawings which Matt had wiped away. Matt was not simply composing variations on a theme—this was new. *More than new,* Kathy thought, *maybe...I don't know...extraordinary.* She quietly herded her team from the room and closed the door behind her. It didn't open again for ten hours.

❖ ❖ ❖

When Matt emerged well after sundown, the area was dark except for one glowing spot on the ceiling immediately above Kathy's cubicle. At the sound of the door opening, Kathy poked her head above the cubicle wall. She walked toward the open door. Her eyes met Matt's as she went into the conference room without saying a word.

All four walls, from floor to ceiling, and the table, layered with handwritten sheets of paper, were filled with the details of Matt's proof. More sheets covered the chairs, some were taped to the walls, and some were arranged on the floor around the edges of the room. Kathy stared open-mouthed.

"What is it?"

Matt scanned the room. His eyes were glistening.

"It's my legacy."

❖ ❖ ❖

Jon arrived Thursday morning at his usual time, well before the large majority of Connectrix employees. As he passed the conference room he glanced at the door and stopped. There was a crude sign posted on the closed door that read:

DO NOT ENTER
BUGATTI

Jon reached for the doorknob, but then thought better of it. He left the room undisturbed and went to his office.

The day before Alvin had promised Jon two things: a quote for a second prototype at a twenty percent price premium, and an advance payment of five thousand dollars to an offshore account. In return, Jon promised information. Since their conversation Jon found it impossible to concentrate. And now there was that mysterious sign on the conference room door. For an hour he busied himself with minor tasks.

At eight-thirty Jon got a visit from Kathy Darling.

"Jon, you need to see this," she said as she walked uninvited into Jon's office.

"See what?"

"In the conference room. Just get in there."

He followed Kathy to the conference room, its door now open and surrounded by a small crowd. They parted to allow Jon to pass, with Kathy close behind.

Matt was on his hands and knees scrutinizing a sheet of paper on the floor. His attention alternated between the sheet and the scribblings on the wall. His laptop computer was on the table. From time to time Matt turned to it and typed frantically before returning to his spot on the floor.

"Matt, what's going on in here?" Jon demanded.

"Shh," Kathy whispered. "I'm not sure he can hear you."

"I can hear you," Matt muttered without looking up. He continued studying his pages and transcribing them one by one into his computer, never rising from his knees.

"I've got to get this into the computer, get it into a form I can analyze." He paused after a short burst of frenzied keystrokes and sat back on his haunches. He spread his arms to draw attention to the equations, text and diagrams on the walls, table and floor. "I can't leave it here. I've got to put it in a secure place."

Jon, Kathy, and a dozen eyes behind them continued to watch, mute, as Matt crawled from page to page, occasionally standing to read some lines from the wall.

"I'll brief you this afternoon. What time is it now?"

"Eight-thirty-five," said a voice from outside the door.

"Eight-thirty-five," Matt echoed. "I should be ready by four. In your office."

❖ ❖ ❖

At four-fifteen Matt had still not appeared in Jon's office. Jon Ames, Josef Hofbauer, and Kathy Darling sat waiting as one of Kathy's developers reported on Matt's activities every few minutes. Every report was the same: "He's still typing."

Matt came in just after four-thirty, carrying a stack of papers and his laptop. He set both on the table in Jon's office, stood facing the three of them, took a deep breath, and exhaled.

"All right," he said, "here's the deal."

For the next ninety minutes Matt described a world of multi-dimensional space and numerical properties that left his audience baffled. He recreated many of the diagrams from the conference room on Jon's whiteboard, filling the entire board, erasing it, and filling it again six times. He talked the entire hour and a half without pause, and no one interrupted him to ask questions. He embellished his rapid-fire delivery with whole-body gestures, looking more like an actor in a performance piece than a mathematician revealing a revolutionary discovery.

At the end of his presentation he paused, laid the marker in the tray at the bottom of the whiteboard and placed the palms of his hands together, the only clue that Jon, Josef or Kathy had that he'd finished his explanation.

They looked at one another uncertainly. Jon spoke first.

"Matt, you mentioned a conversation you had with a mathematician at the conference in Chapel Hill. You said that you and he had a disagreement about whether the search path is connected or not. What was his name?"

"Petrescu," Matt answered. "Marku Petrescu."

"That's right. Petrescu. You said you were going to prove that the search path is *not* connected. Is that what you've done?"

"No, no, no," Matt said, shaking his head. He stopped and looked sideways for a moment.

"Well, yes. Sort of. Here's the funny part. Petrescu is right, but not for the reason he thinks. The search path *is* disconnected in discontinuous *factor* space, but it's *connected* in a continuous *geometrical* space to which the factor space is bound."

The three listeners all wore identical blank expressions.

"This geometrical structure, this *manifold*, is like a tree, with branches and twigs. The factor space is like a flat plane that cuts through the tree. All the intersections with the branches of the tree are like circles in the plane, all disconnected. But they're all part of the same tree. Do you see?"

They didn't.

"What does this mean for your algorithm?" Jon asked.

Matt closed his eyes and smiled as he pressed his fingers to his forehead.

"Jon, it means that the algorithm is deterministic. Give me an encryption key and I can tell you exactly which prime factors are candidates and which aren't. Not a guess, but with one-hundred percent certainty. That means I can restrict the search space to a fraction of what it is now. And I can simplify the tests."

Their perplexed looks gave way to wide-eyed realization.

"And what is the best time, do you think?" Josef asked.

"Too early to tell. Definitely under twenty-four hours, just from reducing the search volume. Probably under twelve when it's all done. Eight hours is not impossible."

Josef stood and put his hand on Matt's shoulder.

"Brilliant!" he said, rolling the *r*. "You see, Jon? Our boy Matt will be the key to our success, no? Well done!"

At that moment Jon forgot about his divorce battle with Hannah, the money he owed Gina, and his covert arrangement with Alvin. For an instant, he thought only about the successful outcome of the Cygnus program. "What's the next step?" he asked.

"I've got to do some more analysis to verify some steps in the proof. That should take me a couple of days. I need to rewrite most of the algorithm to add the geometrical elements. That's at least a three-week job. And of course I have to write up the proof for review."

Josef turned to Matt, peering over his glasses. "Review? What review? Who will review it?"

"Mathematicians," Matt answered innocently. "I need to get the pre-publication draft in the hands of reviewers."

"There will be no review, and there will be no publication."

Matt looked dumbstruck. "No publication? We *have* to publish! This is a breakthrough! This proof has to be reviewed and critiqued." Matt turned from one person to the next looking incredulous. "Josef! Jon! When I write this proof out, it'll be more than a hundred pages. Even after I check it and double check it there could be a dozen mistakes. Any one of them could invalidate the proof. We *have* to get more eyes on this."

"Matt," Josef said gravely, "*are* there mistakes?"

Matt looked again from face to face. He turned back to Josef. "No. The proof is correct."

"Very well," Josef said. "Here is what you will do. You will turn over all your notes to me, along with photographs of the walls in the conference room. Then you will erase the walls. You have captured all this on your computer, no?"

"Yes, it's all in here," he said, holding out his laptop. Josef took it.

"I will turn this over to our information technology department. They will place the file in a secure location that you can access from your workstation. Then they will erase all traces of the document from your computer. You will get this back tomorrow morning. And you will consider this material to be classified, no? *Ja?*"

"I was hoping to work on it tonight," Matt said glumly.

"Tonight you will take a rest, no? You have earned it." Josef placed the laptop under his arm and clapped Matt on the back. "Cheer up, Matt! You have done it! You have reason to be proud of yourself. You rest tonight. Then you come tomorrow and get back to work."

Josef smiled broadly, turned on his heel like a soldier at maneuvers, and left the office. Matt looked blankly at his colleagues before following Josef out the door.

❖ ❖ ❖

Jon arrived at the Target store just before six p.m. on Saturday with an envelope tucked safely in a coat pocket. He sat in the same spot in the coffee shop. He waited another ten minutes before Gina arrived, looking perfectly stylish and maddeningly beautiful.

"Hello, Jon, dear," she said brightly. She opened her coat and began removing her gloves, tugging one finger at a time.

"Could you be a prince and get me a skinny latte, two sugars?"

Jon did as he was told. He retrieved Gina's order, then lay the envelope on the table and slid it toward her. Gina sipped her coffee as she lifted the flap of the envelope and glanced inside.

"Jon, what's this?" she asked, reaching into the envelope and pulling out a key.

"It's the key to your apartment. Don't expect too much. It's not fancy. But it's nice, in a nice area. It'll do."

"Furnished?"

"Furnished and made up. The address is in the envelope. You can stay there tonight if you want."

Gina riffled through the stack of bills, then dropped the envelope and the key in her handbag.

"How convenient. I can't wait to see it. I hope Matt likes it."

"I'm sure he'll love it," Jon said with a trace of sarcasm. "What are your plans tonight?"

"Oh, the usual—dinner, followed by dirty sex."

Jon closed his eyes and grimaced. "I'm sorry I asked." He stood to button his coat and put on his hat and gloves. "He'll be in a good mood tonight. He had a good week. I think you're having a positive effect on him."

"That's nice," she said with a wide smile. "I'll make sure he has a memorable evening."

Jon left the store. Gina finished her latte.

❖ ❖ ❖

Gina arrived at The Commissary restaurant promptly at seven to find Matt in the waiting area, already beaming. They kissed with passion, almost exceeding the limits of decorum. He took her arm and escorted her to their table.

"You look wonderful," Gina said to Matt as she arranged her napkin on her lap. "You must have had a good week."

"You could say that," he said, still beaming. "I had a breakthrough."

"Really? I can't wait to hear about it."

Matt looked down as he positioned his own napkin. "It's an idea I've been working on a long time, a major step forward."

"Well, what was it? Tell me!" Gina said, placing her hand on Matt's.

"It's pretty complicated. I'm not sure I can explain it in a way that makes sense to you."

Gina took back her hand, her face wearing a look somewhere between a pout and a scowl. "I'm not stupid, Matt."

"Gina, that's not what I meant. Of course you're not stupid. Just the opposite." Matt reached for her hand. "I think you're the smartest, most interesting person I've ever met."

"But not smart enough to understand your big idea."

Matt flushed. "I barely understand it myself. And it's really hard to describe." He pushed at his water glass with his fingertips. "Besides, I'm not even supposed to be talking about it. It's sensitive." He took a drink of water. "I'm not supposed to talk about it with *anyone.*"

"You could have said that to start with. If it's a secret, then we just won't talk about it."

Their evening proceeded cordially. Instead of lasting three hours, dinner was over in less than one.

❖ ❖ ❖

Matt helped Gina with her coat and walked her to the parking lot. She turned to Matt and embraced him, kissing him for more than a minute.

"Dear, I'm sorry I acted out like that," she said. "It's not your fault. I know you're a math genius and I couldn't hope to understand what you do."

Matt looked away. "Gina, I really don't know if you could understand this theory or not. It's close to the limit of what *I* understand and I've been working on it for years. I really wish I *could* explain it to you. I wish I could talk about it with *someone.*"

They walked until they reached Gina's car.

"Can I give you a lift, stranger?" she said seductively.

"I was about to ask you the same thing." He took a key from his pocket and pressed a button. The lights flashed on a red two-door sports coupe two spaces away. Gina's face lit up.

"Oh, Matt, you have a car!"

"I bought it today. I figured it's about time I grew up and stopped sponging off my friends. Especially my girlfriend."

"It's really cute!" She pulled Matt by the hand to his car. "It's perfect for you." She kissed him again. "Why don't you follow me to my place?"

"Can I take a rain check?" he said with a hint of weariness.

She knitted her brow. "Are you still upset with me?"

"No, of course not. I just…" He looked up at the sky and sighed. "I just remembered something I have to take care of. It can't wait. I'm sorry."

"Okay," Gina said skeptically. "And you're sure you're not angry with me?"

Matt smiled. "I was never angry with you. Never. I don't think I ever could be." He gave her a parting kiss. "If you're free next Saturday, let's make it a day. I'll drive."

"Count on it, sweetie," she said on her way to her car. She blew Matt a kiss as she drove by.

❖ ❖ ❖

Matt flipped on the lights as he opened the door to the apartment. After taking off his coat and gloves he went to the refrigerator for a beer. He settled into the couch, taking a long pull on the bottle as he punched a few buttons on his cell phone. He set the beer on the coffee table and put the phone to his ear.

"Hello, Anson. How have you been, buddy?" He took another swallow. "Is your security clearance up to date? Good. I've been spending some time at the vertex lately. Want to hear about it?"

❖ ❖ ❖

Agent Gutierrez sat in the cold outside Matt's apartment building trying to make sense of what he'd just seen. He'd observed Matt and Gina at the restaurant and the scene in the parking lot. He watched as they parted, and then he followed Matt to his apartment. He watched him go in— alone. *I don't get it,* he thought. *Why hire a call girl if you're not going to fuck?*

20

THE DISCLOSURE

TAN AND ALVIN sat in their usual meeting place, a dark corner of a lounge near Alvin's office, shortly after their return from China.

"Do you understand your assignment, Xiao Weiguo?" Tan asked, speaking Mandarin and using Alvin's Chinese name, as Alvin insisted he do whenever they met.

"Yes, of course," Alvin replied in a steely manner.

"Repeat it, please."

"What?"

"I asked you to repeat your instructions," Tan said, raising a finger to the waiter, then pointing at his glass, now empty of scotch.

Alvin bristled. "That's not necessary."

The waiter appeared with a fresh glass, then vanished. Tan sipped, then sighed. "Humor me, Xiao Weiguo."

Alvin drank from his glass of ice water. "You know what the system does, and how fast it is, based on..." He sipped again. "Based on the system documents provided..."

"The Mechanized Mind documents," Tan clarified.

"Yes. And you have information about the algorithm from...who? Did you say who your source is for the algorithm? Is it someone inside Connectrix?"

"I have not been told. It's a source who understands Dr. Bugatti's theories."

"All right. Based on this information Wang's cryptology experts calculate the system will take eight to twelve months to break a two-thousand-forty-eight bit encryption key."

"And?"

"And you want me to verify this, the time to break the key." Alvin leaned closer, speaking through clenched teeth, "Do I have that right?"

Tan sipped. "Perfect. I should not have doubted you, Xiao Weiguo."

❖ ❖ ❖

Alvin remembered this conversation a week later as he sat across from Jon Ames at the same table in the same dark corner of the same lounge.

"I would expect this system to break a two-thousand bit encryption key in a matter of months."

"Months?" Jon said. "No. Hours. This system will break a key in eight hours."

"But you haven't actually succeeded in breaking a key, not even in months."

"Our first test is in a few weeks. I doubt we'll meet the eight-hour goal in the first run. Our principal investigator estimates twenty-four hours."

"Dr. Bugatti seems to have made significant progress over brute-force methods."

"Brute force? No, no, no," Jon protested. "He searches for prime candidates based on their properties. He's discovered seventeen different properties of prime numbers. He tests these properties to determine the most favorable candidates. Exactly how he goes about it, no one else knows."

"Yes, of course. But eight hours? When do you expect to reach that goal?"

"We are scheduled to demonstrate the system for the customer in April."

"And who is the customer?"

"I can't say."

Alvin watched Jon gulp his club soda. *He'll tell me all about that machine before he'll tell me who it's for.* He recalled the rest of his conversation with Tan from the previous week.

❖ ❖ ❖

"The National Security Agency is prohibited by law from eavesdropping on American citizens," Tan said, "yet they are doing exactly that. They have listening posts within U.S. borders, in the very facilities through which domestic communications flow. They are accumulating vast quantities of data in secret locations. Much of it is encrypted. They can already break encryption, but at great expense and with much delay."

Tan leaned back in his chair and placed his palm on the table. "So why would the NSA want an inexpensive computer that can decrypt large numbers of secret communications, if not to mine this vast quantity of data, gathered from Americans on American soil?"

Alvin blanched. "You're talking about domestic surveillance by the government, with no oversight. Here, in the United States."

"On a vast scale."

"But why?"

Tan closed his eyes as if meditating. "I'm sure their intentions are honorable. We live in dangerous times, after all. The enemy doesn't stay inside the borders of a single country. They are everywhere." He sipped his scotch. "And the price of liberty is eternal vigilance."

"Liberty?" Alvin blurted. "That's *tyranny!"*

"Tyranny? In America? Impossible."

Alvin sat mute.

"Xiao Weiguo," Tan said, "Do you think that by keeping this technology out of the hands of the Chinese that you preserve it for a more benevolent master?"

❖ ❖ ❖

"Even twenty-four hours seems incredible," Alvin said. "Not even Bugatti can get to eight."

"A week ago twenty-four hours seemed out of reach," Jon confessed. "Bugatti had a breakthrough. He explained it to us but I'll be damned if I understand it. Something about 'manifolds' and 'discrete space' and 'binding.'"

"I would have to see his proof. Have you seen it?"

"I wouldn't be able to judge it if I had," Jon answered. "But it's a moot point. Matt gave us the abridged version, but the detailed written proof is being held under very tight security. The only people who've seen it are Matt Bugatti and Josef Hofbauer."

◈ ◈ ◈

Wang Shutao rarely visited the laboratories of the *Guoanbu* Fourth Bureau, although his name was well known among the researchers who worked there. When he arrived unannounced at the office of Fu Lian, the Chief Scientist of the Encryption Analysis Division and one of the most talented cryptologists in China, Dr. Fu jumped up from behind her desk, nearly knocking over her chair, and rushed to take Wang's hand.

"Wang Shutao," she said, bowing low. "We are honored to have you in our laboratory."

"Fu Lian, my visits are too rare. I must make an effort to call on you more often. And I'm sorry for the surprise. I knew that if I had made an appointment you would have prepared a formal report. It's much more important that you apply yourself to your work than that you waste your valuable time making arrangements for my benefit."

"It's no trouble," Fu said. "But now I'm afraid I've prepared nothing at all."

"As it should be. I need to speak to you and your scientists when you are unprepared. How else will I know the true state of this program?"

Fu led Wang to a large room containing an array of tiny cubicles, each one hardly larger than a coat closet, in which sat the eighty-four scientists of the Encryption Analysis Division. One of the walls of the room had a row of doors, each door leading to a windowless conference room. Two walls were a brilliant, featureless white. The fourth wall was made entirely of glass. Behind it a row of cabinets stood menacingly black and uniform, their shelves filled with the most advanced computers available to the People's Government. As the computers accessed their disk drives their red lamps flickered; as they transmitted or received data their green lamps flashed. The device at the top of each rack displayed undulating patterns of lights as electronic impulses moved through them in incredible numbers and at unimaginable speed.

Fu entered the first row of cubicles, stopping at the first one on the left.

"Yao Shen," she said to the slight young man with disheveled hair. "Mr. Wang is here. He wants to discuss our progress."

The young man walked briskly down the row, almost running, saying simply, "Come!" as he went by. In less than ten seconds a dozen Chinese researchers filed out of the row and into the rightmost conference room.

The scientists of the Encryption Analysis Division sat at attention around a table in the center of the room. Wang walked to the chair at the head of the table and stood next to it, but remained standing.

"Good morning brothers and sisters. For those of you whom I have not met, I am Wang Shutao of the First Bureau. This meeting will be brief. As you know, we have learned more details of the algorithm the Americans have developed. We know the goal the Americans have set, and which they have nearly realized. It is much more ambitious than we thought. You have had this information for one week."

Wang sat down. He looked at Fu Lian. "I am expected in the Minister's office in one hour. I will hear your report now."

The scientists surrounding the table looked at each other nervously. After a few seconds, Fu Lian broke the awkward silence.

"Mr. Wang, we don't believe this information."

"The information is reliable," Wang said, looking grimly at Fu.

"Mr. Yao has calculated that the time required to break a two thousand forty-eight bit key on this hardware would be many weeks."

Wang looked directly at the slight man with the disheveled hair.

"Yao Shen, I assure you, the report is correct."

"To break a key in eight hours would require the search space to be small and bounded," he answered haltingly. "Neither of these is the case."

"And what of the report that their top scientist has proven that in fact this space is limited, and the search is deterministic?"

Yao gulped. "That is the part we don't believe," he said.

"And if I were to provide you with a copy of the proof?"

"That would be of great value," Fu said before Yao could answer. "But to understand how the Americans have accomplished this goal, it's more important that we have the computer code. It's one thing to understand the mathematics. To create an efficient computer program is another thing altogether. Their chief scientist may have proven this theory, but who has written the computer code?"

"Our source has assured us that the person who has proven this theory has also written the program," Wang said. He looked around again. Every head shook in disbelief.

❖ ❖ ❖

"What about the new intelligence?" asked the Minister of State Security.

Wang Shutao stood before him, peering down his nose at his superior. "Minister, our scientists are skeptical. They cannot conceive of any method by which this system, or any system, can break a key in eight hours. They believe it will take many times longer, weeks in fact. They will not be persuaded otherwise."

"Wang Shutao, have you been given false information?" the Minister said accusingly.

"The source is inside the Connectrix Corporation. We are confident that it is reliable."

The Minister scowled as he leaned back in his chair. He removed his reading glasses and tossed them on the desk, rubbing the bridge of his nose.

"There is one thing that would confirm this report, Minister," Wang offered. "If we had a copy of the computer code, our analysts could verify this claim."

"Very well. Direct Tan Yingqun to obtain a copy of the code. Send the order today. Tell him if he obtains the code we will not ask any more of him, and his family will join him in America."

21

Curious

The storm front passed leaving behind a crystal-clear sky and a blanket of new snow. The sun's rays streamed among the leafless branches of the hardwood forest, reflecting off the snow that topped each limb. A bird sang pure notes with no echo—the snow muffled all sound. The breezeless, silent stillness was disturbed only by the rhythmic *swoosh, swoosh* of Gina's skis and Matt's labored breathing.

Gina kept up a steady pace along the tree-lined trail, gliding in long, even strides with no obvious effort. Matt lagged by fifty yards and the gap continued to grow. Unlike Gina, whose technique was graceful and efficient, Matt struggled for every inch of forward progress.

Gina stopped when she reached a clearing. It took Matt another ten minutes to catch up.

"I will never again make the mistake of asking what *you* want to do on a weekend," he wheezed.

Gina flashed a charming smile. "I still can't believe you've never been cross-country skiing. Where I grew up in Minnesota, we started skiing when we could barely walk."

"Where *I* grew up in North Carolina," Matt croaked between gulps of air, "the only winter sport we played was basketball."

"You're not doing it like I showed you. You're not supposed to push off so much as kick forward."

Matt leaned against his ski poles, his face red from cold and exertion, huffing in a cloud of vapor. "I thought these were magic skis that only went in one direction."

Gina's smiled sympathetically, her eyes forming sparkling arcs, crowned by dark lashes tipped with tiny ice crystals. "You'll get it. Just watch me, and remember what I told you." She lifted her scarf over her nose and resumed her cadence.

Matt stayed doubled over, hanging from his poles. He watched Gina recede into the distance. It was the first time Matt had seen her wearing anything that wasn't stylish and expensive. Her ski outfit was purely utilitarian, designed for warmth, comfort and free movement. Yet it was incapable of hiding her femininity. Her wool cap and scarf, drab on anyone else, looked adorable on Gina. Matt blinked his watering eyes, dismissed the burning pain in his lungs, and trudged forward.

◈ ◈ ◈

Matt lit the kindling under logs carefully arranged in the stone fireplace that occupied an entire wall of the cabin. It was just past six o'clock and already dark. The growing flames cast flickering shadows in the dimly lit room, transforming the space from rustic to dreamlike. Satisfied with the progress of the fire, Matt rose from his crouch, stopping midway with a gasp as protesting pains shot through his thighs. He steadied himself against a nearby chair, then worked his way to a standing position. He hobbled to the kitchen where an array of cookware, a large cooler, a bottle of wine and two glasses waited.

Matt still wore his clothes from the trail, damp from sweat and snow that had worked its way into every seam, Gina having commandeered the bathroom. He started his preparations—a pot of water, slowly coming to a boil, olive oil in a pan heating to fragrance, two veal cutlets pounded almost to the point of transparency, and rows of ingredients unloaded from his cooler, all carefully prepared and packaged in advance.

Matt tossed a dish of chopped onions into the heated oil. He stirred the sizzling mixture for a few minutes, strained the onions from the oil and added butter to the pan. The delicious aroma filled the cabin, melding pleasantly with the scent of wood smoke.

"What *is* that wonderful smell?"

Gina leaned with her hip against the counter next to the stove. She held her glass in her left hand and massaged Matt's shoulder with her right.

"Oh, mama, that feels good," he moaned.

"Poor baby," she cooed. She set her glass on the counter and applied both hands to Matt's shoulders and back. He groaned.

"Does that hurt?"

"Hurts good," he whimpered. "Don't stop."

"You were a trooper today," she said, continuing to work Matt's sore muscles. "You were really getting it. You'll be a champion skier in no time."

"I'll have to recover first. I should be all right by the Fourth of July." He slid the cutlets into the pan. The oil sputtered furiously.

"What's for dinner?"

"Veal piccata. Nothing fancy."

❖ ❖ ❖

Matt set a table in the main room, illuminated only by two candles and the fire. Gina was already seated when he served the artfully arranged dish. He seated himself gingerly before raising his glass.

"To new experiences," he offered. They clinked glasses and drank to the toast.

"I hope it wasn't too much of an ordeal," she said with sympathy.

He closed his eyes and winced as he squeezed his shoulder. "Ordeal—that's the word I was looking for."

"Matt, I'm sorry. I wanted this to be fun for you."

"I'm teasing. I had a wonderful time. I wouldn't have changed a thing." He sipped his wine. "Is this what it's like growing up in the north? All burning thighs and frozen buns?"

"Not entirely," she laughed. "Remember, it's only winter in Minnesota six months out of the year."

"Oh god," Matt groaned. "Six months. I'm going to die."

"You'll get used to it. Some of us even like it." Gina took a bite of veal. "Matt, this is delicious! You keep surprising me."

"Thanks," he replied as he raised a fork to his mouth. "Another old family recipe. Almost as good as Mom's."

"I can just picture little Matt at his mother's side in the kitchen, learning all the cooking magic."

He smiled. "What were *you* like growing up? Were you a daddy's girl?"

Gina cast her eyes down. She twisted her fork among the noodles, forming a loose ball, just small enough eat with one bite. She followed it with a sip of wine.

"Hardly."

"Did I say something wrong?"

"No," she said curtly. "I'm just not close to my father."

Matt's stomach turned. "He didn't…"

"No. The idea is too disgusting to think about. He left me alone, thank god. He was a real prick to my mom, though. Why she put up with him I can't understand." She took another bite. "I'll never be that dependent on another human being."

The two continued eating in silence.

"I'm sorry, Gina. I didn't mean to bring up bad memories."

"I don't have bad memories. A memory can't be bad if it's suppressed." She paused for another bite. "Let's just say I couldn't wait to get out of the house. On my own."

Matt said nothing.

"Sweetie," she said, "let's not talk about my childhood. Let's enjoy our dinner and this lovely cabin."

Matt smiled. "Okay."

❖❖❖

By eight o'clock the second bottle of wine had emptied. Matt and Gina sat on the floor in front of the fire, Gina inching closer as they talked. During a pause, she leaned forward to kiss Matt. He pulled away.

"You don't want to get close to me. I haven't showered yet."

She would not be discouraged. She pressed forward and kissed Matt passionately.

"Why don't you get into the hot tub and I'll join you in a minute?"

Matt sighed with feeling. "That works for me on so many levels."

Gina went into the bedroom and closed the door. Matt shed his layers of clothing, ultimately standing naked at the glass door leading to the deck.

The outside temperature hovered just above zero. Matt stepped quickly through the snow, leaving footprints toward the hot tub in the center of the deck. His feet began to numb as he struggled with the cover, heaving it to one side. His feet tingled as he slid slowly into the steaming water. The initial discomfort of the heat gave way to pleasure as the water swirled over his aching body.

Through the door Matt watched Gina walking from the bedroom. She wore a sheer robe that hung to mid-thigh. She paused at the door as she undid the sash and let the robe slip to the floor. The silhouette of her nude body against the fire-lit room was defined by a flickering outline, like the crescent of a new moon setting on a sweltering night. She followed the footprints toward the hot tub and slipped in next to him. They embraced each other and kissed under the starry sky, surrounded by the perfect stillness of the winter night.

❖ ❖ ❖

"I don't think he knows," Anibal Gutierrez said to Josef Hofbauer during his nightly report.

"That she is a prostitute?"

"That's right. Do you know what they did today? They skied. Cross-country skiing, the hard, boring kind. He was terrible at it. He didn't enjoy it at all."

"I don't see the point. How can he not know she is a prostitute?"

"He doesn't know," Anibal insisted. "No man would pay for a whole day with a high-class hooker so they can do something he's no good at and doesn't like. Last week they didn't even have sex. They didn't the first night they met, either. Trust me, a man pays that much for a call girl, he's going to get his money's worth."

There was no sound from the phone for a few seconds other than the irregular hiss of a connection in a remote area with spotty coverage.

"Curious. Perhaps they are really lovers. Are you being too cynical?"

"Sir, I thought of that. I don't think that's the case. Weekends are her prime time. She's given up four weekends in a row. That's a lot of money to leave on the table just for love."

"What do you think?"

"Someone hired her to get to Bugatti."

There was a long, scratchy pause before Josef replied.

"You must find out the arrangement, no? We can't take action without knowing the whole story, no? *Ja?*"

The phone went dead.

Anibal looked out the window of an ancient café from his seat in a booth far from the door. The well-worn tables, stools and counter were illuminated by a single fluorescent fixture which flickered annoyingly. It gave Anibal a headache. The dazzling daytime scenery of bright, snow-covered trees was transformed to a desolate landscape by streetlights' dim illumination. The bleak surroundings compounded the chill he still suffered from a day of traipsing through the woods watching two cross-country skiers at a distance, one well-practiced and the other inept. He would continue to observe them tomorrow. And he still did not know why.

Anibal turned from the window. He sipped his coffee and cursed his life.

22

THE TELL

THE LIGHT ON Jon's phone was flashing persistently when he arrived at his desk on Monday morning. The message was from Josef Hofbauer: "Meet me in my office."

Jon sat down and arranged his desk for his normal Monday routine. An hour later he was satisfied that he had his materials prepared and his most urgent matters addressed. He headed to Josef's office.

Jon found the door to Josef's office closed. Through the adjacent window he saw Josef pacing the room with his cell phone pressed to his ear. It took a few minutes for Josef to notice Jon peering in. He raised his palm and spoke a few more words. He ended his call and waved Jon in.

"What is it, Josef?" Jon said as soon as he opened the door.

"What? Oh, yes. My message. Come in."

Jon took the seat next to Josef's desk.

"How is Dr. Bugatti progressing with his new algorithm?" Josef asked.

"He's doing well, I think. That's what he tells me."

"This is good, no? I have noticed he seems much more…" Josef appeared to be searching for the right word.

"Content?" offered Jon.

"Productive, I was going to say. But you are right, he is more content. He seems to have improved his attitude, no? *Ja?*"

"That's what everyone says."

"This is very good." Josef stopped pacing and sat behind his desk. "What do you think is the reason for this change?"

Jon looked directly at Josef. "Well, he *is* seeing someone."

Josef leaned forward and looked over his glasses. "He has a girl?"

"Yes, for a few weeks now. Eric and Kathy told me."

Josef studied Jon's face. He noted where Jon was looking, how often he blinked, when he swallowed.

"What do you know about her?"

Jon waved his hand as if brushing away a gnat.

"Nothing, really. I've only heard indirectly."

Josef continued to scrutinize Jon. "What is her name?"

"Her name is…" Jon said before halting. His unblinking eyes remained fixed on Josef's eyes. He didn't swallow. "I don't know her name. I can find out, if you're interested."

Josef shook his head as he removed his glasses and cleaned them with a cloth he retrieved from a coat pocket. "No, it doesn't matter. It is only important that Dr. Bugatti is happy and productive, *ja?* Thank you, Jon."

"That's what you wanted to see me about? Nothing else?"

Josef replaced his glasses and peered over them with a look of indifference. "*Ja.* That is all."

Jon stood and looked warily at Josef before turning to leave.

"Oh, Jon, one thing."

"Yes?"

"Please close the door after you."

After Jon left the office, Josef opened his cell phone and entered a number. The call was answered by Stephen Quan of the National Security Agency.

"My apologies for the interruption, Mr. Quan. Shall we go secure?"

Josef pressed a key on his cell phone and entered a seven-digit number. Stephen Quan did the same. For the remainder of the call anyone eavesdropping on the conversation would hear a chirping noise, not unlike the sound of a fax machine.

"As I was saying," Josef continued, "you will have the entire proof this afternoon, delivered by courier."

"It'll be encrypted, of course," Stephen said.

"Certainly. Oh, and I now know who has arranged for Dr. Bugatti's companion."

"Really? Are we at risk?"

"Unknown. But I think not. It's someone in my own organization. He wants Dr. Bugatti to settle down and get to work. I will continue my investigation and report to you my findings."

"All right. I'll turn over the proof to our analyst as soon as we receive it."

"Excellent," Josef said. "I'm looking forward to seeing Dr. Petrescu's evaluation."

23

THE SCHEME

ALVIN XIAO SAT motionless in his office, staring through the window at the St. Paul skyline. It was seven o'clock and well past sunset, not unusual for Alvin who often worked past eight, usually the last to leave. Alvin found his solitary, late-evening sessions to be his most productive, when he could concentrate without distractions, when his most vexing problems yielded to analysis.

This night was different.

Tan Yingqun had directed Alvin to get a copy of Matt's program, and he was specific. He didn't ask for the *machine* code—the incomprehensible ones and zeros that a computer could interpret—but the *source* code, the original text and symbols that Matt had written. With the source code the *Guoanbu* scientists could easily reconstruct not only Matt's theorem, unfathomable to all but the most brilliant mathematicians—but also the means by which he instructed a computer, a fast, unerring, but utterly uncomprehending machine, to achieve the impossible feat of breaking a strong encryption key in a matter of hours.

The source code was kept in a virtual vault, protected by strict security protocols, which Jon Ames had described at a previous meeting.

"It's stored on a single computer," he explained. "Other workstations can access the code, but only if they've been individually authorized. There are exactly four authorized workstations, all locked in place, but even if you could remove them from the building, you wouldn't learn anything. They don't have their own disk drives. The USB jacks are all disabled. Any time someone logs onto a workstation, it's recorded. The time you spend on the workstation is tracked. The auditors go through the records once a week."

Alvin realized that even if there were a way to access the code and secure an unauthorized copy, only someone inside Connectrix could do it. He wasn't yet ready to make that severe a demand on Jon Ames. He would certainly refuse, and Alvin's true intent might be revealed. Even if he agreed, the attempt would fail.

Alvin's thoughts were interrupted by a call to his cell phone. The display flashed *Elaine*.

"Yes, what is it?"

"Do you know when you'll be home?" his wife asked.

Alvin checked his watch. He had thought it was nearer to six o'clock than seven.

"We have guests tonight," he remembered out loud.

"Yes, we do," she confirmed. "They'll be here any minute and I've had no help getting ready."

Alvin turned from the window. "I lost track of time. I'm leaving right now."

Alvin pondered his dilemma during his commute. Every approach he considered was littered with trap doors. He couldn't refuse Tan's request without risking exposure. Convinced that the problem had no acceptable solution, he was left with only one option.

Change the problem.

By the time Alvin arrived home, just minutes ahead of his guests, he had a plan.

❖ ❖ ❖

Jon and Alvin didn't have a standing appointment. They met when either of them had reason to do so, about once a week on average. Although they had met in both Eau Claire and St. Paul, usually it was Jon who traveled.

This Saturday morning Jon was en route to a shopping mall in St. Paul. He'd received a call the previous night from what sounded like a well-attended holiday gathering at the home of Alvin and Elaine Xiao. Jon tried not to think about what Alvin would ask of him. Each time they met the information he provided was more specific—and more sensitive. Each time Jon convinced himself that there was still a line he hadn't crossed. Alvin's skill in eliciting information made this self-deception all the easier. At times it seemed to Jon that he wasn't so much giving Alvin new knowledge as he was confirming what Alvin already knew.

❖ ❖ ❖

Jon found Alvin seated in front of a *Gap* clothing store. The mall had just opened and customers were still sparse. Jon sat next to Alvin on a wooden bench. Alvin smiled but didn't speak. Jon broke the silence.

"I'm here."

Alvin nodded. "As you know, we are shipping the computers for your second prototype this week and next. In fact, you should already have received some of them."

"We have."

"You will receive the remainder by the end of this coming week. All except one. The last computer you will receive the following week. Early in the week, I hope, but it may be delayed."

"Why is that?" Jon asked.

"We are performing some tests. We only need one of the computers for these tests. They do not involve performance or reliability, so there's no need to delay the bulk of the shipment."

"Is this what I drove ninety miles to hear? Couldn't you have told me this on the phone?"

Alvin shook his head, his thin smile never wavering. "No, of course not. I brought you here to tell you this but also to make a request."

"I'm listening."

"You're planning a real-time test of the system shortly, correct?"

"Yes," Jon answered. "Next month."

"The system you'll use for the test, will it be the original prototype or the second prototype we're shipping to you now?"

"I really don't know. Why does it matter?"

"It doesn't, actually, as long as the system includes the last computer we send you."

Jon's face went slack. "What's different about that computer?"

"Nothing. Nothing at all. It will simply have been fully characterized. We're interested in the degree of variation among the computers and the impact it might have on performance in a large parallel system."

Jon clenched his fists, the frustration of weeks of surreptitious dealings rising all at once. "Don't fuck with me, Xiao. That's bullshit. What's so special about that computer?"

Alvin stayed calm "That's not your concern."

"It damn well *is* my concern," Jon growled. "Tell me what you're doing with that computer or I walk out of here and we won't talk again."

Alvin turned away from Jon and looked down the length of the mall. The crowd was growing, columns of shoppers streaming by, bobbing left and right to avoid collision. Mothers with young children camped nearby. At any one time a dozen or more people were within earshot of Alvin and Jon. They could easily have been overheard had they raised their voices.

"That wouldn't be wise. We're engaged in questionable activities. We must cooperate if we're to avoid detection. If you refuse my request I would have no choice but to stop the payments to your account. The money stops but you are still at risk since you have already violated your security clearance. Besides, what I'm asking is very simple. You have my explanation for the request. If you insist on details, you will only implicate yourself further. Why would you *want* to know more?"

Jon weighed his options. Up to that point, he had given Alvin what he considered to be low-value information, a necessary breach of his principles—and the law—to complete the Cygnus program. This was how he justified his actions in the increasingly frequent moments when he thought about his situation. Jon doubted that the authorities would find this argument convincing. But that was how things got done in a startup. *Do whatever it takes. Hang it out over the edge.*

"Fine. Whatever," Jon surrendered. "Anything else?"

"The serial number of the last computer ends in 0147. You'll remember that, won't you?"

"Yes, I'll remember." Jon stood to leave.

"One other thing," Alvin said. "I want to do everything I can to ensure that your test is a success. If any of the computers fails, please send them directly to Mechanized Minds—to my attention."

Jon glared at Alvin. "You do know, don't you, that we erase the programming from any failed computers before returning them?"

Alvin nodded. "Indeed. Very prudent of you."

❖ ❖ ❖

Jon drove back to Eau Claire, stifling speculation about Alvin's motives. Suspicion might compel action. Ignorance was his safest and most comfortable state.

At the sixty mile mark Jon's cell phone vibrated. The console of Jon's car displayed the name: *Gina Bianchi.* Jon pressed a button on his steering wheel to answer.

"Yes, what is it?"

"Jon, dear, why so gruff?" Gina's voice sounded through the car's speakers.

"I've got a lot on my mind. Why are you calling? Don't tell me you've gone through your retainer already."

"You're okay for now. But we'll have to get together soon. I'm spending the weekend with Matt and the meter is running."

"You're with Matt?" Jon said, almost shouting. "Why are you calling me?"

"Don't worry, he can't hear me. We're skiing. The only reason I'm not a mile ahead of him is because I'm holding back. He's a terrible skier. He won't be here for a couple of minutes."

"Great. Wonderful. Why should I care?"

"No reason, I guess. When can we meet?"

"We can't meet in person anymore. Eau Claire is a small town. I can't take a chance on being seen with you."

"That's a problem."

"It's not a problem. I set up an account for you. I'll get you the account number. You'll get your retainers on time, and we don't have to meet."

"Well, all right then," Gina said sweetly. "I'll be waiting for that account information. Got to go now. Matt's almost here. Poor baby. He's not having any fun. I'll have to make it up to him tonight. Bye!"

Jon continued his drive home, his fingers tapping the steering wheel the whole way.

◈ ◈ ◈

Alvin drove directly from the mall to the Mechanized Minds building, but he didn't go to his office. Instead, he went to the prototype shop where fifty high-powered computer assemblies were staged and fully tested, awaiting packaging and shipping to Connectrix. Alvin selected one of them and verified its serial number ended with 0147. He took it to an adjacent room, to a bench with a workstation, surrounded by test equipment, parts, and drawings.

Alvin powered up the workstation. While it booted, Alvin placed the assembly on the bench and plugged a cable into it. As the display came to life, Alvin recalled an earlier time, his first job after college, designing and programming industrial computers. He loved it. What he remembered at that moment was how proud he was of his abilities. He was *good*.

Alvin accessed the computer's on-board system from the workstation. He scanned the contents of its memory, then paused a moment to collect his thoughts. Then he got to work programming two new functions into the computer's operating system. The first was a time bomb that would cause the board to fail twelve hours after being powered up.

The second function would indicate—falsely—that the computer had successfully executed a command to erase its memory.

24

THE TEST

THE CONNECTRIX CHRISTMAS tree still decorated the lobby and festive trim still hung from cubicle walls on the day of the Cygnus test. The goal: to crack a public encryption key in twenty-four hours or less. Eric Reilly supervised the riot of activity like a symphony conductor, calling on each player in perfectly staged order at the precisely planned moment. His competence reassured team members as they performed their tasks. None of them allowed for the possibility that the test might fail. None, that is, except Matt Bugatti.

Matt followed every step of the checklist as Eric called them out. Matt occasionally interjected a question to confirm that a particular task had been completed correctly. Eric responded in good faith, only infrequently rolling his eyes or pausing a little too long before answering.

Eric verified the test environment, with particular attention to keeping the solution to the test (the prime factors of the encryption key) under strict quarantine. He moved on to the System Engineering group under the leadership of Kathy Darling.

"Let's go through the computing module list and verify that the firmware's been properly loaded and verified."

Kathy exhaled sharply. "It's done, Eric. Move on."

Eric remained stoic. "This is by the book. You've got your list, I've got mine. Let's go through them and make sure they match."

Kathy dropped her protest and lifted her clipboard to reading position.

"Serial number 0115102A0010—location zero," Eric droned.

"You know," Kathy said, "it would save a lot of time if you just read the last few digits of the serial number."

Eric came as close to glaring as he had all day. "All right. 0010—location zero."

"Check," Kathy replied.

Eric continued down the list. Well into the drill, Matt interrupted.

"What was that last one?"

"0147."

"0147," Matt repeated. "That's out of sequence."

Eric looked at his list, his pen poised at the entry in question.

"So what? They're all the same."

Matt pressed his knuckle against his lips. "I know they're all the same. That doesn't explain why all the other serial numbers are in sequence and this one isn't."

Eric studied the list for a moment. "I don't know, Matt. I assembled the system myself. I just pulled the modules out of the box in the order they were packed. If they were out of order, they came that way from the supplier."

Matt motioned to Eric to hand him the list. The serial numbers were all in sequence except one—the one ending in 0147. He handed the clipboard back. "I guess it's nothing," he conceded.

Eric continued down the checklist, verifying the serial number and location of every one of sixty-four computer modules in the Cygnus prototype.

"Next step," Eric announced. "Boot the system. Verify system functions."

"Done," Kathy said.

"What do you mean, 'done?'"

"I mean 'done,'" Kathy replied flatly. "As in 'done.'"
"Kathy…"
"I know, I know. By the book."
Eric continued:
"Self test."
"Check."
"Supervisory functions."
"Check."
Eric continued down the list until every component of the Cygnus system had been identified and verified. At the end of the inventory Eric reviewed the list, double checking every entry. He set down the clipboard and looked at his watch. "It's four-ten p.m. Throw the switch."

For eight hours Matt sat transfixed at the system console, four oversized monitors displaying an array of windows showing the progress of the prime factor search in graphs and numbers. Dozens of diagrams presented the search tree from different perspectives, in separate subsets of dimensions, akin to his mental image of the cross section of the frost-covered tree, but vastly more complex. A casual observer might have mistaken the crystalline figures for unusually delicate snowflakes. When Matt manipulated one view the diagrams all rotated in synchrony. Matt studied their interactions as they turned. Their movements reinforced his intuitive understanding of the algorithm as it searched among trillions upon trillions of points in a vast mathematical universe for the single pair of primes that would crack the code.

At one a.m. Matt went home to a fitful sleep.

Matt arrived the next morning at nine o'clock. The level of activity was normal—no commotion that might suggest that the search had ended. He approached the system console in the far corner, where Kathy sat in the operator's position. Eric stood nearby among a few others.

"It's still running?" Matt asked as if he expected otherwise.

"Still cranking along," Kathy responded calmly.

Matt leaned close to the console and examined the numbers. "Seventeen hours, thirty minutes," he read. He stood up and placed his hand over his mouth. After a couple minutes he said, "It should have solved by now."

Eric and Kathy looked at each other, then at Matt.

"It's still got another six or seven hours to go," Kathy said. "Twenty-four hours, that's what you told us."

"Twenty four hours is the ninetieth percentile," Matt explained. "There's a ninety percent chance the problem will solve in twenty-four hours. At seventeen hours the likelihood is eighty percent." Matt crossed his arms and stared at the floor in front of his feet. "It should have finished. Something's not right."

"Don't get too worked up, Matt," Eric reassured him. "There was a failure during the night."

"What kind of failure?"

"Faulty module. It was in alarm when I came in this morning. I programmed a spare and swapped it out."

"Which location was it?" Matt asked.

"Thirty nine, I think," Eric retrieved the log book and scanned his notes. "Thirty-nine—that's the one." He showed Matt the log.

7:22 a.m. Discovered system in alarm, node failure, location 39. Alarm log entry timestamped 4:55 a.m. Programmed spare and swapped out failed unit. System restored 8:12 a.m. E.R.

Matt handed the log back to Eric and bent over to type commands into the console.

"Would you like to sit down?" Kathy asked as she vacated the chair. Matt assumed the position without missing a keystroke.

"The alarm log doesn't show any other failures," Matt said as he leaned back. "A failed node will affect a whole subset of calculations. That could account for the delay. I'll need to verify it, though."

"How goes it so far?" said a voice from behind. All turned to face Jon Ames and Josef Hofbauer.

"Nominal," Eric reported, "other than a node failure this morning."

Josef frowned but said nothing.

"Did the failure affect the test?" Jon asked.

"Matt thinks so," Kathy answered. "He says the test should be over by now."

"Dr. Bugatti, what do you think about this?" Josef said, tapping his lip with his index finger.

"I expected a solution hours ago," Matt said. "The node failure certainly had an effect. I don't know if it accounts for this result. I'll have to analyze it."

Matt got up and walked off to his cubicle. From his workstation he opened the source code file and began tracing the effect of a failure of node thirty-nine for a period of three hours and seventeen minutes.

"Where's the failed module?" Jon asked Eric.

"It's in the computer room, next to the prototype."

"I want you to get it back to Mechanized Minds right away," Jon ordered.

"You will, of course, erase and overwrite the memory, no?" Josef added.

"That's standard procedure," Eric assured him.

"Very well," Josef said. "Jon, alert me when the test is over." He pivoted smartly and walked directly to his office.

"Take care of that module right away," Jon told Eric. "Don't take chances. Send it directly to Alvin Xiao."

"Whatever you say, Chief," Eric responded dutifully. Jon turned to leave, but stopped short.

"Eric, what was the serial number of the failed module?"

"I've got that here," Eric said. He examined the sheaf of notes on his clipboard. "Position thirty-nine. That would be 0115102A0147. Hmm. That's weird."

"What's weird about it?" Jon asked.

"Matt made a big deal out of the fact that one module was out of sequence." Eric held the list of serial numbers so Jon could see it. He tapped his finger over one particular line. "This one—0147—the one that crapped out."

Jon kept a poker face as he recalled a trip to the office he'd made on the previous Sunday. He'd gone early in the morning when it was sure to be deserted, with no one else around when he replaced one computer out of sixteen in one of four cartons holding the sixty-four nodes of the Cygnus test system.

"They probably had a failure at the factory and replaced the dud with this one. It might have been mishandled. Make sure it gets out today. And, Eric?"

"Yes?"

"Make *damn* sure you wipe the memory on that module."

❖ ❖ ❖

Matt threw himself into the difficult task of untangling the impact of a failed node on the solution time of his algorithm. It was possible that the failure *could* explain why the test was taking so long but until he could quantify the effect he had to assume his program was flawed. The analysis was excruciatingly complex, far more so than the original formulation of the algorithm. Building the analytical structure from scratch was phenomenally difficult, but tracing all the implications of this perturbation in a network of interdependent calculations taxed Matt's abilities in new ways. He found himself retracing the same steps with different outcomes as he tried to hold a dozen different factors in his mind simultaneously. At one point he felt himself suffocating under the layers of dimensions, manifolds, and the myriad properties of primes. He flung himself back in his chair and covered his eyes with his hands, trying to clear his mind. His moment of mental quiet was interrupted by a triumphant shout.

"It's done! Time! Time!" It was Eric Reilly, louder and more enthusiastic than anyone had ever heard the soft-spoken man. Matt headed toward the commotion in a trot. A crowd had already converged at the test console. Matt made his way to the front of the mob.

"Twenty-one hours, nineteen minutes, six seconds," Eric shouted, almost giddily, reading the elapsed time clock, frozen at the final duration of the test. Matt supported himself on the desktop, leaning forward to confirm the time for himself. He exhaled sharply, realizing that this team, that *he, himself*, had accomplished a feat many had attempted but none had achieved.

He had made history.

He bowed his head for a moment before lifting it again with another thought—history had been made, but it could not be recorded. The world would not know.

"You did it, goddamn it, you fucking did it," Kathy Darling shouted, punching Matt's shoulder. "How does it feel to be the world's greatest programmer?"

"We need Test Engineering to verify the factors," Eric said loudly.

"Oh, for Christ's sake," Kathy protested. "The thing worked. We'll check the answers tomorrow. It's party time."

"By the book," Eric retorted.

The two prime factors were displayed in windows under the elapsed time clock. Each of them consisted of more than three hundred digits. A test engineer arrived with a sealed envelope containing the prime factors, an envelope that had been carefully sequestered prior to the test. The process of reading each factor and comparing it with the numbers on the screen took nearly thirty minutes, the excitement of the team rising until the final digit.

Every digit matched.

"Go get Jon," Eric demanded of no one in particular. "Get Hofbauer, too."

"We're here," Jon said from the back of the crowd, which by now numbered more than twenty. The commotion ceased as everyone turned to face them.

"Eric," Jon said, "what's the final result?"

"The key was resolved to its prime factors in the time of twenty-one hours, nineteen minutes, six seconds," Eric recited. "The prime factors were verified correct. During the test there was a failure of one node which was repaired and the test resumed after a delay of three hours and seventeen minutes."

"So," Josef asked, "if the node had not failed the test would have taken only eighteen hours, no?"

"I don't think it's that simple," Eric replied. He looked at Matt.

"The impact of a failed node is complicated," Matt explained. "The algorithm doesn't just stop if it loses a node. It tries to continue but with lower efficiency. That means it would have taken less than twenty-one hours but more than eighteen."

No one spoke. Matt continued. "But there's more going on here."

Jon and Josef exchanged concerned looks.

"Such as what?" Josef asked.

"It should have finished faster—a lot faster."

"You said the best time was twenty-four hours," Jon said.

"Twenty-four hours *at most*," Matt replied. "But it can also take less. *Maybe* it was the failed node, or *maybe* it was just the luck of the draw. I need to understand what's happening."

All eyes turned back toward Josef.

"Conduct another test right away," he ordered. "That should tell us, no? *Ja?*"

Having issued his directive, Josef returned to his office.

"Team, I'm proud of you," Jon said with obvious satisfaction. "And you should be proud of yourselves. We challenged you and you delivered. We've got a few loose ends to tie up, but when that's done, we're all headed to Stella's—on me."

The group buzzed with appreciation.

"Eric, set up another test run. Get that module wiped and send it out."

"Roger, Chief," Eric replied.

"Matt, I know you're itching to find out what's going on with your algorithm but that can wait. You're the guest of honor tonight."

Matt didn't respond. He was already at his workstation.

❖ ❖ ❖

By ten p.m. the second test run was well underway. Matt took a break from his analysis to check its progress. At six hours the search tree had developed into a multi-dimensional mathematical structure. Its unimaginable complexity was imperfectly represented in the grid of diagrams that filled the console. It took a singular human mind to understand their meaning.

Matt stared at the diagrams, turning them through every perspective, seeking some tiny influence that would tip the answer from its teetering point, somewhere in the recesses of his mind, to full realization. It was *right there*, just beyond comprehension, like a queasiness in his head. If he thought about it too hard it would tip the wrong way and be lost forever, or—if he were lucky—recovered imperfectly, a flawed facsimile of the truth.

After some length of time during which Matt manipulated diagrams, thought forwards and sideways, stared and meditated, the queasiness vanished. The gap in his algorithm's conceptual structure, which had been invisible, now appeared in high relief, like a flaw in a painting which, once pointed out, can't be overlooked. Matt typed a command into the console and halted the test.

It took Matt ninety minutes to modify the code and reprogram six nodes. He restarted the test from the beginning and noted in the log:

Restarted test after changes to supervisory program and nodes 0, 10, 16, 22, 48, 52. Build 0.121.3. Expected best time 12 hours (90th percentile). 8 hour solution is at the 80th percentile. Expected time 3 ½ hours. Too fucking beautiful for words—Bugatti

Matt checked the time. He rushed out of the building and drove directly to Stella Blues. He sprinted from the parking lot and burst through the door, anxious to announce his achievement, the quantum leap that finally—*finally*—promised to accomplish the eight-hour goal. The test would have to run to completion to confirm his estimate but Matt was as sure of it as he was of his own existence. As cautious as he was by nature, the incontrovertible nature of the breakthrough and the force with which it impressed itself on

Matt's mind merited a premature announcement and another round of drinks.

The bar was nearly deserted, populated only by the usual early January, two a.m. mid-week patrons, none of whom were employed by the Connectrix Corporation of Eau Claire, Wisconsin.

25

Plan B

Alvin Xiao bent over his workbench, peering through a magnifier at the failed module returned from Connectrix. He located a tiny black rectangle, no larger than the nail on his pinky finger, surrounded on four sides by dozens of silver threads all of identical length, parallel and precisely spaced. The device was indistinguishable from a hundred other rectangles on the module.

He directed a stream of superheated air at the chip, watching the silver leads carefully. In a few seconds the solder that held the chip to the board began to liquefy. He held a pair of precision tweezers, its tips hovering over the device, waiting for the right moment. *One chance,* he thought. If he tried to remove it from the board before all the leads were detached, he could damage it. If he waited too long it would fry. At the moment when the reflected highlights on all the leads appeared uniform, when the part shifted almost imperceptibly from the surface tension of the liquid solder, he expertly plucked it from the board in one motion. The leads were all straight, with no solder bridging adjacent wires. *Perfect.*

Next to the board lay a miniature clamshell case of conductive plastic designed to protect sensitive components from mechanical and electrical shocks. It contained a device like the one Alvin had just extracted, identical in every respect but one—it contained no code. Alvin placed it on the circuit board in the open space, aligning it with the tiny traces of copper. With a few seconds of applied heat the chip was reattached. Alvin connected the module to a workstation, restored its original programming and verified that the board was undamaged. He put the precious programmed part in the plastic case and slipped it into his pocket.

Before leaving Alvin replaced the module in its shipping container and left it on the workbench with a handwritten note.

Cliff,
Got this board back from Connectrix. Failed 12 hours into the test. Find out what's wrong with it. We owe them answers!
Alvin

❖ ❖ ❖

Fu Lian had commandeered the largest conference room at the *Guoanbu* Encryption Analysis Division for the purpose of analyzing the memory chip whose provenance could be traced from Alvin Xiao, through Tan Yingqun, to an American bound for China on a student visa, who was detained at the Shanghai airport for supposed irregularities in his travel documents, where the tiny bit of contraband was confiscated by an immigration official and turned over immediately to an agent of the Chinese Ministry of Security.

The researchers under Dr. Fu had extracted the code, unintelligible in its raw form of ones and zeros. They reconstructed the program in the language of the microprocessor at the heart of the Mechanized Minds computer module, known in detail from documents provided by Alvin Xiao. Fourteen programmers and mathematicians had each carved out a section of the code for analysis. Dr. Fu expected progress reports twice a day. Wang Shutao expected reports twice weekly, which he always received in person.

❖ ❖ ❖

Fu Lian's team sat wide-eyed and straight-backed, exchanging occasional furtive glances. Wang Shutao stood at the head of the table, observing them. He thought it unlikely that their report would be satisfactory.

"Brothers and sisters, you have had the American program for more than a month. By now you should have reconstructed the algorithm and prepared a plan to implement the method on our own computers.

"We know that the system is to a great extent the work of one man. Not a team of more than eighty trained and experienced researchers, as we have here at the Fourth Bureau, but one, solitary man. However brilliant he may be, he cannot match our collective abilities and resources.

"You are our finest scientists in a laboratory that surpasses the facilities of the American National Security Agency. I have the greatest of confidence that you will succeed."

Wang sat at the head of the table strewn with notes among four workstations. The walls of the conference room were plastered with equations and diagrams resembling the walls of the Connectrix conference room, somewhat less detailed, and annotated not in English, but in Chinese.

"I will hear your report now," Wang said.

Fu Lian spoke first. "Wang Shutao, we have completed our reconstruction of the program on the device you provided. It consists of routines to calculate properties of prime numbers and to test candidate prime factors against the corresponding properties of the encryption key." She paused as if she hoped that this information would satisfy Wang and the meeting could end.

"Continue," Wang said.

"The code is not complete," she said, her eyes downcast. "Your informant claimed the algorithm evaluates seventeen properties of prime numbers. We found only eleven. Of the eleven calculations, only one of them is complete. The others appear to be missing components."

"Continue."

"These are only calculations and tests. They are important, and they have given us valuable insight into the approach the American scientist has taken. But the actual algorithm for conducting the search is not present.

"This system consists of parallel computers. The American has programmed each computer with different tests. He has also assigned different *parts* of each test to different computers. We believe he does this to gain efficiency."

"Can we make use of this technique in our own development?" Wang asked.

"Yes, Wang Shutao, but it will only give us a small improvement. The real innovation is in the program that supervises the search. That is the key. The code we received does not contain any part of the supervisor, nor does it contain any of the code for the six missing properties."

Wang said nothing. Fu continued.

"If we had the executable code for all sixty-four computers in the system, we could reconstruct the entire program. The complexity of the code suggests that this would take many months to accomplish with only the executable code, even with all our scientists assigned to this task."

Fu looked around the room at her colleagues. She turned back to Wang. "We ask again for the source code."

The corners of Wang's mouth dipped slightly.

"This news is difficult for me to hear," he began softly. "We had hopes that the code we obtained from our American operative was complete. I see now we were naïve to think so."

Wang rose from his chair and left the room.

❖ ❖ ❖

"Wang, what is so urgent that you must interrupt me?" the Minister asked as he closed the door to his office.

"We must escalate the operation. We must breach the American security measures and obtain the original source code."

The Minister placed his hand behind his neck to massage an ache at the corner of his shoulder blade. "Wang Shutao, your enthusiasm is admirable," he said, closing his eyes. "But I counsel patience. These things take time. When I had mission responsibility it was common for an operation to continue for years, even decades in some cases." He rolled his head from side to side. "Continue to work with your assets to gather tiles as you assemble the mosaic. The picture will emerge soon enough."

"Minister, we're not stealing data on cold war weapons that remain static for years or more."

"Wang, give me credit for knowing *something* of our modern times," the Minister bristled. "There are still a few of the old guard who are not either retired or permanently moored in the past."

"Minister, this situation is unique. We have abundant experience penetrating large organizations employing many people with whom numerous relationships can be cultivated at once. When one asset fails, another succeeds."

"Yes, yes, I know," the Minister interrupted. "Why is this operation different?"

"The information we need is not accessible by many. It is in the mind of one man."

The Minister removed his hand from his neck and rubbed his fingertips together as he studied Wang's face. "What do you propose?"

"We must get the code directly from the one who created it."

The Minister shook his head. "Wang Shutao, you are leaping for a jar on a high shelf. If you upset the jar it will come crashing to the floor and its contents will be ruined. Find a stool, or sturdy boxes you can stack to reach the jar safely. It will take more time, but you may find that there are many other jars on the shelf that were previously hidden but which can now be taken with ease."

"I believe there is no other way."

The Minister looked at the man in front of him, thirty years his junior. He recognized traits that he had once possessed—ambition, initiative, ruthlessness—but which had atrophied after decades of rising through the bureaucracy. *Have I become such a timid old man?*

"All right." The Minister massaged a spot on the opposite side of his neck. "Tell Tan to approach the programmer. *But he must be subtle.* Learn about him, what he wants and what he fears. I want to know the plan before he proceeds. If the jar ends up in pieces, we will both have much to answer for."

26

THE RECEPTION

AFTER MATT'S LATEST changes, the team ran eight more tests. The longest completed in less than six hours. The average was three and a half. On the wall at one end of the work area, under a banner which read *BEST TIME,* Jon posted the fastest time of three hours, four minutes. It hung next to another banner which read *DAYS TO DEMO.* Under it was a whiteboard, the number 46 written on it in red. It was impossible to ignore.

The system was far from complete. When finished it would have a slickly styled graphical interface, quite unlike the screen of scattered windows with blinking prompts into which software engineers typed incomprehensible commands. Communication functions would access the digital infrastructure, sniff the torrent of traffic for suspect messages and direct them to a queue from which they were admitted one-by-one to Matt's algorithm for decryption. Once configured, the Cygnus system could collect the private communications of virtually anyone targeted for surveillance. Arranged in arrays of hundreds or thousands of systems, the quantity of intelligence that could be collected, decoded, summarized and reported would exceed the capacity of vastly larger and more costly supercomputers. It was a business model that could not fail—as long as governments had reasons, valid or otherwise, to eavesdrop on their citizens.

No longer on the critical path, Matt spent his days tweaking his algorithm, finding stray bits of inefficiency and purging them from his code, while other programmers worked frantically to test and verify the system. From time to time they asked Matt to make some small changes to his code. But mostly he worked on his proof. He found five flaws in his chain of inference, none of which materially affected its validity. He wrote a monograph of a hundred twenty pages and a fourteen-page journal article. Both were classified and therefore prohibited from distribution. As he prepared the documents, verified his logic, and explained his proof in clear, compelling language, he tried to forget that his work would remain unknown to the world community of number theorists, perhaps until after one among them reproduced his discoveries.

"Matt, I have something for you."

Matt turned his head without altering his position to see Jon in the opening of his cubicle. In one hand Jon held a square ivory-colored envelope; in the other he held four more just like it.

"There's a reception this weekend." Jon held out the envelope. "The management and key associates from Connectrix are invited."

Matt took the envelope. It felt substantial. On the face of the envelope Matt's name was hand-written in a meticulous script.

Dr. Matteo Bugatti

The invitation read:

You are cordially invited to a reception in honor of
Tan Yingqun
Saturday, February 23
Seven O'clock in the evening
At the offices of the Mechanized Minds Corporation

THE GIRLFRIEND EXPERIENCE

"What's this about?"

"One of our board members is a friend of this guy Tan Yingqun. He's in Minneapolis on a book tour and Alvin Xiao —that's our board member—is throwing a party for him."

Matt studied the invitation. "Sure. I guess. Who do I RSVP to?"

"I'll tell Alvin you're coming, Okay? I'll see you there."

"Can I bring a guest?"

Jon hesitated before answering, "Of course."

❖ ❖ ❖

"I don't know what you expect to get from Bugatti," Alvin said.

"What, if anything, we can get from Bugatti will become clear in time," Tan Yingqun countered from across their usual table. "We've been instructed to get the source code, and we've been authorized to make contact with the one person who knows and understands it. My first task will be to know and understand Dr. Bugatti."

Alvin shook his head. "He won't cooperate. Even if he wanted to he couldn't get the code. The reason I sent you the chip was because the code is inaccessible."

"The chip was useless," Tan said evenly.

Alvin bristled. "The chip was *something*. And it wasn't *useless*. You know more now than you did."

"That is true," Tan conceded. "We know now just how clever Dr. Bugatti is. Cleverer than we thought, and our opinion of him was already very high. We know at least some of his strengths. We don't yet know his weaknesses."

❖ ❖ ❖

Matt picked up Gina at her Eau Claire apartment. Under a calf-length quilted coat Gina wore a lime-colored sleeveless dress, nearly knee length, a little shorter than Wisconsinites normally wore in late winter, with a neckline a little lower than needed to attract attention, and heels a little taller than what was safe on icy walkways. Matt wore a jacket, no tie, looking handsome but understated.

"You look awesome," he said as the two of them settled into the car for the drive to St. Paul.

"Thank you," she said, leaning across the console to kiss Matt. She slid her hand down his shoulder and sleeve. "I love this jacket."

"I bought it just for this occasion. Thanks for explaining 'cocktail attire' to me."

"Tell me again—what is this about?" she asked. Matt took the invitation from inside his jacket and handed it to her.

"Who is Tan Ying Kwoon?" she asked.

"I think it's pronounced Tan Ying *choon*. The 'q' is pronounced *ch*."

"Oh," she said as she reread the invitation. "But who is he?"

"He's a Chinese dissident. He spent a year or two in a Chinese jail. Now he lives in America. One of our directors is from China, or maybe Taiwan. He's a friend of his."

"You know such interesting people," Gina marveled.

"I've never met either one of them," Matt admitted. "For all I know we were invited just to fill up the room."

She scrutinized the invitation again in the fading light. "It doesn't say if there'll be food. I hope so. I'm starving."

❖ ❖ ❖

To Gina's relief, the reception featured an impressive buffet and servers passing hors d'oeuvres. Sixty people murmured and mingled with plenty of space between conversations. Large knots of attendees formed near the open bars on either side of the room. At the far end a piano and bass combo played softly.

Matt spotted Jon Ames conversing with a shorter, dark-haired man and an attractive blonde woman.

"There's my boss," he told Gina. "I'll introduce you."

The pair made their way to Jon's group, stopping briefly to accept glasses of wine from a passing server.

"Jon," Matt said as he approached. "This is my friend, Gina. Gina, this is my boss, Jon Ames."

Jon took Gina's hand and smiled, greeting her as if they had never met.

"Happy to meet you, Gina. This is Alvin Xiao and his wife, Elaine. Alvin is our host for the evening."

"Thanks for inviting us, Mr. Xiao," Matt said. "We're looking forward to meeting Mr. Yingqun, although I have to confess I hadn't heard of him before I got your invitation."

"Actually, it's Mr. Tan," Alvin corrected. "Tan is his family name. Yingqun is his given name. I'll be sure to introduce you, but he's not here yet. He's promoting a book, you know. I suppose he's been detained at his event." Alvin looked at his watch. "We expected him here before seven."

The small talk continued for a few minutes before the crowd broke into applause. A tall, lean man entered. On his arm was an attractive, provocatively dressed Asian woman. Tan Yingqun acknowledged the applause with a raised hand and a rare smile.

Alvin took Elaine's hand and made his way to Tan. He broke into an open area with Tan at its center. As Alvin spotted Tan's companion he stopped so suddenly that Elaine's forward momentum carried her into him, nearly knocking him down.

"Alvin, are you all right?" Elaine asked as she regained her balance. "Why did you do that?"

"I was waiting for the applause to die down," Alvin said. "No harm done, was there?" He took Elaine's arm and stepped forward to greet the guest of honor.

"Welcome, Tan Yingqun," Alvin said as he approached. "An impressive entrance."

"Good evening, Xiao Weiguo," Tan replied. "I'm flattered by the attention."

The Asian woman kept quiet, smiling sweetly as Alvin made the introductions. Tan introduced her: "This is Nikki Feng, a friend of mine."

Alvin took Nikki's hand hesitantly. "Happy to meet you, Nikki. I'm afraid Tan hasn't mentioned you at all."

"That doesn't surprise me," Nikki laughed. "We're rather recent acquaintances."

Alvin faced the crowd. "Ladies and gentlemen," he announced. "I'm pleased to welcome a courageous advocate for freedom. His criticism of the many human rights abuses in Communist China attracted the attention of that corrupt regime. As he was to learn, this attention was not the sort which one welcomes. His arrest, his so-called 'trial' and his imprisonment attracted a different kind of attention—the eyes of the world turned toward China, the voices of millions rose in protest, and the power of free nations joined in one cause—to release this champion of liberty."

The crowd was rapt, drawing hardly a breath.

"Now he's told his story in a new book. It's a powerful narrative that exposes the tyranny, the hypocrisy, the moral bankruptcy of this monstrous oppressor. Tan Yingqun—welcome."

The applause reverberated through the hall with double its previous intensity. Alvin and Tan clasped hands and embraced, close enough to speak to each other over the noise.

"That was convincing," Tan said in Mandarin. "You sound like you believe it."

"I do believe it," Alvin replied in the same language. "Parts of it."

"Aren't you afraid that these people will question your sincerity in light of your own ambitions in China?"

Alvin's hand gripped Tan's more tightly, until his fingertips turned white. Tan showed no reaction.

"My hypocrisy is on display for everyone to see. If I'm questioned, I'll defend myself." Alvin squeezed still tighter. "Who questions *your* sincerity besides me?"

Tan winced. Alvin released his grip.

❖ ❖ ❖

For the next hour, Tan stayed where he was as people filed by, shaking his hand and expressing admiration. As the number of greeters dwindled, Alvin reappeared.

"Shall we meet some of our colleagues from Connectrix?"

Alvin led Tan and Nikki toward a group that included Matt and Gina, Eric Reilly and his wife Bridgette, Kathy Darling, Elaine Xiao, and Jon Ames. All of them were on at least their second drink and some were having their fourth. Jon saw Alvin approaching with his guests.

"Here's the man of the hour," Jon announced. The others turned to greet them.

Gina and Nikki simultaneously squealed like two ecstatic middle-school girls. They raced to each other and hugged as Eric and Kathy turned to Matt. Matt shrugged.

"Girlfriend, how *are* you?" Nikki shrieked. "It's good, good, *good* to see you!"

"Nikki, dear, what a surprise!" Gina cried in a high register. "I've missed you!"

Tan sidled up to Matt as the others looked on with amusement.

"It seems our women already know each other," Tan said quietly. "Perhaps you and I should get acquainted. My name is Tan Yingqun."

"I know. I'm Matt Bugatti. Congratulations on the book."

"Thank you," Tan said as he shook Matt's hand. "It seems to be enjoying some success."

Gina and Nikki approached Matt and Tan with linked arms.

"Gina, it looks like you've found a friend," Matt said. The two women giggled.

"Oh, Nikki and I are *old* friends," Gina bubbled. "But I haven't seen her in *ages*."

Matt put his hand out again. "Nikki, I'm Matt," he said, barely getting out the words before Nikki flung her arms around Matt's neck and pulled him close, planting her lips on his cheek.

"Hiya, Matt," she murmured into Matt's ear. She stepped back from the abashed boy.

"Gina, he's a *doll*," she gushed. "Where did you find him?"

"In a bar, of course," Gina laughed. "He was plastered. But cute."

Kathy and Eric exchanged knowing looks. Matt blushed.

"Oh, sweetie, I'm sorry. I got carried away," Gina said softly as she took Matt's arm.

Matt smiled sheepishly. "You're not exactly giving away state secrets," Matt said. Gina kissed his cheek.

"Nikki, you and Gina should get caught up," Tan said. "Matt and I will be getting to know each other." The two women obliged, heading straight for the bar.

❖ ❖ ❖

"Is he a regular?" Gina asked Nikki as she retrieved two cosmopolitans from the bartender.

"Second time with me," Nikki answered. "I don't know if he's had anyone else from the agency." She sipped her drink. "What about Matt? He doesn't look like one of your usual customers."

"He's not," Gina whispered. "Do you see that taller guy in the expensive jacket?" Gina tipped her head toward Jon Ames. "The one with the bald spot? He hired me to be Matt's girlfriend."

"*What?*" Nikki gasped. "Do you mean Matt doesn't *know?*"

Gina giggled mischievously. "It's a sweet deal. Almost full-time, and Mr. Armani Jacket pays all the bills. He even got me an apartment in Eau Claire."

"That's so *bad!*" Nikki said with wide eyes and an impish grin. "How often do you make it with the big guy?"

Gina rolled her eyes. "Never! He doesn't want to get near me." She sipped her cosmo. "It's weird. All that money and he doesn't even flirt. I'd probably give him a freebie if he asked."

❖ ❖ ❖

"What happened to you in China?" Matt inquired. He and Tan had found a table in a remote corner.

Tan nodded wearily, as if he felt obliged, but not eager, to tell his story yet again. "I knew a man who was brutally beaten by the police. One suffers such abuses in China from time to time. Usually we Chinese bear them in silence or complain in private to trusted friends."

"He was a friend?"

"I barely knew the man. But he told me what happened. People are always telling me things. They tell me things they wouldn't tell their own families. It's been that way my whole life." Tan looked past Matt and sighed. "It's a curse."

"So what happened?"

"I complained. The police offered the man an apology and the two officers were reprimanded. Of course, there was no monetary compensation for the man's suffering, but I had achieved my goal."

"What goal?"

"I wanted *them* to say to *me* that they were wrong. I didn't do it for the beaten man, or to resist oppression, or to change the world. It was pure self-indulgence."

Tan took a long drink of scotch. "The man told his friends about my 'courageous advocacy.' His friends, and their friends, came to me with their own complaints. I posted their stories in a blog, but the blogs in China are censored. I found ways to tunnel through China's 'great firewall' where I found a global audience. The more attention I attracted the more people came to me with their stories—and the more notorious I became."

"Notorious? You're a hero."

"I'm not a hero. I'm a celebrity."

"I'll have to read the book."

Tan closed his eyes and shook his head. "The book tells my story a little differently. That was my publisher's suggestion. It's more...*inspiring*."

"Here we are!" Gina and Nikki announced in unison, their arms around each others' shoulders and clutching two fresh cosmos.

"Indeed," Tan deadpanned with a narrow smile.

Gina disengaged herself from Nikki and sat in Matt's lap.

"Nikki knows an awesome club here in St. Paul. Live music and dancing. Want to go?"

Matt put his hand on Gina's waist. "You've never seen me dance. It could ruin our relationship."

"Oh, all you men who think you're such terrible dancers should get over yourselves." Gina kissed Matt's cheek. "It's the men who think they *can* dance who *really* suck."

"I ski way better than I dance."

"I taught you to ski. I can teach you to dance." She nuzzled his ear and whispered *"And the graduation ceremony is even better."*

"In that case, count me in," Matt agreed.

"Oh, good!" Nikki chirped. "Yingqun, honey, can we go dancing?"

"Of course," Tan said. "But my host is expecting me to make a short speech first. And I've agreed to sign books. At least another hour."

❖ ❖ ❖

In his remarks Tan spoke about the corruption of power and the plight of the powerless. He told how he had brought to light horrifying abuses in China and offered his hope that others would take heart from his example and resist oppression. He related the story of his own sacrifice and suffering, and the inspiration he drew from the many brave people of China who shared their stories with him—the inspiration that sustained him through his arrest, trial and imprisonment. In his darkest hour, when surrender seemed his sweetest option, when a confession and recantation would have freed him, he remained steadfast—to honor those for whom his voice offered hope. He was eloquent and sincere. The audience applauded for three solid minutes.

Matt wondered how many in the room besides him knew the truth.

❖ ❖ ❖

"How do you know Mr. Xiao?"

Nikki sat next to Tan in the back of the limousine on the way to the club, checking her makeup in her compact mirror. She snapped it shut and dropped it in her purse, smiling sweetly.

"What makes you think I know Alvin?" she demurred.

"Alvin?" Tan repeated. He returned Nikki's smile, not quite as sweetly.

"We've met before."

"Is he a client of yours?"

"Are you jealous?" Nikki took Tan's arm and pressed her cheek against his shoulder.

"Don't be absurd. I could no more be jealous of one of your customers than I could be of a man in line in front of me at a coffee shop."

Nikki pinched him hard. Tan grunted.

"Why are you so mean?" she complained.

"Let's be adults. I saw how you looked at him, and I saw how he looked at you. It's obvious that you know each other. Is he a customer?"

"Honey, that would be telling." Nikki rubbed the spot on Tan's arm where she pinched. "I may be a hooker but I have some ethics. You wouldn't want me to tell on *you*, would you? A famous author? How awkward would *that* be?"

You've answered my question, Tan thought.

"What about Gina? How do you two know each other?"

Nikki laughed. "I got Gina started. She was working for tips in a bar when we met. I told her with her looks she could make six figures her first year."

"She's an escort?"

"An independent. I tried to get her to sign up with the agency but she went out on her own. And I was right. She told me her first year she made over a hundred thousand."

"I wouldn't have figured Bugatti for the type to hire a call girl."

"He doesn't know," Nikki whispered with an air of wickedness. "His boss hired her to be his girlfriend. Isn't that wild?"

The limo pulled to the curb and halted in front of the club. Tan studied Nikki's face in the light through the window, judging her to be truthful. "Isn't *that* telling? What about your ethics?"

Nikki shrugged. "He's not *my* client."

❖ ❖ ❖

"The programmer, the director, and the entrepreneur—they're *all* involved with prostitutes?" the Minister asked Wang Shutao.

"This comes directly from Tan Yingqun," Wang answered. "It's reliable."

The Minister pressed his thumb and forefinger against his temples.

"This could be very valuable," he said. "Or very dangerous."

"It may provide leverage to ensure cooperation."

"It may force our sources into a corner where they will turn on us."

The Minister released his grip on his forehead.

"Wang Shutao, before we issue threats we must do what we can to entice. Our efforts up to now have had only limited success—that's why I approved the plan to make contact with Bugatti. What did Tan learn about him?"

"He sees himself as a historic figure. He wants to be recognized for his achievements, but he that fears his discoveries will remain unknown, or worse, that someone else may reproduce them and take credit."

"This is what Bugatti said?"

"Not in those words, of course. He and Tan had a long conversation at the reception and at a nightclub afterwards. Dr. Bugatti was quite evasive about his work. He spoke only in very general terms. But Tan is sure of his conclusions."

"Is this a weakness we can exploit?"

"I believe so," Wang answered.

The Minister crossed his arms and leaned back. After decades of experience in high-stakes espionage, he recognized this as a familiar moment. It was the point at which a decision—an *irrevocable* decision—could determine the success or failure of an operation.

"I want you to try again with the sources you have."

"All our attempts to obtain the code indirectly have been fruitless."

"Humor me," the Minister said brusquely. "If you fail, then you can bring me a plan to engage Bugatti."

❖ ❖ ❖

"Did you enjoy the reception, Agent Gutierrez?" Josef asked Anibal at the outset of his report, which Anibal delivered by phone at two o'clock Sunday morning.

Anibal ignored Josef's question.

"Dr. Bugatti and Gina Bianchi arrived at the reception at approximately seven-twenty," Anibal began. "During the course of the evening, Bugatti had an extended conversation with the guest of honor, Tan Yingqun. Following the reception, Bugatti and Bianchi joined Tan Yingqun and his guest at a nearby nightclub. Bugatti and Tan had another long conversation. Bianchi and Bugatti left the club shortly after midnight and returned to Bugatti's apartment in Eau Claire."

"Yes…" Josef said in a distant voice. "We've been watching Tan Yingqun for months."

"Anything you'd like to share with me?"

"Nothing, other than he is a person of interest."

Anibal gulped. "Are we at risk?"

"Pay special attention to any contact between Bugatti and Tan, including secondary contacts. If you need to bring in additional personnel I will authorize you to do so. I'll make the call to your supervisor on Monday."

Oh, fuck me, Anibal thought. *This thing's going to bleed out.*

"Yes, sir. Any other questions?"

"You mentioned that Tan had a guest."

Shit, I forgot about Tan's hooker.

"Yeah. Her name is Nikki Feng. I did a quick rundown on her."

"What did you find out?"

"Sir," Anibal began, "you won't believe this."

27

PRECAUTIONS

"WE'VE COVERED THIS already," Alvin reminded Tan. "The source code can't be accessed without detection."

"Perhaps no one has been given the proper incentive," Tan countered. "I'm sure that with the right reward—or the right threat—Mr. Ames could be persuaded to try. He might even be ingenious enough to find a way around the security measures at Connectrix."

"What kind of reward? He already has plenty of money."

"Indeed? And yet you have been making deposits to an account for several months, an account from which Mr. Ames makes regular withdrawals. Apparently, whatever money he has is not sufficient."

"How did you know that?"

"It wasn't easy to discover. You've covered your tracks well, far better than Mr. Ames has. But don't worry that I'll expose your scheme. Your continued payments are probably necessary to keep Mr. Ames engaged."

Alvin listened silently. *What else has he got on me?*

"I agree with you that he doesn't need the money," Tan continued. "Not for his own use anyway. But he does need to *hide* the money. Have you wondered where those account deposits go?"

"I don't know. He told me there were project expenses that he needed to keep off the books."

"And you did nothing to verify his story." Tan shook his head. "You disappoint me, Xiao Weiguo. Haven't I told you to leave nothing to chance? In this business, only the paranoid survive."

"You seem to know it all. Perhaps *you* know what he's doing with the money."

"I do," Tan answered. "It's a story many would find interesting, and which Mr. Ames would very much like to keep secret."

"Are you going to tell me?"

"Let me say this—judging from your acquaintance with Miss Feng, it's something you would appreciate."

Alvin blanched.

"Xiao Weiguo, no need to worry. Your secret is safe. I won't expose your dalliances. After all, it's a vice we share. Of course, your wife may not be as understanding as I am."

"You fucker."

Tan chuckled lightly. It was the first time Alvin had heard anything from Tan that resembled a laugh.

"For now, let's focus on Mr. Ames. Continue to make payments to his account. You offer the carrot. If necessary, I'll brandish the stick."

❖ ❖ ❖

Jon discovered Matt in the conference room late Thursday. Matt sat facing the far wall, leaning back in his chair with his fingers laced behind his head. The equations and diagrams on the wall appeared to Jon as impenetrable as ever.

"What's all this?" Jon asked. Matt spun slowly in his chair to face him.

"An idea. Actually, it's more like a hunch. It could turn into something. What's up?"

"There's a security audit coming up."

Matt unlaced his fingers and sat up straight. "I know. Three weeks, I think. I heard they wanted one more audit before the demonstration. Are you worried about it? Because we're in good shape, I think."

Jon pulled a chair from the wall and sat facing Matt. "I am a little worried, yes. I don't want anything to go wrong with this demonstration and a finding from the security audit could be a distraction."

"What are you concerned about? We do everything by the book."

"What if we've overlooked something?"

"Like what?"

"I don't know. Something that's not in the policies?"

Matt shrugged with indifference. "If we're following the security policies then what difference does it make? If there's an oversight, that's on the guys who wrote the policies, not us. They can't write us up for missing what the experts overlooked."

"They could always spring a surprise scenario on us."

"You'd know more about that than I would. But if you think that might happen, why not talk to Hofbauer? He stays up nights thinking about that stuff." He turned back toward the wall. "I have other things on my mind."

Jon smothered a small spark of annoyance. "If someone *really* wanted to get a copy of the source code, how would they do it?"

"That would be tough. It's locked up in a virtual vault. Anyone who gets near it leaves a trail. Even if you could somehow manage to copy the code, it would show up in the records. You'd get caught."

"You didn't answer my question."

Matt leaned forward. "You could try to get to the server but that's in a remote location accessible only by the administrator. I wouldn't even think about tapping the secure connection to the server—they'd spot that for sure. Better to get access to an authorized workstation. But you'd still have to add local storage, and you'd have to falsify the logs to cover your tracks, and then cover *those* tracks."

Matt's eyes dropped to the floor. "Too complicated," he said, shaking his head. "No, the simplest way is to copy the code *and for everyone to know about it.*"

"How do you do that?"

Matt shrugged. "Hell if I know, Jon. Make up a story. Tell a lie. Somehow you have to convince Hofbauer, the administrator, and the government auditors that your unauthorized copy of the code is nothing to worry about."

Matt turned back to the wall. He stared at the graphs and equations. "I think you guys are missing the point anyway. You're trying to build this impregnable wall around the code. It's a lot of trouble to prevent something that is highly unlikely. About one out of a hundred hacks involves breaking a security feature. Five percent exploit security flaws. Half are pure guesswork." He leaned back a bit further and looked at Jon over his shoulder.

"The rest happen right under someone's nose."

❖ ❖ ❖

"I've made my last deposit to Jon Ames's account."

Tan Yingqun looked surprised, a rare reaction. "Why?"

"Because he asked me to."

It was the first time that Alvin had seen Tan at a loss for words.

"Did he say anything else?" Tan asked after a pause.

"Only that the money I had already deposited would be sufficient. But the reason is clear."

Tan looked at Alvin inquiringly.

"Dr. Bugatti's girlfriend is a whore, but he doesn't know that. Jon Ames hired her to keep Bugatti happy until the system was complete. Now that the system is nearly finished and the demonstration is only a few weeks away, he doesn't need the prostitute anymore and he can end this messy arrangement."

Alvin watched Tan for a reaction. His conclusion, the connection of multiple dots—his acquaintance with Nikki, Nikki's friendship with Gina, Jon's unexpected request to end payments—was pure conjecture, unconfirmed—until Tan confirmed it.

"Xiao Weiguo, I'm impressed," Tan said.

Finally, Alvin thought. *A level playing field.*

"It's no use threatening Ames. He's convinced that any effort to copy the code will come to light, and he knows that if you expose him, you'll never get the code."

"Unfortunately, he's correct," Tan admitted. "Our bluff has been called."

"You have one option left. But you'll have to move quickly."

"Bugatti."

"Yes," Alvin agreed, "and I can help you. But first we need to discuss my terms."

28

COINCIDENCE

ALTHOUGH HE HAD prepared himself for this day, Matt was fretful. He'd tried to anticipate every contingency, and he felt reasonably confident that he could handle most turns of events, but there were unknowns, weird twists that either could not be foreseen or, if they could, were unquantifiable, with potentially devastating impact. Matt would just as soon have postponed the occasion but Gina insisted. They had been dating for more than four months. She wanted to meet Flora.

The contrast between Wisconsin and North Carolina in mid-March was pronounced. Winter-weary Wisconsinites looked forward to reasonably warm and reliably pleasant weather as they contended with mud and mud-stained snow drifts, which stubbornly persisted in gutters, parking lots, and shadows, looking aged and ugly. When Matt and Gina exited the Raleigh airport, they shed their winter coats and drove with windows open past dense woods already sprouting spring foliage.

"This weather is *fantastic!*" Gina marveled, closing her eyes and raising her face to the sun.

"We should come back next month when the dogwoods bloom. It's unbelievably beautiful."

She turned to him, still squinting and shading her eyes. "Do you think your mom will like me?"

Matt laughed out loud. "She'll smother you with love and stuff you with *braciole*."

❖ ❖ ❖

It was late afternoon when Matt and Gina checked into the hotel, just two hours before they were expected at Flora's house for dinner. Matt was in no hurry. He took a leisurely shower, leaning against the wall as the hot water tumbled over him for a full five minutes, until Gina interrupted, entering quietly, pressing her body insistently against his.

❖ ❖ ❖

The way to Flora's house wound through old neighborhoods of well-kept homes, on streets with curbs and sidewalks amid trees that were old when the houses were new. Gina asked about every school, park, and playground. Matt offered a few words on each, without much enthusiasm. She soon caught on and stopped asking questions. He folded an appreciative hand over hers and held it as they drove on.

Matt parked the car in Flora's driveway and paused with his hands on the steering wheel before turning to Gina and asking gravely, "Are you ready?"

"Why are you being so dramatic?" she said, looking like an exasperated parent.

The temperature had dropped after sunset. Gina and Matt stood on the porch on the verge of shivering, waiting for an answer to the doorbell. Flora opened the door wearing an apron, which she used to dry her hands, and her skin glowed with perspiration, or possibly condensation from steaming cook pots which filled the house with aromas that promised a memorable meal.

"*Matteo caro,*" she said, laying one hand on Matt's shoulder and one on his cheek as she kissed the other, almost hastily, before turning her attention to Gina.

"Hello, Gina. I'm Flora," she said, throwing her arms open and drawing Gina into a hug. "I wish I could say I already know you. But Matteo really hasn't told me much about you."

"Mom, that's not true," Matt protested.

"Oh yes. That's right. You did tell me Gina's a graphic designer and she's starting her own business. What else is there to know?"

"We have plenty of time to get acquainted, Mrs. Bugatti," Gina said as Matt remained silent and chagrined.

"Oh my goodness—who are you talking to? I'm *Flora!*"

Flora guided the couple through the door and into the sitting room.

"Please excuse me. I have a few things to do in the kitchen and then I'll be right back. *Matteo, un aperitivo?*"

Flora disappeared. Gina looked at Matt quizzically.

"An *aperitivo?*"

"A little something before dinner," Matt explained. He surveyed the array of liquor bottles on a sideboard, by a tray with three small glasses.

"That's strange," Matt observed. "No grappa." He turned to Gina. "Do you have a preference?"

She joined him by the sideboard. "I'll have the *Campari.*"

"*Campari,*" he repeated with a chuckle. "That's what Mom likes." He opened the bottle and poured three shots. Matt handed Gina her glass.

"Shouldn't we wait for Flora?"

"She'll be in the kitchen for another twenty minutes," Matt said, holding a glass in each hand. "We'll go to her."

He led the way but was met by Flora coming from the opposite direction, without her apron and looking fresh. She took a glass from the startled Matt.

"Is everything okay?" he asked, looking in the direction of the kitchen.

"Yes, of course," Flora answered, smiling. "Marie is taking care of everything."

"You let someone else cook in *your* kitchen?"

"*Matteo, certo!*" she laughed. "Marie knows what she's doing." She lifted her glass.

"Welcome, Gina. I know already we will be fast friends. *Miei cari, a salute!*"

❖ ❖ ❖

Flora and Gina talked through dinner without ceasing while Matt puzzled over the utter unfamiliarity of the situation. Instead of shuttling between kitchen and table, Flora stayed put as Marie served each course. Instead of hovering and fussing over every detail of its presentation, she enjoyed her meal in leisure. The familiar beef or pork entrée under a layer of cheese was absent; instead, Flora had chosen a seafood dish in a light cream sauce. Flora's favorite themes of marriage and children were missing from the conversation. Flora and Gina talked in animated fashion, and the similarity of their mannerisms and speech was both endearing and disconcerting. The effect was surreal.

After dinner Flora led a tour of the Bugatti home, filled with mementos of their family life. Flora had repurposed Matt's room for houseguests but it still contained a shelf filled with books Matt had accumulated since childhood, topped with a dozen shooting trophies. Matt explained the circumstances of a few of the bigger ones when asked, but Flora did most of the talking.

The hallway was lined with framed photos of Flora, Matt, and his father Giovanni. More than one showed Matt at a pistol competition in a firing stance and full protective gear, looking menacing. There were snapshots from family vacations, and a few professional studio portraits. Flora commented on each of them and paused before a selected few to tell their stories at length.

"This is my favorite." Flora reached out to touch a portrait of Matt and Giovanni, dressed in suits. The man and the boy beamed with pride; the cameo lighting suggested an aura of affection. "We took this picture not long before Giovanni died. Matt had just started college." Her fingers touched the image of Matt's face. It was young and untroubled, resembling his father's, but without its lines and texture, the accumulation of years that exceeded his age. "You looked so much alike back then." She turned to Matt and smiled. "You look even more like him now."

"Ti voglio bene, Mom."

"Ti voglio bene io, caro."

They returned to the sitting room.

"What's this?" Gina asked, looking at a large black and white print.

"Oh, that. I've had it for years. I love that statue. It's Michelangelo, the *Pietà.*"

❖ ❖ ❖

"Your mother is *charming,*" Gina said as she and Matt pulled out of the driveway. "I don't know why you were making such a fuss. She made me feel like part of the family."

Matt nodded absentmindedly. "I think this is the first time my mom has gone a whole evening without treating me like her little boy."

"That's good, isn't it?"

"It's definitely good. I'm just not used to it."

There was a period of silence as Matt retraced the route they'd taken earlier that night.

"Dinner was wonderful," Gina said finally. "But what happened to the *braciole* you warned me about? I was ready for a big, fat roll of meat and cheese."

"That was a surprise. Whenever I come home, Mom cooks all my favorite foods." He looked at her with knowing eyes. "Tonight she didn't. Tonight she cooked all *her* favorites."

"Why would she do that?"

"She wasn't cooking for me. She was cooking for you."

❖ ❖ ❖

The following day dawned as bright and warm as the day before. Gina and Matt enjoyed coffee mid-morning at a neighborhood café, furnished with well-used sofas behind veteran coffee tables covered with magazines and populated by bohemian clientele.

Flora invited them to dinner at her restaurant that night, but they had made no plans for the day. It was Gina's idea to visit the college in Chapel Hill and meet Matt's former teachers—"to fill in the gaps" as she put it.

Matt paused at the entrance to the Department of Philosophy before going in.

"This is the man I told you about. He saved my life."

"Emmett."

Matt nodded. "If it hadn't been for Emmett I would have checked out." He pushed the door open and followed Gina into the reception area.

Jenny sat at her desk squinting first at her computer display, then down at her keyboard as she pecked out a few letters, then back at her display to verify her work. Emmett stood behind her, dictating as Jenny typed. His cardigan was zipped three quarters up his considerable middle, which appeared even more substantial as he pressed both hands into the small of his back.

"Hey, Jenny," Matt said. "Hey, Emmett."

Emmett's attention fell immediately and solidly upon Gina. Jenny looked up with her hands frozen a few inches above her keyboard.

"Matt Bugatti! Look who it is, Emmett! It's Matt!" She struggled to her feet. Emmett appeared stuck in place as Jenny elbowed her way through the narrow passage between her desk and Emmett. Her face radiated joy as she trotted toward the couple. She stopped and stood with her hands folded below her chin and an expectant smile on her face.

"Jenny, this is my girlfriend, Gina. Gina, this is Jenny, one of my favorite ladies."

"Gina, I'm *so* happy to meet you." She spread her arms. "Honey, can I give you a hug?"

"Of course, Jenny. Matt told me to expect a hug."

Jenny pulled Gina into a matronly embrace, not unlike the one she received from Flora, warm and genuine.

"Emmett, I want you to meet Gina," Matt said. "She's heard all about you."

Emmett came about the desk. "Gina, I'm Emmett Komalski." He shook Gina's hand, politely but not enthusiastically.

"Nice to meet you," Gina responded tentatively. A few awkward seconds passed before Emmett broke the silence.

"Well, how did you two find each other?"

"We met in a…" Matt began.

"…in a museum," Gina interrupted.

"What?" Matt challenged without thinking.

"The Art Institute. I was there for a Roy Lichtenstein exhibit. I think Matt wandered in by mistake."

Matt looked from Gina to Emmett and back.

"Ah…sure. I thought it was an art store. I wanted to buy a notebook."

Gina wrapped her hands around Matt's bicep.

"He was so cute. I was admiring a beautiful print when this bewildered boy came up and asked me for directions to the nearest OfficeMax."

"Yeah. Ha, ha," Matt laughed.

"You'll tell that story to your grandkids," Jenny said, still beaming.

"Well, let's not get ahead of ourselves," Emmett added. "So, Gina—you're interested in art?"

"It's what I do. I'm a graphic designer."

"I see." Emmett looked at Matt and Gina as if he were judging the truthfulness of a child's excuse.

"Well, Matt," he continued, "you look content."

Matt looked into Gina's eyes as he replied, "I'm very happy."

❖ ❖ ❖

"Who is Roy Lichtenstein?" Matt whispered on their way out the door.

"I'll explain later," Gina whispered back.

❖ ❖ ❖

"She's lovely," Jenny observed.

Emmett stood in the middle of the room. "I hope she doesn't hurt him."

"Oh, you worry too much. He's a big boy."

Emmett shook his head. "No. That is a fragile young man."

❖ ❖ ❖

Matt escorted Gina along the familiar route from Philosophy to Mathematics. The leaves on the trees weren't yet big enough or dense enough to shade the path but nonetheless held the promise of a vibrant spring and a glorious summer.

"Who are we seeing now?"

"Nels Coffman. He was my major professor in school and my department head when I was a post-doc. He's a really smart guy." His voice trailed off.

"And?"

"He's a self-promoter. But he was really good for me. He pushed me. I guess it shouldn't matter that he did it more for himself than for me."

"He used you."

Matt stopped walking. "He did. But he was never devious about it. Everyone knows that Nels Coffman's number one priority is Nels Coffman. So what? We all made out."

Matt resumed his pace. "If I'm being used, at least I want to know about it."

❖ ❖ ❖

They found Nels in his office with a colleague whom Nels introduced as Dr. Heywood. The four had no sooner exchanged greetings than Nels resumed his recruiting campaign.

"Matt was my star researcher," he told Heywood. "I was ready to put him on the fast track to tenure but he left me for greener pastures."

"I know all about Dr. Bugatti," Heywood said. "I've read most of your papers. Brilliant stuff. What have you been up to lately?"

"I've developed some new theories," Matt said. "I'm not ready to publish."

"I'm looking forward to reading them. Can you send me a preprint?"

"It's a little sensitive," Matt said quietly. "I need to get clearance."

"Don't wait too long," Nels interjected. "I hear Petrescu is ready to announce some new discoveries."

"*What?*"

"Possibly revolutionary, I'm told."

Matt sank into the nearest chair with his hand to his forehead. "That's all you heard? Nothing else?"

"Only that it was big," Nels said casually. "It could just be a rumor. But you know he was investigating properties of primes. I'm sure it's along those lines."

Matt gazed out at the courtyard, now filling with students, some hurrying to class, others gathering in conversation circles. He watched one young man talking excitedly, gesturing to illustrate some difficult concept, while his audience displayed varying degrees of comprehension. Matt imagined himself, the learned professor, in the middle of the discussion, instructing, testing their understanding, and perhaps discovering a brilliant mind to be nurtured.

Matt stood up. "Nels, we should be going. Send me a note if you hear anything more about Petrescu."

"I'll do that," Nels promised. "Gina, I enjoyed meeting you. Matt, remember—we'll always have a place for you here at Carolina."

Heywood waited until Matt and Gina were out of earshot.

"What have you heard about Petrescu?"

Nels returned to his desk and paged through a grant proposal.

"Not a thing," he said without looking up.

❖ ❖ ❖

For the next hour Matt was quiet. Gina knew not to press him, so she held his arm as they strolled through campus and onto Franklin Street. They continued with no clear destination, past restaurants, pubs and shops.

"Matt, look."

Matt felt a tug on his arm as Gina stopped in front of a small bookstore. The sign in the window read:

Tan Yingqun
Wednesday, March 20
3:00-6:00 p.m.
A Father's Debt
Discussion & Signing

"Huh," Matt mumbled. "That's a coincidence."

"It's almost three. Let's say hello."

"Really?" Matt protested. "I'm not feeling very sociable right now."

"We *have* to stop in. We had a wonderful time in St. Paul and you two got along great." She pulled his arm toward the door.

They found Tan in the back of the bookstore, behind a small table holding a stack of books, the title, *A Father's Debt,* visible on the spines. Tan Yingqun stood talking with the bookstore owner.

"Mr. Tan!" Gina cried. Tan turned to see who was hailing him.

"Gina," he answered. "And Matt. So good of you to attend my signing." He leaned across the table to take Gina's hand and exchange a kiss on the cheek.

"How exciting," she said. "Matt and I talk all the time about how much fun we had in St. Paul. Are you staying here for long?"

"I will go to Charlottesville tomorrow—University of Virginia. My publisher has discovered that college-age readers have a special interest in my book." He looked around the nearly empty bookstore. "Although judging from appearances, I would question that finding."

"Do you have plans for tonight? Matt's mom invited us to dinner at her restaurant. You *have* to come too."

"Gina!" Matt whispered hoarsely.

"That would be okay, wouldn't it, Matt? You're mom won't mind if we bring Mr. Tan."

"Please," Tan interrupted, "call me Yingqun. It's what my family calls me." He turned to Matt. "I wouldn't want to intrude on your evening."

"No, it'll be fine," Gina said. "You'll be our guest."

"In fact, my evening is free."

"Wonderful! Matt can give you the address. Is seven o'clock good for you?"

"Perfect. I'm sure it will be the high point of my visit."

❖ ❖ ❖

"Why did you do that?" Matt asked Gina as they resumed their walk.

"Will it be a problem?"

"If so it's too late now."

"I thought you liked Yingqun."

Matt sighed. "I like him. That's not the point. Mom invited us as her guests. She didn't invite Tan."

Gina stopped walking. "If it's going to be trouble we'll go right back to the bookstore and tell Yingqun that dinner is off."

Matt let go of Gina's hand and crossed his arms. "It'll be fine. I'll fix it with Mom."

❖ ❖ ❖

Tan arrived at *Da Flora* shortly before seven-thirty. Flora greeted him personally and escorted him to the table where Matt and Gina had already made good progress on a bottle of *pino grigio*. Matt had explained the situation to Flora and offered to pick up the bill for their friend from out of town, who knew nobody in Raleigh and would otherwise have spent the evening alone, but Flora wouldn't hear of it.

"Matt, I admire the dedication you bring to your work," Tan offered during a lull in the small talk. "That was obvious to me the last time we talked. I find your example inspirational."

"Thanks. It's important work, and I have a knack for it."

"Indeed. After our last meeting I read a few of your papers."

Matt's looked up with a start. "You read my papers?"

"I studied mathematics in university. Calculus mostly—not number theory. But your most recent paper fascinated me. And it seems to have caused quite a stir among your colleagues."

"I'm…flattered."

"Not at all. You should be proud of your work. But I'm curious. Someone as talented and dedicated and…" Tan paused. "…*ambitious* as you appear to be—why have you not published anything new in nearly two years?"

Matt stared at Tan for a few seconds before turning away. "It's sensitive."

"Ah. You don't strike me as one who enjoys laboring in obscurity."

"I don't. That's not how it's supposed to work."

Matt bent forward, leaning against the table. "Mathematics is a dialog. It goes back centuries. You know, we still study Euclid and Pythagoras and they've been dead for thousands of years. Euler, Gauss, Newton—they all built on the old discoveries, and they added their own voices to a conversation that never ends." He leaned back. "Look, I believe that when you're dead, you're dead. But all those names I just mentioned—they're immortal." He looked down and muttered. "If they'd kept to themselves they'd be just a bunch of dead mathematicians—and we'd still be counting on our fingers."

Tan nodded as he took a bite of pasta. "The food is delicious. Your mother is a wonderful chef."

"It *is* good, isn't it?" Gina agreed. "Flora cooked for us last night, too."

Matt kept quiet.

"You know," Tan said, "after reading your papers I decided to do some more research. I came across an article by a man named…*Petrescu?* Does that sound familiar?"

Matt closed his eyes and laughed softly. "Yes. Marku Petrescu. I know him."

"He mentioned you by name. He was writing about how your theories could be applied to the problem of decryption. He was not optimistic."

"Petrescu is mistaken."

"He seems quite sure of himself. And the correspondence in the journals suggests that many others agree with him."

"I see you've made quite a study of it."

"It's my obsessive nature."

Matt drained his glass. "Tan, no offense, but I've been at this for a while. I've read the same correspondence. I know every one of those people personally. And I can tell you they're all on the wrong track."

"But how can you be sure if so many of the experts are in agreement?"

Matt poured another glass of wine and took a generous swallow. "This is mathematics. What counts is not what you *think*. It's what you *prove*."

"But still…"

"Look, Tan," Matt interrupted. "Everyone thinks strong encryption can't be broken because that's what everyone thinks. But they're wrong. I know they're wrong because *I've done it.*"

The corners of Tan's mouth turned up slightly. Gina looked back and forth between the two men.

"Sweetie, is that your big breakthrough? What does it mean? It sounds important."

Matt placed his hand on Gina's. "It's nothing. I've said too much already."

"Matt," Tan said, "if that's true, there are implications beyond mathematics. People's privacy will be at risk."

"Some people forfeit their right to privacy."

"Perhaps. But do you really believe that this power will not be abused? When all of history proves otherwise?"

Matt shook his head. "Here's what I believe. I agreed to an assignment. I agreed to keep it secret. I signed an oath."

"But…"

"Tan. This conversation is over."

An awkward silence followed. Gina took Matt's hand. Tan looked toward the bar. He caught the attention of a young Asian woman, a graduate student from Chapel Hill named Connie. She was the only person in the restaurant to notice Tan's eyes dart toward the door. She nodded an acknowledgement and left.

Flora appeared beside the table.

"Did you enjoy your dinner?" she asked brightly.

"Flora, it was delightful," Tan said. "Matt, thank you so much for allowing me to intrude."

"We couldn't let you eat alone. That's a sin in Italy."

"I know you won't allow me to pay for dinner, so I brought a small gift for each of you."

Tan produced three copies of his book, each signed with a personal message. Flora opened the cover to read the inscription.

To Flora
My best wishes
Your hospitality will be a treasured memory forever

It was followed by the Chinese characters for his name, *Tan Yingqun.*

"Thank you, Mr. Tan. I'm looking forward to reading it." She turned a few pages.

"What does the title mean—*A Father's Debt?*"

"The message of my book is that the next generation will inherit the consequences of our actions. There's a familiar Chinese expression—'a father's debt his sons repay.'"

❖ ❖ ❖

Tan followed close behind Matt and Gina as they left *Da Flora.* A stretch limousine waited at the curb. The driver came around the back and held the door as he waited for Tan.

"Nice ride," Matt said.

"My publisher treats me very well on these trips," Tan said. He faced Matt. "I apologize for my prying questions. I meant no offense. I hope you'll allow me to take you somewhere for a drink. You've been so gracious and I've behaved badly."

"Not at all," Matt said smiling. "I should apologize for how I acted."

"Then you'll accept my offer?"

Matt struggled to find a way to decline gracefully when Gina made the decision for both of them.

"Of *course* we'll come. Matt can show us all his favorite spots."

"Excellent," Tan said. "My driver will take us anywhere you like."

The driver opened the door and motioned for Gina to enter. Matt followed, bending low. He looked up and froze, his face just inches from the barrel of a forty-five caliber semi-automatic pistol.

The Asian man brandishing the gun sat on the forward seat facing rearward. Gina sat across from him between two other men, one of whom had an identical pistol pressed into Gina's ribs. Gina had a hand wrapped around each arm and a look of terror on her face.

"You'll need to remain calm if you want to avoid bloodshed," Tan whispered in Matt's ear. "We will be taking custody of Gina for a little while. She will be treated well. We'll return her to you when you have satisfied our demands."

"What demands?" Matt rasped, still motionless.

"The source code for the Cygnus project. We don't need all of it—just the code for your factoring algorithm."

Matt turned slightly to his left, keeping his eyes on the gun. "How do you know about that?"

"Please, now is not the time for questions." Tan put his hand on Matt's shoulder and pulled him back from the car.

"Look in the book I gave you. On page one hundred is a phone number. You may call that number at any time to arrange a meeting to exchange the code for Gina."

Tan got in the car and sat on the forward seat.

"I recommend that you make the arrangements as soon as you're able. Our patience is not unlimited. Of course, I don't need to warn you about doing anything that might endanger Gina's life. I feel we've grown close. It would be painful for me if we were forced to harm her."

The door closed. The car pulled out of the parking lot. Matt watched the taillights recede in the distance.

29

THE RUSE

THE FINAL DAYS before the NSA demonstration were a maelstrom of activity. Eric ran the hardware through dozens of dry runs, which by then had become routine. Kathy posted a graph of bugs discovered, analyzed, and fixed. Jon carefully scripted every aspect of the demonstration and pulled the team away from their preparations twice a week to rehearse until he was satisfied with the content and presentation.

Eric had encased the Cygnus prototype in sheets of black metal, behind a pane of tinted glass which obscured the modules, but through which dozens of flashing lights were visible. Nine fans drew chilled air from under the floor, through the cabinet and out the top, ridding the modules of heat generated from enough power to illuminate a neighborhood of twenty homes. All extraneous material in the computer room had been hidden or carted away, leaving the black monolith standing alone amid an expanse of pure white.

Amid the commotion only Jon had noticed the change in Matt's behavior. He had reverted to his previous sallow, disheveled appearance. His performance during the rehearsals was listless and rambling. Jon coached him patiently but never pushed him. Something else was going on with Matt and he didn't want to disturb it.

Matt had resumed his obsessive work habits, bent over his computer for hours without a break, often late into the night and sometimes through the next day. Jon wasn't sure what Matt was working on—perhaps he was developing the theories he'd scrawled on the conference room walls—but he didn't pry. He figured Matt deserved some slack.

After all, Jon's retainer with Gina was exhausted more than a month ago, and he hadn't made a payment since. He hoped Gina had let Matt down gently. It would have been devastating to Matt if she had simply disappeared.

❖ ❖ ❖

Jon called the team together the day before the demonstration. He climbed a stepladder near the middle of the far wall. From his vantage point he scanned the faces, all with the look of marathoners at the twenty-third mile.

The whiteboard under the *DAYS TO DEMO* banner now contained the numeral *1*. Without a word Jon scrubbed the whiteboard clean and tugged at the banner until it fluttered to the floor to the sound of cheers. He raised his hands for silence.

"Team, I've been doing this for twenty-five years, and I have never experienced a moment like this. Because I've never been part of a team who's accomplished what you have. Congratulations—not just for being the best in this business—not only for doing what no one else has ever done. I congratulate you for doing the *impossible*."

The applause resumed until Jon motioned for them to stop.

"You all know how important tomorrow is. There's nothing more you can do to prepare so I want you all to take the afternoon off, relax, get some rest. We'll need you all here at eight tomorrow. If everything goes as I know it will, tomorrow afternoon we'll have a reason to celebrate. Team, I could not be more proud."

Jon descended the ladder to the sound of clapping, making his way through the crowd, shaking hands individually, offering acknowledgement and thanks for specific contributions, and receiving congratulations in return. He looked around for Matt but didn't find him. As the last few people dispersed, he found Matt in his cubicle tapping away on his keyboard.

"Matt, you should take some time off before tomorrow. It's your big day."

"Sure, Jon," Matt muttered without missing a keystroke.

"Seriously. Go home. Get some rest."

"In a minute."

Jon watched Matt as he continued typing. "What are you working on?"

"My new idea. Could be huge. I'm at the vertex."

"That's great." He waited to see if Matt might slow his pace. He didn't.

"Matt, really. I need you fresh for tomorrow."

"No worries, Jon. I'll be sharp as a tack."

Jon stood silently for another minute. "How's Gina?"

The keystrokes stopped. Matt lifted his eyes but didn't turn away from his display. "Gina's fine."

"Good. I hope I'll see her again soon."

"Yeah. She wants to see you, too."

"All right. Good. I'll see you tomorrow. Eight a.m."

Jon walked away.

Matt resumed typing. *She'll be just fine*, he thought.

The entire staff arrived well before eight the next morning. To the old hands, this moment was familiar; they at least *appeared* relaxed. First-timers grinned and chatted and fidgeted–all except one. Matt sat to one side with his laptop and a cup of coffee, speaking to no one.

"Folks! It's show time!"

Jon stood in the doorway to his office. He held a sheet of paper in one hand and a USB memory stick in the other.

"I've just received the encrypted test message from the NSA. I've transferred it to this thumb drive. Kathy, transfer the test to the system queue." He looked at the wall clock.

"It's now five minutes to eight. Our instructions are to initiate the test exactly at eight o'clock. Let's get started."

Kathy retrieved the device from Jon and headed to the computer room in a brisk walk, Eric close behind.

"Our guest will arrive at nine," Jon announced. "After introductions we'll begin the presentation. You're all welcome to wait in the board room."

The crowd moved together past the windows to the computer room where Kathy and Eric sat at adjacent consoles. They stopped to watch.

Kathy finished a succession of keystrokes with a blow to the *Enter* key sufficiently vicious to raise the keyboard from the table. She lifted her hands as Eric continued until he hit *Enter* with comparable force. Both turned to the clock, which read precisely eight o'clock. With a high-five they turned to the audience to offer two thumbs-up. *Yesssss!* they hissed and pumped their fists in unison.

Matt had already found his assigned seat in the board room, near a console in the corner. The wall display was a larger duplicate of the console, which at the time read:

Project Cygnus
Rapid Decryption System Demonstration
Connectrix Corporation
Eau Claire, Wisconsin

Matt gazed at the screen, then slowly scanned the room. He took his seat and opened his laptop just as the rest of the team entered. Chairs arranged in rows at the back of the room quickly filled with Cygnus team members, still whispering nervously. Matt, alone at the table, went through the presentation on his laptop, rehearsing it in his head. The time was eight-fifteen. Over the next half-hour Kathy and Eric silently took their places at the table and opened their computers.

The chatter ceased instantly at five minutes to nine. A stocky, unfamiliar Asian man entered the room, followed closely by Josef Hofbauer, Jon Ames, and the remaining three members of the technical committee. Josef showed the stranger to his place, front and center. Josef walked to the front of the room.

"Welcome to the Cygnus demonstration," he said loudly. "You have all worked very hard for this day, no? You are ready to show off your achievement, no? *Ja?* You have done very well. You should be proud. First I will introduce our guest, Mr. Stephen Quan, from the National Security Agency. Mr. Quan, I have invited the Cygnus team to meet you."

The back rows stood as Stephen Quan rose halfway and turned to nod in their direction.

"Our senior leaders are at the table—Kathy Darling, our system leader, and Eric Reilly, hardware. And of course, we will hear from our Dr. Matt Bugatti, whom we have to thank for this breakthrough."

All sat down as Stephen rose. "Thank you, Josef, for the introductions. Congratulations to your team. We at the NSA are very excited about this demonstration. I'm looking forward to reporting your success."

He looked out on the rows of smiling, nodding faces. "As you know, this program has the highest priority and is protected by strict security measures. For these reasons I must ask two things before we begin." He turned to Josef. "The discussion may touch on some extremely sensitive subjects. I know you all have clearance, but those who are not actually presenting must leave the room."

Josef nodded and with a look from him the audience filed out.

"Also, your laptop computers, cell phones or other electronic devices must be turned off and stored away from the table."

Matt, Eric and Kathy obliged. Once Stephen was satisfied that the discussion couldn't be surreptitiously recorded, he sat.

"Please—begin."

Jon took his place up front. "Mr. Quan, what you will see during this demonstration is nothing less than historic. The Cygnus system is a parallel computer constructed from the most sophisticated technology available. Its design is the culmination of years of research, drawing on two centuries of combined experience in high-performance parallel processing."

Jon stood to one side as Eric stepped up in a well-rehearsed move. For the next half-hour Eric described the complexities of the Cygnus system, emphasizing the speed and power of its computers and its massive communications bandwidth, the equivalent of a full-length, high-definition movie every two seconds. He explained the system's unusual configuration with pride, making certain to mention that he had filed for sixteen patents—all classified, of course.

Kathy took Eric's place in the next choreographed switch. She used the next hour to lay out the features of the application software. She demonstrated the simplicity with which an operator could target any individual or group for surveillance, based on any number of factors, and the efficiency with which suspect messages could be queued up for decryption.

At the end of Kathy's presentation Jon took over. "This machine is impressive, but what it *does* is astounding. What we will show you was thought to be impossible a year ago. At exactly eight o'clock, less than two hours ago, an encrypted message and its public key were submitted to the queue of the prototype system. Today's supercomputers, many times larger, more powerful, and more expensive than Cygnus, using a brute force approach, would take centuries to decrypt this message. Cygnus will break the key, decrypt this message and reveal its contents *before lunch."*

Jon took his seat as Matt rose.

"Testing random pairs of primes is impractical for the reasons Jon has explained," Matt began. "It's possible to accelerate the process by limiting the search to a space that is more likely—but not *guaranteed*—to contain the prime factors. Our breakthrough is a revolutionary discovery in the field of number theory and the properties of primes. We have determined that the search space can be limited to a small fraction of all the possible pairs of primes.

Furthermore, it can be shown that this space *must* contain the solution."

Matt turned to the console and tapped a few keys. The display on the wall filled with the tree-like search path. Matt enlarged the diagram and rotated it to show thousands of tiny clusters of points.

"Although the clusters in this diagram appear to be disconnected, they are in fact all adjacent points on a geometrical construct."

The display flashed white and went dark. Matt looked concerned as he bent over the console. As he typed Stephen Quan looked first at Jon, then Josef for an explanation.

"Matt, what has happened?" Josef asked.

"I'm not sure," Matt replied, still typing. "The program is running but the display has stopped."

Jon spoke up. "We've been testing this configuration for weeks with no problems. Has anything changed?"

Matt typed and didn't answer.

"Matt—has anything changed?"

"Nothing significant."

"What about anything *insignificant?*"

"I added some enhancements to the display code last night. I thought I'd tested it well enough."

"Matt!" Jon exclaimed.

"I think I can revert to the old version without interrupting the decryption algorithm, but I'll need to get to my workstation. It'll take about an hour."

Josef was displeased. Jon was frantic.

"It would be faster if I did it from here," Matt said. "I've got my laptop with me and it'll boot much faster than the workstation."

Josef and Stephen traded looks. Stephen nodded.

"Very well," Josef said. He took a cell phone from his jacket pocket and placed a call. "Hello, this is Josef Hofbauer. Please grant temporary authorization to this computer for the next…" He looked at Matt who held up two fingers and a fist.

"Twenty minutes." Josef motioned to Matt for the laptop. Matt handed it over.

"Are you ready?" Josef turned the laptop over and read the sequence of letters and numbers that uniquely identified Matt's computer among all the computers on all the networks in the world.

Once the authorization was confirmed, Matt removed the network cable from the console and plugged it into his laptop. He opened a window and began to download the source code. In fifteen minutes he'd located the offending section, modified it, built a new version and installed it in the prototype system. Satisfied that the problem was corrected, he transferred the network cable back to the console and restarted the application. Matt's tree diagram reappeared, more densely populated than before but otherwise identical.

"I see Dr. Bugatti has restored the presentation. I assume we may proceed, no? *Ja?*"

"Ready," Matt said. "Sorry for the delay."

Matt continued describing the details of the factoring algorithm in terms as comprehensible to the layman as he could make them. Jon followed Matt's presentation with a summary. Josef closed out the agenda, describing the potential of Cygnus for covert surveillance at a scale unimaginable until now. He waited for the response from Stephen Quan.

Stephen had scribbled notes almost without ceasing over the course of the program, asking only an occasional clarifying question. He kept writing for another three minutes after Josef finished, then laid his pen aside and rested his chin on his folded hands.

"This is an impressive set of claims, especially your test results indicating an average decryption time of less than four hours—half the goal you proposed. Frankly, I never expected this program to get close to that goal. If you can verify this level of performance to my satisfaction…"

The console chimed. A window on the screen popped open displaying the decrypted text of the test message:

No leader has ever become great without daring. If the leader is filled with high ambition and if he pursues his aims with audacity and strength of will, he will reach them in spite of all obstacles.

Stephen silently mouthed the text of the message.

"Carl von Clausewitz, no?" Josef asked. "An interesting selection."

"I couldn't say," Stephen answered. He pulled a sealed envelope from his bag and tore it open. Inside was the clear text of the message, unknown to Stephen until he had read it from the display just seconds before.

"How long did that take?" he asked. Josef called his attention to a time in the corner of the screen: *3 hours 37 minutes 03 seconds.*

"Does this meet with your satisfaction?" Josef asked, sounding triumphant.

Stephen nodded. "You may call the rest of your team into the room now."

Once the back rows were filled, Stephen addressed them from the front of the room.

"This demonstration exceeded my most extreme expectations. I will report this to my superiors, who, I'm sure, will want to discuss an agreement to supply as many Cygnus systems as you are able to produce. You've done a great service to your country."

Stephen turned to Matt. "Well done, Dr. Bugatti. The United States of America is in your debt."

The team applauded as Stephen shook hands with Josef and Jon and then with each team member one by one. In the commotion that followed, Josef found Matt and put his hand on Matt's shoulder.

"Dr. Bugatti, you have amazed all of us, no? Your country has a new weapon against her enemies and we will all become rich, no? *Ja?*"

"I'm glad it worked out," Matt answered quietly.

"Not without a glitch, no? But you took care of that, too."

"Oh, yes. Sorry about that."

"It's nothing. What is the expression? 'No harm, no foul?'"

Matt grinned. "Glad you feel that way."

"Of course," Josef said, clapping Matt on the back. "Now I must have your laptop computer."

Matt looked into Josef's face. Josef was smiling benignly.

"My laptop?"

"Yes. Since your computer had access to the secure server, it must be inspected by the IT administrator and cleared of any classified information. You will have it back on Monday."

Matt removed his computer from its bag and handed it to Josef with a deliberate motion. Josef tucked it under his arm, smiled, and left.

The room emptied, leaving Matt alone. Through the door he could see his teammates, now collecting their things to leave for a celebratory banquet. As the voices outside the room died down, he took his right hand from his pocket and inspected a small memory card. It matched a slot on the front of his laptop. The card contained the source code for the Cygnus system and a utility which erased all evidence of the transfer from his computer. For more than two hours the previous day he had practiced the maneuver of ejecting the card and palming it while holding the laptop with one hand.

Matt put the card back in his pocket and left the room. He would join the celebration later. First he had a phone call to make.

30

THE DROP

"Wang Shutao, I believe you have lost your mind."

The Minister was not given to fits of rage, but he was as close to losing control as Wang Shutao had ever seen him.

"Minister, I am confident that this will turn out well."

The Minister pushed his fingers through his hair, laced them behind his head, and pressed his chin into his chest. He undid his fingers and slammed his hands flat on the desk with enough force to scatter papers. "You are extorting information from the programmer by threatening harm to his girlfriend. Now he's in a desperate position and his actions cannot be predicted. If this situation *does* end well it will only be through remarkable luck."

"She's not his girlfriend. She's a whore."

"Wang, you really are shameless," the Minister shouted. "What difference does that make? I counseled patience and you took this reckless course. The programmer could have been a valuable asset. Now, even if he turns over the code we will get nothing more from him."

Wang Shutao stood stoically, enduring the Minister's tirade. He waited for a pause before saying, softly, "Minister."

"What? What can you possibly say? Perhaps some incantation to restore my confidence in you—which was very high, I could add, but is now in shreds?"

"Bugatti has the code. He has already arranged for an exchange."

The Minister glared but stopped shouting. "When?"

"Immediately, this evening. Tomorrow morning American time."

The Minister bit his knuckle, still looking fierce. Wang kept talking.

"My instructions to Tan Yingqun were to appeal to Dr. Bugatti's vanity, but if in his judgment this approach couldn't succeed to go ahead with his alternate plan."

"This was Tan's idea?"

"No. In fact, it was proposed by Xiao Weiguo."

"Xiao?" the Minister screamed. "That rice bucket? Are you taking advice from white-eyed foreigners now? Really, Wang Shutao, I believe you *have* gone insane."

"Minister, allow me to explain and you will see that this plan has a very high likelihood of success."

"Oh, please," the Minister commanded, his voice dripping with sarcasm. "Explain away."

Wang related the plan that Alvin had offered to Tan in the days following the reception. The Minister listened reluctantly at first, then with a spark of interest and finally with grudging acceptance.

"All right, Wang, perhaps I was hasty. Not that I approve. In time I believe you could have succeeded without acting so impulsively. We could have retained the programmer as our operative. You may win your prize, but you will have poisoned the well. And you will leave tracks."

"No, Minister, we will erase our tracks."

❖ ❖ ❖

Anibal Gutierrez drove slowly past the building where Matt Bugatti rented an apartment. Matt's car was parked in its usual spot. During his morning rounds Anibal confirmed that Matt had not left the building to which he had returned late the previous night, coming directly from the party at which the Cygnus team raucously celebrated their triumph. Matt gamely took part. None suspected that Matt had already arranged to turn over state secrets to covert Chinese agents in return for the freedom of the woman he loved.

Agent Gutierrez *did* suspect as much, but had he no proof. He'd observed the Cygnus celebration from a distance, trailed his man to his residence and confirmed that he was secure in his apartment before retiring for the night. Now, just past eleven in the morning, Matt's car remained where he'd parked it less than ten hours earlier. *Sleeping it off,* Anibal concluded. He drove on.

❖ ❖ ❖

Anyone paying attention might have wondered about the gaunt young man sitting alone at mid-morning on a bench by a rarely traveled path of Minnehaha Park. Men looking lonely and spent were commonplace in the park but rarely were they as young or as well-dressed as Matt.

He had arranged a meeting at ten. It was just past noon. During those hours, Matt had acknowledged the nods of one jogger, one dog-walker and two cyclists.

At a quarter past noon a lone hiker came into view. When he sat at the other end of the bench Matt recognized him as the man who had threatened him with a pistol in the limousine outside Flora's restaurant.

"You have something for me Dr. Bugatti," the man said with a heavy accent.

"Where's Gina?"

"She is safe."

"I want to see her."

"She is safe."

"I've been sitting here for two hours. I'm not in a mood to be fucked with. If I'm not face to face with Gina in one minute I'm walking."

The man reached into his pocket and produced a cell phone. He entered a number and handed the phone to Matt. He put it to his ear.

"Hello?" said a voice Matt recognized as Gina's.

"Where are you?"

"I don't know. I'm not even sure what state I'm in."

"Are you all right?"

There was a long pause. "I'm okay," she answered at last. "They're making me comfortable. They haven't hurt me."

She sobbed softly. "Honey, I'm scared," she whispered. "I'm so scared. I want to see you again."

Matt leaned forward until his head was almost between his knees. He pressed the cell phone to his ear and shut his eyes tightly, but tears escaped. They moistened his cheeks and dripped from the tip of his nose.

"I'll take care of you. It's almost over."

He choked back a sob of his own. There was a sound of someone taking the phone away from Gina, followed by a beep signaling the end of the call.

Matt held out the phone. The Asian man took it. Matt pulled a miniature brown envelope from his pocket containing a memory card on which the highly classified source code of the Cygnus system was stored. The man opened the flap and inspected its contents. Without a word he pocketed the envelope and resumed his walk down the trail.

"When do I see Gina?"

The man stopped and turned back. He tapped his shirt pocket. "When we have verified the contents of this device."

❖ ❖ ❖

Matt returned to the lot where he'd parked Eric Reilly's car that morning. Eric never questioned Matt's story—his new car needed repairs, he had urgent business in Madison, could he use Eric's car just for the day?—and allowed Matt to pick up the car at his house. *No problem,* Eric told him. *I'll drive Bridgette's car.* Matt walked three miles to Eric's house before eight o'clock after escaping unnoticed from his apartment building.

He spent most of the afternoon in a haze, unwilling to make the drive to Eau Claire; to his apartment where he would wait alone for events outside of his control to unfold. He alternately walked aimlessly along Minneapolis streets and sat on sidewalk benches. He imagined he saw Gina wherever he looked—every woman with dark hair and average height was an involuntary distraction. Sometimes the impression was so compelling he walked toward the woman until he reminded himself of the absurdity of the thought or the woman turned to reveal her face.

Matt sat at a table in a diner for more than an hour, nursing his third cup of coffee, having abandoned a grilled cheese sandwich after one bite. It was impossible to suppose that his contact could have transferred the source code to someone capable of analyzing it, much less verifying its completeness, in the few hours since the drop, but he hoped for a call on his cell phone anyway, so at least he could make the drive home knowing *something*. Every few minutes he reached for the phone in his pocket, often responding to a phantom vibration generated not by the phone but by his own mind. The sensation became so annoying that he put his phone on the table and stared at its display, still reaching into his pocket from time to time without thinking.

At five p.m., weary but wired on caffeine, Matt left payment for his check, two hours after the waitress scrawled it and placed it face down with ill-concealed impatience. He collected his phone and dragged himself out the door as he buttoned his coat. Eric's car was in a parking ramp seven blocks away; though light was beginning to fade he walked slowly with hunched shoulders, still hoping for some word, dreading the lonely drive, the empty apartment and the long, uncertain wait.

He looked up to judge the traffic as he came to an intersection. Pedestrians bunched at the corner, until the signal changed and they moved forward. He followed the crowd, glancing furtively left and right, trying to avoid making eye contact but doing so inadvertently, coming face to face with a woman walking from the opposite direction. His breath caught and his heart quickened. His eyes widened in astonishment.

And so did Gina's.

31

THE MESSAGE

GABBY NORQUIST, FOURTEEN, of Story City, Iowa, made doll clothes. She made them for all sorts of dolls—baby dolls, little girl dolls, fashion dolls, action figures—she even took commissions. She enjoyed making doll clothes and she was good at it. She'd already placed her product in shops in Iowa Falls and Ames, and gotten inquiries from as far away as Des Moines. She employed friends on a piece-work basis to cut fabric but insisted on doing the final assembly herself, having found the quality of her friends' work wanting. After all, she had a brand to maintain. *Teensy Togs Doll Fashions* were premium products with a premium price.

Gabby had plans for expansion. For her channel to market she chose CraftersMall.com, a website specializing in hand-made items. The process of setting up an online store, building a catalog, and promoting a business fascinated her. When she placed an ad in *World of Dolls* magazine the number of site visits climbed and her first orders came in.

After two months and her second *World of Dolls* ad Gabby received an email announcing her first order from overseas—two ensembles at eighty dollars apiece for *American Girl* dolls, one of her most profitable lines. The buyer was from China.

Gabby hurriedly logged onto her CraftersMall.com account anticipating her first international transaction. Her account page popped up, its banner announcing:

You have 1 message(s)

She clicked on her inbox. There was one unopened message with no subject line. The body of the email was incomprehensible to Gabby, who could neither speak nor read Chinese.

Curious and excited, Gabby copied the text and pasted it into Google Translate. The English version of the message read:

Our scientists has been confirmed that the contents of the device. The code is complete. Programmer and girl continue to plan termination. When they reported success. Your family is eager to see you again.

"Mom!"

Gabby's mother found Gabby at her desk peering at a computer display surrounded by doll clothes in all stages of completion. She stood behind Gabby's chair and read the message.

"Where did that come from?"

"I thought it was from a customer in China. I translated it and got that."

Gabby's mother read the message again. "Did you see who it was from?"

Gabby copied the foreign characters in the *From:* line and pasted them into Google. It returned

Wang Shutao

"Is that your customer?" her mother asked.

"No. The name of my customer is Sandy Walton. Should I reply?"

"Never reply to any email unless you know the sender," her mother said gravely.

Gabby clicked the image of the trash can at the top of the message. She went to her order queue and verified the payment credentials of Sandy Walton, an ex-pat resident of Shanghai, China, who was anxious to receive her *American Girl* fashions.

❖ ❖ ❖

"What does this mean?" Alvin asked Tan, after hearing the news that *Guoanbu* scientists had verified the Cygnus code.

"Your enterprise is highly important to the Chengdu economy. Its success is of interest to the People's Government, which has granted your company favorable tax status. Your computers will be specified in future government projects." Tan seemed even more glum than usual as he relayed the message from Wang Shutao. "You stand to become a very wealthy man."

Alvin crossed his arms and leaned back in his chair. He mentally projected sales volumes in China assuming conservative market growth rates and penetration, factoring in the effect of privileged treatment by the Chinese regime. To this he added the anticipated revenue from Cygnus modules based on the expected volume of system sales to the NSA.

I did it, he thought.

❖ ❖ ❖

Wang Shutao stood by as the Minister read the report from the Encryption Analysis Division. At last the Minister laid down the report and removed his reading glasses, pressing his lips to the back of his hand.

"Are you certain that the code is complete?"

"Yes, Minister."

"And that it hasn't been doctored in any way?"

"There is no evidence of that, Minister."

"I didn't ask you if there was evidence, Wang Shutao. I asked if you were certain. Is it possible that the programmer could have changed the code in some subtle way such that we would conclude that it is correct when in fact it's not?"

"Fu Lian's scientists considered that possibility. According to the report they found no evidence of it."

The Minister stood and leaned with his closed fists on the desk. "I know what the report says, Wang. You stood there for fifteen minutes while I read the report. I'm not asking about the report. I'm asking what *you* believe. I want to know what *you* will commit to. Will you stake your reputation on these conclusions?"

"Yes, Minister. Fu Lian's scientists conducted a test on a sample key. It took many days to break it but it's reasonable to expect that the American's specialized hardware would shorten that time to a few hours. The code is complete."

The Minister stood erect and put his hands behind his back. "Very well. You may close out the operation. Send Tan his instructions. Have him report back when he is successful. And tell him that his family is eager to see him again."

"I will send the message by the usual means."

The Minister sat as Wang turned to leave.

"Wang Shutao."

Wang turned back. "Yes, Minister?"

"You have accomplished the mission with daring and efficiency. Had we proceeded as I had wished, we might still be waiting for the code, and the Americans' advantage would have widened." He pursed his lips, then gave Wang a closed-mouth smile. "From an old man to a young man: Well done."

32

MISDIRECTION

THE HANDBAG WENT flying, its contents scattering on the pavement among the feet of a dozen pedestrians crossing the street. Some stopped; a few knelt to help gather up the belongings of the woman whose bag had flown inexplicably from her hand. The rest ignored the commotion and walked on.

Gina crouched in the midst of the crowd, thanking each person who handed her an item from her bag. Matt knelt beside her and grabbed her arm.

"Gina, what…"

Gina put a hand behind Matt's neck and pulled him close enough to whisper in his ear.

"Don't talk. We're being watched."

A helpful bystander offered Gina her wallet. She pulled a card from the wallet as she thanked the man. Another handed her a pen. She scribbled on the back of the card and pressed it into Matt's hand.

"Don't follow me."

Gina slung her bag on her shoulder and hurried across the street. Matt stood where he was, until a car honked and he jogged back in the direction he came from. Gina was no longer visible on the crowded sidewalk, but he knew she was there, just ahead, not in an unknown location under the guard of Chinese spies. She was there. He had touched her.

He looked at the card.

Top Flight Escort Service
Minneapolis-St. Paul
(612) 555 8888
Highest Standards – Complete Discretion

He turned it over. On the back Gina had scrawled a name:

Nikki

33

THE CONTRACT

IT WAS THE sort of meeting that usually drove Jon crazy, filled with endless details: all the clauses, paragraphs, and addenda that make up a contract, which, though necessary, held no interest for Jon. He could talk endlessly about technology or for hours about product development, but business matters put him to sleep.

But in this meeting, now in its fourth hour, of which the last twenty minutes were devoted to the topic of spare parts, Jon was engaged and focused. He felt as if a part of him was standing in the corner of the room watching himself at a table next to Josef Hofbauer and Cooper Hodge, opposite Stephen Quan and two others from the NSA, wondering who that person was who looked exactly like Jon Ames but who acted like the founder and Chief Technology Officer of a fantastically successful company. *So this is what it's like.* The years of hard work, long hours, risky gambles, a failed marriage; of minor successes and major disappointments; of coming so close and falling short—all led to this moment, the reward that had eluded him for nearly three decades. It was knowing that he finally *had* succeeded, but also that others knew it, showing it in the only way that mattered. In this case it was a letter of intent to purchase eight hundred Cygnus systems over a period of two years at a price of three million dollars each. All that stood in the way of Connectrix becoming a billion-dollar company were a few details about indemnification and *force majeure*. It was a prospect so tantalizing that Jon picked through every syllable of the draft contract without having to talk himself into paying attention, while his alter-ego watched from the corner.

"The language of the final two clauses is boilerplate," Stephen Quan said. "We don't normally negotiate on these terms."

"What do you mean 'normally?'" Jon asked.

Stephen frowned. "It's standard language for government contracts. Almost no one objects to it and everyone lives with it."

"Our general counsel will have to review them, of course."

"Of course," Stephen acquiesced.

"You will send us the final version of the contract with the changes we discussed, no?" Josef said. "We will prepare the addenda with the model numbers and price schedule, and after we execute the agreement you will have your first Cygnus systems in twelve weeks."

The six men stood and shook hands across the table. They collected their papers and stuffed them into their portfolios and briefcases. All made for the door except for Stephen and Josef.

"I will stay a little longer to talk with Mr. Quan," Josef explained.

Cooper and Jon shrugged to each other before leaving the room.

"Two point four billion dollars," Cooper whispered to Jon. *"One point two billion a year for two years with an option to extend."*

"The timing couldn't have been better," Jon said.

"Why's that?"

"The divorce decree is final. I signed the papers last week. It cost me a quarter of my assets and the house but Hannah gave up any claims on future earnings. Once I pay her off, everything from Connectrix is mine."

Cooper looked down and pursed his lips. "Well, I'm sure you're relieved to have that behind you. I'm glad for you. And I'm sorry."

"Thanks," Jon said. "And thanks."

❖ ❖ ❖

Josef closed the door, leaving him alone with Stephen. He opened a side door to admit Agent Gutierrez. Josef made the introductions.

"Agent Gutierrez, it's time we brought Mr. Quan up to date on your investigation."

Anibal remained grim-faced as he shook Stephen's hand. "Yes, sir. Mr. Quan, what do you already know?"

"I know that anal son-of-a-bitch who just walked out of here gave classified information to the Chi-Comms." He looked at Josef. "I know that one of your directors, the primary contractor for the system we're about to pay north of two billion dollars for did the same. I *don't* know why I shouldn't blow the whistle on both of them and throw them into federal prison for five hundred years."

"Sir," Anibal said, "I have to agree. Give me the word and I'll reel them in. We have the evidence we need to convict them. And the other two, as soon as I find them."

"What other two?" Stephen asked as he leaned forward.

"The programmer, Bugatti, and his girlfriend," Anibal answered. "We think they're in on it."

"Are you fucking kidding me? Jesus Christ on the cross. Bugatti? But why? We know the deals Ames and Xiao are working, but what's Bugatti's motive?"

"It's complicated," Anibal demurred.

"God damn it, Josef," Stephen growled. "I gave you a free hand to manage this program—*my* program. The Director told me your history and what you did for us in the Cold War. He vouched for you. I figured you knew what you were doing. How did you let it get to this point?"

Josef didn't reply.

"Well?" Stephen insisted. "Tell me. Tell me why we shouldn't round them all up today and end this disaster."

"Stephen," Josef said softly, "we can't afford to be impulsive. We know most of what has been turned over to the Chinese. Once we have the report from your analysts we will have all the pieces of the puzzle."

Josef stood and paced. "Things are not always as they seem, no? And with people's lives at stake we must be certain. We could arrest these—these *spies*—but then we would be unable to gather more information. And we would *never* know the one thing we *must* know."

"And what's that?"

"We must know whom we can trust."

The room fell silent. Stephen looked at Anibal who rolled his eyes sympathetically. He turned back to Josef.

"The Director has absolute trust in you. So I'll play along. But I'll have to report the situation to him."

"Of course, Stephen. You have no choice. It is your duty, no?"

Stephen stood, picked up his briefcase, and walked to the door. As he reached for the doorknob he froze in mid-motion. He looked at Anibal. "Wait a minute. What did you mean, 'as soon as I find them?'"

"Bugatti and the hooker," Anibal answered. "They've disappeared."

34

THE SESSION

TAN YINGQUN'S TASTE in sex ran along conventional lines. What variety he enjoyed came not from *what* he did but from how, where, and with whom he did it.

He had a preference for Asian girls but he held no prejudice against girls of any race. His date for the evening was Trish, a blonde. It was their first session together.

The evening began with a blow job in the kitchenette of Tan's hotel suite, followed by drinks in the living room. Trish gave him a tug in the back of the limo on the way to the restaurant, where she buried her bare foot in Tan's crotch through dinner. On the ride back Tan reciprocated, slipping his hand into Trish's panties as she moaned convincingly.

She was equally convincing in Tan's hotel room, bent over the arm of the sofa as Tan entered her from behind.

"God, baby, you're so big—oh *baby*, fuck me!" she said breathlessly as she scanned her surroundings. Her body jerked forward with each thrust, disturbing her concentration.

"Oooh, not so fast baby. Make it *last.*"

Tan slowed his pace, restoring Trish's focus. She took account of the room arrangement—the layout, the position of the furniture, the objects on the desk—a lamp, some papers, and a laptop computer. On the corner was an envelope stuffed with a thousand dollars in twenties, and next to it, in exactly the same spot it had been when she first arrived, was a spare key card for the suite.

"Mmmh. That's it baby. *Yeah.*"

❖ ❖ ❖

"Nikki, what have you been up to?"

Denice French, proprietor of Top Flight Escorts, had called Nikki Feng to her office after overhearing chatter between two of her girls: Trish, a tall blonde who'd been with Top Flight for nearly a year, and Angie, a petite redhead just a few months with the service.

"Can you narrow it down a little, Denice?" Nikki retorted. "I'm a busy girl."

"Angie and Trish and our client, Mr. Tan. Is that narrow enough?"

Nikki pulled a compact from her handbag and checked her makeup.

"You know what I'm talking about Nikki. Just tell me and save us both some time."

Nikki dressed the line of her lipstick with her pinkie before snapping her compact shut and returning it to her bag. "I can't tell you."

Denice heaved a sigh. "Don't take advantage of me. I don't care if you are a top earner. There are hundreds of skinny Asian girls in the Twin Cities who would love a chance to make some real money."

Nikki pouted.

"And don't mug for me. I've seen that look a hundred times. You've worn it out."

"I really can't tell you, Denice," Nikki answered with uncharacteristic sincerity. "I have a friend in trouble. I'm trying to help her out. That's all I can say."

"What kind of trouble could possibly justify spying on one of our clients?"

Nikki sat in the chair next to Denice's desk and leaned forward with her hands between her knees. She had a desperate look on her face.

"It's really, really bad. And I really can't tell you what it is." She put her hand on Denice's. "I wouldn't have done it if it wasn't serious. Please—don't make me say any more."

It was a side of Nikki that Denice had never witnessed, with none of her usual fawning, overblown attitude.

"Our clients rely on our discretion. Compromise our reputation and we're fucked. Do you understand?"

"Yes."

Denice paused. "How bad is it?"

"Life and death."

Denice consulted a calendar on her desk. "You're with Mr. Rodolfo tonight, seven o'clock. Don't be late."

35

OFF THE GRID

THE OPERATION HAD grown to include six divisions and forty agents, their activities coordinated by Agent Gutierrez from the Minneapolis field office. Josef Hofbauer called every day, sometimes more than once. The Director called twice during the week. Now that he was getting raw reports directly from Anibal, the Director became more worried and his calls grew more frequent. There were many unanswered questions–that was normal for an operation such as this–but Agent Gutierrez was not finding the answers. That gave the Director fits.

Anibal scanned the photographs posted on the walls of his headquarters. Tan Yingqun's movements were easy to track. He continued his well-publicized tour, returning to his Minneapolis hotel room between circuits of bookstores and lecture halls. Alvin's weekly sessions with Tan in the darkened St. Paul bar had ceased. *As long as Xiao doesn't try to leave the country, he'll never know he's being watched.* Jon's activities were unremarkable—his routine took him from his apartment to Connectrix in the morning and back to his apartment in the evening. The agent assigned to Jon filed the same report nightly, almost verbatim.

Gina hadn't been seen since her abduction. Anibal kicked himself for weeks after losing track of the limousine that night in Raleigh. *The wheels are off the fucking cart at the Charlotte office—I should have tailed them myself.* The flow of money from Alvin to Jon to Gina had also stopped, and the balance in Gina's account remained unchanged since she vanished. Her cell phone mailbox was filled with messages from existing and prospective clients, all unanswered. He was sure that Gina, wherever she was, remained in the hands of Chinese agents, but he staked out her apartments in Minneapolis and Eau Claire just to be safe. Anibal had pleaded with Josef to allow him to take Tan into custody after Gina's disappearance but Josef refused. "We must allow events to unfold, Agent Gutierrez," Josef told him patiently. "There is too much we do not know."

Too much we do not know, Anibal repeated silently as continued down the gallery.

Under each photograph Anibal had posted background information on each person of interest, a chronology of events and, in bold lettering, a description of the classified information believed to have been compromised. *Cygnus system specifications: general features, performance targets, technical approach* read the list under Jon's photo; *Cygnus computing module: detailed design* under Alvin's. Anibal wasn't sure what it all meant but his NSA contacts considered most of these revelations to be of minor concern.

There was one item of more than minor concern, under the final photo in the series. Anibal had scrawled *CYGNUS SOURCE CODE* in large red letters. It was this item that weighed on Anibal's mind, and on Josef's, and on the Director's. It was the focal point of the operation and the quest of forty special agents of the FBI.

Anibal stared at the portrait and asked himself the question he'd pondered daily for the last two weeks: *Where is Matt Bugatti?*

❖ ❖ ❖

The chatter in the kitchen was muted and limited to one topic—what was up with Flora? She'd been a terror for days, lecturing the waiters, inspecting every dish on its way to the table, and second guessing the sous-chefs. The tension built to a steady hum and radiated into the dining room until customers could sense the change. A few remarked quietly that their dining experience was not what they'd come to expect at *Da Flora*. Some among the staff said they'd seen Flora this way only once before, in the weeks following Giovanni's death. They nominated Marie to approach her. She found Flora in the cooler, inspecting a bundle of asparagus.

"These stems are like wood," Marie overheard Flora saying to no one. "Am I going have to buy the produce myself? My lord, look at this zucchini. I just know it's all seeds."

Marie took a step forward, making sure that her footsteps were audible. Flora looked up.

"Yes? What is it?" she snapped.

Marie stepped back. "We're worried about you."

Flora stared fiercely but said nothing. Lit from behind by the single bulb at the far end of the cooler, her graying hair formed an electric halo that made her appear even more menacing.

"Don't be." Flora tossed the asparagus and zucchini into their bins. She wiped her hands on her apron and placed them on her hips.

"Anything else?"

"We're worried about you."

Flora remained stern for a moment before her features softened. She closed her eyes tightly, folding her hands together and pressing them to her abdomen. Her breaths came in short convulsions until she recovered her composure.

"You're in charge. Close up for me," she said curtly as she walked past Marie, out of the cooler, and out of the restaurant.

She was about to start her car when she stopped and allowed the thoughts to return, the dark thoughts that had plagued her since the visit from the FBI agent, the thoughts that she had tried to banish by immersing herself in her work. The agent was polite but vague. *We'd like to talk with your son*, he told her. *If you hear from him, please contact me.* Her daily calls to Matt had gone unanswered.

She gripped the steering wheel and pressed her forehead against her knuckles as she sobbed for five minutes, after which she drove herself home under the watchful eye of an FBI agent from the Charlotte field office.

❖ ❖ ❖

The lobby of the downtown Minneapolis Residence Inn was sparsely populated early Saturday evening, making it all the more difficult for Anibal Gutierrez to remain inconspicuous. But the lack of people did have an upside—it was easier to spot a suspicious person. Anibal took a stool at the end of the bar. Nearly the entire lobby was observable, and his visibility was shielded by four loudly enthusiastic Minnesota Twins fans. Anibal read a newspaper but kept one eye on the comings and goings while occasionally sipping a club soda. The cheers and catcalls that erupted periodically from his bar-mates interfered only slightly with the reports coming through his earphone from an agent stationed on the sixth floor where Tan Yingqun rented a suite. Since late afternoon, when Tan returned to his room, the door had remained closed.

"Mic check," the voice in Anibal's ear announced. "No movement."

"Acknowledged," Anibal mumbled into the microphone concealed in his collar. He sipped his club soda, cast one eye toward his paper and the other in the direction of the lobby entrance.

For more than an hour Anibal scrutinized every movement in his field of view. Every ten minutes his earpiece chirped *mic check* to which he replied *acknowledged*. He endured an endless loop of mic checks, club sodas, close plays at second base, and the same drab people shuttling from entrance to desk to elevator. He forced himself to notice details the untrained eye would miss, a trick he used to avoid complacency when observing a person of interest. As people drifted into sight, he mentally described each one with a short phrase.

Big-haired woman. Red-headed hooker. Black businessman. Horny teen couple. Pizza guy. Wannabe cowboy.

Anibal dropped his newspaper.

Pizza guy.

He wore a red and yellow uniform with a red cap and carried what looked like an extra large pie. *What is it about that pizza guy?* Nothing definite—his height and build and the way he walked seemed familiar. He came through the door and headed directly for the elevators hidden around a corner.

Anibal left his paper on the bar and trotted toward the elevators. He turned the corner in time to spot a narrow red and yellow stripe between the doors of the elevator as they closed.

"Tan has a visitor," his earpiece crackled. "Caucasian female, mid-twenties, five-four, one-ten, red hair."

Red headed hooker.

"What's their status?" Anibal whispered hoarsely into his mic.

"The female is in the room. The door is closed."

Anibal kept his eye on the floor indicator of the pizza guy's elevator. It stopped at six.

Fuck me.

"Anyone else up there?"

"Pizza delivery man just exited the elevator. He's headed down the hallway."

"Which way?"

"The other way. Away from me."

The elevator was at floor three on its way to the lobby.

"Keep your eye on him. I'm headed up there."

The elevator doors opened. Anibal rushed in, colliding with the car's passenger who nearly walked over him before stopping to help him up.

Black businessman.

"Oh man, I'm sorry. I left something in my car. I was in a hurry. I wasn't even looking."

The large black man lifted Anibal from the floor and brushed his clothes with the back of his hand.

"Tan and the female are leaving the room," the earpiece said.

Shit.

"Are you all right?" the businessman asked.

"I'm fine. Let go of me."

The man held Anibal's arm a little too tightly for comfort and continued to beat the dust from his clothes.

"Let me clean you up, man. I feel terrible, just terrible. Are you hurt?"

"I told you, I'm fine." Anibal twisted his arm free too late to board the elevator.

"Tan and the female are on their way down," said the persistent voice in his ear. "Have you got them?"

"No, god damn it, I haven't got them," Anibal shouted.

"What?" asked the confused businessman.

"I'm on my way down," the voice said.

"No! Stay on the pizza guy!"

"Shit, man, you're crazy," the businessman said, shaking his head. He walked out the door leaving Anibal fuming.

"I've got Tan and the female," the voice announced.

The door to the second elevator car opened. Tan Yingqun emerged with an attractive redhead on his arm giggling seductively. Anibal turned away from them but kept them in his peripheral vision. The first elevator arrived a few seconds later carrying an inconspicuously dressed FBI agent who immediately left the hotel to follow Tan and his companion from a discreet distance.

Jesus.

Anibal took the vacant elevator, urging it to go faster for the thirty seconds it took to get to the sixth floor. He rushed from the elevator and looked left and right down each hallway. Both were deserted.

He stood by the elevator vestibule at the intersection of two hallways as he pondered his next move. *He wouldn't have gone into the room if he were delivering a pizza—would he? Did we pass each other in the elevator?* He knew there were only three ways in or out of the hotel. He radioed for an agent to cover the back and side doors. He had the front entrance.

Anibal returned to the lobby and took his spot at the bar. *If that pizza guy comes through here I'll spot him.* He picked up his paper. As he reinserted himself into the endless loop another urgent question pricked his mind.

Where have I seen that black guy before?

❖ ❖ ❖

The phone in room 620 rang once. Matt Bugatti answered it.

"He's back at the bar," the caller said.

"Thanks," Matt answered.

Matt checked the hallways before he left the room and headed for the elevators. Next to the elevators stood a table on which an arrangement of silk flowers sat next to the house phone. Matt lifted the phone to find a key card placed there minutes before by an attractive redhead from the Top Flight Escort service of Minneapolis. It was the spare key card for Tan Yingqun's suite.

Matt entered Tan's room and scanned it quickly, confirming the layout, which had been described to him the week before by another Top Flight Escort, a tall blonde. Tan's computer was on a desk in the main room of the suite, turned off and closed. On the opposite side of the room was a couch with tables at either end. Matt took a cell phone from his pocket to which an extended run battery had been attached. He turned on the phone, removed the paper from an adhesive strip and pressed it into place under the couch. Before leaving he replaced the spare key card on the desk next to the computer.

In room 620 Matt got out of the outrageously colored pizza delivery uniform and put on jeans and a sweatshirt. He took the elevator to the lobby and walked quickly to the entrance. Within minutes he'd disappeared into the streets of Minneapolis. Had Agent Gutierrez not been momentarily distracted by a three-run homer, he might have noticed—*kid in a hoodie.*

❖ ❖ ❖

Wang Shutao waited impatiently outside the Minister's office. When the door opened, he rushed in, pushing aside the *Guoanbu* Domestic Affairs bureau chief.

"Wang, my time is limited," the Minister snapped. "Can we get to the point quickly?"

"Some information has come to me, which I must share with you immediately."

"The point, Wang Shutao. Get to it."

"The programmer has disappeared."

The Minister looked pained but not surprised. "Continue," he said.

"He has not contacted Tan Yingqun for nearly two weeks, and our agents have not been able to locate him."

"I was afraid of this. The programmer knows he's in a desperate position and he has taken action. Should we be shocked that he was not content to leave his fate in our hands? Now there is another unknown factor we must account for. And we have lost the initiative."

"Minister, I agree that this development is troubling. But the overall plan is sound."

"Oh yes, the plan," the Minister said wearily. "Xiao's plan. Tell me, Wang, how is the prostitute?"

"That situation at least is under control."

The Minister nodded tentatively. "Locate the programmer. Report to me daily with your progress. As long as his whereabouts are unknown, we are exposed."

◈ ◈ ◈

Monday afternoon was not peak time at the Chippewa Valley Shooting Club. A few regulars were target shooting in the range. The proprietor sat on a tall stool behind the counter with the latest issue of *Shooting Times*, reading an article on polymer handguns. *What Have You Got Against Polymer?* the title asked. The subject had been a regular topic of discussion at the club and it was one on which he'd taken no strong position. He was in the process of forming an opinion when he was interrupted.

"Are you Chuck?"

Chuck looked up at the speaker, a tall man with a pleasant face. "Do we know each other?"

"We have a mutual friend. What have you got in a small, light handgun, easy to conceal?"

Chuck set his magazine aside and pushed himself back from the counter, examining the tall man asking about concealable weapons.

"Who's our mutual friend?"

"Matt Bugatti recommended this place. He told me to go to Chuck if I had, let's say, *special requirements.*"

Chuck eyed the stranger with suspicion. "Yeah. Matt Bugatti. How is the Doc? I haven't seen him in months."

"The Doc has some special requirements."

Chuck decided to play along. "Small and light, right? Easy to hide? Do you want a revolver or a semi? Twenty-two or something bigger?"

"Actually, Matt suggested a SIG P938."

"Nine millimeter. That'll do some damage." Chuck walked to an adjacent display case, placing a mat on the glass top and removing a small semi-automatic pistol from the case.

"This is the *Extreme* model. Three-inch barrel, single-stack seven round clip. A really nice piece. The Doc knows what he's talking about."

"I'll take it."

Chuck touched the gun lightly with his fingertips and turned the pistol grip away from him.

"Don't you want to try it out? Pick it up at least, see how it feels?"

"Nope. Wrap it up. And two hundred rounds of ammo."

Chuck silently replaced the miniature pistol in the glass case. He retrieved four fifty-round boxes of nine millimeter ammunition.

"I can sell you the ammo today. There's a waiting period for the gun. Fill out this paperwork and you can have your weapon in forty-eight hours."

The man leaned slightly closer and spoke softly. "Matt told me you could keep this, you know, out of the system."

Chuck shook his head. "We have rules for a reason."

The man opened his wallet and took out a business card bearing the logo of the Chippewa Valley Shooting Club. He showed Chuck the writing on the reverse side:

Doc, here's my home phone. Call me if you need anything. <u>Anything</u>.
Chuck.

Chuck recognized the card immediately. "Who are you?"

The man held out his driver's license. "I've got nothing to hide."

Chuck accepted the driver's license and verified that it belonged to the man standing in front of him. He took the pistol from under the glass and placed it in its plastic carrying case, bagging it with the ammo.

"That'll be seven-twenty for the gun and sixty for the ammo. Plus tax. I assume this is a cash transaction?"

The man laid nine hundred-dollar bills on the counter. Chuck made change and handed over the bag. He inspected the driver's license one more time before giving it back to its owner.

"Nice doing business with you, Mr. Anson Polk. Give my regards to the Doc."

36

THE CLOUD

MATT BUGATTI'S TYPING slowed, then stopped, overcome with fatigue from another sleepless night. He draped himself across the small kitchen table of Anson Polk's apartment, his arms heavy and his thoughts muddy, after fourteen straight hours of parsing computer code among a dozen different cloud servers, and programming pipelines through which hacked communications could be routed to his makeshift decryption system. Matt rested his head in the crook of his elbow amid an array of computers and a tangle of cables that served as the nerve center of an impromptu surveillance network.

After two weeks the detritus of two bachelors had accumulated in corners where it couldn't be kicked further. The odor of stale laundry and discarded Fritos bags had long since reached a steady state to which both Anson and Matt had become desensitized. Matt remained sequestered in the one-bedroom apartment for the entire time, venturing out just once to plant a modified cell phone in Tan Yingqun's suite, whose purpose it was to monitor the wireless communications between Tan's computer and the hotel Wi-Fi network, and to relay it bit for bit to a secure storage location. The entire cache of data was encrypted, of course, but that was a small obstacle to the man who had discovered how to do in hours what had previously taken centuries. Still, it took some work to adapt his factoring algorithm to a computing platform not built from dedicated hardware specifically designed for the task.

Matt rubbed his forehead and closed his eyes. He cleared his mind and slipped into unconsciousness.

❖ ❖ ❖

"It's damn good to know that even with the whole world hunting your ass you're still keeping up with the latest doll fashions."

Matt woke with a spasm. He took a deep breath and shook his head, then looked to his left to see Anson in the early morning light, bent forward, scrutinizing one of four computer displays on the table. He was completely naked.

"Put your pants on."

"Jealous, amigo?"

"Annoyed. Every morning I have to look at your bare butt. Have a heart."

Anson laughed in a familiar way that comforted Matt. It was almost the same laugh Matt had known before the accident, but a little slower coming, not as loud, not quite as bright. They had talked about the accident just once. Anson never volunteered a word on the subject and Matt was unsure how to bring it up, until one night he asked "How are you doing?" He didn't have to be specific. "I'm okay," Anson said and then he talked for an hour. One *how are you doing* after months of holding back was all it took. The man poured himself out.

"That memory is always with me," he finished. "Whether I'm thinking about it or not."

Anson found an unoccupied pair of pants on the arm of the couch and pulled them on. "What's that thing you're looking at?"

Matt repositioned his keyboard and started typing again. "CraftersMall.com. It's an online store for handmade stuff. As far as I can tell, the Chinese use it to exchange messages."

"No shit. What are they saying?"

Matt stopped typing just long enough to rub his eyes with the heels of his hands. "Don't know yet. I just hacked in a couple of hours ago. I built a pipe to my decryption routine and it'll be a little while before I can break the key."

Anson pulled up a chair. "A little while? I know your hot shit program can crack secret codes but don't you need a big, bad computer to run it on?"

Matt kept typing another six minutes before answering. His fingers flew as he shifted his eyes from one console to another, mindless of his surroundings. Anson leaned back with a nod and a sense of déjà vu. *Don't interrupt when Matt's at the vertex.*

"I partitioned the code out to a dozen cloud servers," Matt said at a break in the typing. "I used your credit card. I hope you don't mind."

"Of course not!" Anson said with mock enthusiasm. "Mi cash es su cash. But just so I won't be shocked when I get my statement, how much am I into this for?"

"A couple of hundred, give or take. I'll pay you back."

Anson laughed in disbelief. "Didn't you say you're selling those boxes to the NSA for three million a pop? And now you're telling me you can put it out in the cloud and do the same thing for chump change?"

Matt rested his head against his forearm, fighting off fatigue for a few more minutes.

"Not *exactly* the same thing. It's not as fast or efficient, but it does the job." Matt stood, took two steps to the couch and collapsed on it. He threw his arm over his eyes.

"Fortunately, it doesn't have to be all that fast. The Chinese are only using two-hundred-fifty-six-bit encryption. It's cooking now. When it's done I'll know."

Within seconds Matt was asleep.

❖ ❖ ❖

Anson turned off the shower and reached for his towel. As the rush of the shower died away he became aware of a persistent beeping. He wrapped himself in his towel and went to find the source.

The scene in the living room was almost the same as Anson had left it twenty minutes earlier, the differences being the ear-splitting tone and the computer display flashing *COMPLETE*. Anson roused Matt, who took a few seconds to awaken and recognize the sound. His computer was signaling that the covert communications that Tan Yingqun had transacted over the past seven months were now readable in clear text. He leapt from the couch and sat in front of the flashing display.

Both Matt and Anson focused on the screen as Matt opened a file stored on a server located in India, not far from Bangalore. It contained a long list of messages, perhaps sixty or more. They scanned the entries, each of which consisted of the date of the communication followed by the subject line. They were all incomprehensible.

Anson turned to Matt. "Do you know anyone who reads Chinese?"

"I do. Someone I knew in grad school. Her name is Connie."

❖ ❖ ❖

Although the problem wasn't overly difficult, the student had obviously struggled with the solution. He'd made no errors, but the proof was missing some steps. The support for some steps was not properly cited, and his language was muddled.

Connie Hu ticked off each step, added comments, and wrote the final score:

Content—7/10
Presentation—3/5

She set the paper aside and pulled the next one from the two-inch stack.

"Connie Hu?"

Connie looked up at a large black man she didn't recognize, standing in the doorway of her office.

"My hours are from ten until twelve."

"I'm not a student. I'm here to ask for your help. Matt Bugatti sent me."

Connie froze for several seconds. "Close the door, please," she said, gesturing for Anson to enter.

Anson took a chair facing Connie.

"What help do you need from me?" she asked.

Anson opened a letter-sized portfolio and removed a folder. "I have some emails I'd like you to look at. They're in Chinese." He placed the folder on Connie's desk and laid his hand on top of it. "Before you look at them, I should tell you they're very sensitive. But Matt told me that you can be trusted. Can you keep this to yourself?"

She tried to swallow but her mouth was too dry.

"Of course. I owe a lot to Dr. Bugatti."

Anson opened the folder. "We tried running these through a translation program but that didn't work very well. We need to know exactly what these emails are saying."

He spread the papers out, pulling one sheet from the middle of the pile. He pushed it toward Connie.

"We're especially concerned about this one."

Connie translated the Chinese characters to herself.

We are pleased with your preparations for the final stage of the operation. The location you have chosen is acceptable. Advise us of the day and time once the programmer contacts you. You are not required to perform the assassination. Our agents will kill the programmer and the prostitute and dispose of the bodies. We rely on you to assure the prostitute that she and the programmer are in no danger. She has been cooperative but it is most important that she suspects nothing.

The sheet of paper began to shake. She laid it on the desk and folded her hands over it.

"Well? The translation looked pretty ominous. There was something in there about *assassination* and *disposal*. It didn't sound good."

Connie picked up a pen and wrote on the paper. She turned it toward Anson.

Davis 9:00 DS774

"What does…"

She shook her head and glanced at the door. Anson rubbed his lip as he studied the woman in front of him. She appeared to be hardly more than a girl. And she looked scared to death.

Anson stuffed the papers back into the portfolio, left the office, and closed the door behind him.

❖ ❖ ❖

Anson entered the Walter Royal Davis Library at 8:45 p.m. It took him a few minutes to locate a sign titled *Stacks Guide*. The fourth line read

DE-GV Floor 4

He took the stairs to the fourth floor. The smell of dust and old paper triggered memories of the hundreds of hours he'd spent in libraries indistinguishable from this one. He made a quick circuit around the stacks. The floor was deserted.

He searched the rows until he came to one labeled

DS550 – DT110

The books on the shelves ranged from old to ancient. The titles on the spines meant nothing to Anson—they were all in Chinese. He came to a section of books labeled with numbers that began with *DS774*. He waited.

Anson was nearly dozing when he was startled by a touch on his arm. As he turned, Connie shrank from him, looking as terrified as she had that afternoon.

Anson pulled the papers from the portfolio and held them out to Connie. "What do these mean?"

She took another step back, then spoke in a whisper. "Dr. Bugatti is in danger. The men who wrote these letters expect him to call to arrange a meeting. When he arrives they will kill him." She looked nervously to either side. "Please, tell him to be very careful."

He held the folder out. "There are dozens of emails here. What else do they say?"

She shook her head. "Not here." She slipped her backpack off her shoulder. She pulled a folded sheet of paper from an outside pocket and handed it to Anson.

"I can translate another one or two. No more. Log onto this account and put the text in an email. Save it as a draft. *Don't send it.* I'll log on once a day and leave you a reply." She shouldered the backpack.

"We can never meet again."

Connie disappeared through an exit. Anson opened the note.

https://www.craftersmall.com
doctor_prime
mersenne57885161

He pocketed the paper, then he drove back to his motel and made a reservation for an early flight the next morning.

❖ ❖ ❖

Connie kept her eyes down as she approached her dormitory. She didn't notice the man in dark clothes waiting in the shadows. She was a few feet from the entrance when he stepped in front of her. He spoke to her in Chinese.

"Hu Zhixian, come with me."

Connie briefly thought of running before nodding meekly and following the man to a nearby car. A second man waited in the back seat. No one spoke until the car was underway.

"Tell me about your meeting with the black American, Hu Zhixian."

Connie looked straight ahead. "He came to my office with copies of emails in Chinese. He asked me to translate them."

"What emails? What did they say?"

"I didn't read them all. I only read one."

The man placed a hand on Connie's arm. "Sister, tell us what you know."

Her eyes remained forward. The streetlights of Chapel Hill gave way to the darkness of the wooded countryside.

"The email said that a programmer and a prostitute would be killed."

"What do you think of that, Hu Zhixian?"

"I don't think anything about it," she said, her voice quavering. She turned to the window. "I was not aware that the People's Government did such things."

The man's hand closed around Connie's arm. "Where did he get the emails?"

"I asked him. He refused to tell me."

"And what did you tell him?"

"I told him his translation was flawed, that he had no need to be concerned."

"That was wise, Hu Zhixian. And what did the two of you discuss at the library?"

Connie looked at the man. "The library was his idea. He insisted." She looked forward. "I told him nothing."

The man patted her arm. "You did well, sister. I'm pleased. Gong Yang, you may stop here."

The driver pulled to the side of the road. The man got out as another car pulled alongside.

"Gong Yang will take you back to your residence."

Connie settled into the seat. The driver put his fingers in his ears. The man drew a pistol from a shoulder holster and fired a bullet into Connie Hu's brain.

37

Change of Plans

Anson sat mute while Matt stared at the note for a long time.

"CraftersMall.com."

"Yeah."

"Have you logged on?"

Anson shook his head. "Not yet."

Matt laid the note on the table amid the tangle of wires. He walked to the window and peeked through a slit in the closed curtains.

"She was scared?"

"Petrified."

Matt turned from the window.

"Here's what we know," he began, counting off the points on his fingers. "The Chinese Secret Service is out to kill me. Connie is collaborating with the Chinese. Yet she confirmed the plan and offered to help us."

"That sums it up."

Matt bit his lip as he looked at the floor.

"Log on to the account. Upload the email with the location of the meeting. Let's find out if Connie's being straight with us."

"Right away, Chief."

"But use a proxy."

Anson grinned. "No tracks, no trail. You're not the only one who knows his way around the Internet."

Matt picked up the note. "Connie and I have been friends for six years. I never suspected." He dropped the note on the table.

"Fuck. First Gina. Now this."

❖ ❖ ❖

A door and two windows were the only points of entry or exit from Anson's apartment. One man watched the windows. Two stood at the door. At three a.m. the only illumination was from a streetlight a half-block away—the parking lot lights had been disabled by shots from silenced pistols.

The layout of Anson's apartment was identical to the one immediately below it. That apartment was vacant. An interested party, the first in weeks, had toured it the previous morning. The serious-looking Chinese man spent an hour in the small flat before deciding he was not interested. He pictured the arrangement in his mind as he stood in the dark at Anson's door.

He stepped back. That was the signal for his companion to kick the door open with one well-practiced blow. He rushed through the door and down the hallway to the rear bedroom. The second man followed him through the door and turned to his right, facing the couch. They fired almost simultaneously. The muffled shots ripped holes in the couch and bed. Both men stopped firing and retreated to the nearest wall, holding their guns at the ready.

They shared the same thought: *That didn't sound right.*

They stood silent and motionless for ten full minutes. The men gingerly made their way along the wall to a central spot, checking each door along the way. They met near a light switch listening for another minute before turning it on.

The living room looked like it had been ransacked. The table was covered with a rat's nest of wires, keyboards and monitors. Two computers lay disassembled on top of the heap, missing their disk drives. The couch was demolished, its stuffing scattered and protruding through gaping tears ripped open by forty-five caliber ammunition. A chair in the middle of the floor sat surrounded by white dust, the by-product of a large rectangular opening that had been sawed in the ceiling.

The Chinese man cursed.

"Report to the ministry that we have failed. We will proceed with the original plan."

❖ ❖ ❖

"Look at this."

Matt turned his laptop so Anson could see it.

The Minister has canceled the planned assassination programmers and prostitutes. It's too dangerous. Loosen the prostitutes at the appointed time and place. Do not hurt her or programmer. This is the minister's direct command.

"What do you make of that?" Anson asked.

"Either they've changed their minds about rubbing me out or they want me to think so." Matt shifted in his chair. "We need a Chinese speaker to look at this."

"It's not your friend Connie," Anson said. "I posted that email three days ago. I just checked it. Nothing."

"God damn it." Matt sat silently for a moment. "Get me one of those phones."

Anson fetched a pre-paid cell phone, one of ten burner phones for which Matt had paid thirty dollars apiece, intending to use each one exactly once. He punched in a number.

"Nels Coffman, please. This is Matt Bugatti calling." A few seconds passed. "Dr. Coffman, it's Matt. I'm fine, thanks. I'm trying to reach Connie Hu."

Anson thought he saw Matt turn pale.

"How long ago was that? And you never talked with her directly? All right. Thank you, Dr. Coffman. Goodbye."

Matt clicked off the phone, holding it in his hand without laying it down.

"What did he say?"

"Coffman got a call from the Chinese consulate. Connie's left the country—for 'personal reasons.'"

"She's dead."

"Yeah. That's a real possibility." Matt opened his wallet and pulled out a business card for the Top Flight Escort Service.

"Time to go to our backup plan." He handed the card to Anson. "Call Nikki again."

❖ ❖ ❖

In his Chapel Hill office Nels Coffman hung up his phone. He also held a business card—*Anibal Gutierrez, Special Agent, FBI.* Nels stared at the card for a moment, then tapped it on his desk. He opened the desk drawer, put the card in it and closed it. Then he went back to work.

❖ ❖ ❖

"This is some crazy shit," Nikki Feng said.

"Tell me," Anson agreed. "How it got this fucked up I don't know."

Nikki paged through the printed emails. "Why didn't you bring these to me in the first place? I could have read them for you."

"We had someone else, someone we've known for years. Anyway, be glad we didn't come to you first. The last person who saw these is probably dead."

"Oh, fuck." She re-read the most recent email.

"This last one definitely says the killing is off…but…" She scanned the email again. "It's different from the rest."

"Different how?"

"Different style. It's not natural. It's almost like they *wanted* to make it easy to translate."

Anson nodded. "That seals it. You'd better get word to Gina."

He took the emails and laid them on the nightstand before getting out of bed and pulling on his pants. He took an envelope containing three hundred dollars from his pocket and held it out.

"Gee, honey, after all we've been through it doesn't feel right to take money from you," Nikki said as she accepted the envelope.

❖ ❖ ❖

Matt and Anson spoke little during the drive to the Prairie Lake Sportsman's Association, a little more than forty-five minutes from their motel. The long, straight stretches of road en route provided unhindered visibility—anyone following them by car would be easy to spot. Anson pulled into the gravel parking lot and took a space to the side of the main building, hidden from the road.

Matt and Anson had become familiar faces at Prairie Lake, a private club which nevertheless allowed non-members to shoot, providing they paid a fee and obeyed the rules. As they entered the range they were greeted by name—*Frankie* and *Duke*.

The pair went through the usual ritual before entering the firing range. Each emptied a magazine into the target before either spoke a word. Anson's competence had improved markedly under Matt's instruction but still fell far short of Matt's deadly skill. As Matt reloaded the magazines, Anson broke the silence.

"So, what's the plan?"

Matt continued to click the cartridges into place, filling one clip and starting on the second. "I don't know." He pressed the bullets into the clip one after the other as he whispered the count to himself—*seven, eight, nine…*

"Are you going to shoot your way out?"

"I don't know," Matt repeated. He finished filling the clip —*fifteen*—and snapped it into the grip of the Beretta. He chambered a round and aimed at the target.

"Shooting is stress relief as much as anything else," Matt said. He squeezed off four shots, each finding the center of his target. "But if I get in a scrape, I want to be at the top of my game."

Anson watched Matt shoot the rest of his rounds. He ejected the empty clip, checked the chamber, and inserted the second magazine. He offered the pistol to Anson. He took it and studied it as it lay in his hand.

"They're going to try to kill you," Anson said. "You have two options—fight or flee. And you don't look like you're fixing to run."

"Once you start running it's hard to stop. The longer you run, the harder it gets."

Anson wrapped his hand around the grip, pointed the gun at the target and sighted down the barrel.

"Fight," he said.

"I've already set up the meeting."

Anson looked at Matt with his eyes wide.

"No shit."

Matt nodded.

Anson aimed again and fired six rapid shots. He removed his finger from the trigger and lowered the pistol to judge the result. There were six neat, round holes scattered in the vicinity of the target's center. It was a respectable performance, especially compared with his first session just three weeks before. He'd never held a pistol in his life—of the fifteen shots from his first clip just four hit the target. *Jesus, I'd be safer downrange*, Matt joked. Anson recalled the quip with a smile as he went through the rest of the magazine, satisfied that if the target were an enemy every round would be either incapacitate or kill.

"I'm coming with you."

"No you're not."

"Yes—I *am*."

Matt took the pistol from Anson and ejected the clip. He began reloading. "I've got to go alone. They're expecting me to come alone. If you're with me they'll freak. If you come separately you'll be followed."

"I never did hear such a crock of shit."

Matt slapped the clip into the pistol and took aim. Anson put his hand on Matt's forearm. Matt turned toward him. He relaxed his grip on the pistol and laid it on the shelf.

"You're not in this alone," Anson said.

"It's my problem. Mine." He let go of the gun. "I got Connie involved and she's dead."

"You don't know that."

Anson tightened his grip on Matt's arm, just enough for emphasis. "You can't do this by yourself."

"The only one I can count on is me."

"That's your dad talking."

"So what if it is?"

"So do you want to die because your dad was a rugged individualist?"

Matt grabbed the gun and began firing, emptying the clip in less than six seconds. The pattern was scattered. One shot missed the target entirely. He ejected the clip and dropped the pistol on the shelf.

"God damn it. God *damn* it." He shut his eyes tightly, tears escaping the corners. "That stubborn bastard. He never could take help from anybody. And he worked himself to death." He walked away from the barrier and dropped into a chair. "The meeting is tomorrow night. We've got work to do."

38

THE REWARD

JON MASSAGED THE cramp from his hand after signing the last of a half-inch-thick stack of papers, the closing documents on a magnificent twelve-thousand-square-foot home in a fenced lakefront compound near Chippewa Falls. The three-million-dollar price was more than he wanted to pay, and there would be another hundred thousand or so on top of that for redecorating and improvements; furnishing the main house and the various out buildings would probably set him back a hundred thousand more. The sheer magnitude of the dollar amount Jon found difficult to square with his sensibilities—the closing procedure, with its interminable procession of forms, had a rarified feel that Jon found unfamiliar and exciting. *I'll have to get used to this*, he thought. During the signing ritual his mind returned again and again to the conversation he'd had with Cooper Hodge a month before.

❖ ❖ ❖

"This valuation is conservative, maybe overly so," Cooper said. "The contract with the NSA *alone* justifies this stock price. Additional sales from other product lines are all upside."

Jon studied the spreadsheet. It showed sales projections and cash flows for the next ten years. The return on capital was high, in the "too good to be true" range. But the phenomenal numbers were easy to defend. The revenue was guaranteed by contract—and the profit was obscene, the value of the company derived from the intellectual products of its people, who would reap the reward.

Cooper's model spat out a price per share at the initial offering and each year for ten years. Jon mentally multiplied the price by the number of shares to which he was entitled as the founder of Connectrix. His mind reeled. "Am I reading this right?"

Cooper grinned with avarice, his eyebrows bouncing. "It's not that complicated, Jon. Do the math." He pointed a pen at a figure on the sheet. "When this stock hits the street, you'll be worth north of six hundred million."

❖ ❖ ❖

"With the recent large order from one of our key customers, and the expansion of our sales in China, we anticipate strong growth in revenue with increased profitability continuing for the foreseeable future."

Alvin leaned close to the speaker phone as he read his prepared remarks, his opening to the analysts' conference call. The news was good—Mechanized Minds had beaten expectations for both revenue and profit by wide margins. The stock had risen fifteen percent over the past month on rumors of booming sales in China. Alvin expected the price to spike another ten percent before the stock market closed that day.

"I'll take questions now."

The operator announced the name of a technology stock fund manager.

"Mr. Xiao, your results in China are truly impressive. You went from a standing start to over fifteen million in sales in less than twelve weeks. But last quarter you warned against overly optimistic expectations of sales in China. You reported startup problems and unforeseen expenses. It was a bleak picture, and now you're blowing away your sales plan. It's hard to believe."

"You can believe it," Alvin said sharply. "The figures have been certified by our auditors."

"Of course we believe the numbers, Mr. Xiao," the analyst said slowly. "I'm complimenting you on your leadership." There was a moment of static-filled silence before the analyst continued. "I just want to know—what's your secret?"

❖ ❖ ❖

At the conclusion of the call Alvin circled the table shaking hands and congratulating his officers until Alvin's assistant interrupted.

"Mr. Xiao, the car is here to take you to the airport."

"Thank you, Melissa." He recovered his briefcase from the table and announced, "Everyone, I'm on my way to Chengdu to celebrate our success with Jimmy and his team. We'll have a proper celebration here when I get back."

He left the room to the sound of applause, turning back once to wave goodbye.

❖ ❖ ❖

The check-in line for the flight to Chicago threaded through the rope lanes and snaked into the distance. Alvin bypassed the line and approached the First Class counter, stepping up and offering his itinerary and passport. The agent took them with a smile.

"Minneapolis-Chicago, Chicago-Beijing, Beijing-Chengdu. Long trip, Mr. Xiao!" He verified Alvin's passport and checked his visa.

"How many bags?"

"Just one to check," Alvin answered, placing his bag on the scale.

The agent tapped his keyboard before coming to a sudden halt.

"Is there a problem?" Alvin asked.

The agent stared blankly at his terminal. "Nothing, sir. Will you excuse me?"

Alvin craned his neck after the agent as he walked the length of the counter to a doorway at the far end. He emerged a few seconds later following a short woman with glasses and a scowl. The two of them examined the screen. The woman peered over the terminal at Alvin.

"Just a moment, Mr. Xiao," she said. She pointed, drawing the agent's attention to the terminal screen. The agent bent forward, then stood, looking first at the woman then at Alvin.

"There's been a mix-up, Mr. Xiao," the woman said. "It seems your seat on the flight to Beijing has been assigned to another passenger."

Alvin frowned. He was about to speak when the woman cut him off.

"It's not a problem, sir. We'll take care of it. We'll find a place for the other passenger. Donald will print your boarding passes."

The agent completed the transaction and handed three boarding passes to a relieved Alvin. He picked up his briefcase and made his way to security.

Donald and the woman watched until Alvin was out of sight.

"What do we do now?" Donald asked.

"Put the bag aside," the woman said. She pointed to the terminal again. "And call that number."

❖ ❖ ❖

Alvin gulped the last of his gin martini as he heard his flight called in the airline lounge. He reached the gate just as the general boarding announcement was made. He joined the First Class line, reaching into his jacket to retrieve his boarding pass. As he did so he felt a hand grip his right arm. He jerked instinctively but the grip remained firm. A second hand grabbed him from the left.

"Mr. Xiao," said the shorter of the two men, the swarthy one, with dark, wiry hair. "We need you to come with us."

Alvin looked at each of the men in turn. "I'm getting on this plane!" he objected, trying unsuccessfully to break their grip.

"We can't let you do that." The man produced a wallet and flipped it open. It bore a gold shield and an ID with a photo of the wiry-haired man, the name *Anibal Gutierrez* and *FBI* in letters so large they turned Alvin's stomach. The two led Alvin away, leaving behind a crowd murmuring speculations.

❖ ❖ ❖

Alvin sat quietly at the table in the middle of the small room, eyes down, not looking at the FBI agent sitting in the corner. He closed his eyes but couldn't close his ears to the tapping of the agent's fingers on the frame of his chair, or the fluorescent light buzzing overhead, boring a hole in his brain.

He replayed the past ten months in his mind. He considered his options—deny, bargain. It was a short list. He thought up explanations and excuses, repeating them to himself, biting his knuckle as he imagined how they would sound to someone else. He squeezed his eyes shut and bit his knuckle harder as he realized that he was no longer in control —and would not likely be again in the foreseeable future.

Twenty minutes after he'd been pulled from the boarding gate, the door to the room opened. Anibal Gutierrez entered. He held the door for Josef Hofbauer.

"Josef!" Alvin cried. "What's this all about?"

Josef closed the door behind him. "I didn't intend for it to happen this way but your travel plans have forced my hand."

"I don't know what you mean," Alvin said anxiously. "I've got to get out of here. I've got a plane to catch."

"Alvin, before you say anything, you should listen to what Agent Gutierrez has to say, *Ja?*"

Anibal read from a card he had ready, one that he carried with him at all times. He read carefully, word for word, so there would be no mistakes and no misunderstandings.

"You have the right to remain silent. Anything you say can be used against you in a court of law. You have the right to an attorney and to have an attorney present during any questioning."

As Anibal read from his script, Alvin looked from face to pitiless face. He bent forward, head in hands, and sobbed.

❖ ❖ ❖

"Anything interesting?" the agent asked.

The contents of Alvin's briefcase were laid out on the table. The FBI technician was taking photographs.

300

"Laptop. It's encrypted but nothing our guys can't unlock. The usual pile of accessories. File folders—a bunch of reports and graphs and stuff." He continued down the length of the table.

"Then there's this." He picked up a flat, square object. It was cardboard, covered with patterned paper. The surface was worn and the edges frayed. The agent took it from him.

It opened like a book. Inside was a monochrome photo in sepia tones—a family portrait of a man, his wife, and their infant son. Along the right border was a column of Chinese characters.

"I don't suppose you've translated this writing."

"Not yet," the technician replied. He took the last of his pictures. "Funny thing. Most of this stuff looked like it was tossed in the case without much thought." He pointed at the portrait. "That thing was in a pocket all by itself."

39

Suspicion of Espionage

THE EIGHTY-MILE drive north of Eau Claire took Matt along back routes through dense woods, far from human habitation. He was running on pure adrenaline, having slept little since the previous evening, his mind churning through alternate scenarios with different likelihoods, hoping he could construct an equation with a known outcome. He could not. There were too many variables—*independent* variables—over which he had no control.

I'll just have to trust.

He thought back to the call he made to Flora that morning, his first in nearly a month. Constructing an alternate reality for his mother's sake was vastly less complicated than his real life. *I'm all right*, he lied to her, and *it's not as bad as it sounds* when she told him about the visit from the FBI agent. Flora wept with relief and with renewed dread and Matt made a promise to call her again the next day without knowing if he could keep it.

Near the halfway point Matt's phone chimed. The display read *Anson*. He answered, "How does it look?"

❖ ❖ ❖

The last stretch of road led across an old bridge over a broad and deep creek bed, wet with early summer rain but many times wider than the flow it contained. After crossing he took a sharp turn to the north and slowed to a crawl. To his left was a dense stand of trees; to his right was an open field, broken by the creek bed, bordered by more trees he judged to be fifty yards away, the waxing moon hanging just above them, the far side of the clearing cloaked in shadow.

Matt turned his car from the road. As he turned, the beam of his headlights swept the distant tree line. He stopped when a flash caught his eye, the reflection of his headlights off the grille of a black SUV.

❖ ❖ ❖

The man stepped behind a tree as Matt's headlights swept by. From where he stood he could see the entire field—the black SUV he'd left forty-five minutes earlier, the red coupe on the far side of the field, and the broad ravine that separated them. He aimed his rifle at the coupe and sighted through the scope at the driver's side window. He didn't have a clear shot, but it wouldn't have mattered if he had. The agreement was to wait until the programmer and the prostitute were together and to take them at the same time. With a second sniper waiting in the trees to the south, aiming from a different angle, the chances for a successful kill were high.

The man had no time to think as the weapon pivoted upward, the rifle torn from his hands, the eyepiece of the scope digging into his eye socket, an arm encircling his neck. He raised his hands to grab the head of his attacker and throw him forward but the move was anticipated. The two of them fell backwards and hit the ground hard. The man saw a flash as a rifle butt crashed into his cheekbone before he passed out.

Anson Polk stood over the unconscious Chinese agent and the man who disarmed him. They appeared in shades of green in his night vision goggles.

"That was damned impressive," Anson whispered.

"Thanks," Chuck whispered back.

❖ ❖ ❖

The lights of the SUV flashed on. Its door swung open and Tan Yingqun emerged, half hidden by the open door. Lifting his hand to shield his eyes from the light, he surveyed the scene, then, after a few moments, circled the vehicle and opened the passenger door. He helped Gina out of the SUV, holding her by the arm.

Her appearance was distinctly less stylish than usual. She wore a sweater and jeans, and running shoes instead of heels. A backpack replaced her ever-present handbag. Tan held her arm tightly and Gina didn't resist. Even in the dim light Matt could see fear in her eyes.

"Dr. Bugatti," Tan cried out, "are you alone?"

Matt pulled the handle of the door and pushed it open. He leaned slightly out of the opening.

"I'm alone," Matt answered. "Gina, are you all right?"

"I'm scared, Matt." Her voice was thin and quavering in the still night.

"It's almost over," Matt called back. He stepped from the car but remained behind the open door. "What happens now, Tan?"

"Our scientists have verified your code. You've fulfilled your end of the bargain."

"Then let her go."

Tan pulled Gina forward and let go of her arm. She gave Tan a brief look before walking toward Matt, reaching the edge of the creek bed after a few steps. She turned sideways to make her way down the side of the depression, stepping gingerly.

❖ ❖ ❖

Anson and Chuck watched Gina approaching the ravine; to the south, two more members of the Chippewa Valley Shooting Club watched and waited, one with a rifle and the other with a pistol pressed against the head of a Chinese *Guoanbu* agent.

❖ ❖ ❖

Gina's footing faltered as the gravel gave way. She hit the ground and slid down the side of the creek bed and disappeared into the darkness.

Oh Jesus, Matt whispered. *Not part of the plan.* He bolted from the car toward the ravine.

❖ ❖ ❖

"Shit," Anson said. "Now what?"

Chuck raised his rifle and aimed. "We improvise."

Two puffs rose from the ground near Tan's feet where rifle rounds struck. Tan spun in the direction from which the shots came, looking confused, then terrified, as a third bullet hit the ground, missing his foot by inches. He dived into the SUV and slammed the door closed.

❖ ❖ ❖

Matt ran hunched down toward Gina, finding her crouched on the ground in ankle-deep water. Matt wrapped one arm around her, positioning himself between Gina and the SUV, pulling her to the side of the creek just as the *crack* of three rifle shots echoed.

"Here," Matt whispered, pressing a SIG P938 nine-millimeter pistol into her hand. "Get to the trees. I'll give you a signal when it's clear. We've taken care of the two guys in the woods."

"You mean three."

Matt's jaw dropped. "Tan?"

She shook her head. "No, not Tan. Someone else. They had me blindfolded but I'm sure there were three men besides me and Tan."

Independent variable, Matt thought. "Get going," he said.

Matt signaled to Gina to move downstream with a gentle push. He moved quickly and silently in the opposite direction, bent over slightly to avoid the glare of the headlights. As he walked, nearly running, the fingertips of his right hand touched the center of his chest and slid along the curve of his torso until they contacted the grip of the Beretta cradled in its holster under his left arm. He felt the serrated texture of the grip under his fingers, as familiar to him as the feel of his own stubbled chin. His index finger came to rest alongside the trigger guard as his other fingers curled around the grip. His thumb found the safety and released it as he drew the pistol from the holster in a smooth motion, practiced to the point of unconscious proficiency, all in the space of a half-second.

"Doc!"

Matt raised his head to see a Chippewa Valley shooter step out of the trees near the south end of the clearing, holding his rifle at his side. Before Matt could react he heard a rifle shot from behind him, on the opposite side of the road. The man in the clearing jerked backwards, dropping his rifle and clutching his chest as he collapsed to the ground.

His companion holding the Chinese agent at gunpoint jumped up without thinking but took only a step before his captive tripped him. He'd rolled on his side when a knee came down on his neck with terrible force. After convulsing for a few seconds he lay still. The Chinese agent lifted his arms and thrust them downward, forcing his arms apart and snapping the plastic ties that bound him. He retrieved his pistol and crouched at the edge of the clearing.

"Fuck me," Chuck said under his breath. "Put your goggles on, Mr. Polk. Time to take the high ground." With two shots he took out the headlights of Matt's car.

Matt understood. He took aim and shot out the headlights of the SUV.

Fourteen he counted down the rounds. *Thirteen.* The clearing was in total darkness.

Matt took up a new position further upstream, feeling his way along the rough terrain. He stopped and remained still. Minutes passed in the night, as soundless as it was dark.

Matt tensed as he heard the sound of rocks sliding down a slope, followed by silence. After a breathless moment the sound repeated.

"Anson?" he whispered.

Four shots erupted from close range. Matt plastered himself against the wall of the ravine as the shots struck the ground, showering him with debris. Without thinking he returned fire.

Twelve. Eleven. Ten.

Matt scrambled further upstream, struggling to maintain his footing. Another shot struck the ground behind him. He fell back against the ground, rolled, and fired.

Nine. Eight.

He heard a cry of pain. He moved on.

❖ ❖ ❖

The agent grabbed his thigh. He could feel the blood seeping into his pants as he pressed his fingers into the wound. It was a deep crease in his flesh—a grazing hit; painful, but not disabling. He considered binding the wound with his shirt but time didn't permit it. The programmer was getting away.

❖ ❖ ❖

Matt kept moving, staying low, putting more distance between him and his pursuer. The slope became steeper and his footing more precarious. He struggled to keep his balance when his foot came down on a baseball-sized rock. It rolled under his weight.

Matt's left leg folded under him as he fell. He felt a sharp pain in his knee just before he pitched forward. His fingers dug into the soil as he slid down the slope, off the edge of a fissure and into empty space. He landed on his back, half submerged in the creek.

His gun hand was empty.

Two bullets flew over him, close enough that he felt a disturbance in the air, followed by a shower of gravel as they buried themselves in the wall.

Matt began to search for his pistol on the creek bottom. He tried to reconstruct his fall, estimating the point at which he lost his pistol and guessing at possible resting places for the gun. Waves of panic welled up as his search grew more frantic. Over the soft splashing he heard footsteps running toward him—just one set, he thought. He stopped his search and kept still.

The footsteps approached in a run, increasingly louder, until they stopped, followed by a thud and a grunt as a Chinese agent fell into the ravine, landing at Matt's feet.

The agent's arm was pinned under his body, his gun inches from his fingertips. Before he could free his hand he saw a flash of light and felt a searing pain, his head snapping back as Matt's heel struck him full in the face.

Matt landed a second blow before the agent recovered. He wrapped his hands around Matt's ankle and pulled himself on top of him. Matt tried to strike back with his other foot but each attempt sent an agonizing wave up his thigh and into his back. He was trying to pull himself away when a hand closed around his throat and forced his head under water.

Matt grabbed the arm that held him under with both hands but he had no leverage—the man trying to drown him held him under with all his weight. He nearly managed to pull the man's fingers away when a second hand encircled his throat and squeezed until Matt began to feel his consciousness slip away.

No, he thought. *Not now. Not like this.*

His field of vision brightened, filled with vague shapes that sharpened into focus. He stood next to Flora at Giovanni's bedside, the life-support machinery performing its function, sounding mechanical and entirely un-human. *No heroic measures*—that was Giovanni's wish. Flora nodded a signal and the doctor flipped a switch. The machinery went silent except for a soft beep at each heartbeat. After a minute the rhythm faltered and the beep became a continuous tone. *Is that all there is to it?* Matt wondered. *Can it be that easy to let go?*

Matt's struggles weakened. One arm fell to his side as he tried to lift himself out of the water. His hand instinctively searched the creek bottom for a firm handhold when it came across a hard object.

Half aware, his hand closed around the thing, acting as much out of instinct as deliberate agency. It had a familiar feel—his hand recognized its shape and texture and communicated the realization to his semi-conscious mind.

Beretta.

Matt's hand broke the surface of the water, unnoticed by the man on top of him until the muzzle of the pistol pressed against his breastbone. He pulled the trigger.

He vaguely perceived the muffled report, followed by the loosening of the grip on his throat and the weight of a lifeless body pressing him down. He grappled with new found strength, rolling the dead man off of his chest. He sat up, sputtering to catch his breath.

Seven.

Matt froze with the body of the Chinese agent still pinning his legs, cold water flowing around him, gurgling softly. The pain in his leg had subsided to a dull ache. Then he tried to stand. He felt a jolt from his leg like an electric shock. He inhaled sharply and bit his lip to avoid crying out. Inch by inch he slid himself out from under the dead agent, each movement causing another blast of searing pain. At last he freed himself and struggled on his good leg to a standing position.

From his right came the sound of rocks splashing into the creek. Matt spun and fired at the sound.

"Jesus, Matt, hold your fire! It's me!"

Matt recognized Anson's voice. As he looked up he could just make out a silhouette against the stars and a ghostly green glow from Anson's night vision goggles. The glow moved closer. Matt felt a hand grabbing his forearm.

"Do you want to take your finger off that trigger?" Anson said, straining to pull Matt from the ravine. "I know you're firing blind but you could still hit me at this range."

Matt put his finger on the outside of the trigger guard and engaged the safety. He slipped the gun into his holster. Anson surveyed the scene, his gaze settling on the dead man in the creek.

"Shit. Did you…"

"Yeah," Matt said. "He didn't give me a choice."

Anson lifted Matt's arm around his shoulder and began the climb up the wall of the gulley. "Where's Gina?" he asked.

"In the trees, I hope. What's the situation up there?"

"Chuck has one of the Chinese guys under guard. I have to assume that the other one is still in custody. One of our guys is down." He stopped and looked over his shoulder at the corpse. "Sorry we missed that one."

Matt grunted with each step but said nothing.

"We'll get out of this hole and circle back to Chuck. Then…"

Anson stopped. In the distance he saw a bright green glow —an infrared lamp attached to a pair of night-vision goggles. They were worn by a Chinese agent who at that moment had a pistol aimed directly at Matt and Anson.

Matt screamed in pain as he and Anson hit the ground, just under the paths of two bullets. Matt drew his pistol and released the safety. He laid down a pattern of fire in the darkness, emptying his clip. The agent crouched as the bullets flew around him. Every shot missed its mark.

I'm sorry Dad, Matt thought. *I lost count.*

As the agent stood and took aim Anson leveled his pistol at the glowing figure. Before he could pull the trigger his field of vision was flooded with intense light. He shut his eyes tightly as he tore the goggles from his face.

The Chinese agent did the same. Before he could recover Chuck stepped from his Humvee and trained his rifle on the Chinese agent in the full glare of his off-road lights. The agent gently lowered his pistol to the ground and raised his hands.

"Doc, Polk, are you okay?" Chuck shouted.

"Matt's banged up," Anson shouted back. "But we're cool."

The driver's side door of the SUV sprang open. Tan Yingqun tumbled out, shouting, nearly stumbling, waving a weapon crazily. He fired in Matt's direction, missing wide to the right. He steadied himself and aimed again.

A shot hit Tan and spun him around, his gun flying from his hand as he lost his balance and fell forward, a bullet from Gina's SIG P938 lodged in his shoulder.

Gina stepped from the shadows of the tree line with her pistol still aimed at the writhing Tan. "Six," she said, loud enough for Matt to hear.

A commotion of light and sound filtered through the trees at the south end of the clearing. An assortment of vehicles rounded the corner and lined up along its length: three squad cars and an ambulance flashing and squealing. They left a space in the middle where a dark late-model Ford appeared, stopping just forward of the line.

The sirens stopped as the doors of the squad cars flew open. Six officers in full body armor took positions with weapons raised and ready. The flashers continued to paint the trees in red and blue as the door of the unmarked car opened and Special Agent Gutierrez stepped out. He had no bullhorn or other means of amplification. He didn't need them.

"FBI. On your knees. Weapons on the ground. Hands behind your heads. Do it!"

❖ ❖ ❖

One officer helped Matt and Anson hobble up the embankment, while a second officer followed with a rifle. As the four of them approached the line of vehicles, Chuck and Gina disappeared into one squad car and the last Chinese agent was corralled into another. Tan lay on a stretcher by the ambulance, moaning. The officers led Matt to Anibal.

"Are you Matteo Bugatti?" he asked.

Matt looked directly into Anibal's eyes. "Yes."

"Dr. Bugatti, I'm Agent Gutierrez, FBI."

"Yeah," Matt answered, "You're the guy who's been following me around for the last year."

Shit, Anibal thought. *I'm losing my game.*

"Tell me, Agent Gutierrez. What happens now?"

Anibal signaled the officer, who pulled a pair of handcuffs from a pouch on his belt. The officer pulled Matt's arms behind him and snapped the cuffs into place.

"What happens is I place you under arrest," Anibal answered. "Suspicion of espionage."

40

COMPLIMENTS OF THE PEOPLE

IT WAS A quiet night in the infirmary of the Hennepin County Public Safety Facility. Angie Dowell, the nurse on duty, treated the usual mid-week clientele: three bar brawlers too drunk to feel pain as she sutured their wounds—they'd sleep it off and be out by midday; one *resisting* with scalp lacerations, a cracked rib and two broken knuckles. None were life-threatening, but nothing ever was—critical cases were taken to Emergency. Her job was to administer *reasonable and medically necessary care*—just enough to relieve pain or avoid loss of function. Stitches and pain killers were the mainstay of her medical repertoire.

Angie's last case cleared at two a.m. By two-thirty her paperwork was done. By three she was on her second crossword puzzle. The routine had become familiar after twenty-seven years.

"Hi, Angie."

Angie looked up at the night officer, behind him a young man, mud-stained from head to foot, favoring one leg, hands manacled behind him and eyes cast down. At his arm was a third man in khaki pants and a zippered jacket, which bore the badge of a U.S. Marshal.

Angie's eyes shifted from one man to the next.

"What've we got here, Dennis?"

"Federal arrestee. We're holding him here for arraignment."

"Federal, eh? Haven't seen one of those in awhile."

"Five more upstairs, Angie, and four went to the hospital. Two of them to the morgue. Guess there was some nastiness up past St. Croix."

"You don't say." Angie looked over the young man, who never looked up. "Well, Dennis, I guess you and the marshal need to get this young fella in the exam room."

Angie observed the man's movements as he limped forward. He obviously felt intense pain any time his left foot contacted the floor, which it did for only a split second at a time. She followed him and the two officers into the room.

"On the table, gents," Angie commanded. They lifted the injured prisoner over the edge of the table and slid him across the cracked vinyl. He leaned forward to accommodate his handcuffed wrists behind him.

"Left leg, son?"

He nodded. "Yeah."

"Dennis, can you get his pants off of him?"

The marshal held the man's arm as Dennis undid the man's pants. He grimaced and drew a sharp breath as they came off.

Angie studied the disfigured left knee, swollen and purple.

"Does this hurt?" she asked in a clinical tone as she pressed an index finger into the spot she judged to be location of the lateral collateral ligament.

The man pinched his face and gave out an involuntary groan.

"You got a sprain, son. I can give you some Motrin and a cortisone shot—that'll ease the pain and keep the swelling down a little bit. Dennis, I don't suppose you could get him some ice, could ya?"

Dennis shrugged. The marshal remained impassive.

"Ya, I thought not. He should see a doctor, you know?" She turned back to the young man. "Did that knee make a popping noise when you hurt it?"

"I don't remember," Matt answered. "I was being shot at when it happened."

❖ ❖ ❖

No natural light penetrated to the holding cell where Matt spent a fitful night and some part of the following day. The events of the previous day slipped in and out of Matt's thoughts like stills from a movie that flashed for an instant, caused a surge of adrenalin, and then faded as he pushed them aside until they forced their way back into his mind. The mug shots. The body search. He surrendered his clothing and personal things in exchange for the orange jumpsuit that hung on him like a drop cloth tossed hastily over a spindly chair. He was offered a phone call, which he declined—four in the morning was the wrong time to break the news to his mother that he was a federal prisoner, and anyone else he might have called he was sure had abandoned him or was in custody. The night officer escorted him to his cell where he lay for twelve hours, stripped of all possessions and dignity.

"Bugatti, you have a visitor."

Matt picked his head up off his cot and blinked wearily at the guards. There were two of them, a big, doughy white man holding a key and shorter black man holding what looked like two pairs of cuffs connected by a length of chain.

"Who is it?"

"I don't announce 'em by name, inmate," said the white guard. "Get up and stand in the middle of the cell."

Matt obliged. The white guard opened the cell and stood with one hand on the door and the other on the butt of his pistol. The second guard entered and manacled Matt's feet and hands. Matt shuffled forward as the two guards led him to the visiting area, covering just over twelve inches with each step, the maximum distance the chain on his legs would allow.

The room was narrow and long, lined on one side with a shelf, steel stools bolted to the tile floor between dividers on which hung phones tethered to the wall by cables. Through the thick glass barrier Matt could see an empty chair across from each stool. They were ordinary chairs, not fastened to the floor.

The guards led him to the farthest position. Occupying the chair on the visitor's side of the window, looking fresh and well-rested, was Gina Bianchi.

She looked startled at the sight of the gaunt, chained figure in the absurd orange jumpsuit. Her mouth dropped open and her eyes moistened.

Matt took the seat on his side of the glass partition. He took the receiver in both hands and pressed it to his ear as Gina did the same.

"Hi," he said.

"Matt, are you all right?"

"I'm okay." They looked at each other uncertainly before Matt continued. "What happened after they took you in?"

Gina looked sideways as she answered. "They questioned me for an hour or so. They released me but they told me not to go anywhere. They haven't charged me with anything but I'll probably have to testify."

She turned back to Matt. Her hand inched forward until her fingertips touched the glass. "A lot of what I told them they already seemed to know."

"That makes sense," he laughed. "They watched every move I made for months."

She smiled. "You had them guessing for a while, though. They asked me where you were. I don't think they had a clue."

"What did you tell them?"

"That I didn't know. I told them how Nikki kept us in touch after you found me in Minneapolis." She pressed her palm to the glass. "I told them about the messages from China. I told them we knew they were going to kill us."

She leaned forward, pushing her hand further up the glass. The look in her eyes took Matt by surprise—a look of caring, but unlike any he'd seen in the entire time he'd known her. He realized he was seeing, perhaps for the first time, a sincere expression of feeling.

"I told them what you did for me," she said. "I told them you saved my life."

"You didn't look like you *needed* help. When did you learn to shoot?"

"Right after our trip to the shooting club. I took some lessons. It seemed like a useful skill."

She looked down. She dropped her hand to the ledge in front of her.

"Gina."

She looked up. "Yes?"

"How much did they pay you to be their prisoner?"

"It was a lot," she said factually. "Even the half they paid me up front was seven figures." She paused and clenched her jaw. "I didn't know that they never intended to pay me the rest."

Matt shook his head. "I can't believe they let you run free. Why didn't they keep you locked up?"

"They kept a close eye on me, but lock me up? That's a deal-breaker." She smiled. "It's all about the negotiation."

"What are you going to do now?"

She looked toward the ceiling as if she were considering all her options. "I like what I'm doing."

"I'll bet," Matt said, looking away.

Gina put her hand back on the glass. He turned back to her. "I loved you, you know."

She looked hurt. Matt couldn't tell if the look was genuine or pretended.

"I loved you, too," she said.

"Gina, after all we've been through, can we at least be honest with each other?"

"Matt, I love all my clients—when I'm with them."

Matt nodded as if he were accepting, finally, what he should have known all along but couldn't admit to himself.

"Gina, why are you here?"

"I wanted to see if there's anything I could do for you."

He thought about the question. "Do you know any lawyers?"

She smiled. "Yes. Quite a few, actually."

❖ ❖ ❖

More time passed. Matt judged it to be a day based on the number of meals the guard brought. Each meal was delivered with the same declaration, invariably followed by a laugh as the guard amused himself with his own cleverness:

"Compliments of the people!"

Matt forced himself to eat everything despite his lack of appetite. He tried to make conversation with the guards, hoping they would divulge some information about his status, but they volunteered nothing. From the time he was taken into custody the only information he was asked for were his blood type and next of kin. Apart from Gina's visit, Matt was isolated from the world. He would spend another restless night and eat another breakfast—compliments of the people—before that would change.

"Hey, Bugatti. It's your lucky day. You're getting out."

The same two guards who'd taken him to the visiting area stood outside the cell. Neither of them carried chains.

Matt sat on the edge of his cot, hands between his knees, looking at the officers with suspicion. "How can I be getting out? I haven't even been charged yet."

"Fuck if I know," said the pasty white guard. "I *follow* orders. I don't *analyze* them." He unlocked the door and swung it open. Matt sat erect but remained on the cot.

"Well, come on, come on, let's get going."

The three of them left the lockup single-file with the white guard in the lead and the black guard bringing up the rear. They took an elevator up one floor and followed a circuitous route through corridors with blank walls and occasional doors of frosted glass, some with numbers and some with titles—*Public Defender, Deputy Detention Officer*—each of which reminded Matt of where he was and how much he wanted to be someplace else.

At the end of the last hallway the three of them trooped through a door into a room Matt recognized as the same one he'd entered days before. As he turned the corner he recognized his benefactor, who stood and greeted Matt with a nod and a smile on a face lined with concern. Matt smiled back.

"Well, Dr. Bugatti, I'm sure you're anxious to get home, no? *Ja?*"

41

ILLEGAL RETENTION

JON AMES TURNED in before nine p.m. anticipating an early start in the morning. Since vacating his house after the divorce, he'd lived alone in an apartment, a situation he hadn't had to endure since his first job out of college. He hated it. But this was the last night. In the morning he would move to his estate.

He had no household goods to speak of—the furnishings went to Hannah in the settlement. What he did take with him he'd have delivered from storage the next day. He would spend most of the morning going through the punch list with the contractors, and the afternoon overseeing the preparations for the housewarming party that evening. He would rely on the event planner and the caterer to do most of the work (under his personal supervision, of course). It would be a celebration to remember, marking the endpoint of a long journey that started with the founding of Connectrix, the pinnacle of a twenty-five year career. Jon slept soundly.

The doorbell failed to wake Jon—it took a full minute of persistent knocking to rouse him. Jon had a hard time getting his bearings but after a few seconds he located the clock on the dresser. It glowed *1:47*.

Jon pulled on a robe and stumbled to the door. Through the peephole Jon could make out the hazy image of two men in dark jackets, each with yellow block letters over the left breast. The letters were partly obscured by the folds of their unbuttoned lapels but Jon thought they read *FBI*. He opened the door just wide enough to expose his face, and for him to see the two men clearly, and the four men behind them in riot gear, carrying automatic weapons.

"Are you Jon Ames?" the agent in front asked.

Jon blinked hard to clear his vision. He shook his head to wake himself up. "What's this about?"

The two men brandished badges and IDs. "I'm Agent Lémieux, FBI. This is Agent McMullen. Are you Jon Ames?"

Jon's drowsiness dissipated. He gripped the edge of the door and narrowed the opening until just half his face was visible.

"I can't let you in unless you have a warrant."

Agent Lémieux closed his ID and slipped it into his jacket. He removed a paper with the same motion and held it at eye level.

"In fact, I do have a warrant authorizing me to search these premises and to detain Jon Ames for questioning on a charge of espionage." He held the warrant closer. *"Are you Jon Ames?"*

Except for the name, and the description of the particular place to be searched and the things to be seized, the warrant was identical to the one Agent Gutierrez was serving to Matt Bugatti at that same moment, eighty miles to the north.

❖ ❖ ❖

Josef Hofbauer's taste ran toward luxury touring cars, preferably of German make. He drove a BMW 7 Series sedan. He was satisfied with its features and performance, and he especially appreciated its comfortable, quiet ride on long drives, such as the one from Minneapolis to Eau Claire.

It was early afternoon before they began the drive. Matt wore a fresh change of clothes that Josef had brought to the jail. After processing out of custody and changing out of his government-issued jumpsuit, Josef drove Matt to a hospital where a doctor examined him and his knee was x-rayed. *No permanent damage*, he assured Matt. *Stay off it.* He immobilized the leg in an air cast, prescribed medication, and recommended that he see his own doctor if his condition didn't improve. The entire procedure took less than an hour. It was clear to Matt that Josef knew the doctor well, and had personally prevailed upon him to see Matt on short notice.

The first thirty minutes of the drive passed wordlessly. Matt was distracted by his throbbing knee until the pain killers kicked in. Josef was content to drive until Matt broke the ice.

"Josef, what's my situation?"

Josef pursed his lips, keeping his eyes ahead. "That's a little complicated. After all, you turned over classified information to a foreign power. How do you think you should answer for that?"

Matt studied Josef's profile for some sign of his temperament. He found none.

"I did what I had to do."

"You could have gone to the authorities, no?" He glanced at Matt. "You could have come to me, no? *Ja?*"

"Could I? I don't think so." Matt looked out his window at the passing scenery. "Look at it from my perspective. Jon, Gina, the NSA, the FBI, the Chinese—*you*—all of you have your own agendas. It took me awhile to figure that out, but I realized that, for all of you, my well-being was not a top priority. I suppose I could have come to you, or the FBI. But not without knowing one thing." He turned back from the window. "I had to know who I could trust."

Josef's head twisted quickly toward Matt, eyebrows raised.

"Indeed?" He faced forward. A faint smile appeared on Josef's face as he nodded. "*Ja.* That is a sentiment I can appreciate."

They drove in silence for a moment before Josef continued.

"To answer your question, I have arranged for the espionage charge against you to be reduced to *illegal retention of data.* In exchange for your cooperation, this charge will be dropped."

"That's very generous. But why? What about the classified information? What about state secrets I gave to the Chinese?"

Josef gave Matt a look of as if the two of them shared a secret known by no one else. "But that's not exactly true, *ja?*"

Matt nodded, leaning back against the headrest and smiling.

"You've kept dozens of NSA scientists quite busy over the past year, Dr. Bugatti. They have analyzed and verified and debated your theories. They have studied and tested your computer code. You have many admirers at the NSA, Matt. More than a few of them don't want to see you blamed for this." He glanced at Matt. "Especially after your most recent changes to the code."

Matt reclined his seat slightly. "What did they tell you?"

"I congratulate you on your ingenuity. The way you changed the algorithm to only work on a small subset of prime numbers—that took ten NSA analysts a week to understand. They would be unaware still if they hadn't already analyzed the previous version of your code." Josef shot him another quick look. "That's an advantage *we* have over our Chinese counterparts, no?"

Matt thought back on the anxious days between Gina's staged abduction and the NSA demonstration. The changes to the code took him three weeks of twenty-hour days.

"Thanks for the compliment, but I took a risk."

"That the Chinese might actually perform a test using an encryption key that your code couldn't break. That's true. In fact, they did perform such a test. But you needn't have worried."

Matt looked at Josef uncertainly. *That code can only break one out of a thousand of all possible keys* he thought. *If they'd actually tested it they would have known...unless...*

"What key did they use for the test?"

"One chosen by our operative on the Chinese team—one that our NSA analysts provided. It worked beautifully."

❖ ❖ ❖

Wang Shutao stood outside the Minister's office. After a wait of ten minutes the door opened. The Minister glanced at Wang but said nothing as he returned to his desk. A haze of cigarette smoke hung in the office. The Minister rarely smoked.

Wang entered and stood in front of the Minister's desk. The Minister picked up a cigarette from an ashtray as he sat and drew one last puff before crushing it out. He exhaled slowly through his mouth, letting the smoke curl around his face. He shook another cigarette out of the pack, put it to his mouth, and lit it.

"Wang, how do you think I should regard these unfortunate events that occurred in America?"

"This was the regrettable result of a miscalculation in an otherwise successful operation."

The Minister laughed. "A *miscalculation* you call it. How clinical." He took another deep drag. "Tan Yingqun is wounded. Two of my agents are in custody. Another is dead."

The Minister stood and rested his closed fists on the desk. His head was bowed; his smoldering cigarette hung from his lips. "Now I must arrange for the return of my surviving agents. We have already taken an American operative into custody to bargain with. I must conclude this transaction quickly before it erupts into a public incident." He stood and turned to the window, continuing in a calm, even tone. "I tell you these things, Wang, to make a point. I advised patience and you proceeded recklessly. Oh, you are not the only one at fault. I knew your plans and I did not forbid them. No, in fact, I *praised* you for your initiative. We are both answerable. And both of us must learn from this error in judgment."

Wang said nothing as the Minister continued.

"We will recover. But the rehabilitation of our reputations will take much time."

The Minister returned to his seat behind the desk. "We can be certain that Xiao Weiguo is telling everything in a futile attempt to save himself. The Americans know what he knows." He put out his cigarette and lit another. "Everyone involved will be closely watched. Of course, the programmer and his prostitute cannot be harmed."

The Minister paused long enough for Wang to speak. "What of Tan Yingqun, Minister?"

"I'm not inclined to permit his family to join him in America. I doubt they could make a life out of occasional visits to prison in any case. But I'm open to allowing Tan to return to China. I'm sure the Americans would be willing to discuss it."

Wang sensed that the meeting was over but ventured one last comment.

"Minister, I can report that we are nearly finished with our system. We will run additional tests on randomly selected encryption keys within the month."

"I'm happy to hear that, Wang Shutao. The fact that we were able to obtain the computer code in spite of all these troubling events—this is the only reason the two of us are still alive."

❖ ❖ ❖

Matt slept for most of the drive. He awoke just as Josef exited the Interstate.

"You are feeling better now, *ja?*"

"*Ja*, I mean, yes, much better. Thanks."

A silent minute passed.

"Josef."

"Yes, Matt."

"What about my friends?"

"Mr. Polk and your paramilitary friends have caused a bit of trouble for us. It will take time to untangle. But I think I can protect them, too."

"What about the man I shot? And what happened to Tan?"

Josef frowned. "That man is dead. I'm sure there will be an inquiry but if you had not shot him, what then?"

"He'd have drowned me."

"Indeed. No one will fault you for defending yourself."

Matt turned to the window. "And Tan?"

"Oh, yes. Tan Yingqun. He will recover from his wound. What happens to him next is not clear."

The car came to a stop at an intersection. Josef turned to Matt. "Since Tan's arrival in America he has been an informant of ours—a condition of his immigration. Most of what we know about this whole affair we learned from Tan Yingqun. He told us many things—but not everything. We knew he had family in China. We suspected the Chinese might use them to manipulate him. For this reason there were things he chose to hide. We didn't learn about the plan to kill you until we were told by Mr. Xiao."

Matt's jaw dropped in surprise. "Alvin Xiao? He was part of this?"

Josef nodded. "Indeed. Most of this plan was his."

The light changed. Josef drove on. "He's being very cooperative now. But I think he will be spending some time in prison."

The car turned onto the street where Matt lived. As they approached the building Matt recognized his car, parked in its usual spot. Its headlights had been replaced.

"I arranged to have your car returned to your home. You were a little tied up."

They pulled into the parking lot. Matt opened the door but remained seated. "So, Josef—where do we stand?"

"I'm afraid you can no longer be a part of any classified operation. Your employment with Connectrix is at an end."

"I expected as much."

"But I can tell you that some parts of your proof have been approved for publication. After all, posterity demands it. Only some aspects of the theorem are too sensitive to be released, according to our chief analyst. I believe you know him—Marku Petrescu? He'll be in touch with you to discuss the details."

Matt closed his eyes and pressed his hand to his mouth. After a moment he whispered, "Thank you."

Matt stepped out of the car, holding onto the door and supporting himself on his good leg. He lowered his head into the car. "Thanks, Josef—for everything."

He was about to close the door when Josef spoke.

"One other thing I should tell you, Dr. Bugatti. Since you are being separated from Connectrix, I persuaded the board to make you an offer for your shares. Given the circumstances, the stock must be discounted from its expected future value. I'm sure you understand. They would only authorize an amount of twenty-two million dollars. You will let me know if this is acceptable, no? *Ja?*"

Epilogue

SUNLIGHT STREAMED THROUGH the slats of the metal blinds and cast stripes on the opposite wall of the modest office of Professor Matt Bugatti. Matt sat at his metal desk reviewing the lesson plan for Math 270, *Introduction to Discrete Mathematics*. Classes would commence in three days and students were already migrating to campus. He'd had less than a month to prepare his syllabus and lecture notes. He knew the material but that wasn't enough. Just knowing the material would do for research, but he also had to explain it clearly enough that others would know it as well. He had to teach. *I've got to get this right*, he thought as he fussed over his papers.

"Welcome home, Professor."

Nels Coffman stood in the doorway, holding a bottle of scotch and two glasses. "I'm here to christen the office." He set the glasses on the desk and the bottle next to them. He pulled a rectangle of plastic from his pocket and held it forward. It was inscribed

DR. MATTEO BUGATTI

"With your permission, of course."

Matt took the nameplate, running his fingers over the engraved letters. Nels poured two shots of liquor, handing one to Matt.

"To the next recipient of the Fields Medal."

Matt and Nels clinked glasses and sipped their scotch.

"Isn't that presumptuous?"

"Not too," Nels replied, tapping his glass on the desk to punctuate his speech. "I read the preprint of your paper. So have some on the IMU committee. It's brilliant—groundbreaking. I know the committee, *and* I know your competition. You may not be a shoo-in, but you *are* the frontrunner."

Nels scanned the office. "Sorry we couldn't put you in better surroundings. It's standard issue for our associate professors. But don't worry. Once you get tenure we'll move you up." He put a hand on his hip and held out his glass. "I expect you to be the youngest tenured professor in the history of this department."

The two toasted the prospect.

Nels glanced at the papers on the desk, rotating the stack so he could read it. "Matt, you do know, don't you, that under the terms of your grant, you can hire a graduate assistant to teach your classes? Especially this one." He tapped the paper with the bottom of his glass. "An *introductory* course? Not even our associates teach them."

Matt smiled sheepishly. "I'm looking forward to teaching. I thought I'd start small."

Before Nels could respond he was interrupted by a joyful shriek.

"Matt Bugatti, my prayers are answered! You are just a *five minute* walk away!"

Jenny squeezed past Nels and engulfed Matt in her arms. Emmett Komalski followed her through the door.

"Jenny, you look wonderful."

"Oh, go *on*," she protested. "What about *you?* You used to be so skinny." She pinched his cheek. "Look at you now."

"My mom likes to feed me. And I like being fed."

Matt hugged the woman again before disengaging and approaching Emmett. The two men hugged like brothers.

"Welcome back, Matt. You look happy."

Matt laughed out loud. "I am, Emmett. I'm happy."

"Dr. Coffman?"

Everyone turned toward the voice at the door, where a young woman with an inquisitive smile stood.

"Terri, come in," Nels said. "You need to meet our newest faculty member. Matt, Terri is a post-doc from Cornell. She's doing some fascinating work with group theory."

The young lady strode confidently into the room and extended her hand.

"Dr. Bugatti, it's a pleasure. Your work is inspiring."

Matt accepted her handshake. "It's my pleasure, Terri— I'm sorry, what's your last name?"

"Cavinato. I'm Terri Cavinato."

Matt held her hand and smiled at her beaming face.

"Well, Matt, what do you think of that?" Emmett mused. "A nice Italian girl."

About the Author

ACKNOWLEDGEMENTS

INDEPENDENT AUTHORS FACE a challenge. Every function of a traditional publisher falls to the author. These functions are no less necessary, but they require skills other than writing.

I wrote *The Girlfriend Experience* because I had a story to tell. I was unprepared for the effort needed to package and promote the book. It's been exciting and difficult at times, and it's been educational.

At least I didn't have to do it alone. Like Matt Bugatti, who learned almost too late that he can lean on others, I found a whole community of supporters and fellow Independents willing to encourage me and share their experience.

The other Independents on the Kindle Support Forum have been wonderful. Ken, Marti, Notjohn, 1001, JT, Andre, Cy, Marcy—I can't name you all but you know who you are. Thanks for your advice and encouragement. Special thanks to all of you who liked my Facebook page early on.

Jun Ares, my cover designer, taught me that writing and cover design are two different skills and that I possess one of them at most. Thanks for a great first impression.

Every writer needs an editor, and every writer deserves an editor who can tell him the truth in a way that makes him want to be a better writer. Thank you, Cornelia, for telling me what I did wrong, what I did right, and teaching me the value of another pair of eyes. This is a different book because of you.

Sincere appreciation to all my friends and family who read *The Girlfriend Experience*, offered praise and wrote reviews. To my brothers and sisters who left reviews on Amazon and Goodreads—Jacki, Dan, Jodi, and Robin—bless your hearts. Know that I'd do the same for you. To the early readers—Franc, Gary, Keith, Ty, Bruce, Mike, and Mike—thanks for reviews by people not named O'Donnell.

Special thanks to my Chinese friends who endured my endless questions about Chinese culture, language and politics. I'm sure I asked more than a few uncomfortable questions. To my daughter Brie and her husband Kirk, who lived for four years in Harbin, China, thanks for sharing your experience in a language I actually speak. It's so good to have you back near us.

And, of course, thanks, Helen.

Charles O'Donnell
May 10, 2019

GUIDE TO CHINESE PRONUNCIATION

THE CHINESE NAMES and the few Chinese words (*guanxi, baijiu*) in *The Girlfriend Experience* are written in *pinyin*, a system of representing Chinese characters phonetically. Chinese characters represent syllables and must be learned by heart; a literate Chinese reader normally knows 3,000 to 5,000 symbols.

The difficulty of entering Chinese characters directly using a keyboard should be obvious. Instead, computer users enter characters phonetically using their pinyin equivalents. It's not a straightforward process for a couple of reasons. First, there are many Chinese characters that bear no resemblance to one another but are pronounced identically, and have the same pinyin spelling. Substituting one homonym for another changes the meaning of the written language but not its pronunciation. Second, Chinese is a tonal language—each syllable is pronounced with one of four tones, either level, rising, falling, or falling followed by a rising tone. In pinyin these tones are represented by marks:

mā, má, mà, mǎ

Tonal marks have been omitted from the book, and they aren't normally entered when keying pinyin into a computer. Instead, as the user enters the pinyin spelling a list of Chinese characters appears and the user selects the correct one.

All educated Chinese can read and write both Chinese characters and pinyin. In fact, my son-in-law, who taught English in northern China for four years, tells me that school children are taught pinyin before they're taught Chinese character writing.

A syllable in pinyin consists of an *initial*, a consonant, and a *final*, consisting of vowels or vowels and consonants. The following tables list pinyin initials and finals with their approximate pronunciations.

Pinyin Initial	**English Approximation**
b	*p* as in s<u>p</u>in (unaspirated)
c	*ts* as in ha<u>ts</u>
ch	*ch* as in chur<u>ch</u>
d	*t* as in s<u>t</u>op (unaspirated)
f	*f* as in <u>f</u>un
g	*k* as in s<u>k</u>ill (unaspirated)
h	*ch* as in lo<u>ch</u>
j	*ch* as in chur<u>ch</u>yard
k	*k* as in <u>k</u>ill (aspirated)
l	*l* as in <u>l</u>ay
m	*m* as in <u>M</u>ay
n	*n* as in <u>n</u>ay
p	*p* as in <u>p</u>it (aspirated)
q	*chy* as in pun<u>ch y</u>ourself
r	*r* as in <u>r</u>ay
s	*s* as in <u>s</u>ay
sh	*sh* as in <u>sh</u>irt
t	*t* as in <u>t</u>op (aspirated)
w	*w* as in <u>w</u>ay
x	*sh* as in <u>sh</u>eep
y	*y* as in <u>y</u>es
z	*ds* as in rea<u>ds</u>
zh	*j* as in junk

Pinyin Final	**English Approximation**
a	*a* as in f<u>a</u>ther
ai	Pronounced like *eye*

an	*ahn* like c<u>an</u> in British English
ang	*ahng* like s<u>ong</u>
ao	*ow* as in c<u>ow</u>
e	*uh* as in d<u>uh</u>
ei	*ey* as in h<u>ey</u>
en	*en* as in tak<u>en</u>
eng	*ung* as in h<u>ung</u>
er	*ar* as in b<u>ar</u>
i	*ee* as in b<u>ee</u>
ia	*ya* as in y<u>a</u>rd
ian	*yen* as in y<u>en</u>
iang	*yang*
iao	*eow* as in m<u>eow</u>
ie	*ye* as in y<u>e</u>t
in	*yeen*
ing	*ying*
io	*yo*
iong	*yong*
iu	*eo* as in L<u>eo</u>
o	*oh*
ong	*ohng*
ou	*o* as in s<u>o</u>
u	*oo* as in m<u>oo</u>
ua	*wa* as in <u>wa</u>sh
uai	*wai* like *why*
uan	*wahn*
uang	*wahng*
ue	*we* as in <u>tw</u>enty
ui	*way* as in <u>way</u>
un	*won* as in <u>won</u>
uo	*wo* as in <u>won</u>'t

As you can see, the pronunciation of pinyin is not always obvious to an English speaker. For example, *Wang* rhymes with *song* not *sang*.

Chinese names begin with the family name followed by the given name. Tan Yingqun's family name is Tan; his given name is Yingqun. Chinese address each other in a variety of ways. It's very common to address someone using his full name, even in informal situations. Some address each other by just their given names or their family names. I have Chinese colleagues whom I address in all these ways, as well as by their adopted English names.

Charles O'Donnell
May 10, 2019

www.ingramcontent.com/pod-product-compliance
Lightning Source LLC
Chambersburg PA
CBHW060855210726
48293CB00006B/1808